GRYPHON'S EYE

Kevin Weston

Wave Train Books

BRIGHTON, MICHIGAN

Wave Train Books LLC
6194 Sundance Trail
Brighton, MI 48116
www.kevinwestonbooks.com

Publisher's Note: This is a work of fiction. Names, characters, places, and incidents are a product of the author's imagination. Locales and public names are sometimes used for atmospheric purposes. Any resemblance to actual people, living or dead, or to businesses, companies, events, institutions, or locales is completely coincidental.

Cover by Matthew Jay Fleming
Map by Conor Smyth
Book Layout © 2017 BookDesignTemplates.com

Gryphon's Eye/Kevin Weston. -- 1st ed.

For Allison and Lindsay

1

Threadbare

A shroud of resignation settled over Jessalyn Suntold as she climbed the winding stone staircase to the room where her father waited. Once, not so very long ago, she had regarded these visitations to the top of the north tower as little more than nuisances to be indulged. But now? After so many disappointments? After so many crestfallen sighs and muttered oaths? Now her father's calls to his side felt like harbingers of resentments and sorrows to come.

Jess glanced to her left, where Gwyn was matching her stride for stride despite her huffing and puffing. The presence of her longtime governess was always reassuring. It made the echoes of their footfalls against the tower's stone walls seem not quite so forlorn. Made the shadows cast by the lanterns spaced at regular intervals seem not quite so bleak. But even Gwyn's companionship could only provide so much consolation. It did nothing to lessen the ache of dread in her chest—an ache that seemed to swell with each step they ascended.

Upon reaching the landing, they found themselves standing before a thick oaken door banded with iron. Gwyn stepped forward and opened the door, then stood aside for Jessalyn to enter. Jessalyn swallowed hard and forced herself forward. She cast a quick glance at Gwyn as she passed by, trying to arrange her face in an expression of world-weary bemusement despite the unpleasantness to come. But Jessalyn abandoned the effort when she saw the downcast aspect of Gwyn's broad features. These rituals had taken a toll on both of them over the past few years.

"Ah, there she is now!" King Owyn cried with forced cheer as Jessalyn entered the room. "You look lovely today, Jess." Affixing a wan smile to her face, she stood obediently as her father strode forward and embraced her, his long arms holding her with what Jess knew, despite everything, was a deep and abiding love. Somehow that made it all worse.

After a long moment, her father turned her loose and smiled down at her. His crown gleamed in the afternoon light pouring in through the tower's open windows, as did the golden clasps that adorned his dark tunic and cloak. Owyn's short beard was a blend of gray and white now, as was the hair that cascaded down to his shoulders and the shaggy eyebrows that adorned his wide, heavily lined forehead. But he still possessed the high strong cheekbones and square jaw that had long made him such an easy subject for artists in Kylden, from the sculptors and portraitists of Mercy Square to the pamphleteers of Wyndlass Row.

Two steps behind her father stood Marston Pynch, high votary to the Throneholder. Jess felt her spirits further plummet as she contemplated the scowling old man. She understood that Pynch was an asset to her father. His cool pragmatism helped temper her father's more fanciful notions and impulsive ways, and his deft diplomacy with the various lords and casters scattered across Fyngree had helped the king navigate many thorny problems of governance over the years.

But while Jess grudgingly conceded the value of Pynch's service, she resented the traces of condescension with which Pynch sometimes treated her—and even her father, on occasion. And Pynch apparently had no objections to the upcoming ritual, the latest in her father's desperate bids to circumvent the known laws of magic where his daughter was concerned. Though in truth, Jess had no idea if the high votary supported these endeavors, either. One certainly could not glean his feelings from his countenance, which was as dour as ever.

Jess turned and surveyed the rest of her surroundings. Here in the north tower's topmost chamber, the stone walls were bare of the tapestries and banners that adorned much of the rest of Kylden Hall. But the high arching windows carved into the wall at regular intervals offered glimpses of the great castle's parapets and gate house, as well as of blue skies, distant woodlands, and a gleaming sliver of the Whetstone River.

As her gaze lingered on the Whetstone, Jess felt a sudden swooning impulse to hurl herself out the window and toward its beckoning waters. Who knows? Perhaps if she did so she would sprout wings, take flight, and disappear forever. Was such a fantasy any more absurd than her father's delusion that the Thread might yet take root in his daughter?

Jess felt her father watching her, and something rose up from deep inside her—a scream? a sob? a bitter laugh? she honestly didn't know—that she had to swallow hard to keep at bay. Throughout her childhood, her father's eyes had shone with a deep and uncomplicated love every time his gaze turned her way. But she was no longer a child, and different emotions swam behind those mild brown eyes now. There was still love there, to be sure. But she glimpsed darker things as well. Fear. Frustration. And disappointment too. But with his daughter or himself? These days, she never quite knew.

She forced herself to turn to the far end of the room. There were six birds of prey in the tower today. Three hawks, two falcons, and a single great gray owl, all wearing black leather hoods to keep them calm and still. They stood silently on tapered black marble pedestals arranged about ten yards apart in a semicircle around the inner wall of the turret. The pedestals stood about five feet high and were topped with black cork so the birds could grip their perches. To Jess the birds looked like sleek sculptures carved out of dragon oak or polished stone. Despite the years of frustration and heartache the creatures represented for her, she could not deny their beauty.

In the middle of the semicircle of raptors stood her father's lead falconer and animal trainer. Bearded and slope-shouldered, Brundy Sevenshade supervised the care and training of Kylden Hall's many birds and beasts. Brundy was reticent with his own kind, but her father regarded the falconer as the finest animal trainer in all of Fyngree. Jess suspected that her father was right; she had once seen Brundy stroll through the banquet hall during a raucous holiday feast with an enormous lion padding behind him like an obedient hound, seemingly oblivious to the riot of smells and sounds around him. Today, though, Jess observed with a sort of grim satisfaction that Sevenshade looked like he would rather be anywhere but in this tower. She knew exactly how he felt.

Jess turned back to her father, who was approaching her with a cobalt blue goblet of heavy blown glass that he had retrieved from a nearby table. Owyn held the goblet out to her. "I think I've finally got it this time," he said. "Rynelle Tremeny found a transforming incantation of which I'd not heard tell in one of the ancient texts from her library and she was kind enough to send it my way last night. She is aware of our efforts in this matter . . ."

Jess nodded absently and took the cup from her father's hand as he continued, though she wasn't really listening. Tremeny was high sentinel of Tydewater, second only to Kylden among Fyngree's cities, and she ranked first among her father's allies. Jess had no reason to doubt her loyalty. Still, it was unsettling to learn that her father's desperation had reached the point that he was willing to tell Tremeny of his daughter's secret.

". . . and selecting a creature of the desired species will help facilitate the spell," concluded King Owyn. Jess looked at him blankly. "So?" he said with a hint of impatience, spreading an arm behind him to the assembled birds on their perches. "Which one suits you best?"

Jess shot a quick glance over at Gwyn, who gave her a nearly imperceptible shrug. Jess glumly returned her attention to the birds. "Uh, the one on the right, I guess."

"Very good!" her father said with forced enthusiasm, as if the exercise in which they were engaged was finally gathering some forward momentum. "He's a beauty, isn't he? Master Sevenshade! Bring him to us!"

Brundy briskly strode over to Jess and strapped a leather falconer's glove over her right forearm. He then went to the hawk Jess had selected and transported the hooded creature to his left forearm, which was also sheathed in black leather. Brundy then returned to Jess and transferred the hooded hawk, a smallish fellow with spectacular red and black plumage, to her glove before retreating to his position among the pedestals.

Jess felt a rising flush of embarrassment on her face. Holding the bird on one upraised arm and the goblet in the other, she felt like a piece of ridiculous statuary. Her dismay deepened when she peered down at the contents of the goblet for the first time. The liquid within reminded her of nothing so much as a miniature bog. An unhealthy-looking film had already congealed on the dark surface, which was flecked with floating bits of matter that looked like remnants of vegetation and bone—and was that a piece of *feather*? And the bitter odor wafting from the goblet smelled like the contents had come directly from the city's sewers. She looked up at her father, anger flaring anew in her heart. "I'm not drinking this," she said flatly.

"Now Jess," Owyn said soothingly. "You promised." He turned for support to Pynch, who adopted an impassive expression and clasped his hands behind him.

Owyn scowled. "You're no help."

"I'm sorry, Your Majesty, but I've no authority in this matter," Pynch said. "This is between you and the princess. Besides, you know my perspective on these . . . exercises. "

Jess leaped at this unexpected opening. "You see, father? Even Pynch recognizes that this is folly." Her hands were full, so she gestured with her chin toward Gwyn—loyal Gwyn, her confidante and comfort throughout her childhood and adolescence—and the falconer. Jess felt the heat rising in her, and this time she let it slip its leash.

"Father, spare me this indignity. You have watched me swallow vile potions, smoke vile tobaccos, suffer defilement of my body with vile symbols conjured from vile paints, soak in vile baths, and chant vile passages from vile tomes for five years now, and what has come of it? Nothing!" Jessalyn paused guiltily as a cloud of unhappiness settled over her father's craggy features. She proceeded more gently. "I'm sorry, father, but it's hopeless. Please accept it. The truth of the matter is that I'm not meant to carry the Thread. The gift has passed me by. "

Owyn shook his head. "That is nonsense," he said. "Remember the example of Jerylyl Fjorsus. His familiar did not appear to him until his sixteenth year!"

"Father, you know that the Thread comes later to boys. And I am seventeen now! Have you ever, in all of your studies, come across an instance where a girl gained her familiar so late?"

"Jessalyn, we have to keep trying," Owyn said. "Your place on the throne depends on it."

"And what of Rylla Tallwyst?" Jess countered. "Queen Rylla ruled Fyngree for two decades without virtue of any sorcerous powers! How can you ignore that?"

"We have had this conversation before, Jess. Rylla reigned during a fallow period for casters in Tempyst's history. Few wizards or witches roamed the continent during her time. Even Rojenhold was led by a threadbare during those years."

"Noll Whytewender was not threadbare."

"Well, a stoat hardly counts." Owyn sighed. "I'm sorry, Jess. I wish it was not so. But we must keep trying. It is not just your future that hangs in the balance, but that of Fyngree. If Thylus Whytewender and the Faithful Shield were ever to learn that a *threadbare* sits on the throne . . . " Her father's voice trailed off, but Jess saw how his features curdled at the thought.

Jess looked down again at the foul liquid she held. Smoke and Ash, she thought resignedly. This stupid hawk is getting heavy anyway. And who knows? Maybe this time it *will* work. Maybe her father *had* finally unlocked the secret of the Thread.

Besides, arguing with her father was *so* exhausting.

"All right," Jess said, breaking the lengthening silence. "You win." She glanced around at the other faces in the room, trying to ignore the hollowed-out feeling that she always felt in her gut in these final moments. "Cheers!" she announced with forced good humor, as if the whole affair was a lark. Then she closed her eyes, brought the goblet to her lips, and took a great quaff from its contents.

As soon as Jess took her first swallow, the color of the room changed, as if a pale golden veil had fallen over her surroundings. She heard a rising roar in her ears, and beneath it a faint, almost musical sound, as if she was hearing notes from some strange and seductive instrument being played on the other side of the world. She turned her head to the hawk sitting on her right forearm. The bird still wore its hood, but she could *feel* the hawk's eyes on her, blazing deep into her being, searching like powerful twin lighthouse beams. The beams spilled into every corner of her body, washing her bones and muscles and organs in a fearsome white light that grew in intensity with each passing second.

Then she felt it—a force that was both the hawk and something else entire. A force frantically pulling and tugging at her insides, like a thief rifling through the deepest corners of her being. And as the frenzied ransacking continued, an icy finger of fear touched her heart. That spell, whatever it was, might tear her apart in its quest for the nonexistent Thread it was seeking.

A hard nugget of pain abruptly sprouted in the center of her chest and began radiating outward, expanding in tandem with the swelling cacophony in her ears. The musical notes were gone now, drowned out by a rising, crashing tumult of sound. She felt as if the beams of light were flaying her insides as they lashed violently back and forth, deeper and deeper, in their frantic quest. Jess moaned in distress and swayed on her feet, her eyes rolling up in her head. Dimly, she felt a wave of shudders roll through her body, followed by painful tingling over every inch of her body, as if she had stumbled into a dense cloud of wasps.

And then suddenly it was all gone, snuffed out in the blink of an eye. Jess opened her eyes blearily, turned away, and vomited a huge gout of black liquid out onto the stone floor. The heavy glass goblet slipped from her left hand and shattered on the stones.

"Get this damned thing off me," she said thickly, thrusting her gloved right arm, still adorned with the hooded hawk, toward Brundy. Never had she felt so hollowed out, so completely empty of possibility.

The room was silent as the falconer relieved Jess of the hawk and gear, then withdrew to his position at the far end of the room. She wheeled on her father. "That's it," she said, her voice shaky but hoarse with conviction. "No more. Never again." She turned on her heel and stalked toward the open doorway to leave, Gwyn dutifully falling into step behind her. Just before they reached the doorway, though, she heard the murmur of her father's voice. An instant later the oaken door slammed shut in front of her.

Jess stared at the door, a hot ripple of impotent anger washing over her. She felt the sting of tears in her eyes and cursed, roughly swiping one hand across her face. She would *not* further add to her humiliation by crying in front of her father and Pynch and Sevenshade. "I hate it when you do that," she said in a low voice, keeping her back to him. "Please let me go."

"Jessalyn—"

"*Please.*"

She heard her father mutter under his breath, and the oaken door swung open slowly. Jess stepped forward but when she reached the doorway she paused and turned back to her father. "I'm going to Percy's tonight," she said. She made an effort to keep her voice calm, but she could hear the tremble of fury and shame running through every word. "Don't wait up."

Owyn's face darkened. "Of all the pamphleteers in Kylden, why must you keep company with Percyval Muncenmast? That man is nothing but an agitator. I ought to take an axe to that press of his, he's brought me nothing but grief over the years."

"I think you just answered your own question," Jess spat, only to feel her throat further knot up at the stricken look that flashed across her father's face. And with that she and Gwyn fled the tower, the echo of their footfalls drowning out anything more that her father might have said.

2

The Falcon's Shadow

Traejon Frost cursed softly as he steered his mount through the dark wood, brushing past the rain-drenched boughs in his path. The falcon usually charted courses over more hospitable terrain, such as the rolling fields, pastures, and hedges of the Loaf. Or the serpentine valleys of the wild Marching Mountains. Or the Gilded Hills, where the trees grew so tall that their canopies blocked the sun for miles. Until autumn, that is, when steady gusts off the Amaranthine Sea poked holes in the forest roof and tossed leaves to and fro in swirling slashes of vivid color. On those days, that entire land shimmered with a simultaneously elegiac and celebratory air.

This was not the Gilded Hills.

Instead, Nomad had plunged him into a dense wood of scrub pine, gnarled oak, and thorny vegetation that tugged and pulled at his clothing every few seconds. The day's cold and steady rain, only now trailing away into a light mist, added to his discomfort. But Traejon pulled the dark hooded cloak he wore a little closer around his broad shoulders and pressed onward. He trusted Nomad had a reason for dragging him through this infernal tangle of forest. And if he had his bearings right—and he always did—then they should soon be hitting the north branch of the Whetstone River, the brawling waterway that ran from the high aeries of the Marching Mountains all the way to Kylden itself. If nothing else, the open river corridor would give him a little relief from these cramped and clutching woods.

A few moments later the sound of running water reached Traejon's ears, and he quickened his pace. But as they moved closer to the still-unseen river, the wind shifted and Traejon straightened up in his saddle.

Smoke in the air. And a foul undercurrent of something else.

Traejon moved forward slowly, his eyes scanning the murky shadows around him, until he caught a glimpse of fast-moving water through the trees. A moment later they reached the edge of the wood. Still hidden in the shadows of the tree line, Traejon reached over his shoulder and took the longbow off his back, then notched one of his arrows onto the string. Only then did he lightly nudge the horse with his heels, the weapon held ready in his lap.

As Traejon emerged into the open, he looked up and down the river for movement before sparing one brief glance up into the low-hanging sky in search of Nomad. Nothing. Brushing off the glimmer of irritation he felt at the falcon's continued absence, he considered the tableau before him. The north branch rushed past him from right to left, its broad surface a rippling pewter gray. Even here, miles above its junction with the mainstream, the tributary was a good forty feet wide, and the far bank displayed the same dark confusion of woods from which he had just emerged. Both riverbanks, though, had been cleared of the heaviest vegetation, allowing for easier walking or riding up and down the river's churning length.

Traejon turned his mount upriver to the source of the smoke, and a short time later he came upon the blackened husks of a small cluster of buildings tucked in a bend in the river. There were three buildings in all. A good-sized home, a small stable, and a workshop of some sort, to judge by the tools scattered about. But there was little left now but a few stray blackened timbers, curls of smoke trailing from them like banners of desolation. Whoever the raiders were, they had been sure of their work.

Traejon approached to the outskirts of the homestead, pulling up at the edge of a bed of bulrushes tucked along the inner curve of the river. The charred carcasses of a horse and several pigs littered the hardpacked ground. Several vultures and crows hopped about on their blackened bodies, filling their bellies. And at the far end of the small clearing, Traejon glimpsed a broken wagon tipped on its side in high grass, next to a well-worn path that disappeared into the woods to the east.

As he took in the dismal scene, Traejon felt unwelcome memories come skulking unbidden to the ragged edge of his thoughts. Memories that he had no wish to revisit, on this or any other day. As far as he was concerned, his past was a plague ship, a vessel heavy with cargo that reeked of pain and misery. No good had ever come of wandering through its squalid hold or over its blood-shellacked decks. So whenever that cursed ship drifted out of the fog toward him, he doused it with oil, set a torch to it, and watched it burn down to the waterline, making certain that nothing escaped the fire of forgetting that he set.

But there was no manifest to consult to make sense of the ruination before him now. This was someone else's dark story, with a power all its own. A power to call out to his old plague ship of memories, fill its black sails, and beckon it closer as if it were some unholy lighthouse.

Traejon felt a ripple of cold uneasiness run down his spine. And just like that, he knew that he could not tarry on this blood-soaked ground much longer.

Not unless he wanted to climb on board that ship of horrors for a good long spell.

A gust of wind swept down the river corridor, sending Traejon's cloak billowing and spurring the bulrushes into a swaying dance. Sensing a sudden flash of color in the periphery of his vision, his mind snapped out of its grim reverie. He brought the longbow up, aiming it past the remains of the main house. But he lowered it again when he saw the body floating toward him.

The wind must have dislodged it from the bulrushes or an upstream eddy and released it into the main current. The dead man floated swiftly past him, bearded face to the sky, arms splayed as if he had been crucified. He wore a craftsman's apron and an expression of anguish, his eyes wide and glassy. The shafts of two arrows stuck out of his chest, their bright red fletchings a stark contrast to the otherwise charcoal-colored landscape of the day.

Traejon watched the body float downriver, lazily spinning in response to logs and stones lurking below the river's surface. The corpse disappeared around a distant bend just as Nomad alighted in a nearby tree. He turned in the saddle and regarded the falcon for a moment. Nomad was a gyrfalcon, to be precise, and a magnificent example of her kind. Even in repose, Nomad's broad white wings and chest, each heavily dappled with gray, gave off an aura of vitality, as did her gleaming black talons and beak. And her unblinking black eyes stared back at Traejon with an inscrutable gaze that, even after four years, he found mildly disconcerting. They looked at each other for another moment before the falcon spread her wings and soared out above the river, cutting an arc that set her on a westward course.

Traejon nodded to himself and turned his horse back into the woods, leaving the bleak riverside scene behind with no small measure of relief. The falcon would be returning to Kylden Hall to show her master what she had witnessed. King Owyn took a dim view of lawlessness of any kind in Fyngree. He would waste little time in rousing patrols to hunt down and punish the bandits responsible for this carnage.

Traejon would have taken satisfaction in pursuing that duty himself. His tracking abilities were what had brought him under consideration for shadow work in the first place. And he knew well the ways of bandits. But he knew his responsibilities lay elsewhere. And so Traejon pushed through the woods until he came out the other side, then rode on, the land rolling away beneath his horse's galloping hooves as he chased the familiar's shadow westward.

They pushed on until night overtook them. After seeing to the needs of his tired horse, Traejon built a small fire and prepared his supper. "Nasty business out there today," he said to the falcon, who had circled back to him as dusk fell. She watched him go about his activities now from a perch high in a nearby birch. Nomad shook her wings briefly in response to his voice but otherwise maintained her stony silence.

It was late and Traejon was tired when he finally lay down next to the fire and pulled his blanket up around him. But sleep was slow to come. Since as far back as he could remember, spasms of violence had flared across his life like malignant comets. What was one more death to him? But it had been some time since such a comet had burned his eyes, and he found himself unable to shake the image of that single body floating downriver. It dug at him, like a thorn in his boot.

What kind of craft had the man plied? Traejon wondered as he stared up into the trees and the night sky beyond. Carpentry, perhaps? And had he been a husband or father? And if so, where was his family now? Had any of them somehow escaped the marauders that had descended on their home?

Other questions came on the night winds as well. Where was the man's body at this moment? Had it been snared by a fallen tree and become a feast for the fish and the creatures of the forest? Or was the Whetstone even now carrying him past slumbering riverside villages toward the arched stone bridges of Kylden, and finally out to the eternal expanses of the Amaranthine Sea?

Sleep finally did arrive, but it gave Traejon no relief from his troubled thoughts. Instead, a nightmare coiled around his mind as he slept, leaving him to twitch and twist under his blanket. A nightmare in which he found himself pinned to the deck of a dark ship sailing toward a distant, blood-rimmed land. And he wanted so much to stand and fling himself off that ship, for he recognized the voices calling to him from that shore, echoing across the dark waters through which he passed. But his limbs no longer obeyed him. He was dead, after all. So he just lay there on that cold deck, staring with lonely, sightless eyes at the moon and stars drifting by above.

3

The Pamphleteer

J ess had chosen her usual workplace, a battered old table located midway between the crackling fire in the hearth and Muncenmast's hulking printing press. The dark wood of the press gleamed in the firelight, in marked contrast to the shopworn and mismatched tables, chairs, jars, buckets, and bins scattered elsewhere around the high-ceilinged room. Hunched over the table, Jess looked down on the galley plate that she had been working on for the last hour, then picked another letter from the rack of tiny lead tiles at her right elbow.

A moment later, Jess straightened up and stretched her arms and shoulders in pleasure. A big smile of satisfaction flashed across her face as she looked down at the finished galley. "I'm done!" she announced happily, turning to her bespectacled host.

"Wonderful!" Percy Muncenmast said, shifting his soft bulk off the stool where he had been waiting patiently for her to finish. The pamphleteer and the princess spent the next several minutes scurrying around the printing press. They placed Jess's galley on the wide bed of the printing press, next to seven other typeset plates that Muncenmast had already prepared. They then examined every inch of the galley set, employing little mallets to knock uncooperative tiles into level with neighboring letters, and locked the plates into place. He then poured black ink over the galley plates while Jess set a great billowing sheet of paper for printing. Once the paper was in place, they gripped opposite sides of the big iron handle connected to the top of the screw press itself, revolving it downward until the screw press pushed the paper into the galleys. They then reversed the screw to its original position, carefully removed the sheet from the press, and laid it out to dry on a nearby table illuminated by two hanging lanterns.

Muncenmast's spectacles shone in the lamplight as he looked over each page set in the galley. He stood up and beamed at her, his eyes scrunching into little slits of delight. "Perfect!" he said. "Lord Bracey is going to be so pleased." He dropped his voice conspiratorially and gave Jess a mischievous nudge. "Of course, his thesis is perfect dreck. His contention that the ancient elvish races were killed off by plague is essentially a rehash of Peel's discredited scholarship, and he completely misinterprets Brystlebrow's findings in the Tomorrow Islands. Now *there* is a scholar." The printer paused. "Still, Bracey did select a nice woodcut image for the cover. So his book will have *that* going for it."

"I just finished reading *Chronicles of the Bolde Temple* last night," Jess volunteered. "Thank you again for letting me borrow it. Remind me to give it back to you, it's in my satchel. So you agree with Brystlebrow's theory that the elves actually fled from Tempyst to the east, across the Uncrossable Sea? Brystlebrow himself describes that as only a provisional conclusion."

Muncenmast nodded. "Yes, that's true. But I believe Brystlebrow's theory to be the most plausible one I've yet heard! And I've always respected Brystlebrow's refusal to engage in irresponsible speculation about *why* the elves left Tempyst. Perhaps if Thylus Whytewender ever permits an exploration of the Elvish Islands, scholars will be able to uncover some of the mysteries surrounding their disappearance." He clapped his hands together. "All right, enough about Brystlebrow and elves of ages past. We have more work to do! I'm to deliver 200 copies of Bracey's manuscript to the bindery by the end of the week!"

As they turned back to the printing press, a familiar feeling of contentment came over Jess. She loved these evenings, perched out here in this unassuming shop on the far southern outskirts of the city, basking in the magic of the written word—and it *was* a sort of magic to her, even if it did not have a supernatural basis. She loved the smell of wood and ink and paper around her. And those twinkling eyes behind Percy's ink-smudged spectacles. The old printer's booming laugh and his penchant for speaking in exclamations. The generous and patient manner with which Percy taught her not only about printing and pamphleteering, but also about the great philosophers, poets, and playwrights of Tempyst, past and present. Percy brought their lives and passions to life in a way that none of her tutors had ever been able to manage.

Most of all, Jess loved her weekly visit to Muncenmast's shop because here, working inside walls festooned with yellowing broadsheets and playbills from printing jobs of yesteryear, she felt more at home than she ever did in the ornate banquet hall or cavernous throne room of Kylden Hall. Here she could bury herself to the elbows in words and ideas. Learn about the composition and capacities of the inks that Percy used to create the deep blacks and vibrant yellows and rich purples of his illustrations. Get ink and oil and dirt on her face, hands, and garments without eliciting scandalized titters from the bejeweled, gimlet-eyed ladies of Kylden Hall's court. Slouch if she felt like it and fart if she needed to. And here she could forget—at least for a short time—the gnawing guilt and resentment she felt about her threadbare condition.

They worked quietly for the next hour, occasionally exchanging remarks about one aspect or another of the work at hand. Finally, though, Muncenmast turned to her with a gentle smile. And in that moment Jess felt her spirits plummet, for she knew what was coming. "The hour is growing late, Jess. King Owyn will not be pleased at your tardiness in returning to the castle. And you were late in returning home last week as well."

Jess turned away and gazed out the front window, a frown slipping across her features. Several of the soldiers who had accompanied her to the shop were standing guard outside, and the backs of their helmeted heads blocked the bottom half of her view. In the upper panes, however, the lights of the city gradually sloped upwards to the distant ramparts of Kylden Hall. "Just a little while longer, Percy," she said softly. Then: "Tell me again about my mother."

Muncenmast smiled at the obvious ploy but played along. "Oh, your mother was a wonderful queen, Jess," he said expansively. "She had a naturally regal bearing that no amount of instruction can impart! And Queen Ayleth was a beauty, too—just like you," he added. "The men and women of Kylden—aye, of all of Fyngree—still miss her terribly. You know, I never saw your mother and father together except at ceremonial holidays. But everyone agrees that their marriage was a singularly harmonious one. They doted on one another. And she was no ornament to your father's throne, either. On several occasions, in fact, people say that her wise counsel kept King Owyn from making impetuous decisions that he might well have later regretted. Surely you've heard about the role she played in keeping the House of Tusk from throwing in with Whytewender some years back."

Jess nodded. "That was right before I was born."

"Yes, that sounds right," he paused. "I've always been curious. . . . Do you remember her at all?"

Jess smiled wistfully, and her eyes became distant as she ferried herself across the currents of childhood memory. "Some. Fragments of this and that. I remember her smile. I remember holding her hand when we walked in the garden. She loved to tell me about the different kinds of flowers growing there. I remember how she used to sing me this one lullaby before bedtime. Something with dancing foxes and candles in it. I loved that song."

Jess turned to him, that faraway look gradually receding until she was seeing him again. "I wish she was here," she said simply.

"I know you do, Jess. Your father does too. After Ayleth's funeral service, he did not emerge from Kylden Hall for nearly two months. Fortunately for Fyngree, your father did not permit his grief, great as it was, to distract him from his obligations any longer than that. I sometimes think that he incorporated some of your mother's kindness and wisdom into his rule as a sort of tribute to her. He's certainly been a good king in the intervening years."

Jess's eyes widened in surprise. "How can you say that, Percy? He imprisoned you for five months!" She strode over to an old piece of paper tacked up on the wall and took it down. "For a pamphlet!" Jess thrust the paper toward him angrily, as if the event had somehow slipped out of his memory.

Muncenmast looked down at the wrinkled paper in her ink-stained hands. The bottom of the page consisted of printed words, but the top half depicted a crippled soldier looking up from the ground, tugging beseechingly at the hem of a king's garments. The king, clearly drawn to resemble her father, was gazing imperiously in the other direction, his left arm holding a jewel-encrusted goblet while his right rested on the hilt of his sword.

"Yes, he did, didn't he?" Muncenmast chuckled, shaking his head. Jess's bewilderment deepened. River and sea! What was so amusing about being thrown in shackles? Before she could further voice her dismay, however, the old man raised his hand. "I was wondering when you'd bring that up. There is more to that story than you've heard, I think."

Muncenmast pulled himself up onto a table next to the hearth, where the fire had burned down to a bed of glowing coals. He patted a spot beside him. Jess slowly walked over and joined him, her expression one of impatient skepticism.

"Seven years ago," he began, "I began to hear disquieting rumors that elderly and crippled veterans of the king's army living in and around Fellen had fallen into deep impoverishment. Do you know the place?"

Jess shook her head.

"Fellen is a small village in the northwest quarter of the Loaf. The sort of tranquil, quiet place that attracts weary old soldiers after they set down their shields. In any case, I began to hear vague mutterings on the wind that some of the village's injured and elderly veterans had been reduced to selling valued medals and other keepsakes from their years of service in order to feed themselves! I confess that I dismissed these rumors initially. Several years before, you see, your father had decreed that a generous pension be extended to all aged and infirm soldiers who had once worn the blue and gold. He assigned various officials to ensure that the veterans received their pensions, made the necessary notifications to his treasury, and so on. Now the man responsible for dispersing these pensions in Fellen was a soldier himself—one who continued to wear Kylden's colors despite the loss of an eye in a clash with bandits some years earlier. As a soldier who had suffered such a ghastly injury in service to his king, the fellow seemed an ideal choice for the position!

"As the months passed, however, dark hints of malfeasance continued to filter down from the Loaf to my ears, possibly because of my modest reputation—yes, even back then!—as a pamphleteer who did not quail at the thought of publishing controversial material. In any case, the whispers finally piled up to the point that I decided to ride up and investigate—quietly, of course." Muncenmast shook his head. "It was horrible. Some veterans were slowly starving to death. I found others, bedridden and without family to care for them, who suffered from bedsores that had become infected or who had been lying in their own filth for days."

Jess's imagination flooded with images of the events described by the pamphleteer, and she felt her pulse quicken in outrage. "That's awful!" she cried.

"Yes," Muncenmast said, grimacing at the memories. "I eventually discovered that this one-eyed soldier was diverting a large portion of the pensions into his own purse. He had been able to avoid notice, however, by limiting his targets to the most isolated veterans—widowers without families and such—and bribing officers and officials all the way to Kylden Hall itself. Unsure of who to trust in the military and unable to gain an immediate audience with your father, I finally published this"— Muncenmast raised the paper in his hand—"and distributed copies of it all around the city. I felt that I couldn't wait, you see. "

Muncenmast sighed heavily. "Well, the uproar was enormous. The people of Kylden were outraged by my account, of course. It was a hard time for King Owyn. Your father is a proud man, and he suffered deep embarrassment as a result of my revelations. Most of all, though, I think he was furious with himself for being unaware that those proud old veterans who had served him so well were being treated so grievously. Within a matter of days, he uncovered the identities of the officials who had accepted the one-eyed soldier's bribes, and they were dealt with. Harshly. Unfortunately, the soldier who orchestrated the vile plot escaped into the Speartip Mountains and over the border into Rojenhold just ahead of his pursuers. I'm sure your father is looking for him still."

"And for revealing this corruption to him you get thrown into prison!" Jess erupted, her eyes flashing with anger.

"Jess, you have to understand. My pamphlet was seen in many quarters as an attack on King Owyn as an uncaring tyrant, not as a desperate effort to alert the kingdom to an evil scheme. Whytewender watched the whole affair unfold with keen interest from his throne in Stormheel, I'm sure. And not just him. I wager that some of Fyngree's more powerful casters studied hard on the affair, watching to see if King Owyn was no longer able to fend off attacks on his authority. Would your father allow me to publish such an embarrassing work without any consequences at all?"

Muncenmast patted Jess's arm consolingly. "If your father had not punished me for what was seen in some quarters as brazen insolence, Whytewender and his Faithful Shield might very well have begun testing Fyngree's defenses and alliances with even more vigor. He would have taken it as a sign of weakness, for force and intimidation is all he understands. And who knows? If he could ever lure one or two of your father's traditional allies to his side, Whytewender might finally be tempted to move against King Owyn. He's certainly made no secret of his belief that the continent entire should bow to Stormheel Keep, as it did long ago."

"But you did a brave and good thing!" she cried, her mind still swirling with indignation at the unfairness of it all. "You didn't deserve to go to prison! He should have held a ceremony in your honor!"

"Perhaps," Percy said, shrugging his shoulders. "But if I had published such a pamphlet in Rojenhold, King Thylus would have had me tortured and executed. The printers of those cities dare not publish *anything* that does not meet with the approval of the Faithful Shield."

He smiled down on her. "We live in an imperfect world, Jess. Your father did the best he could. He arrested me and tossed me into prison, yes. To this day I think he believes that I should have tried harder to inform him of the conditions I found. Or poked him with a stick that was not quite so sharp. But his jailers placed me in a clean and comfortable cell, and I was well-fed and cared for. And when the fuss surrounding Fellen died down and Whytewender's gaze finally turned elsewhere, King Owyn quietly released me without placing any restrictions on my printing or pamphleteering. And these days, I daresay that there are not any old soldiers of the blue and gold that are going cold or hungry. Their pensions are now under the direct supervision of your father's accountants. So I have no regrets, you see."

Jess sat quietly, absorbing everything that Percy had told her. She was still sitting there when she heard a muffled series of bumps to her left. She turned her head just as a small gray goose came flying out of the chimney in a welter of flapping wings and ash cloud. Jess and Percy jumped away simultaneously in surprise, then watched as the goose settled itself on a table. Only then did Jess notice that a gleaming wooden box hung suspended from a leather strap around the goose's neck. "It's carrying a Tiding Horn," she said in amazement. "Is it for you or me, do you think?"

Muncenmast stepped toward the goose, eyes wide and sparkling. "I guess there's only one way to find out."

4

The Ties That Bind

As the late-afternoon sun dipped behind Kylden Hall's ramparts, it drew a curtain of shade over the multitude of shops arrayed outside the eastern walls of the sprawling fortress. Reminded of the approaching evening, the people crowding the streets rushed to complete their errands for the day. Merchants and customers haggled in shop doorways. Horse-drawn wagons and carts pushed by young boys and old women clattered forth in fits and starts down the wide cobblestone streets. And an assortment of soldiers, priests, craftsmen, and other visitors of indeterminate purpose and vocation picked their way through the wider cacophony in desultory fashion. Some talked intently with one another as they went, while others eyed the comely young ladies who dipped in and out of the shops like brightly colored swallows. And amid them all, tucked into the shadows of a narrow alleyway, Traejon sat on his horse, his gaze trained on the sky above the castle.

Far above Kylden Hall's topmost spires, Nomad was carving runes into the heavens with each beat of her wings. This was customary behavior on the falcon's part in the final moments before she entered one of the castle's many towers, and Traejon watched her without concern. But not without a certain melancholy. For truth be told, he had come to feel that Nomad's arabesques over the castle had a wistful quality to them. As if the familiar was coaxing as much joy as she could out of her last moments of flight before submitting to the world of walls, ceilings, and doors below.

Finally, Nomad disappeared inside a high arched window of a tower on the castle's north side. Traejon lowered his gaze to the bustling street before him. His work was done now. If form held, he would have two or three days to himself until he received word that Nomad was heading out again.

Traejon guided his horse out of the alley and into the main current of traffic heading away from Kylden Hall. He kept his hood up over his head as he made his way, aware that his appearance might otherwise attract unwanted attention. True, his skin was light enough to pass for a mainlander. But his smooth jawline, jet-black hair, and piercing sea-green eyes all marked him as *Koah*—a native of the Tomorrow Islands, perched far out on the eastern edge of the Fyngrean Empire. Sightings of the Koah were not commonplace in Kylden and the other cities of western Fyngree, and Traejon had no wish for any keen-eyed observer to notice that the same Koah had a pattern of visiting the outer walls of Kylden Hall every week or two. It had been impressed on him from the start that the identities of past shadows had unraveled on smaller clues.

Within an hour Traejon had made his way through Kylden's honeycombed streets to a quiet inn tucked away on the eastern outskirts of the city. The rooms here were simply furnished but clean, the stable boys gave competent care to the two fine horses provided for him by Treadlow, and the keeper—a somber older woman who ran the inn with military efficiency—was incurious about his comings and goings. She also set a good table, and in return for a modest fee, she washed his clothes and prepared baths for him as well. Traejon smiled as he handed his horse over to one of the inn's stable boys. He had only been gone six days on this occasion, but the prospect of clean sheets, a warm bath, and a hot meal prepared by someone other than himself still filled him with anticipation.

Traejon slept hard and well that night, and after enjoying a late breakfast the following morning he set out to collect his pay. He rode to a small stable on the city's north side and left his mount, then walked several blocks in the general direction of Kylden Hall until he arrived at a small, nondescript tavern sandwiched between the shops of an apothecary and a clockmaker. Traejon glanced briefly at the three wafer-thin rings circling the middle three fingers of his left hand, their black surfaces like tattoos against his bronze skin, then slipped inside and made his way across the sawdust-covered floor to the bar, where a bald, heavily tattooed man with a curly beard was already pouring him a flagon of hard cider. It was only early afternoon and the tavern was nearly empty of other patrons.

"The boats in the harbor were stirring early this morn," the tattooed man said, looking off into the distance. "Tis a beautiful day for sailing."

Traejon nodded, his body relaxing almost imperceptibly. Any mention by the barkeep of incoming stormy weather would have meant that something was off—perhaps a stranger from the previous night asking questions about the tavern's clientele, or a raven that had taken up residence on a roof across the street—and Traejon would have been forced to return another day. Or make his way to another of the secret passageways to Kylden Hall that ran beneath the city. But there were only two other such passages of which Traejon was aware, and the next nearest one was halfway across the city. So he was pleased to hear the report of fine weather, for it meant that he was free to proceed.

Traejon finished his cider in one long draught and flipped a coin on the scuffed and worn bar top. He walked out of the tavern's main room and down a long hallway to the back, where a weathered but sturdy-looking door awaited. A door undetectable to most everyone—even most casters— due to a powerful warding spell. But Traejon walked straight to it.

After one final glance backward to ensure that he wasn't being observed by any curious eyes, Traejon opened the door and stepped inside. Closing the door behind him, Traejon briefly surveyed the cluttered storeroom, then strode over to a tall and dingy wardrobe in a corner. Blackness descended when he stepped inside and closed the doors behind him, but his fingers quickly found the mechanism hidden in the closet's upper right corner. A second door slid open at the back of the cabinet, revealing a flight of rough stone steps illuminated by flickering torches. He started down the stairs, reflecting as he often did whenever he entered this passageway on the strangeness of the life he now led.

Many aspects of the relationship between casters and their familiars remained a mystery to Traejon. Whether they hailed from Fyngree or Rojenhold, the continent's wizards and witches had erected such a complex web of deceptions, disguises, and precautions surrounding the identities and powers of their familiars that pinning down the specifics of the caster-familiar bond felt like trying to catch smoke in your hands.

But one essential element of that bond was known to everyone. When wizards and witches die, whether from sickness or old age or violence, their familiars expire as well. And when familiars die, so too do their human companions—their *compeers*—at the other end of their Threads.

Traejon knew that even King Owyn himself could not escape this iron rule of magic. Owyn could call tens of thousands of soldiers to his side from Kylden and the other provinces of Fyngree. He also ruled from behind the walls of the continent's mightiest fortress. And Owyn himself was said to possess magical powers sufficient to obliterate entire divisions, even after nearly a half-century on the throne.

And yet if Nomad perished, so too would Owyn. Instantly and irrevocably.

Little wonder, then, that witches and wizards took such extensive precautions to protect their familiars. He had heard tell of families with non-noble bloodlines who relocated to remote rural areas when sons or daughters—their young minds and bodies already thrashing in the heavy currents of their transitions to adulthood—woke up to find strange beasts curled up at the foot of their beds. And Traejon had heard stories of casters who roamed the length and breadth of Tempyst's two kingdoms for their entire lives, never residing in a single city or village for more than a few months lest their familiar be identified by a jealous neighbor or ruthless business competitor.

The high sentinels who ruled over the individual cities of Fyngree did not need to resort to such extreme measures of self-preservation, of course. Since in most cases they owed their station to magical powers handed down through their bloodlines for generations, the question was not *whether* they possessed the Thread. The question was *which* creature soaring over the treetops, running through the woods, or departing from a castle tower or royal garden was their familiar. And it was the answer to this question that Tempyst's leading casters, whether they resided in Fyngree or Rojenhold, had become so masterful at hiding.

Traejon had heard that even some minor witches and wizards maintained small sets of highly trained but non-magical birds and animals to conceal the true identities of their familiars. But in Fyngree at least, these decoys—masks, in the argot of those gifted with the Thread—were most often employed by King Owyn and the powerful casting houses that swore fealty to him. Traejon guessed that the king's trainers had as many as three-score beasts of various shapes and sizes that they regularly released into the wild to disguise the significance not only of Nomad, but also of whatever familiar Princess Jessalyn commanded. And each and every one of those creatures was treated upon its release as if Owyn's own heart beat within the animal's breast.

All across Fyngree, for example, sweeping prohibitions against hunting were strictly enforced for numerous wild species—and especially for falcons, eagles, owls, and other birds of prey closely associated with Fyngree's leading casting families. Violations of these hunting bans were viewed as acts of attempted assassination—and punished accordingly. And all the great casting houses maintained heavily guarded towers and groves for masks and familiars to come and go unmolested.

Of course, it would all be so much easier and safer for people gifted with the Thread if their familiars appeared in the form of domesticated animals like cats, dogs, or horses. But for whatever reason, such familiars did not seem to exist except in folktales. Familiars have always been wild creatures, taking the forms of beasts that roam Tempyst's mountains and forests and rivers and seas.

And Traejon had long since surmised that casters do not have the option of caging their familiars for safekeeping.

In the four years he had served as Nomad's shadow, the gyr-falcon had never spent more than two successive nights at Kylden Hall. Perhaps familiars rebelled when threatened with prolonged exposure to humans. Or perhaps they simply lost their vitality—or even their magical properties—if kept from the wild for extended periods. Like so many aspects of the Thread binding familiars to their compeers, the truth of the matter seemed walled off from threadbares such as himself.

Whatever the reasons for permitting familiars to roam free, though, Traejon had reaped considerable financial benefit from the situation. Whether the familiars that wandered the lands of Fyngree followed courses charted by their masters or their own mysterious instinctual imperatives, they needed as much discreet protection as it was possible to give them on their sojourns. And they needed that protection for years and years, since familiars did not grow old and die like their non-magical counterparts. Or like their compeers, for that matter.

And so in addition to the hunting laws and the use of masks, Fyngree's wealthier casters sought out and recruited men and women with specific skill sets to follow both their familiars and their masks. Usually the individuals who served in this role were experienced scouts, trackers, and marksmen plucked from the military. These "shadows" pursued their assigned creatures through the wilderness with single-minded devotion, as if they alone bore the responsibility for the life of their employer. Which for all they knew, they did.

Of course, no shadow was supposed to know whether the animal he or she was tracking was a mask or an actual familiar. That was all part of the symphony of misdirection, deception, and mystery so carefully scored by the casters of Fyngree.

But Traejon has known for more than two years now that Nomad is King Owyn's familiar. And the man waiting for Traejon at the end of this passageway knows it.

It was with this thought running through his mind that Traejon arrived at a heavy oaken door heavily banded in iron. He pounded on the door with his fist, and a moment later the door swung open. The silhouette of a massive body filled the doorway.

"Ah, there you are," rumbled Fyfe Treadlow, commander of Kylden Hall's secret Shadow Guard. "Come in. We've got a lot to talk about."

Traejon stepped into the sparsely furnished room, glancing sidelong at Treadlow as the captain settled into a massive leather chair behind a similarly massive desk, a hint of a wince flashing across his face. As always, Treadlow presented an imposing appearance. He was a giant of a man, layered in great slabs of muscle that carried only the slightest layer of middle-aged fat on them, and his black skin gleamed like obsidian in the light cast by the chamber's hearth fire. Years of scowling, meanwhile, had set the wrinkles lining Treadlow's face into a perpetually forbidding expression. Indeed, he always looked to Traejon as if he had just received news of a particularly disagreeable nature.

Traejon had no doubt that if Fyngree ever went to war, hundreds of soldiers would march under Treadlow's command. And if the captain's eyesight was better and he did not limp so badly in wet weather, he would probably be a shadow himself. Perhaps even Nomad's shadow. But the kingdom was at peace, Treadlow squinted whenever he looked across the room, and there probably wasn't a horse in all of Tempyst blessed with both the strength to carry Treadlow's bulk and the speed to get him anywhere swiftly.

And so here Treadlow sat, tucked away deep in the bowels of Kylden Hall, wielding nothing but a ledger, a quill pen, and an inkpot to orchestrate the comings and goings of the masks and shadows belonging to King Owyn and Princess Jessalyn—as well as the handful of Fyngrean spies that had managed to burrow themselves into Rojenhold over the years. Not for the first time, Traejon wondered how Treadlow felt about his lot. The work was vital, to be sure; but he thought that such dreary duty—so far from the open skies, deep-running rivers, and silent forests that he had come to think of as his home—would drive him mad in a matter of weeks.

"So," said Treadlow as he tossed a heavy leather purse across the desk toward Traejon. "What's the latest?"

Traejon smiled to himself. Treadlow had never been much for idle chatter. The shadow tucked the coins away and told Treadlow about Nomad's discovery of the gutted homestead on the north branch of the Whetstone.

"Do you think we have a bandit problem over there?" Treadlow asked after he was done.

"Hard to say. They didn't leave a lot to sift through. Not far to the Marching Mountains from there, and that's always been a favorite refuge for those with a taste for robbing and pillaging." He paused, his eyes searching Treadlow's face. "But you don't think it was bandits."

Treadlow sniffed. "I don't know whether it was bandits or not. But if so, they've been busy. There have been two similar incidents in the last few weeks, one on the Gryndstone and one east of Treffentown."

"The Gryndstone could be the work of the same bandits. It runs right out of the Marching Mountains. But Treffentown is hundreds of miles away. That's not the same group."

"No, I suppose not." Treadlow rose and turned to a long wooden table behind him. He poured two glasses of water from a pitcher and handed one to Traejon. "Did you hear that Karon Marsho is dead?"

Traejon raised his eyebrows. Marsho had long been one of King Owyn's most important allies in Fyngree's eastern provinces. It was widely rumored that the prosperous Tydewater merchant had built his fortune through enchantments that ensured smooth passage for his own trade vessels and stormy seas for those of his competitors. But whether that was true or the grousing of jealous competitors, Marsho's loyalty to the Throneholder had always been unquestioned.

"What happened?"

"No one knows exactly except that his Thread was snapped. His familiar was a kestrel, by the way. No reason to keep that a secret any more, I suppose. Marsho was down at the Tydewater docks yesterday morning, supervising the loading of one of his ships. He was talking with the ship's quartermaster when his eyes suddenly rolled up in his head and he collapsed in a heap, just like that." Treadlow snapped his fingers.

"I don't see a connection to the raids."

"Nor do I. But that doesn't mean there isn't one."

"What are you hearing from the northern outposts?"

Treadlow snorted. "Other than the news about the attack outside of Treffentown? Nothing. None of the garrisons along Tucker's Front are reporting any unusual activity. All quiet from Valyedon as well. But we haven't heard from any of our agents in Rojenhold for several weeks. That's unusual. And troubling."

Traejon pondered the matter for a moment. "Have you thought about asking the king to send his familiar up there?" he asked carefully.

Treadlow fell silent. Traejon studied the man across from him impassively. He knew that Treadlow was wary by nature, and that keeping his shadows in the dark about whether they were tracking a true familiar or a mere mask was part of his job. But he felt a glimmer of irritation at the captain's evasiveness. Why continue to maintain this pretense that Traejon was unaware of Nomad's true identity?

His thoughts drifted back to a crisp fall day nearly two years past, when he and Nomad had been traveling along the coast of the Amaranthine Sea, across the black sand beaches of Vanguard Bay. The gyrfalcon had been soaring high above the sands when a golden eagle appeared out of a stand of trees along the beach and began pursuing her. The familiar changed course and flew down directly toward Traejon, as if seeking protection. And Traejon obliged, shooting the streaking eagle out of the air from forty yards. As remarkable as Nomad's behavior had been, though, his suspicions about her magical nature were not confirmed until a few days later, when Traejon was summoned to Kylden Hall by royal courier so that the king and his daughter could express their personal gratitude to him for saving Nomad's life. Expressions of gratitude that had been given over the objections of Treadlow, no doubt.

And yet, the captain continued to maintain this half-hearted charade that Traejon was unaware of Nomad's importance. Why bother? Traejon opened his mouth to challenge Treadlow on the point, only to have the words die on his lips. For the captain's expression had changed to that of a man reluctantly preparing to enter uncharted waters.

"I'm not certain the Throneholder would survive such a separation," Treadlow rumbled irritably. "Four or five years ago? Perhaps. But King Owyn's not as young and vital as he once was. It is at least a fortnight's journey just to the eastern reaches of the Speartips from here, even for you. And that doesn't even account for the return trip. Surely you've noticed that Nomad's travels have become more circumscribed over the last two or three years. She's almost never gone from the king's side for more than a week now."

"What about Princess Jessalyn's familiar?" Traejon suggested. "If he possesses the power of flight and you have faith in the capabilities of his shadow, perhaps it could be sent instead."

Treadlow hesitated for the briefest of instants, and understanding struck Traejon like a thunderbolt: Princess Jessalyn had no familiar. She was threadbare.

"King Owyn would never approve such a scheme," Treadlow snapped. "And I don't have enough evidence to convince him or Pynch to make such a request of any of Fyngree's other casters. Besides, few of their familiars have the power of flight. One might as well send human scouts."

Treadlow pushed himself out of his chair and began pacing the room. "So that's what I've done. They left last week. But until they return—or I receive word from Treffentown or our agents in Rojenhold—there's little I can do."

"If they made contact up in the northern provinces with a caster that you trust, they could send a Tiding Horn," Traejon suggested. "Shave several days off the time it would take for them to inform you of anything they find."

"You think I didn't think of that?" Treadlow growled testily. "I approached Pynch about that possibility last week. He rejected the idea in his usual condescending way. Said that making a Tiding Horn was advanced magic, beyond the capabilities of any known casters living north of the Loaf. Other than Thrynjack Brymborne, and who knows where his allegiances lie? Besides, no one's seen him in years. And there's Aleyda Tusk over in Valyedon, but that's a fair distance north of Treffentown and even farther from Tucker's Front. Pynch said that there probably aren't more than two dozen casters in all of Fyngree with that kind of power. How am I supposed to know?"

The captain stopped pacing and leaned against the corner of the table. He looked off into the distance, an expression of genuine puzzlement on his face. "That surprised me, actually. Doesn't it seem like Tiding Horns used to be more commonplace? When I was a young soldier, our garrison commander used to get one or two a month. Perhaps it's true what some people are saying: That casters are dying out, slowly but surely. That someday there won't be any witches or wizards left. That would be a strange world, wouldn't it?"

Dismissing the thought with a wave of his hand, Treadlow returned to his chair. "In any event, I've been informed that Nomad is departing tomorrow morning at dawn. So make your preparations." He paused, then plunged ahead. "You need to be careful, Frost. It feels like something's gone sour out there. Laugh if you want. I'm just an old bookkeeper these days. But something's in the air. Something that has my hackles up. And I don't like it."

Traejon met Treadlow's gaze. "I'm not laughing, Captain. Because I can feel it too."

5

A Visitor in the Night

Ben Thystle and his family had just settled in for a late supper when the evening quiet was broken by the hard rapping of a fist on the front door. Ben's gaze darted to his father at one end of the table, then his mother at the other. On each of his parents' faces he saw the same flare of fear. Visitors were a rarity after sundown in this remote precinct of Rojenhold. And their family no longer enjoyed unexpected company.

"Someone's at the door, " said Ben's younger brother, a button-nosed towhead of five years. It was an absentminded observation, though; the bulk of his focus remained on the chunk of potato that he was chasing around his plate with his fork.

"I know, Rowan," their father said. "Eat your supper."

Ben closed his eyes, cursing the sudden lurching thud of his heartbeat. It always did this now, whenever someone knocked on their door. But tonight it was pounding so hard that it felt like it might splinter his ribs. And he knew why. When the sun went down in Rojenhold, its roads, woods, and fields emptied quickly. Only predators or fools would be out there now. And the hard rapping on the door did not sound as if it belonged to a fool.

Ben was seventeen, and the spindly build of his early teen years had finally begun giving way to lean muscle and broadening shoulders. But his cheeks were still soft and free of whiskers, and at this precise moment, Ben wished that he could just be a young child again. A youngster who could chase the nightmares of his dark bed away by curling up in the comforting lap of his murmuring, cooing mother or pipe-smoking father.

"Calm yourself, Ben," Ben's father muttered. "It is nothing, I'm sure." Ben opened his eyes, face flushing at the quiet rebuke, and watched his father push himself away from the table.

Ben stole a glance at his mother, who was sitting rigidly in her chair, eyes wide as they followed her husband's progress to the door. River and Sea, he thought miserably. She was even more frightened than he was at the prospect of receiving a night visitor. But perhaps they were both wrong, he told himself. Perhaps it was only a neighbor, come to seek advice or share a morsel of gossip. Maybe it was Dorya Frendfell from down the lane. Or even Roland Overbeek, who was forever arguing over the price his father paid him for his wheat. Any of their neighbors would do.

Then Ben's father opened the door. He said something indistinct, his voice muffled by the door and the sounds of the rising wind outside. And horses too. Ben could hear them now, snorting and clopping about in the darkness. He looked to the right of the door, to a small leaded glass window that looked out into the front yard. Torches bobbed in the blackness like monstrous fireflies, at least a half dozen of them.

The man at the threshold of their home had brought friends.

Then he was inside their home, wiping his boots on a rough rug as his father quietly shut the door behind him. The stranger was a broad-shouldered man of medium height, with a spade-like black goatee that accentuated the hard lines of his face. And over his left eye, a patch of oxblood red that matched the color of his cloak. His right eye, meanwhile, seemed intent on doing the work of both itself and its ruined twin. It examined the room with a kind of feral intensity, stalking across every cupboard and chair and plate as if it were hunting down some cowering quarry hidden among the home's domestic trappings.

Yet the man's ravenous eye was not the most frightening aspect of his appearance. For emblazoned on the back of the man's cloak was a roaring gryphon in black silhouette—the symbol of Stormheel's Faithful Shield guard. The emblem was such a shattering sight that Ben almost groaned. But then he heard his mother clear her throat, and he forced himself to look sideways in her direction. She was staring at him—no, *glaring* at him—and Ben well knew the message in her eyes. *Stay calm. Don't panic. Let's see what he wants. It may have nothing to do with us. With you.*

"As I said, the mill is closed for the evening," Ben's father said, and he could hear the faint tremble in his voice. "But you are welcome to warm yourself at our fire, Captain. And if you have any business to discuss I'd be happy to meet with you come the morrow."

The one-eyed man grinned at him. "You'll deign to fit me into your busy schedule tomorrow, you mean? Is that really the tack you want to take with an officer of the Faithful Shield, Master . . . Thystle, is it? Wynston Thystle?"

Ben saw his father's face go pale. "I-I meant no offense . . . "

The man clapped Wynston on the shoulder, as if they were old friends sharing a few pints down at the tavern. "None taken! But I do have a few pressing questions about your mill for which I'm seeking answers tonight. And I would very much appreciate the opportunity to chase away the chill for a moment. It's turning into a perfectly dreadful evening."

"Yes, of course," Wynston said quickly. He glanced toward the closed door. "Would your companions. . . ."

"—Like to join us? That's very generous of you, Master Thystle. But I don't think that is advisable." The soldier leaned in toward Ben's father, as if he were sharing a great confidence. "The gentlemen outside are not cut from the same civilized cloth as you and I, I'm afraid. To be candid, I think you'll be much happier if they remain outside."

The one-eyed man turned his attention to the dining table where Ben, Rowan, and their mother were still seated. Ben felt unable to move, though his eyes flitted about the room like trapped moths, unable to alight on anything for more than an instant. The younger boy, though, was staring at the stranger in goggle-eyed fascination, his face a flushed mix of excitement and apprehension.

"Good evening!" the stranger said with what seemed to be genuine enthusiasm. He gazed around the room again, his expression one of complete delight at the simple but well-made furnishings, the crackling fireplace, the glowing lantern suspended above the table, and the food laid out below. His one good eye then turned to Ben's mother, shining on her face like the light from some alien moon. "What a lovely home you have!"

"Thank you," she said quietly.

"Yes, lovely, just lovely." He turned back to Ben's father. "And who is this handsome woman before me? And these fine strapping lads?"

Wynston cleared his throat and stepped forward. "This is my wife Malkyn. And these are my sons, Rowan and Ben."

The one-eyed man bowed to Malkyn, then turned to the boys, nodding first to Rowan, then to Ben. "Hello, young masters."

"Hello," said Rowan, his voice muffled by a hunk of half-chewed bread in his mouth. The man reached over and lightly tousled his hair with one gloved hand, casually glancing across the table at the boy's mother as he did so. Ben saw his mother tense, but she said nothing.

Ben forced himself to meet the stranger's eye when it swung his way. *Stay calm. Maybe his visit has nothing to do with you.* "Hello, milord," he said, his voice a croak.

The soldier smiled down on him. "Oh, no 'your lordships' for me, young master. I have no estate or title to trumpet. I've earned every coin in *my* purse."

The man walked over and settled heavily into a large cushioned rocking chair by the hearth. "Now then—", he said, only to stop when he saw that Wynston was still standing indecisively by the doorway. He gestured to the table. "Please, Master Thystle! Sit! This won't take long." As Ben's father slowly returned to his seat, the one-eyed man pulled the heavy leather gloves off his hands. He wiggled his thick blunt fingers before the fire. He has strangler's hands, Ben thought dully.

"I am Faxon Glynt, captain of the Faithful Shield and humble servant of Lord Thylus Whytewender," the one-eyed man said. "And it is in that capacity that I'm visiting you tonight."

Glynt shifted forward in the rocking chair and grabbed the poker at the side of the hearth. He leaned into the fire and pushed a few of the logs around. "Master Thystle?" he said, addressing Ben's father without taking his attention from the fire.

"Yes, captain?"

"Until about a year ago, you owned a mill along the Monument River in Hanken, isn't that correct?"

Wynston sat perfectly still for a second, then slowly nodded. "Yes, that's right." he swallowed hard and rubbed his hand along his mouth. "You see, we—"

"Now my understanding is that your mill there was a very successful enterprise," Glynt said, giving the logs a final poke before turning to face the room. "And no wonder, considering its location. Close proximity to the corn and grain growers of the coast. Regular sales to buyers in Stormheel. And the mill itself! I visited it a fortnight ago. You must have been very proud of what you built there. You'll be pleased to hear, I'm sure, that that magnificent water wheel is still churning away, still driving those millstones for the new owners. They are doing quite well for themselves, just as you did during your time there."

"Yes, we enjoyed our years in Hanken, but—"

Glynt raised a hand and Ben's father fell silent. It was as if the one-eyed man had closed the lid on a music box. The captain carefully laid the poker against the wall by the hearth and leaned back in his chair. He began rocking, the chair creaking each time his weight shifted back on its rockers. "I find it so odd," he continued, as if his host had not said a word, "that a successful mill owner would voluntarily leave such a thriving location while still in the prime of his working life. And why would such a devoted father and mother deprive their children of such a comfortable and secure future?"

Ben felt his hopes flicker and gutter out as Glynt lazily batted his father around. Listening to them was like watching a barn cat play with a crippled mouse. There was only one way this visit was going to end. Ben saw that now. He bowed his head in silent despair, as if preparing his neck for the executioner's axe.

But as Ben bent his head he saw the gleaming cutting knife that his father had brought to the table for supper. It sat only a few feet away, perched on the same platter as the venison that his mother had prepared. He studied the blade, which his mother kept honed to a fine edge. And then his heart began thudding in a whole new way.

Ben forced himself to block out the voices of Glynt and his father. Only by wiping his mind clear could he hope to coax the cursed magic that had infiltrated his bones out of hiding. He stared at the knife as if everything else in the room had vanished. As if he had awakened from a dream to find that of all the things in his life, only that blade was real. His hands began to move in his lap, twisting and jerking of their own accord. A moment later he felt strange words alight on his lips. They floated out in whispers so faint that even Ben himself could barely hear them. A feeling of lightheadedness washed over him, and some dim part of his mind wondered if he was going to faint. But the lightheadedness dissipated, vanquished by a sudden surge of exultation.

For the knife had moved. It now hovered about an inch above the platter, its silvery blade trembling in the lamplight.

And then Ben heard, as if from a great distance, the rhythmic creaking of the rocking chair come to a halt.

Glynt remained seated, but his feet were planted firmly on the floor, and he leaned forward so that his forearms rested on his thighs. "And why leave your mill in

Hanken for this?" he said to Wynston in a tone of bewilderment, gesturing with both hands to the shadowy corners of
the room. He cocked his one good eye at his host. "I took the
liberty of peeking at your mill operation next door before announcing my arrival," he said in a confidential tone, "and that
only added to my confusion. Your mill here is horse-powered!
What a modest operation this must feel like after leaving
Hanken. And the volume of grain raised in this valley pales
next to what the growers on the coast produce."

Ben risked a glance over at his father. The polite
smiles that he had mustered upon Glynt's arrival were absent
now, and he could see the fear rising in his eyes.

"Lord Whytewender works very hard to provide opportunity and security to the people of Rojenhold, Master
Thystle," Glynt said, baring his teeth in what Ben now saw as
a grotesque parody of a smile. "It . . . *disturbs* the king when
word reaches him of such developments. To leave a prosperous business and community for a more impoverished
existence in one of the most remote and inhospitable corners
of the empire. . . . Well, as I said, it is all quite puzzling from
afar. So the king asked me to make the long journey out here
to inquire about your decision to relocate. What would you
like me to tell him?"

"I understand King Whytewender's confusion, captain," stammered Wynston. "And perhaps it *was* an impulsive
decision. Foolish even. But I was born and raised not far from
here, and we had often talked of turning to a simpler, less
frantic life."

Glynt stared at Wynston, that terrible grin slipping
from his face as if it were some dark, marauding leviathan of
the sea returning to the depths from whence it sprang.

Malkyn frantically rose from her seat. "Captain,
please. Wynston forgets to mention that Rowan fell very ill

last year. He never stopped coughing, you could hear the sickness in his chest. We thought that perhaps a respite from the river air would be helpful."

"Yes, that's right," Wynston hurriedly agreed, "He's been sleeping so much more soun—"

"Tell me, young master," Glynt interrupted, turning his single glittering eye toward Ben's younger brother. "Do you like your new home out here?" The captain's voice was silky now, soothing.

"Yes, sir," Rowan said, glancing anxiously at his mother. Even in his distracted state, Ben could tell that he was unnerved by the abruptness with which he'd become the center of attention.

"Good, good. And do you like exploring the woods with your brother?"

"I'm not allowed in the woods. And Ben can't play with me very often. He helps father in the mill." Suddenly his face brightened. "He reads to me at night sometimes."

"What a good brother you have! It's probably a good idea to stay out of those woods. No telling what kind of nasty beasts are out there, prowling around."

The little boy nodded, eyes widening slightly.

"Did you know that some wild animals might even be attracted to your father's mill? For the grain inside, I mean. Rats, for instance. Rats love grain."

Wynston set both of his hands on the table. "Captain, I really—"

"Hush," Glynt said softly, his good eye never leaving the little boy, and once again the music box snapped shut. "Do you ever see rats creeping around your father's mill?"

The boy shook his head, and everyone in the room could see how he wanted to go to his mother. Yet he remained seated, pinned to his chair by the gaze of the one-eyed man.

"No? Well, that's good! Maybe you have a pet that keeps the rats away. Tell me, young master. Do you have a pet that keeps the rats away? Like . . . a kitty?"

Ben heard his mother groan audibly, saw out of the corner of his eye as she staggered back into her chair. Glynt smiled and stood, shoving the rocking chair behind him so that it rocked crazily at the edge of the crackling fire, its back banging against the stone hearth. He walked casually over to the table, shaking his head as if in great sorrow. Glynt stopped next to where Ben was seated.

"This charade has become tiresome," the captain said as he pulled his gloves back on, his shadow falling over the boy. "The hour is growing late and the nearest inn of any consequence is miles away."

The one-eyed man looked to Wynston at the far end of the table. "The Faithful Shield sees everything, Master Thystle. Did you and your wife really believe that you could just slip away and that no one would inform the Shield? Could you have been that foolish?"

Now Rowan did go to his mother. He silently slid out of his seat and shuffled over on stiff legs to his mother's side, where he slipped under the curve of her sheltering arm.

Doing his best to ignore Glynt's looming presence, Ben willed the knife higher. A fresh gust of whispers floated out of his mouth, and an instant later the blade rose another inch. It was hovering about three inches off the tabletop now. *Do it, Ben,* he told himself. *Slit this bastard's throat.*

Glynt pivoted and slammed the knife to the table with one gloved fist, the blow rattling the dinnerware. Ben jumped in shock, and he felt the magic that he had conjured up drain out of his body as if it had never been there.

The soldier leaned down until his good eye was mere inches from Ben's pale, frightened face. "I bring an invitation from Lord Whytewender, young master," he said in a low and ugly voice. "An invitation for you and your family to fill an important role in the defense of Rojenhold from those who would do it harm, both within and without. It's a great honor, really. I'd counsel you in the strongest possible terms not to spurn it. So why don't you invite the fifth member of your family out here to join us and hear my invitation, Ben? Or would you rather that my companions use their torches to smoke your friend out? Perhaps there will be room for all of you at the inn after your home is a blackened husk."

Ben looked over at his father, who nodded grimly. He turned away from Glynt and looked to the back of the main room, where a short hallway led to the bedroom that he and his younger brother shared. "Wynk?" he called in a heartbroken voice. "Come out, Wynk. It's ok."

They all waited silently, and for a brief panicked moment Ben wondered if Wynk had fled. But then the leopard padded slowly into the room, her light gray eyes burning with the reflections from the lantern and the hearth fire. The beast was huge, with paws that looked as big as dinner plates and a thick, twitching tail. Her fur was a blanket of white dappled with inky black spots. The spots on her head were small, and they trailed away from the base of her broad nose and her whiskers to the top of her head like ash on snow. On her broad flanks and shoulders, though, the spots widened into great whorls of gray and black.

Wynk sat a few feet away from the table and turned her inscrutable gaze on Glynt. The one-eyed man returned the creature's look, his good eye traveling up and down her length. "Oh you are going to be useful indeed," Glynt breathed, that ravenous grin breaking to the surface once more.

Ben looked over to where Malkyn sat, expressionless but for the tears rolling down her face. *She knows it, too. My life is over.* And with that thought echoing blackly in his mind, Ben turned away to hide the rush of his own bitter tears.

6

Dream Come True

Brundy Sevenshade cleared his throat and glanced over at Pynch. Their eyes met for a moment before the king's high votary turned away with a shrug. Good luck, the gesture seemed to say.

King Owyn caught their wordless exchange out of the corner of his eye and felt a prick of irritation. But he found himself unable to muster the energy to bark at them. Instead, the brooding monarch merely slouched deeper into his chair and returned his gaze to the crackling fire before him.

They had gathered this evening in Owyn's spacious private chambers. The room itself was spectacularly framed, with gleaming marble floors and a vaulted ceiling supported by massive arched beams carved from dragon oak. Aside from a handful of sumptuously overstuffed chairs and a few bright tapestries and heavy rugs, however, it was modestly appointed. Even the bed upon which the king laid himself to sleep every night was a relatively understated affair, with blankets, sheets, and pillows that had been chosen for comfort and warmth rather than ostentatious display. Tucked into the far corner of the room behind a half-closed curtain, the bed waited for him now like an obedient hound.

Owyn, though, had turned his chair away from the room. He had placed it only a few feet away from the massive stone hearth, then cast a spell that had turned the fire within into a virtual bonfire, one that radiated heat and light into every corner of his chambers. Owyn watched the flames intently, eyes unblinking despite the fierce heat that blanketed him.

"We have many fine raptors on hand, sire," Brundy concluded. "I'm confident that the training that I can provide, augmented by your spell work, will produce a bird of such apparent authenticity that no one outside of this room will ever suspect that it is a mask. All the world will believe that Princess Jessalyn carries the Thread—and a powerful one at that."

Brundy's words hung in the air for a lengthening moment, and Owyn scratched at his beard. The falconer would hover at his side for the rest of the evening if he did not offer some sort of response.

"I appreciate your efforts, Brundy," said Owyn. "But creating a mask capable of fooling the enemies of Kylden Hall is only a half-measure. It does not provide my daughter with the magical powers that—sooner or later—she will need to defend herself and Fyngree when I'm gone."

Owyn abruptly rose from his seat. This conversation was getting them nowhere. He strode toward the gleaming oaken door that provided the only entrance into his chambers. Recognizing that the king was bringing their audience to a close, Pynch and Sevenshade fell in behind him like ducklings.

"Good night, gentlemen," he said, opening the door. "We'll talk again tomorrow."

Owyn watched the men disappear down the hallway, then turned to the nearest of the two guardsmen standing watch outside his door. "Has Princess Jessalyn returned yet?"

"Not to my knowledge. We haven't yet received notification from her attendants."

"Very well," Owyn said. "Let me know when she does so."

"Yes, Your Majesty."

Owyn shut the door and wandered over to a long table of polished black stone, upon which sat an assortment of goblets, bottles, and flagons. He poured himself a half-glass of red wine and returned to his seat in front of the fire. It was pointless to go to bed until Jess returned to Kylden Hall. He would just toss and turn until Gwyn sent word. So he took a sip from the goblet and watched the fire dance. And as he did so, he felt his mind slip away to years long past.

† † †

It hardly seemed possible to him now that the primary emotion he had felt when the Thread failed to appear in Jess was relief. When she had first been born, of course, he hadn't thought about the Thread one way or the other. He had been too lost in the all-consuming love he felt for the amazing creature in his arms. Even his love for his wife Ayleth, as great as it was, had been eclipsed by the devotion he felt for Jess when she entered their lives as a squalling, red-faced infant. And he remembered how Ayleth had been similarly transformed by Jessalyn's arrival.

After those first joyful months of parenthood, however, their thoughts gradually turned to the future. And when they did, their brows clouded with the knowledge that once their daughter reached adolescence and her familiar appeared, her life might be extinguished at any moment by events hundreds of miles distant.

The knowledge filled them with a dread that seemed to swell with each passing day. How did the parents of young casters "blessed" with the Thread live with such a threat looming over them? How had their own parents made peace with that? How were they not paralyzed by the knowledge that their child could keel over dead at any moment if his or her familiar met with misfortune in its travels?

As the months passed by, they found themselves increasingly preoccupied with tales of parents who had been so devastated. Parents like Lord and Lady Grandyse, who lost their teenage son in precisely such a manner. The boy had been out riding with his father a few months earlier when he suddenly slid from his saddle and crumpled to the ground, his life snuffed out in the blink of an eye. The House of Grandyse never found out what happened to the boy's familiar. All they knew was that their son was suddenly, mysteriously . . . gone. Did this same anguish lie in wait for them?

Their anxiety was further amplified by the knowledge that, like virtually all of Fyngree's ruling class, they both came from long lines of casters. Owyn was the scion of the Suntold family, rulers of Kylden for most of the last two centuries. Ayleth hailed from the Tremeny clan, the most powerful casting house in Tydewater, and her familiar—a great fierce-eyed heron named Coyn—was of no mean consequence. Since they both carried the Thread—and powerful Threads at that—they never doubted that a familiar would someday enter Jess's life. She would wake one morning shortly after her first menarche to find a fox curled up at the foot of her bed, or an owl hooting from the sill of one of her bedroom windows, or a marten burrowing under her covers.

And then Ayleth died one night while he was on official business in Thryn, hundreds of miles away. Attendants found her body in their private chambers, unmarked but lifeless. The only explanation was that she too had been carried to the Far Shore as a result of some misfortune suffered by her familiar. But Coyn's shadow could shed no light on the heron's demise. The familiar had been out of his sight, flying over a fog-shrouded lake, when he had met his mysterious end.

When Owyn had received word of his wife's death, his grief had nearly undone him. For the next several months he felt as if he was drowning in a raging cataract, swallowing great gulps of cold black water with every breath. Life without the only woman he had ever loved seemed impossible. He spent his days in a numb haze and his nights staring into the dark, bleakly imagining all the different ways that Coyn might have perished.

The mysterious circumstances of Ayleth's death also underscored with shattering impact just how vulnerable his daughter was. Jessalyn's Thread would someday uncoil from the hidden den in which it slumbered. And on that day Jessalyn would feel the first tingle of magic in her fingers and Owyn would embrace her with a wide smile of congratulations. Knowing all the while that the world had just gained another avenue by which it could break his heart.

But the Thread never came.

Jessalyn experienced her first menarche, and nothing happened. Weeks and months passed by, and even as Jess began to blossom into the young woman she was now, her Thread refused to show itself. Does this mean I will never be a wizard like you, father? Jessalyn would ask, and he would tell her to be patient. But he was filled with a secret joy. It felt like a dream come true. If Jess did not carry the Thread, he would never have to worry about her heart stopping in mid-sentence—or on her wedding day or in the midst of giving birth to his first grandchild—because her familiar had been slain by a poacher or killed in a storm hundreds of miles away.

But then came the day when his relief turned to ash.

It arrived on a sunny day a little more than three years ago, during an ordinary meeting with Pynch and the other members of his Votary Council. The discussion had ranged over the usual topics. Harvest prospects for the Loaf. Progress on harbor, bridge, and road projects. Reports from Tucker's Front on the movements of the perpetually restive armies of Rojenhold. But then a votary from Talonoux had hesitantly asked if anyone else had heard a rumor—a whisper of a rumor, really—that Thylus Whytewender was violating his own edict against exploring the derelict towers and ruined monasteries that dotted the interior of the Elvish Islands.

That had been a disquieting rumor indeed. The ruins of the Elvish Islands were understood to be relics of a bygone age of dark and alien magic. After the elves vanished, the rulers of Rojenhold had imposed a total ban on travel to the islands, which squatted closer to their capital of Stormheel than to any other city in either kingdom of Tempyst. And they had enforced the ban for more than three centuries.

The ban had always galled Owyn for its presumption. Stormheel Keep had no more authority over the islands than did Kylden Hall. The Elvish Islands were not officially part of *either* of Tempyst's two kingdoms. The islands had such forbidding reputations that neither Fyngree nor Rojenhold had wanted them after the elves had disappeared. Claiming them would have been like inviting an adder into one's own bed.

On occasion, though, Owyn had grudgingly conceded that imposing the quarantine had been a wise move. It was true that few people had any desire to go anywhere near the islands. On several occasions, however, Rojenholdean patrol ships had intercepted vessels approaching the islands' misty shorelines. In every case, the vessels had been commanded by madmen—wizards or pirates or religious fanatics—who had convinced themselves that they could tap into the dark magic of the islands without being consumed.

The fact of the matter was that the ban had been effective, and it was widely supported throughout Fyngree. What of it if the ban was enforced by Stormheel rather than Kylden? The main thing was that the quarantine existed. And as Throneholders had come and gone without directly challenging Stormheel's authority to impose and maintain the ban, its unofficial status as gatekeeper of the islands had calcified into reality.

In recent years, however, the historically chilly diplomatic relations between Rojenhold and Fyngree had fallen to depths not seen since the two-century-old Broken Wing Wars, the blood-drenched conflict that had established the present borders between the two nations.

Most Fyngreans did not realize just how badly the relationship had curdled. Why would they? After all, the two kingdoms remained sworn to the common defense of Tempyst in the event that the sails of an invading fleet ever materialized on the horizon. And trade between the two nations remained as robust as ever—though that stemmed more from Rojenhold's meager domestic stores than any mutual warmth. Rojenhold was largely a land of rock and clay and ice, with only a narrow strip of coastal land well-suited for farming. Unable to grow sufficient volumes of food on their own, Stormheel and the other cities of Rojenhold depended for their very survival on the bounteous foodstuffs generated by the green fields and pastures of the Loaf. Fyngrean complacency was further fed by the knowledge that ever since the Broken Wing Wars, the combined military and magical might of Fyngree had always exceeded that of Rojenhold by a comfortable margin.

In the twenty years since Thylus Whytewender had ascended the throne at Stormheel, though, his resentment of Rojenhold's subordinate status had become more and more evident to Owyn. Mostly, Whytewender expressed himself with fits of pique. He rejected all invitations to visit Kylden or any other Fyngrean city. He refused to send representatives to appear before Owyn and the Votary Council for all but the most pressing trade negotiations. He introduced new licensing policies that were so expensive and serpentine that Fyngrean theatrical troupes and musicians stopped performing in Rojenhold.

In more recent years, however, Whytewender's hostility had begun to take more unsettling forms. Fyngrean spies operating in Stormheel and Strovenstaff reported that his Faithful Shield, the elite corps of warriors that served as the beating heart of the king's security forces, were intercepting and burning shipments of books and pamphlets from Fyngree. Meanwhile, the tracts and leaflets coming out of Stormheel's own print shops no longer clung to the comforting if delusional fiction that the kingdoms of Rojenhold and Fyngree were equals. Instead they spoke resentfully of Fyngree's power and prosperity, and implied that its stature could be traced to centuries of Fyngrean treachery and greed. Some of their broadsides even began to drip with scorn for Owyn himself.

It was against this backdrop of escalating tension that the votary from Talonoux had raised the possibility that

Stormheel was violating its own Elvish Islands quarantine. Little wonder that the rumor caused an immediate uproar around the council table. The clamor did not subside until Owyn conjured a crash of thunder that rolled across the hall with such violence that the votaries cringed and covered their ears. The thunderclap stunned everyone—even Pynch was startled—but it served its intended purpose of restoring order to the gathering.

Over the next several minutes Owyn had canvassed every council member. No one else had heard the rumor. By the time the last votary had spoken, the assembled men and women had convinced themselves that the rumor was nothing but a phantasm spawned by the increased tensions between the two kingdoms.

But Owyn had not been so reassured. The next day he sent Nomad to the Elvish Islands. The bird was gone for nearly a month, and by the last week of Nomad's absence Owyn was bedridden. But early one morning the gyrfalcon returned, and when he laid a trembling hand on Nomad's wing, he felt the life and vitality return to his limbs and organs, as if the familiar had brought a long cool rain to drought-parched soil.

At the same time, he felt Nomad's experiences of the Elvish Islands wash over him in an exhilarating rush. Gazing at the islands through the familiar's eyes, he soared over dense forests, swooped along fog-shrouded ruins and rocky cliff walls, gazed down at a lone man tramping through the forest in pursuit, always following following following. Nomad's shadow, a former soldier named Frost.

When Owyn released Nomad from his touch, he had felt enormously reassured. The islands had been as silent and still as ever, untouched by human activity.

But the following evening he had been tormented by a nightmare in which some great winged beast flew under cover of night toward Kylden, a ball of roiling green-tinted fire in each misshapen hand. As the beast surged forward through the sky, the very constellations seemed to tremble in its wake. And somehow, as Owyn tracked the monster through the fathomless blackness of his own dream, he realized that the monster was coming for his daughter. That was when he awoke, his body coated in an icy film of sweat.

The nightmare had shaken him to his core. It had felt like an omen. And so over the next several weeks he sought out any spell or ingredient or potion that held even a remote prospect of awakening the Thread within his daughter. But each effort failed. And with each failure, he felt the pressure in his chest increase, as if his heart was being squeezed in a vice.

He was an old man now, and Jess would become Throneholder when he finally departed for the Far Shore. But without her own casting powers to draw from, how would she be able to withstand predations by Whytewender and his armies of the north? Or by treacherous casters and high sentinels within Fyngree itself? Would the death of Owyn Suntold mark the advent of a bloody new chapter in Fyngree's history? One that would buffet his beloved but helpless daughter like a leaf in a storm?

King Owyn stared into the flames, his goblet empty now. His dream had come true. His daughter was threadbare. And tonight the knowledge filled him with bleak sorrow. For in some dim corridor of his being, he felt the truth of that night vision. Something was approaching. Something with gleaming eyes and sharp fangs and a terrible, terrible appetite.

7

A Message

Jess watched as Percy grasped the leather strap hanging around the goose's neck. He carefully lifted the Tiding Horn over the bird's head and set it on a nearby table. They both regarded the box silently for a moment, studying the runes scrawled across its gleaming surface.

Jess felt a sudden burst of impatience. Was he going to open it or not? "Go ahead, Percy," she said. "The goose came here, it must be intended for you. The message would have gone to Kylden Hall if it was for me."

"I'm savoring the moment. I can't imagine who this would be from, I don't think I know any casters remotely capable of this." Percy's face brightened. "Maybe it's your father telling me to kick you out of my shop for the night!"

"Come *on*," said Jess.

"All right, let's see what we have here."

Percy reached out and touched the lid with one fingertip. The lid dissolved and a tendril of glowing light emerged from the dark opening. The tendril thickened into a rolling wave of white vapor, its depths sparking with little flashes of light. As the fog poured forth from the dark interior of the horn, it rose up and solidified into countless swirling grains of sand orbiting one another. Almost imperceptibly, the sand began coalescing into the rough outlines of a human face, and within a matter of seconds the disembodied face of a weary-looking man of roughly middle age was gazing out at them. The top of his head was as free of hair as a polished stone, but his chin was adorned with a well-kept blonde goatee.

"River and Sea, it's Bryscoe Rygaard!" exclaimed Percy, his face shining with astonished delight. But then his expression changed to one of puzzlement. "But how did Bryscoe—"

"Hello, old friend," the image said, the voice as clear as if it were right there in the room with them. "I hope this message finds you doing well. I wish that I could be there in person to greet you and hear that laugh of yours once more. But I'm afraid that this is the best I can do for now. " The man's expression hardened. "Percy, I'm sending you this tiding because Fyngree is in peril, as is the Throneholder."

Jess felt her pulse quicken at the mention of her father. She snapped a brief look of concern at Percy, then leaned forward toward the image.

"I've learned that a secret war is being waged against Fyngree's wizards and witches," Bryscoe continued. "A war that is being carried out for the purpose of toppling Owyn Suntold from his throne and bringing all of Tempyst under the dominion of Thylus Whytewender."

"What?" Jess cried. "What is the nature of this plot?"

"He can't hear you, Jess," reminded Percy. "Remember, we are merely hearing what Bryscoe said when he filled the Horn."

"—that there is a traitor stalking the halls of Kylden Hall," the image continued. "Someone in the king's inner circle. Possibly more than one. King Owyn and his daughter are in grave danger. I have much to tell you, old friend. Much more than I can fit into this Horn. So I ask that you make haste to the Widow's Torch. There you will find Gydeon Gloomwater, an old and trusted friend. He is a man of middle years, thin as a flute, with a great blade of a nose. He will tell you much more than I can here. And if you need to find me, Gydeon knows where I am." He smiled crookedly. "And just so you know—he'll see you before you see him."

Bryscoe paused and glanced off to the side, as if listening to someone. He gave a brief nod, then continued. "I'm told that the Horn is almost full, so I must bid you goodbye. Travel safely, old friend. Be careful who you trust. And make sure that printing press of yours is in good working order."

The image began to lose its shape, the sand sheering off and breaking apart like the edge of a dune in high wind. In a matter of seconds the image was gone altogether, as was the sand. Jess touched the box with one finger and it crumbled like a carving of white ash.

Percyval turned to the goose. "I will begin my journey to the Widow's Torch this very night. Please let Bryscoe know."

The small gray goose honked, shook her wings, and dropped to the floor. She waddled over to the fireplace, planting her webbed feet right at the edge of the glowing coals. And then the goose was gone up the chimney, leaving nothing but two feathers lazily fluttering to the floor.

Percy and Jess looked at one another for a long moment.

"Percy, what are we going to do?" Jess said, her thoughts a twisted tangle of fear and excitement.

"Well, the first thing we need to do is get you back to Kylden Hall. Your father can provide much more protection to you than I can, and you need to alert him to the plot described by Bryscoe."

Jess stared open-mouthed at him. He wanted to send her back to the castle? Absolutely not. Once her father learned of this threat, he'd sequester her so deep in the castle that she'd smother to death. Here was an opportunity to take her rightful place on the ramparts of Fyngree's defenses, and she fully intended to take advantage of it.

"Alert him to what plot, Percy?" she exclaimed, fighting to keep the desperation out of her voice. "Your friend's dire warnings were as insubstantial as the image in the horn! We must go and talk to this Gydeon—"

"We?" Percy said. "I must go alone, Jess. Your father would never allow you to accompany me without an escort, and if I arrive with a company of soldiers in tow this Gydeon fellow might well disappear, certain that they have come to arrest him. Remember what Bryscoe said about traitors within Kylden Hall?"

"All the more reason to take me with you! You can't ask me—" Jess stopped, distracted by sudden shouts from the street. They both turned to the front window just as it shattered inward, blown apart by the impact of a body that skidded to a stop at their feet. It was one of Jess's armored guards, and he no longer had a head. Jess started to cry out in horror but Percy clamped a hand over her mouth and dragged her to the floor behind a heavy table. They stared wide-eyed at each other as shouts and screams and the ringing of swords floated through the broken window to their ears.

The bodies of two more guards, a man and a woman, came hurtling into the shop in a tangle of broken and bloody limbs, followed by another riot of confused sounds. Grunting men and screaming horses. The repeated chiming of swords. The wailing of mothers and children, their cries becoming fainter as they fled the area in terror. And the sound of wood and metal being crushed and torn asunder.

Percy grabbed Jess's hand and pulled her to a door at the back of the shop, only to find it jammed. Something heavy was blocking the door on the other side. They turned back into the room, searching frantically for some other means of escape.   Then Percy spotted one of the buckets of water that he kept around the paper-filled shop as a precaution against fire. He bent down and grabbed it, then turned and flung half its contents directly onto Jess's face and chest. Jess gasped from the cold and looked at him in shock.

"Turn around," he whispered fiercely.

"What?"

"Turn around!"

Jess did as she was told, her mind tumbling in terror and confusion. Cold water drenched her hair and back as Percy emptied the rest of the bucket on her. "What—" she gulped, but her jaw snapped shut as the pamphleteer grabbed her arm again and wrenched her back into the main area of the shop. They both looked to the broken window at the front as they ran forward.   A huge form flashed across the open window frame and disappeared again, followed by another scream and the clattering of steel on cobblestones.

Percy stopped them in front of the wide hearth. He grabbed her shoulders and looked her squarely in the eyes. "I'm hiding you in the chimney."

"What?"

"You're small, Jess. You can do it. It will still be hot in there, I've had the fire going all day, but it is down to coals now, and the water should help. When you get far enough up, brace yourself against the walls. Use your shoulders, knees, feet, whatever it takes."

"Percy, I don't underst—"

"Listen!" he hissed, his gaze darting back to the front window for an instant. "Whatever's out there is coming in here any second now. And I'm not going to see you kidnapped or killed. But you need to be silent up in there. Not even a sniffle. No matter what you hear. Stay hidden until you're sure it's gone."

Tears glistened in Jess's eyes, "But Percy . . . " She couldn't say it. He was going to die, and he knew it.

Percy smiled and leaned forward to kiss her forehead, then cradled her face in his hands. "You're going to have a wondrous life, Jess," he whispered. "I just know it. Now up you go."

Jess ducked into the interior of the hearth, hiking up her dress in her hands to keep the hem away from the glowing coals as best she could. She squirmed up into the flue, tears streaming down her cheeks, Percy pushing her up from underneath. As she shimmied upward, the material of her dress began bunching up, making it difficult for her to make any progress. She could feel Percy reach in and frantically rip at the material. The lower half of her skirt tore away and she resumed her struggle upwards.

The slippery, sooty stones inside the narrow chimney shaft burned Jess's bare hands, so she pressed her fists against her chest and used her elbows and legs to inch her way upward into the blackness. The walls were still hot from the day's fire but the wet fabric at her elbows and knees provided a little protection. As she struggled onward she tilted her head at an angle so that she could look up the shaft. A tiny rectangular opening of stars floated far above her, framed by the blackness of the towering chimney walls overhead. It was like being at the bottom of a deep and hopeless well. And still she pushed upward through the heat and dark, panting with effort, beads of sweat pouring down her face.

"Stop moving." A whisper from below. Percy's voice.

Jess stopped and wedged herself into the left side of the chimney, her heart hammering in her chest. She could feel the heat from the creosote-caked stones and the coals below pulsating through her clothes, and she realized that she needed to clear at least a small opening in the chimney shaft for air to escape. Otherwise the bottom of her dress would act as a damper and trap the smoke from the dying coals until it drifted out into the shop, alerting the invader that something—or someone—was blocking the chimney. Snaking her right arm down to her side, she grabbed a fistful of material in her hand and pulled it close to her body. It was enough to create a little opening in the shaft for the smoke to rise upward and out into the night sky.

Jess could feel the heat from the stones on her back, but Percy had been right; with the fire reduced to glowing embers and her dress drenched with water, the heat itself was tolerable. The air in the shaft was hot and cottony, though, and she had to fight back the awful sensation that the cramped chimney walls were squeezing in on her. The oily creosote caked on the chimney walls was slippery too, forcing her to continually adjust her points of leverage. But she cast these distractions aside and focused her attention on the sounds coming from the room she had just left.

A minute of silence passed, and another. Then she could hear the sound of heavy footsteps making their way into the shop through broken debris, crunching on shards of glass and pieces of pulverized wood. The footfalls stopped a few feet from the hearth.

"Well, you certainly know how to make an entrance." Percy's voice, trembling but clear.

Jess strained to hear a response. At first she thought she heard nothing. But then she realized that she could hear a faint undercurrent of sound. Heavy breathing, like the bellows of a blacksmith's forge.

Jess swallowed hard, and as she did so she realized with mounting panic that she had to sneeze. She had stirred up a cloud of ash during her ascent, and the particles were floating around her head now, dancing on currents of warm air rising from below. Jess bent her head down and clamped two fingers down on her nose until the sensation passed.

"I've not seen a gargoyle before," came Percy's voice. "In fact, I daresay there hasn't been a reputable sighting of one of your kind this far south in a century or more. To what do I owe the honor?"

Jess heard a deep, throaty growl in response, and her blood ran cold. A gargoyle! Jess's mind reeled at the horrifying revelation. But even so, she dimly recognized that by identifying the creature, Percy was trying to help her understand the nature of the threat that she and her father faced.

"I'm going to have to ask you to leave," she heard Percy say. "You've made a terrible mess, and I've got some cleaning up to do. So I'm asking you nicely. Or do I have to toss you out on your ass?"

Jess felt her eyes grow wet again. Percy was antagonizing the gargoyle. He knew that she could not stay in the chimney forever. Sooner or later she would cough or sneeze or shift in a way that revealed her presence. He was giving the beast no reason to linger.

"Very well, have it your way." Percy's voice again, trembling but defiant. "You can't say you weren't warned." Then Jess heard the sound of running feet, followed by a tremendous roar and the sound of flapping wings. Something slammed into the wall with such shuddering force that flakes of stone and hardened soot from the upper reaches of the chimney rained down on Jess's head. She heard a low groan that was cut off by the sound of several more heavy blows in quick succession.

Jess held her breath, even as tears of sorrow streamed down her soot-smeared face. Her back slipped against the slick wall and she braced herself with renewed force, her legs trembling with the effort now.

She could hear the gargoyle shuffling through the remains of the devastated shop. And far in the distance, the sound of galloping hooves and war horns. Soldiers coming from Kylden Hall. Lots of them. A lantern shattered on the floor near the back of the shop, where Percy kept his paper supplies. Even from inside the chimney shaft she could hear the *whump* as the shelves went up in flames. A moment later, she could hear the gargoyle tossing tables and chairs aside as it pushed back to the front of the store. And then somehow she could sense that it was gone.

Jess waited another two minutes before she shimmied back down the chimney. When her feet touched the floor, she thought for a moment that she might faint. But she shook it off and stumbled out into the shop, coughing and tamping down smoldering spots on her torn and soot-blackened dress. Jess limped over to the body of the pamphleteer, whose eyes stared sightlessly up at the ceiling. She reached down and gently closed Percy's eyes. "Goodbye, my friend," she whispered. Then she straightened, her eyes red but dry now. The hoofbeats and horns of her father's soldiers were closer now, only a couple of blocks away. She ran a hand through her hair, grabbed her leather satchel off the peg from which it had been hanging, and staggered out of the obliterated storefront into the cool night air, the flames rising and roaring behind her.

Jess gazed down blankly at the broken bodies of the soldiers sworn to defend her, then looked up over the city to the lights of Kylden Hall. The castle looked a million miles away now, and she realized that she could no more return there than she could slip into the scenery of a painting. Her path lay to the east. To the Widow's Torch, where a man named Gydeon carried news of traitors and conspiracies and murderers. And perhaps of the monster that had slain her friend.

Less than thirty seconds later, the first horsemen from Kylden Hall pulled up before the blazing inferno that had once been Percy Muncenmast's pamphleteering shop. But by that time the princess was gone.

8

Marooned

Owyn studied the image on the rough paper in his trembling hands, eyes scanning every detail of the woodcut of his daughter's face. "It's a fair likeness, is it not?" he said finally, looking across his chambers at Pynch, who was slouched against one of the room's great oaken pillars.

"An excellent likeness, Your Majesty."

"Yes," Owyn said, nodding in satisfaction. "Very well done." And so it was. The pamphleteers of Wyndlass Row were an arrogant lot, and Owyn knew that there was no love lost between them and Percyval Muncenmast. They had long sneered at his ink-stained wardrobe, so unlike the expensive silken trappings in which they draped themselves. And they had seen Muncenmast's decision to keep his print shop down on the far southern outskirts of Kylden, far from their more affluent addresses on the Row, as a judgment on the value of their company—which of course it had been. Most of all, though, they had resented Muncenmast for his craftsmanship, which had kept many of Fyngree's most discerning poets, scholars, and polemicists knocking on his door.

But his death two nights ago had changed all that. When news of the gargoyle's attack reached Wyndlass Row late that night, the printers had leaped into action. They had enlisted the finest artists in the city to create woodcuts of Jess. And when Owyn selected the woodcut that most closely resembled his daughter, Wyndlass Row entered another frenzy of activity. As the city awoke to the cataclysmic news that a murderous gargoyle had been in their midst—and that Princess Jessalyn had apparently been abducted by the loathsome beast—the printing presses had pumped out broadsheet after broadsheet bearing Jess's image. And at the bottom of each page, a promise of riches to anyone who could help bring her home alive—and identify the sorcerer responsible for the murder of Muncenmast, whom his fellow printers now described as "their fallen brother" and "a pamphleteer without peer."

Other steps had been taken as well. After Owyn had been informed of the attack, he had immediately ordered a full-scale sweep of the city and the surrounding countryside. He had then called Pynch and Sevenshade to the east tower. Over the next two hours he filled eight Tiding Horns with grim accounts of the evening's nightmarish events, then cast spells of pilgrimage on Brundy Sevenshade's eight strongest birds. By the time they slipped out the tower and into the moonlight, rune-covered boxes swinging around their necks, and began making their way to Tydewater, Talonoux, Parsca, and the other great cities of Fyngree, Owyn was nearly at the point of collapse.

And still there was more to do. Beating back the panic clawing at his heart, Owyn marched to his throne room to meet with his generals, consult with Captain Treadlow of the Shadow Guard, and interview terrified witnesses to the carnage that had whisked his daughter away into the abyss.

As the morning sun climbed into the sky, couriers were dispatched to the military garrisons strung across

Fyngree's borders with Rojenhold, their saddlebags carrying tersely worded orders to stand ready against possible incursions. Sailors and fishermen dragged their nets along the bottoms of the Whetstone River and Vanguard Bay. Search parties galloped out of the city, radiating outward in all directions. Meanwhile, Nomad and her shadow set out for the rugged highlands north of the Whetstone, while the three other casters in Kylden known to have flying familiars sent them off to other points of the compass. Arrangements were made to provide food and shelter to the traumatized survivors of the fire, which had claimed most of a city block before being extinguished, and for the burials of the eight guards who had been slain in the gargoyle's attack.

Through it all, Owyn had been decisive and resolute. His voice never quavered and his hands never shook. But once all the commands had been given and Kylden Hall emptied out, Owyn had returned to his chambers and taken another Tiding Horn in his hands. After muttering a series of low incantations to prepare the Horn for his message, he had filled the box with a warning to Thylus Whytewender. A warning that if Rojenhold was found to be in any way responsible for the previous evening's events, then retribution would be swift and severe. Eyes gleaming with fury, he sealed the Horn and tossed it to Pynch. "Here," he had said. "Find a horseman, if there's anyone left around here. Send it."

"Your Majesty, I really don't think that's a prudent message—"

"I said, SEND IT!" roared Owyn, and that had been the last he had seen of Pynch until the morning.

††††

Since then, another day had come and gone with no word of Jessalyn. A three-quarter moon hung suspended in the night sky now, shining down over Fyngree with a cold light that brought him no comfort. Until his daughter's disappearance, Owyn had always enjoyed nighttime strolls atop the walls of Kylden Hall. He would smoke his pipe and greet passing watchmen, all the while gazing down on the silver-washed city at his feet. Tonight, though, the moonlight cascading down on Kylden seemed to drape everything it touched in a deathly pallor. And so he remained inside, pacing back and forth in his chambers.

"We are certain that there is no caster in Rojenhold with sufficient power to have a gargoyle as his or her familiar?"

"Your Majesty, the light by which we view affairs in Rojenhold is a dim one," said Pynch. "They guard their secrets jealously, and our knowledge of the witches and wizards who roam its lands is incomplete. But none of our agents has heard of anyone so Threaded. We have to entertain the possibility that the gargoyle was the familiar of an unknown caster here in Fyngree. Or perhaps it was no one's familiar at all. Perhaps it was just an ordinary gargoyle that went mad."

"Nonsense," Owyn spat. "I'd wager that there hasn't been a gargoyle spotted outside the Speartip Mountains in fifty years or more. And even there, sightings are so rare that those foul beasts have nearly become creatures of myth! They skulk about at the most forbidding heights of those desolate mountains, brooding like carvings of stone for hours at a time. If one of them didn't swoop down into the valleys occasionally to carry off a horse or a bear, no one would ever see one. And you're telling me that one of those creatures, without any magical guidance, flew all the way down here and just by chance carried off the heir to the throne of Fyngree?"

"I am just raising various possibilities to explain recent events, however unlikely they might be," Pynch said coolly. "I beg your leave, Your Highness, if my ponderings strike you as foolish."

Owyn fought to control his temper. "Oh, don't carry on so, Marston," he grumbled. "I've a right to be a little cross, I think." Pynch's face colored at the mild rebuke, and Owyn felt a small measure of satisfaction that his words had struck home.

He crossed the room and poured himself a goblet of wine, then took a long deep draught before turning back to his advisor. "Do you think," he said slowly, "that it's possible that Whytewender has fooled us for all this time? About his familiar, I mean?"

"No," Pynch said. "The king of Stormheel is threaded to a large black owl. Whytewender is cunning, but the reports are clad in iron and go back many years, to when the Thread first came to him as a boy. And all indications are that his son's magical abilities are not those of a man Threaded to such a beast. King Thylus has guarded the identity of Faeros's familiar far more zealously than his own parents did for him, but you yourself have stated that his familiar is likely a wolf or coyote."

Owyn turned to the sputtering fire. "What was the name of Thylus's other boy?"

"The one who drowned? Teryk."

"That's right. You know, I always thought that Whytewender's rule hardened after that. The boy's funeral was the last time I set foot in Stormheel. They conducted the ceremony right along the banks of the Monument, just downstream from where he drowned. I remember how blank and pale Whytewender's face was that day."

Owyn reached to the side of the hearth for a poker and began rearranging the mostly spent logs, coaxing the flames back to life by hand. "A father should never outlive one of his children, Marston," he murmured. "Especially such a young child. That boy must not have been more than five years old when he perished. That must haunt Whytewender still, even after all these years. To always wonder what your child might have grown to be. . . ."

They heard a knock.

"Yes?" said Owyn, whirling away from the fire and striding quickly to the door.

The heavy oaken door opened and a guard poked his head in. "I'm sorry to disturb you, Your Majesty. Gwyn requests an audience, if you please."

Owyn's shoulders slumped a little. He felt as if every knock that failed to reveal his daughter ground him down into the floor a little more. But he recovered quickly. "Gwyn? Why yes, of course."

The door opened wide, and Jess's governess entered the room, her head bowed. She carried a handkerchief that she was kneading nervously in both hands.

"Your Majesty," she said, bowing to Owyn, then turned to his venerable counselor. "Master Pynch."

Both of the men greeted her, then Pynch turned to the king. "Your Highness, by your leave. . . ."

"Hmm? Oh, yes. Thank you, Marston. Get some sleep. I will see you on the morrow."

Pynch left the king's chambers, closing the door quietly behind him, and it suddenly occurred to Owyn that he and Gwyn had never been in a room alone together before.

Jessalyn had always been there with them, the sun around which they both orbited.

"What can I do for you?"

The corners of Gwyn's mouth turned down, and Owyn saw with considerable alarm that she was on the verge of tears. River and sea, a sobbing servant was the last thing he needed tonight. "Can I get you something to drink?" he said hastily. "A glass of wine, perhaps. Or some water?"

"Thank you for your kindness, Your Majesty, but no." Gwyn glanced at the fire, then rolled her gaze up to the ceiling, despair etched on every inch of her features.

"It's my fault, Your Majesty," she said forlornly. "I should have gone with her."

"With Jess?" he said, puzzled.

"Yes," Gwyn said, croaking out the word. "The princess asked me to go with her to Master Muncenmast's shop that night. She said it would be fun. She fancied herself a matchmaker between the two of us, I think." Gwyn tried to smile through her tears. "She was always doing that, Your Majesty. Always looking for someone to court me."

"Gwyn, I don't see how—"

"I could have helped her!" she cried. "Begging your pardon, Your Majesty, I've completely lost my manners, but if only I'd been there I might have been able to, I don't know, distract the beast or convince her to return home at an earlier hour or—"

"Gwyn."

"Your Majesty, the princess, she's been, she's been like a daughter to me—oh my goodness, I can't believe I said that, of course Queen Ayleth was her only true mother, and I don't mean to suggest that I could be anything other than a poor substitute—"

"Gwyn."

"I should have *been* there, Your Majesty, and now she's vanished! And now I feel as if, as if—"

Owyn reached out a hand and placed it gently on the matron's broad left shoulder. "As if you're marooned," he said quietly. "As if you're marooned on some desolate shore and Jess is drifting away on the waves and she's calling out to you but you can't do anything but watch as she disappears."

Gwyn stared at him silently, her eyes wide and glistening.

"I know whereof you speak, Gwyn," he said. "I do. But Jessalyn needs us to be strong. She needs us to maintain hope. Jess is alive, Gwyn. I believe that. And I believe she'll return to us."

A tired smile appeared on Owyn's exhausted, aged features. *This* was what he needed, he realized. He had spent the last two days absorbing earnest reassurances and vows of justice from an assortment of lords, advisors, and military officers, but their well-meaning words had done nothing to salve the awful sense of helplessness battering his soul. What he should have been doing, Owyn realized now, was comforting *them*, reassuring *them* that all was not lost. And in so doing, armor his own heart against the darkest whisperings of his mind.

"You know my daughter as well as anyone, Gwyn! She's a fighter. She's clever. She's—"

"She's resourceful," Gwyn jumped in, and at that Owyn's smile broadened.

"Yes, Gwyn," he said. "Yes, she is."

9

A Campfire Story

Tabytha Fyncloud watched the moonlight play over the broad back of the horseman riding in front of her, her unease deepening with each passing moment. During the two weeks that she had been forced to endure Tossoah Pentce's company, she had gained a deep understanding of the man's essential nature, and she had been appalled by what she had learned. How such a man had risen to become a shadow of Tydewater was beyond her. True, he was likely only a "mask"—a tracker charged with following a decoy rather than a genuine familiar. Nonetheless, the fact that Pentce had any role *at all* in protecting the city's small population of casters had been profoundly disillusioning to the young cadet.

And now here the two of them were, quietly circling a small campfire tucked in the lee of a massive wedge of stone, one of many that jutted from the bony spine of the Whetstone Highlands. Pentce's circuit kept them just out of the light cast by the fire, and he used the shaggy firs and thick-trunked maples ringing the clearing for further cover. But eventually his avarice would prod him to move in for a closer look. The figure lying next to the fire had not moved since their arrival, and the two horses tied at the edge of the campsite were fine-looking animals. Sensing that her companion was not above horse theft when it suited him, Tabytha grimly pondered her options if Pentce attempted to rob the sleeping traveler.

She didn't have all that many. Tabytha would not passively stand by and allow the robbery to take place. That was the coward's way—and she was not a coward. But she could not defeat Pentce in a swordfight. She prided herself on her strength and fitness, but her blade work remained a work in progress, and she suspected that the veteran soldier would dispatch her with relative ease.

Perhaps she could get the drop on him with her bow, though. Such a move would infuriate Pentce and spell doom for her already faint prospects of receiving a positive evaluation from him. But at least she wouldn't be complicit in a robbery—or worse.

And then a third option occurred to her. Pentce had kept them downwind of the horses in the camp, but there were other ways to alert yonder traveler to their presence. Tabytha quietly veered out from behind Pentce's lead and directed her horse underneath the boughs of a towering maple. As her horse trod forward, several fallen branches cracked under its heavy hooves. Pentce whirled in his saddle and glared at her, muttering a low oath. Tabytha made a vague gesture of apology and steered her horse back behind him, her gaze now trained squarely on the form laying by the fire. River and Sea, the man still was not stirring!

Tabytha had just reluctantly concluded that she was going to have to reach for her bow when the voice came floating out of the darkness.

"Come forward slowly and state your business. Reach for a weapon and I'll drop you out of your saddle. Especially you in the front. You'd be pretty hard to miss."

Pentce halted, forcing Tabytha to follow suit. Another hissed curse escaped Pentce's lips before he squared his shoulders and slowly turned his horse toward the fire. He walked his horse into the light, his posture deceptively casual. Tabytha came in behind him with both hands on her reins, well away from her bow and sword hilt. As they approached the fire she glanced down at the prone form that had aggravated her so much. She could see now that the hooded cloak covered naught but saddlebags and other traveling gear.

"That's far enough," the voice said from above their heads. Pentce and Tabytha halted and craned their necks toward the huge outcropping on the far side of the fire. A tall man stood atop the slab of stone. The firelight only partially illuminated his features and clothing, but Tabytha could see that the arrow strung on the man's bow was fully pulled back—and that the tip of the arrow it held was trained on the center of Pentce's chest.

"You are not welcome here," the man said calmly. "You were given ample opportunity to announce your presence, as is customary with travelers of good will. The fact that you failed to do so leaves me little choice but to conclude that you are roaming the highlands tonight with other motivations."

Tabytha felt a wave of humiliation wash over her at the man's assumption that she and Pentce were cut from the same predatory cloth. But she kept silent.

"So I bid you farewell and safe travels," the stranger continued. "But if we cross paths again, I will not provide you with warning before I loose my arrow."

Tabytha breathed a sigh of relief. The man was clearly not to be trifled with. Still, he was letting them go, despite their suspicious behavior.

But Pentce did not move. He just kept staring up at the man atop the rock. "Traejon?" he called after a moment. He flipped the hood of his cloak back to reveal his face. "Traejon Frost, is that you? It's Tossoah Pentce!"

The man above them slowly lowered his bow, and Pentce gave a short bark of laughter that echoed off the surrounding rock.

Oh that's just wonderful, Tabytha thought with dismay. They *know* one another.

† † †

One hour later, Tabytha still did not know quite what to make of Traejon Frost. After Pentce had identified himself, the archer had come down from his vantage point atop the rock and invited them in to share his campfire. But there had been a clear undercurrent of reluctance to the invitation. And Frost had spoken little since then, even as Pentce filled the night air with coarse jests, blusterings about past exploits, and bitter ruminations about various people who had let him down over the years.

Pentce had introduced Tabytha only at Frost's prodding, and then only dismissively. He described her as a "speck"—a demeaning term used at garrisons across Fyngree for new recruits—for whom he had been forced to serve as nursemaid. The entire exchange had been mortifying, but when Frost had shaken her hand, they had locked eyes and Tabytha had not looked away. It was hard to convey "I'm not like Pentce!" in a single look, but she hoped that somewhere in her forthright gaze she had managed to communicate just such a message to Frost.

Tabytha had been spared the worst of Pentce's tedious prattling because, as usual, he had ordered her to tend to their horses. That task had taken the better part of an hour, and she had only joined the men around the fire a few moments ago. She quickly poured herself a cup of hot tea, then gratefully accepted a small plate of fruit, cheese, and bannock offered by Frost. It was much tastier fare than the salt-saturated jerky that Pentce had packed for the two of them.

She studied their host now over the rim of her cup. Frost sat on the other side of the campfire at apparent ease, leaning back against his saddle with his forearms crossed over his chest. He was younger than she anticipated. Indeed, she guessed that he was not much older than her twenty-two years. Judging by his high cheekbones, whisker-free jawline, and shining green eyes, the man's ancestry ran at least in part through the Tomorrow Islands. His raven-black hair, though cut considerably shorter than the norm, also suggested Koah blood. And he looked every bit the warrior in his prime, thanks not only to his tall and muscular build—also typical of the Koah—but his intimidating wardrobe. Indeed, Frost carried an unsettling array of weaponry on his person, including a quiver of three throwing knives strapped to his right side and knives sheathed to both forearms. The hilt of a mid-sized sword jutted out of a scabbard that lay on the ground beside him, right next to the bow and quiver that he had brought down from the rock.

"So you're out here looking for the princess, I take it?" said Pentce as he filled his tin cup from a goatskin. Unlike she and Frost, he was drinking liquor, as was his nightly habit. It was his fourth or fifth cup of the evening, and he showed no signs of slowing down.

"Like the rest of Fyngree?" said Frost noncommittally.

Pentce laughed. "It seems that way, does it not? I think there are more farmers than soldiers looking for her! Who can blame them? The reward for her safe return is astounding. Even the reward for finding her lifeless body would be enough to purchase a small estate. Myself, though, I think all this fuss is a colossal waste of time. In all likelihood, she's sitting in the stomach of that gargoyle."

When Frost did not respond, Pentce leaned forward toward the fire. "Of course, I don't blame men such as yourself from seeing if there's gold to be had. If perchance she's locked away in some wizard's tower . . . well, if anyone could find her, it would be you, Frost."

Pentce turned to Tabytha abruptly. "Let me tell you how Traejon and I got to know one another, speck."

Tabytha started in surprise at her sudden inclusion in the conversation. "I was wondering about that. . . ," she allowed, glancing over at Frost.

"Well, you know of the goblins of the Black Marsh, right? A treacherous, vicious lot, they are. But most of the time they only rob and murder their own kind. A sensible policy of self-preservation, when you think about it. Their numbers are small compared to us, and they don't possess the Thread. So they skulk about in that foul marshland year after year, avoiding contact with humans."

Pentce took a long drink from his cup. "Now to be sure, the occasional human travelers who skirt the Black Marsh on their way to and from Thryn or Parsca sometimes *hear* the goblins hidden in the marshlands. I've heard that their frustrated mutterings and gnashings of teeth sometimes follow riders for hours. But goblin *sightings* are rare— unless you are one of those wretched merchants who occasionally trade for the strange plants and creatures the goblins harvest from the swamp. And so we coexist with them, yes? They leave us alone and we leave them alone.

"Once in a great while, though, a goblin stalks forth from the swamps to gorge itself on the depravity that others of his race barely keep at bay," Pentce said with enthusiasm, warming to his tale. "And five years ago, just such a goblin emerged from the Black Marsh. Myk, his name was, and he killed and mutilated six members of two different traveling parties before anyone had an inkling that anything was amiss. Didn't even eat some of his victims. Just killed them for the pleasure of it, draping their body parts over trees like party streamers."

Tabytha glanced over at Frost, who was looking into the flames of the campfire with hooded eyes. Where was this story going? she thought uneasily.

"So the high sentinel of Thryn dispatches two separate military patrols to run Myk down, but he just vanishes into the swamp. And after a while, Myk starts picking off scouts, stragglers, and watchmen from the patrols. Takes five of them all told, if I remember right." Pentce smiled unpleasantly at Tabytha. "So two weeks later, another patrol is ordered into the Black Marsh. But the members of *this* expedition do not come from the soft and pampered barracks of Thryn. No, these men hail from a garrison in the Marching Mountains, where soldiers are forged of steel rather than paper!" Pentce glanced over at Frost, and it dawned on Tabytha that however it turned out, this entire monologue was an effort on Pentce's part to ingratiate himself with the younger man.

"In less than a day our lead scout found Myk's trail," Pentce continued. "He kept on the goblin's scent for the next two days and nights, even as the creature fled through the dankest, darkest depths of the marsh. But we stayed in relentless pursuit, tracking him on foot or in canoes. Until dusk of our fourth day in the marsh, when our scout signals us to halt. I watch him as he stands there, strung bow at his side, and scans the marsh ahead. None of the rest of us can see a thing in the failing light and swirling fog, but we've seen the man ply his craft before so we keep silent. Then the scout suddenly brings his bow up and fires deep into the marsh. We hear a splash off in the distance, then nothing. So the scout signals us to move forward and about ten minutes later we find Myk's body slumped over a half-submerged log, his scaly limbs floating in the water. The fletching of the scout's arrow is pressed up against the back of Myk's skull and the shaft is jutting out of the goblin's left eye socket."

Pentce looked at Tabytha expectantly. "That's quite a shot," she acknowledged slowly.

"Yes it was, speck. To cap off an equally impressive feat of tracking. And then no more than a week later, that scout leaves our lonely little garrison, mysterious new orders from Kylden Hall in his pocket. And I never saw that scout again—until this evening."

Tabytha turned to Frost, who had remained silent throughout Pentce's tale. "That was a long time ago, Toss," he said finally. "And I was lucky. You overstate my abilities. I didn't even recognize you at first."

"Now you are being modest," scoffed Pentce. "I didn't shave my head back then, and I'll be the first to admit that I'm a little thicker in the middle these days. But you? You look no older tonight than the last time I saw you. And I'd wager that you remain just as adept at tracking sign as you were back in the Black Marsh."

Understanding flashed across Tabytha's mind. Pentce meant to discard their orders from Tydewater and attach himself to Frost's own quest. It was a craven scheme, but understandable in its way, she supposed. If Princess Jessalyn *was* still alive, who had better odds of finding her than this . . . what? Soldier? Mercenary?

Pentce drained the last of his cup's contents. "I have a proposal," he said. "I propose that Tabytha and I join you in your search for the princess. Three sets of eyes are better than one. And if we were to find her in thrall to the gargoyle or his master, we could aid you in the battle that would certainly ensue. You know my skill with a sword, Frost. And Fyncloud here is quite adept with a bow herself from what I've heard. What say you?"

Tabytha smiled to herself. It was the first time in days that Pentce had referred to her by name rather than as "speck," or acknowledged any of the attributes that had brought her to the attention of Tydewater's Shadow Guard in the first place. She was uneasy with the idea of casting aside the instructions they had received in Tydewater. But she doubted that it would come to that. Frost had been civil throughout the evening, but he seemed like a loner—and a man who probably knew from previous experience that Pentce was not the most trustworthy of companions.

"I appreciate the offer, Toss," Frost said. "Tis a generous one. But as you may also recall from our time in the Marching Mountains, I generally prefer the sound of the wind to the sound of men. And I do not wish for you and Tabytha to run afoul of the authorities in Tydewater. Punishments for desertion are severe."

Pentce managed to keep a grin pasted on his face, but it teetered on the edge of a snarl. Tabytha could see that his temper was rising. Pentce did not like it when people defied his wishes. "Come now, Frost. We've been comrades-in-arms in the past, why not again? There's a possible fortune in gold waiting if we join forces."

"You've misunderstood the purpose of my travels, Toss. Tis true, the mountains and valleys of Fyngree are full of men and women seeking Princess Jessalyn. But I'm not one of them. I'm a courier in the employ of Kylden's merchant guild, and my destination is Talonoux. I'm not interested in the princess. As you said earlier, searching for her is a fool's errand. She's likely dead and gone, and the sooner that the Throneholder accepts that, the better for everyone."

Pentce flushed and leaped to his feet. "You dare lie to my face?" he spat, his hand resting on the hilt of the longsword that hung at his waist. "Why would a courier of the guild stray from the main road to Talonoux? Damn your insolence, Frost. You always did put on airs, and I see that has not changed with the passage of time. Perhaps you need to be taught a lesson about respecting fellow soldiers—not to mention comrades in arms."

"You are not my comrade, Toss," Frost said calmly, even as he rose to his feet himself. "We shared the same barracks for a few months. We went on a couple patrols together, captured the odd highwayman, and hunted down a solitary murderous goblin. That's it. Does that provide sufficient mortar for a lifetime of obligation? Does that make us brothers? I do not think it does."

Tabytha got to her feet as well, her pulse quickening. Given the anger crackling between the two men, she thought that remaining seated was unwise. She needed to be ready to react to whatever came next.

"Now I've shared my fire tonight with you in deference to our past history, and I was happy to do it," Frost continued. "But when I depart for Talonoux tomorrow morning, I'll be doing so alone."

Pentce unsheathed his sword, shaking his head disbelievingly in a way that reminded Tab of a bear that had just received a snoutful of porcupine quills. This was not going to end well, she realized, and felt her heart kick into a full-on gallop. Pentce was a lecher and scoundrel, a man who in both appearance and disposition was unappealing in the extreme. But at least he was known to her, and during their travels she had managed to impress upon Pentce that his compensation for instructing her in shadowcraft did not include a place under her blankets.

But Frost? About all she knew about the man was that he once shot a goblin through the eye. And while his appearance was certainly pleasing to the eye, handsome men were just as capable of rape or murder as their homelier counterparts.

Pentce stepped forward menacingly. "You'll not dictate my travels, Frost," he snarled.

Tabytha stepped in his path, hands held out appeasingly. "Sergeant Pentce, this is not—"

Pentce backhanded her across the face, spinning her to the ground. Stunned by the blow, she looked up in an uncomprehending daze as Pentce loomed over her, his sword arm raised high. And then he staggered back with an inarticulate roar, the hilt of a dagger suddenly buried in his left shoulder. Tabytha rolled away and regained her feet, her left ear still ringing from the force of Pentce's blow.

"I could have put that between your eyes, Toss," Frost said coolly, nodding to the dagger that had sprouted as if by magic in Pentce's shoulder. "Let this end now. I've no wish to spill any more—." And then he stopped because Pentce was stalking around the fire, his entire being suffused with murderous intent. Frost brought up his own sword just as the enraged soldier reached him. He parried two thrusts from Pentce, then stepped in close as he blocked a roundhouse swing. Frost whipped one leg around against the back of Pentce's knees, sending him sprawling on his back, then swiftly put the tip of his sword to the fallen man's throat.

Pentce grew still, and Tabytha could see the fear swimming in his eyes.

"Don't make me spend the night cleaning my sword as well as my dagger, Toss," Frost said levelly.

Pentce let the sword slip from his fingers. Frost kicked it away, then bent down and pulled the dagger out of the prone man's shoulder. Pentce groaned and clutched at the gushing wound as Frost straightened and walked over to the soldier's gear. He pulled out Pentce's bow and snapped it over his knee, then returned to the fire and threw the pieces in the flame. "Goodbye, Toss."

Pentce slowly got to his feet, muttering darkly. He refused to meet Tabytha's gaze as he staggered over to his horse and gear, blood dripping down his left arm. Tabytha watched him prepare the horse for riding, her apprehension rising. She was not welcome here, but how could she go with Pentce? The man's towering humiliation would make him an exceedingly dangerous traveling companion. She would have to strike out on her own and make her own way back to Tydewater, keeping an eye out for Pentce the entire time.

"You are welcome to stay for the night, Tabytha."

She turned to Frost, her thoughts caught in a confused undertow of relief and uneasiness at the offer. He was looking at her steadily. "Or you may go. The choice is yours. But you understand that I'll have to keep your bow if you leave with Toss."

"I'll stay then," Tabytha said. "Thank you." She had no idea if she was making the right choice. But it was not lost on her that Frost had spared Pentce when he could have easily sent him to the Far Shore. It was an indication—perhaps—that the man possessed at least some semblance of a moral grounding. And besides, Frost hadn't come blundering into *their* camp. In all probability, the man simply wanted to get some sleep.

Pentce spat as he mounted his horse. "Your dream of being a shadow died tonight, speck," he said, glaring down at Tabytha. "When they read my report back in Tydewater you'll be drummed out of the army altogether. Or thrown in Rynelle Tremeny's dungeons."

Tabytha and Frost said nothing, and after a moment Pentce turned his mount and savagely kicked his horse's flanks. The horse broke into a startled canter, and in a matter of seconds Pentce disappeared out of the firelight and into the darkness. They listened as the horse's hoofbeats faded away in the night.

Tabytha looked cautiously at Frost, whose mouth was set in a grim line. But when he sensed that she was watching him, he turned to her with a wry smile. "I don't know about you, but I miss him already."

Tabytha laughed, and as she did she could feel the coiled tension of the past hours—and the heavy strain of the last several days—loosen in her chest, like a fever that was finally breaking.

10

The Warden House

J ess watched the cabin intently from the fringe of the woods. Five more minutes, she thought. Just to be safe.

As she settled herself back in the bushes to wait, she found herself reflecting once again on how surreal the last five days had been. Her life back in Kylden now seemed as illusory as a dimly remembered dream. Out here in the wilderness, the ever-present struggle to avoid detection and care for her basic needs had left Jess with little time to ponder the people and places she had left behind. Since fleeing the city she had spent her days eating up the miles on horseback, her evenings conducting raids on apple orchards and vegetable gardens, and her nights shivering in remote fields, stables, and barns.

Back home, platters of fresh-baked bread, succulent fruits, and savory meats and cheeses all stood ready for delivery at a single beckoning word, as did an assortment of fine wines and juices and teas to wash it all down. But last night she had dined on a few handfuls of wild blueberries and sips of water from a farmhouse well. Out here, her existence had quickly boiled down to the essentials of safety, food, water, and shelter—all things that she had taken for granted in Kylden Hall.

The stealing bothered her. A lot. And she'd had to do quite a bit of it. Within minutes of fleeing Muncenmast's shop she'd taken a big chestnut-colored mare out of a nearby stable that had been left unattended in the tumult. She'd saddled it frantically and then urged it out onto the dark plains east of Kylden.

Jess had ridden for hours in the moonlight that first awful night. As if the black horizon line promised refuge from the memories of her terror-filled minutes in the chimney and of Percy's sightless eyes. At one point the drumbeat of the horse's galloping hooves became so hypnotic that Jess could feel her stunned and ragged mind float free and drift into a pool of perfect blankness, one that offered refuge from the howling wreckage of her thoughts. She had not snapped back into the present until the sound of her horse's labored panting—so like the bellows-like breathing of the monster that had slain her friend—reached in and pulled her out of that cocoon of blankness.

As Jess's mind cleared, she also changed course. In her first feverish hours of flight, Jess had charted a direct course for the Widow's Torch, one that would take her across the broad southern expanse of the Loaf. Gradually, though, she comprehended that she would be easily sighted if she kept to that exposed route after sunrise. If not by the gargoyle, then by someone else. And if that happened, she would be forced to return to Kylden Hall without an opportunity to find Gydeon and learn more about the forces menacing her father and country.

And so Jess had swerved south, racing toward the Whetstone River. By the time the first glimmerings of the sun appeared on the horizon she had reached the heavy forest that girded the river banks. She spent the next two days using the forest canopy for cover from flying familiars and avoiding established trails and lanes altogether. Only at the gloaming hour did she return to the open country of the Loaf, where she could pluck food out of the gardens and fields and seek nighttime refuge in dark stables and towering sheaves of wheat.

The next several days had been marked by other acts of thievery. Plain but sturdy work clothes, and a frayed but otherwise serviceable cloak to ward off the night chill. A pair of boy's boots that fit her small feet perfectly. A tin of cooling muffins. All taken from modest farmsteads, cottages, and shops. The knowledge that she was stealing from people who did not have much, and who worked hard for what they did have, shadowed her every time she skulked away with her booty. And so Jess salved her troubled conscience by memorizing the location of each home and hamlet. Someday I'll come back, she promised herself, and compensate these people properly.

Jess spotted several companies of soldiers during her travels, as well as an assortment of other riders who were clearly searching for her. Most of the latter search parties seemed comprised of farmers or tavern drunks on a treasure hunt. Which Jess supposed they were, in a way, for she had no doubt that her father had posted a considerable reward for her return. But two of the groups carried the well-worn weaponry and dead-eyed demeanor of mercenaries, and she gave these riders a particularly wide berth.

On her fourth day out Jess finally reached the beginnings of the Whetstone Highlands. Her spirits lifted as she ascended out of the woodlands and onto the plateau, which marked the western approach to the Marching Mountains. When she saw those distant peaks for the first time, she whispered a quiet prayer that Gydeon—whoever he was—was still waiting for Percy at the Torch.

The cover wasn't as extensive up on the highlands as it was down its southern escarpment, where heavy woods continued to flank the river. Nor did it offer the same opportunities for larceny as the Loaf. But the broad spine of the plateau featured a generous assortment of rocky ridges and strips of woodland into which she could disappear for rest or cover. Moreover, the rocky soil of the Highlands did not support farming or cattle ranching, so the plateau was practically empty of humans.

Except for the odd warden, Jess mused now, eyeing the door of the cabin before her. Five minutes had come and gone. Time to see if anyone was home. She pushed cautiously out of the woods and into the clearing, absently massaging the back of one sore thigh as she went. She was an accomplished rider, but never had she spent so much time in the saddle before. Her thighs and bottom throbbed with every step she took.

The cabin itself was a relatively understated building, though it looked to be in good condition aside from a light fur of moss on the north side of its steep eaves. A weather-beaten wooden sign emblazoned with "Warden House No. 11" hung from one of the front porch's supporting beams. Most of the outer west wall was taken up by the exterior of a great fieldstone chimney, the top of which remained as empty of smoke as it had been when she had arrived at the compound an hour earlier. On the far side of the cabin stood a corral-shaped wall of waist-high fieldstone, with a small stable attached at its southern end. A stone well sat next to the stable.

Stumbling upon a Warden House was a mixed blessing. On the one hand, Jess thought that it would almost certainly be stocked with useful items for her final push to the Widow's Torch. But Fyngree's wardens were seasoned woodsmen and sworn defenders of the Throneholder. Indeed, their reputation for rectitude and loyalty was known far and wide. If she was discovered, the warden would detain her and return her to Kylden, no matter what sort of protests or threats she offered.

Yet despite her fears of being identified and apprehended, Jess had to admit that a part of her thrilled at the thought of actually spotting a warden in his natural habitat, so to speak. Most wardens lived solitary lives, although she had occasionally heard of married couples who managed outposts as a team. Wardens rarely set foot in Kylden, let alone within her father's audience hall.

As Jess moved forward through the tall grass she imagined peering inside one of the cabin windows and seeing a warden sleeping inside on a bed of itchy wool blankets, or drinking bitter tea as he repaired some complicated snare. She imagined him as a tall, square-jawed, and solemn-looking fellow, with a wild ginger beard and twigs tangled in his hair.

Bypassing the cabin itself, Jess sidled up instead to the side of the stable and peered inside. Every stall was empty, a sure indication that this particular warden was out patrolling his or her territory. Jess trotted back to where she had emerged from the woods, then returned into the clearing a moment later with her horse in tow. She walked the steed over to the stable, pulled some water from the well and poured it into a trough, gave her a big armful of hay, then made her way back to the cabin, her satchel slung over one shoulder. When she was about ten yards away from the front porch, however, she stopped. She studied the building intently, hands on her hips.

Wardens occupied a unique place in Fyngree, for they straddled multiple worlds. Unlike most Fyngreans, they had considerable discretion to slay wild creatures. But their primary role was to protect the kingdom's wildlife, and this stewardship included authority to enforce the strict hunting laws that prevailed across Fyngree. In addition, wardens enforced animal protection laws that were specific to the particular territory they managed. Most of these latter laws were handed down by regional high sentinels to protect themselves or other casters.

Most of Fyngree's hunting laws were relatively uncontroversial. All birds were protected, since powerful witches and wizards often had winged familiars. But since even the largest of the raptor breeds did not prey on commercially valuable livestock, farmers and ranchers had no reason to hunt them in the first place. And a few rare creatures were so widely despised or feared that they also could be killed on sight, the reasoning being that any wizard with such a familiar must surely be a horribly black-hearted one. The gargoyle was such a beast, as was the dreaded cockatrice, the cunning jackal, and the eerie kelpie.

Small and abundant foraging animals like hares and squirrels could be added to the stewpot of any skilled hunter or trapper without penalty. Apparently familiars did not take such harmless forms—or if they did, their masters had never possessed sufficient political power or influence to extend legal protection to such creatures. Still, hunting pressure on those mild-mannered members of the animal kingdom remained light thanks to Fyngree's vast deer and cattle herds. For nearly a century now, Fyngrean rulers had made thrice-annual disbursements of high-quality venison and beef quarters to families across the kingdom. It was a simple policy, but most Fyngreans—and especially its casters—understood it to be a cornerstone of the kingdom's familiar-protection efforts.

The wardens' lives also were made considerably easier by the fact that although familiars looked just like their wild brethren—albeit very large and healthy versions of same—they behaved in ways that set them apart. Familiars did not need to sustain themselves by eating. When a wolf, bear, or catamount forsook its usual wild prey for livestock or the odd farmer, it was understood that the offenders were non-magical creatures that could be hunted down and killed without snuffing out the life of some distant caster.

Even then, though, wardens were often called in to trap or track down those troublesome beasts. Unless a Fyngrean actually caught a beast with its muzzle buried in a freshly killed cow carcass or dragging a family member into the darkness, it was preferable to call in the territorial warden to make certain that the fox lingering on the edge of their woods was the one picking off their chickens, not some caster's familiar innocently crossing their land.

Jess recognized that the harsh punishments for slaying a protected animal were an important factor in curbing such impulses toward vigilantism. But as she had grown older she had also come to understand that Fyngreans were generally loath to take the life of a familiar in error. Casters were sometimes viewed with fear or jealousy, but they were also prized military resources. Most Fyngreans understood that every caster, no matter how modest their Thread, added to their kingdom's defenses against Thylus Whytewender and the armies of Rojenhold.

Jess circled the house slowly now, eyes lingering on every board and window frame. She studied the ground as well, peering down into the grass and up into the branches of the two trees that cast shade on the north side of the cabin. Then her gaze settled on the fieldstone corral next to the cabin, and she smiled and quickened her stride.

The other Fyngrean worlds that wardens straddled were its magical and non-magical ones. According to her father, wardens did not usually possess magical abilities themselves. But it was not uncommon for Fyngree's most accomplished casters—including her father—to provide wardens with powerful enchantments to help them carry out their duties. These alchemic spells bottled magical energy into small items that could be carried by a warden or hidden in his or her home, such as an enchanted candlestick to give its owner the gift of night-sight, or ledgers for recordkeeping written in ink that vanished if opened by anyone other than the warden.

Most Fyngreans had a vague understanding that wardens and their outposts enjoyed magical protection. They received periodic reminders of this protection, usually in the form of stories of thieves who tried to break into an empty warden house--only to awaken hours later in nearby woods with blurry vision, splitting headaches, and a pressing need for new undergarments.

But Jess was one of very few threadbare Fyngreans who understood how this branch of the magical arts actually worked. Her father had insisted on tutoring her on the history and mechanics of alchemy, even as she remained threadbare. For years he had patiently guided her through Tempyst's most important wizarding scrolls and books, instructed her about the preparation of magical potions, salves, paints, and metals, and showed her how the Thread, when properly applied, could invest these items with enduring power.

And now, for the first time in her life, all those hours of instruction might finally turn out to have some practical value.

Jess placed her right hand at the corner of the field-stone corral wall nearest the stable. She slowly walked forward in the direction of the house, testing the sturdiness and stability of each rock along the top of the wall. She was two-thirds of the way around the wall when she felt the rock under her hand shift. Jess stopped and placed both hands on the wedge of stone. She applied pressure and felt it move in its cradle of hardened mortar. Carefully lifting the stone out of the wall, she peered down into the hollow space left behind.

A tiny scale model of the Warden House sat on a bed of wood shavings, dried flowers, and feathers in a dark recess in the wall's interior. No more than three inches high, the model had been carved with such exquisite detail that it looked identical to the actual house behind her, all the way down to the fine coating of moss on the model's tiny eaves. Jess carefully lifted the model out of the hole, placed it in the palm of her hand, and brought it up close to one eye so that she could peer inside through one of its miniature windows. She was amazed to see a fully furnished room, complete with table, chairs, and books that were little more than grains of sand. She half-expected to see a tiny warden strolling around in its interior.

Jess gently placed the model back on its bed of shavings, flowers, and feathers. But she did not put the stone back. As long as the miniature warden house was uncovered, she would be able to freely enter the real building and take what she needed.

Jess walked up on the porch, opened the front door, and stepped inside, a small smile of satisfaction spreading across her face. Here she was, far from the walls of Kylden Hall, unprotected by any retinue of soldiers, and without even a thimble-full of spellcasting abilities to call upon. Yet despite all that, she was strolling into a Warden's House as if it were her own home. And she was closing the distance between herself and the Widow's Torch every day. Perhaps her father was wrong. Perhaps a threadbare *could* rule Fyngree, provided she used her wits and knowledge to full advantage.

Jess emerged fifteen minutes later, her satchel stuffed with supplies, an apple in her left hand, and a small crossbow in her right. She carefully replaced the stone in the wall and retrieved her horse. Before setting forth again, though, she gave a final lingering look back at Warden House No. 11. And when she did finally turn the horse away, her thoughts were not of Percy or the gargoyle or traitors or the Widow's Torch. They were on the contents of the letter that she had left on the warden's desk.

11

Into the Marching Mountains

O n the morning of their first day riding together, Traejon admitted to Tabytha that he was not really a courier bound for Talonoux. There was no point in maintaining that fiction, since Nomad's flight path was such a meandering one. The gyrfalcon was pressing generally eastward to be sure, but with forays to the north and south that sometimes extended for two or three miles. A drunkard could have charted a straighter path to Talonoux. So he told Tabytha another lie—that he was, as Pentce had guessed, one of the many soldiers of fortune who had ventured into the wilderness to search for Princess Jessalyn.

Tabytha had accepted the story with a nod of understanding. "Well, it's certainly a large reward," she said. "Half of the soldiers in Tydewater would have asked for leave to join you out here if they weren't already under orders to take part in the search." And then Tabytha had sighed so heavily that Traejon had turned to look at her. "Poor King Owyn," she said, looking off into a stand of rustling pines. "I just hope that someone finds the princess's body so that he can find a measure of peace."

As the next two days unspooled across the green canvas of the Whetstone Highlands, Traejon learned the basics of Tabytha's background. The daughter of a former Tydewater army captain who had built a thriving carpentry business in his retirement, she had enjoyed a loving if rough-and-tumble childhood with two older brothers. And like her brothers, Tabytha determined from an early age to enter the military herself. She'd been able to parley her high training scores and the Fyncloud family name into a coveted cadet slot with Tydewater's Shadow Guard. Where she'd had the awful misfortune of being assigned one Tossoah Pentce as her instructor.

At the close of their second day together, they finally reached the westernmost palisades of the Marching Mountains. As Traejon laid out his bedroll that night, he resolved to cut her loose the following day. After all, Toss Pentce was long gone. And although Traejon was confident that the young soldier was not a threat to himself or Nomad, taking on a riding companion was the last thing that a true shadow should do—especially one sworn to protect the familiar of King Owyn himself. Moreover, the task of following Nomad for hours on end without revealing that he was doing so had been more taxing than anticipated, and he was not looking forward to maintaining the charade for a third successive day.

But the following morning, as he watched Tab pack up the last of her gear into her horse's saddlebags, he felt his determination waver. For the truth of the matter was, he didn't *want* to bid her farewell.

He supposed that Tabytha did not have the appearance of a young woman about whom sonnets or poems were usually written. Her form was lean and broad-shouldered rather than curvy or lissome. Her hair, cut short so that it barely reached her shoulders, was a nondescript ash blonde color. And her face was adorned with faint smudges of dirt and a fine spray of freckles, not the milky-white skin favored by Fyngree's troubadours and painters. But her features were generally pleasing, her smile was as quick and appealing as her wit, and she had proved herself an able rider and campmate. Over the last two days and nights, in fact, she had carried herself with an understated confidence that surprised him, given her youth and the circumstances under which they had met. And after more than four years of solitary travel as Nomad's shadow, he found that having human company at the end of a hard day's ride was a welcome change. This human's company, at any rate.

And just like that, Traejon's vow to send her back to Tydewater melted away like a late-spring snow. He and Nomad could still carry out their mission with Tab in tow. He'd just have to be careful. And he'd have to leave her behind in another day or two anyway, when Nomad began her return journey to the Throneholder. They could just take leave of one another then.

Tabytha gave the cinch on her saddle a final tug and turned to him. "Ready to go?" she asked with a smile, the usual hint of a rasp in her otherwise girlish voice.

Traejon took in Tab's open and guileless expression, and noticed once again—quite despite himself—how pleasing her voice sounded in his ear. "Yes, ready to go," he said briskly. He nodded to his two horses, already saddled up. "And they're ready as well."

They rode deeper into the shadow of the mountains in companionable silence, each of them riding off short distances at various points to inspect rocky couloirs and tangled blowdowns. But as they approached the high pass that would take them off the highlands and into the mountains proper, Tabytha pulled her horse up by his side.

"I want to thank you for your kindness, Traejon. I needed some time to think, and these last days have been a balm in that regard. But tomorrow morning I intend to begin my journey back to Tydewater. My father will be expecting me, and I suppose I need to find out just how many lies Pentce will have told about me in my absence. If he's been riding hard, his words may be in Captain Brocham's ear before the week is out."

Traejon nodded. "As you wish," he said readily, doing his best to ignore the twinge of disappointment he felt at this unexpected announcement. "Probably wise. You'll need to be careful of Toss down there, you know. He's a grudge-holder, and he has a couple of beauties that he's nursing against the two of us."

"I will. It's a shame, really. I think Toss might have been a capable teacher of shadowcraft under different circumstances. "

"Why do you say that?" said Traejon, cocking his head obliquely in the direction of a high mountain wall to his left. Out of the corner of his eye he watched as Nomad floated on past.

"He actually provided some worthwhile instruction the first two days we went out in the field," Tabytha said. "But on the evening of our second night out he got a little drunk and a lot . . . amorous. I was lucky to get my knee up and scramble his eggs that night. And the next night I made sure he saw me take my knife to bed with me. From then on Toss guarded his yard. But after that I was 'speck.' If I'd been a man we'd have been fine once I acknowledged that his sword was bigger than mine."

Tabytha abruptly swept her hair back from her face, and now Traejon could see the anger in her eyes. "My father warned me that there were soldiers like Pentce. Men who think so little of their oath and their country that they stalk their fellow soldiers for pleasure or profit. Men who are so blighted in spirit that they can see such looting as their just due."

She looked down and drew a long shuddering breath, then turned back to Traejon. "It rankles to think that such a man could seek to dictate the river I choose for my life. *I* choose the river. Not him. So I'll go back and I'll deal with his lies. I won't be drummed out of the Shadow Guard without a fight, that's for certain. And I'm reporting him. At the very least, maybe Brocham will think twice before he places another woman cadet under Pentce's authority."

Tabytha and Traejon pushed onward, and at midday they arrived at Spiteful Pass, the primary western entranceway into the Marching Mountains. They stood on the crest of a rocky but worn path bracketed on one side by massive pillars of stone reaching into the heavens, and on the other by a sheer drop of several hundred feet. The path trailed off in a generally northerly direction, twisting along the midsection of an otherwise sheer mountain face until it descended into a narrow, lightly wooded valley far in the distance.

Traejon ran a hand through his hair as he surveyed the knife-like ridges and towering peaks arrayed before them. "I respect your stand, Tab," he said carefully. "But Toss outranks you, and he undoubtedly has allies in Tydewater's barracks. I'm not saying you can't win, especially given what you've told me of your father's reputation. But if you're going to war, you might as well bring all the weapons that you can to bear." Traejon fell silent for a moment, and he could feel Tabytha's eyes on him.

Then Traejon raised his eyes to hers and plunged ahead. He might as well put his position as a shadow to good use for once. "I know the captain of the Shadow Guard of Kylden Hall," he said. "If you'd like, I can arrange for Treadlow to send a formal statement of endorsement to this Captain Brocham of yours. Or perhaps you'd consider a transfer to Kylden Hall's Shadow Guard. I think it could be done. You'd have to begin your shadowcraft training all over again. But I can promise you that with Treadlow, you'll rise or fall on your own merits."

Tabytha stared at him wide-eyed for a moment before a slow grin spread across her face. "Well, look who's been hiding their political connections," she said. "Do you make a regular habit of rescuing forlorn cadets?"

"Just the ones facing long odds," said Traejon, returning her grin. River and sea, she really was quite fetching when she smiled like that . . .

"I appreciate the offer, Traejon. And I'll take you up on that. But I still need to go back to Tydewater and confront him. No one's going to tell lies about me unchallenged."

"Fair enough."

Traejon nudged his heels against his horse's flanks and pulled ahead onto the path, Tabytha's horse falling in line behind. They rode in silence as they passed beneath the stone spires marking the range's western edge. The Marching Mountains had a far different character and appearance than those of the Speartips, Tempyst's other major chain. Whereas the peaks of the Speartips were long and sharp and worn to an icy, incisor-smooth gloss by the relentless winds of the far north, the Marching Mountains reminded him of a graveyard of broken pillars toppled to earth. And many of the hulking massifs were honeycombed with bat-infested caverns that whistled and moaned when the wind was right.

"So tell me, Traejon," said Tabytha, taking advantage of a widening in the rocky path to pull up alongside him. "What's it like being a true shadow?"

Traejon felt his pulse kick up a notch at the question, but he responded with a smirk, as if she had said something amusing. "Friendship with a captain of the Shadow Guard does not *make* one a shadow, you know."

"No," she allowed. "But you're no mask. You're a shadow, and the familiar that you have been alternately following and studiously ignoring is that big falcon up there." She pointed to Nomad, who was cutting a graceful arc over the valley floor about fifty yards to their right.

Traejon's smile vanished. "Smoke and Ash," he muttered to himself. "I knew I shouldn't have mentioned Treadlow."

Tabytha recognized that he was vexed. "It wasn't the mention of your shadow captain," she said hastily. "Although I'll admit that further confirmed my suspicions."

"What, then?"

Tabytha laughed and pointed toward Nomad. "It was the bird that tipped me off! Or its flight patterns, to be more precise. It took me awhile to notice the falcon at all, to be honest. But by yesterday afternoon I could tell that we were following it—despite your valiant efforts to disguise the fact. Mostly because the falcon usually took a course that you could follow fairly easily—and when it didn't, it always reappeared after a few moments, as if it was letting you know where it was. Which I guess it was!"

Traejon said nothing, but he felt anger at his carelessness bloom like a dark flower in his chest. This is why they discourage shadows from acquiring companions during their travels, he thought dourly.

"What's it like? Being the shadow to such a powerful familiar, I mean?"

Traejon turned to her, studying her features. Her cheeks colored in a slow flush, and he saw that she was wondering if she had been too bold. Yet she did not look away. "It's . . . all-consuming," he said finally. "But if that doesn't frighten you off—if you can handle the solitude—it's not such a bad life." He gestured to the surrounding mountains and trees with one hand. "Fyngree is a fine kingdom, and she likes to fly over most of it. And I've never been one for cities."

"Do you ever get to see your family?" Tabytha asked, then dropped her eyes, recognizing immediately that the question might be construed as a clumsy attempt to ferret out whether he had a wife tucked away somewhere. "Parents or siblings?" she added quickly. "Or old friends?"

Traejon's mind clouded over at her words. He could feel that old plague ship out there, creaking and groaning. But it was far offshore, and he aimed to keep it that way. "That's not a consideration for me," he said obliquely, then offered her a chilly smile full of warning. "I'm ideal for shadow work in that respect."

Tabytha blinked and brought her horse to a halt, aware that she had transgressed in some mysterious way. "I apologize. I should have known better than to badger you for details."

She smiled regretfully at Traejon, who had stopped as well. "Would it be better if we parted company now? It's probably bad form to permit a cadet to tag along with you like this, isn't it? I wouldn't want to get you into trouble. I know how to reach Cloven Pass from here, I think. And from there it's only a few miles to the Gryndstone River. If Pentce is lying in wait for me, it will be further west. He'll never expect me to return to Tydewater via the Gryndstone."

Traejon looked down at his gloved hands, then out across the valley spread before them. He knew he should feel relieved. Tab's offer to remove herself from his company would spare him the discomfort of disentangling himself from her a day or two hence. And although he did not believe she posed a threat, he still felt a little off-balance from her continued presence. He was accustomed to the rhythms of solitary travel, comfortable with them.

And yet he still didn't want her to go. "I don't—"

Traejon's mouth snapped shut as Nomad streaked across their line of vision, no more than ten yards in front of them. They followed the gyrfalcon with their eyes as it circled around in a small arc, then swooped down and strafed them again. Traejon turned to Tabytha, green eyes glittering.

"Nomad's found something she wants us to see."

12

News from the
Highlands

K ing Owyn slumped in his throne chair, absently
tapping the walking staff clutched in his right
hand on the black marble floor. The throne sat
atop a wide dais at the northern end of the spacious audience hall. From this high vantage
point, Owyn held a commanding view of the length of the
hall. Massive braziers billowing with flames lined the midsection of the hall at regular intervals, casting warmth and light
into every corner. Farther back, long, ornate tapestries hung
from the rafters and left wall. On the right side, weak light
filtered down onto the stone floor from tall stained glass
windows that depicted past rulers of Fyngree. And down at
the far end, a half-dozen sentries stood guard, their blue and
gold tunics flashing as they moved beneath the arched doorway that gave entrance to the hall.

Owyn's eyes tracked the movements of the sentries in
the distance, but his thoughts were, as usual, on his absent
daughter. The spark of hope that he had felt when he had
comforted Gwyn had long since departed. Eight days had

now passed since Jessalyn's abduction. Eight days of soul-wrenching despair and impotent fury during which time he had learned nothing more about his daughter's fate. Had the gargoyle flown her high above some remote wilderness, then dropped her to be pulverized on the rocks below? Had the creature dragged her off to Whytewender's dungeons up in Stormheel? Or to the lair of some unknown caster who intended to ransom her for money or power? Or perhaps gargoyle and master were at this moment flaying the flesh from his daughter's limbs as part of some depraved retribution for the real or imagined sins of her father.

Owyn had received no answers to any of these questions. The world had gone silent, and so his mind pitched and heaved from awful possibility to awful possibility like a broken-masted sloop on a lightless, storm-ravaged sea.

His torment had been further heightened by Whytewender's response to Owyn's angry Tiding Horn. Oh, his words had been diplomatic enough, full of murmured condolences and concern. And King Thylus had promised to alert his military forces to Jessalyn's abduction and expand the search for her across Rojenhold. But his closing words had struck a discordant note in Owyn's heart. "It is my deepest wish that you and your daughter soon be reunited," Whytewender had said in the last seconds of his message, before his image frayed and spun away into sparkling dust. Had there been a hint of mockery in those last words? Owyn had no idea.

Owyn's gaze slid down to the walking staff in his hand. He hated relying on it, but he was weakening quickly in Nomad's continued absence. In another three or four days it would be a struggle for him just to climb the dais to his throne. Back when he had first ascended the throne of Fyngree, he could have gone four, even five weeks without touching his familiar and experienced few ill effects. Now he was not even sure he could ride a horse out of the city. Smoke and Ash, he hated growing old.

A mild commotion broke out down at the far end of the audience hall, interrupting his reverie. A moment later a bearded man came walking briskly down the hall toward him, bracketed by halberd-wielding sentries. As they drew closer, Owyn straightened up in his seat a little. Of medium height and lean build, the man was dressed in the garments of a woodsman.

The stranger and his escorts came to a halt before the dais, and the man quickly bowed. "My liege, I bring news, though it is of uncertain value."

Owyn leaned forward, his forearms resting on his knees. "News of my daughter?" he asked, his heart suddenly thudding in his chest.

"I-I think so," said the man hesitantly, and he pulled two envelopes out of his vest. "I am a warden in the Whetstone Highlands, sire. My name is Wylem Brasse and I maintain Outpost 11. Three days ago, I returned in the late afternoon from my usual regular circuit of my territory. Takes me three or four days, I do it once a week or so."

Brasse paused uncertainly.

"Yes?" Owyn said. "Out with it!"

"I'm sorry, Your Majesty. I just want you to know that if this is some cruel hoax I had nothing to do with it."

"What's that supposed to mean?"

Swallowing hard, Brasse forced himself to meet Owyn's gaze. "When I returned to my Warden House this last time, I immediately sensed that someone had been in there in my absence."

"Had you secured your post before your departure?"

"Yes, Your Majesty."

"Go on."

"As I said, someone had been inside. My pantry had been disturbed, for one. The chair to my desk wasn't as I left it, either." Brasse drew in a deep breath, then exhaled. "And on top of my desk someone had left two envelopes. One was unsealed, but the other had been sealed in wax." Brasse looked down at the unsealed envelope. "This envelope was addressed to 'Warden House No. 11.'"

Brasse looked up at Owyn, who was standing on the edge of the dais now, looming over him with his walking staff clenched in both of his hands. "What does it say?"

The warden took a piece of paper out of the envelope, shook it open, and began to read.

To the Proprietor of Warden House No. 11. I hope you will accept my apologies for entering your home without your permission, and for absconding with a few items for which I have temporary but considerable need. I will make every endeavor to ensure that the kingdom of Fyngree compensates you for your losses. In the meantime—and I know this is quite bold of me considering the circumstances—I must ask a favor of you. Please take this sealed envelope to Kylden Hall and present it to King Owyn Suntold—my father. Under no circumstances are you to open this second letter yourself, or permit anyone other than my father to take it from your hand.

Yours Truly,
Jessalyn Suntold

The sentries exchanged glances with one another as Brasse lowered the letter. Then they all looked up at Owyn, who swayed ever so slightly on his feet.

"Show me the second letter," he said hoarsely.

Brasse promptly stepped forward, reached up, and placed the second envelope in the king's trembling hand. "I confess that I was suspicious of the first letter, Your Highness. But then I noticed the insignia on the seal of this one."

Owyn raised the envelope and turned its back into the light from the nearest brazier. It had been sealed by a coin-sized dollop of dried wax. Squarely in the middle of the wax was the detailed impression of a peacock in silhouette. The impression exactly matched the latest seal matrix that Jessalyn had been given to authenticate messages from her hand. Only four weeks ago, her seal had been a leaping stag.

Heart pounding, Owyn tore open the envelope. The seal itself did not prove that the letter came from his daughter. The matrix might now be in the possession of kidnappers or grave robbers or some other tormentors. But if nothing else, the seal showed that this letter—whatever its contents— came from *someone* who had seen Jessalyn since her disappearance.

Owyn turned away from Brasse as he opened the letter. His heart soared when he saw the precise handwriting, which he immediately recognized as that of his daughter.

Dear Father,

I miss you so. And I wish I was home with you now. But the events at Percy's shop demanded that I take a different path, and it may be some time before I can return to your side.

You are undoubtedly aware that the creature who despoiled our city was a gargoyle. What you may not know is that its attack on Percy's shop was preceded by a visit from a caster's familiar—a small goose. I am unaware of any wizard who is so Threaded, but perhaps you know to whom that familiar belongs. At any rate, the goose brought a Tiding Horn from a man who was unknown to me, but who clearly harbored great affection for Percy. The man warned Percy of a plot by Rojenhold to conquer Fyngree. A plot that hinges on eliminating our kingdom's casters—whether by murder or other means, he didn't say. He also claimed that Kylden Hall has been infiltrated by agents of Whytewender who mean to do you harm.

The Tiding Horn closed by urging Percy to rendezvous with another loyal Fyngrean who could provide additional information about the plot. I think that they hoped to enlist Percy in a campaign to alert Fyngree—and you, Father—to the approaching threat.

I don't think the gargoyle knew of my presence at Percy's shop. Its quarry was that grey goose, and when the gargoyle failed to intercept the message it was carrying, it chose instead to murder its recipient. But I would have died too were it not for Percy. He gave his life to protect me.

So I am going to seek out the man that Percy was supposed to find. I don't know whether he will still be at the promised meeting place, or whether he will flee when I arrive in Percy's stead. But I have to try. I am sorry I cannot tell you where I am going, but I cannot take such a risk in the event that this letter is intercepted by Fyngree's enemies.

Trust no one, Father. Take steps to protect Fyngree's loyal casters. I will write again when I am able. I love you.

Jessalyn

Jess was alive! And free, at least for the moment. Owyn raised his head and stared out above the heads of Brasse and the guards, to the stained-glass windows lining the hall. He felt tears spring to his eyes and abruptly turned away, swiping at his eyes as he shambled back to his throne. It would not do for them to see their monarch weeping, even if it was in relief. By the time he sat down he had regained control of himself, and he sat pensively for a moment, his thoughts racing to and fro.

"Is it from your daughter, Your Highness?" Brasse asked cautiously. "Is she all right?"

Owyn turned to the warden. "It is," he said brusquely. "And she is well. Or at least she was when she composed this note." He looked to the guards that had accompanied Brasse into the hall. "That will be all," he told them. "Leave us now and return to your posts."

Once the guards had retreated down the hall far enough to be out of earshot, Owyn leaned forward toward Brasse. "You say that your post is in the highlands? Would that be above the north branch of the Whetstone?"

"Yes, Your Highness."

Owyn allowed himself a small smile. "Evidently she has been putting all those hours of riding lessons she insisted upon to good use. What did she take from you?"

"Some food and a waterskin, Your Highness. An enchanted candlestick for night-seeing. A crossbow. And two maps of the Marching Mountains."

13

Lessons

In the first weeks after Faxon Glynt descended on their home, Malkyn Thystle tried to go on as if nothing had changed. She prepared her usual hearty breakfasts for Wynston and Ben to sustain them for their daily labors at the gristmill. She sat at the table with Rowan, instructing him in sums and reading. She busied herself with housework and with pickling the ripening vegetables she plucked from their modest garden. She baked bread and gathered eggs from the coop and cut her sons' hair and washed their clothes.

But every week Glynt returned. And with each visit, the masquerade of normalcy became more difficult to maintain.

For Glynt did not come empty-handed. Each time he brought a leather purse that jingled with coins. Wynston accepted those purses from behind a mask of studied casualness, but Malkyn was not fooled. The first time, Wynston had accepted Glynt's payment with evident reluctance. But that was no longer the case. Whatever qualms he might have once had, they were no longer in evidence. Instead, Malkyn had begun to notice how her husband's spine straightened and his shoulders squared every time he took ownership of one of those purses. She knew that they didn't really have any option but to accept the terms of the transaction that had been presented to them—payments in return for Ben's training and eventual enlistment in Whytewender's Faithful Shield. Still, she was dismayed by the speed with which Wynston seemed to have become comfortable with the arrangement.

Malkyn was also disturbed by the fact that whenever Glynt visited, the officer would take her husband outside for long strolls up and down the rough road that ran past their home. She watched them sometimes as they walked and talked, and with each passing week her curiosity about these conversations increased. As did her frustration at being excluded. For Wynston refused to share any meaningful information about their little chats. He would just mutter platitudes about how much King Whytewender valued their son's gift and how Glynt wanted to be sure that their son's Thread was developed "properly." But he rarely met Malkyn's eyes when he talked of such things.

The visitations from Ben's new tutor were even more disruptive and ominous. Dendra Tumdown was not imposing physically. Thickset and jowly, with a mane of wiry gray hair that spilled to her shoulders, Tumdown was even shorter than Malkyn. And she was unfailingly polite when coming and going from their home. But beneath her veneer of civility, Tumdown possessed an imperious manner that she could not fully disguise. Or she just didn't bother. Malkyn wasn't sure which.

Tumdown had accompanied Glynt on the captain's second visit to their home. Glynt introduced Tumdown as one of Rojenhold's finest wizards, and he described the caster's assignment to their son as a tremendous boon to the entire family. The Thystle family would do well to recognize their good fortune, Glynt said, his one good eye gleaming with its usual dark mirth.

Since then Tumdown arrived two or three times a week—always without any advance notice, as if to keep the family in a state of perpetual unease. She always arrived in the early afternoon, in a sleek black carriage pulled by four equally black horses under the direction of a member of the Faithful Shield. Then she and Ben would disappear into the boys' small bedroom, which Tumdown had appropriated as a study area, until finally emerging four or five hours later. Tumdown always appeared to be in good humor after these sessions, and when she bid them goodbye at the end of the day, she did so with a faint smile on her face. Ben, on the other hand, looked wan and tired, as if he had just awakened from a night of ghostly visitations. On many nights now he just pushed his food listlessly around his plate after Tumdown's departure, his eyes lost in some faraway place.

Tumdown made it clear on the first day of her arrival that she and Ben were not to be disturbed. During Ben's second day of instruction, however, Malkyn's anxiety and curiosity got the best of her. About an hour after Tumdown began the lesson, she realized that she could hear the murmur of voices. The door to the room must have been left slightly ajar. She left her kitchen stool perch, crept across the main room and down the hallway, and peered into the boys' room.

Ben and Tumdown were seated in chairs facing one another, their knees nearly touching. Both teacher and pupil were tossing potato-sized stones from one hand to the other. The stones did not touch their hands, however; instead they hovered in the air, moving back and forth in a pendulum motion as teacher and pupil moved their hands. They were both talking softly, but Malkyn could not make out any of their words.

She watched them for perhaps fifteen seconds, the hairs on the back of her neck tingling in fear and fascination, until Tumdown slowly turned her head to the doorway. Their eyes met for a moment. Then Tumdown's stone stopped moving. It hung suspended in the air above her upturned left hand for a moment before dropping into her palm. Whereupon Tumdown made a slicing motion with her right hand and muttered a string of words that Malkyn could not quite catch. And then the door slammed shut in Malkyn's face.

It remained closed for Ben's lessons after that.

Malkyn tried to question Ben after Tumdown left that day, but her queries about the lessons were rebuffed. As they were every other evening when she tried to broach the subject. Each time, Ben just gave her a hollow-eyed look and mumbled generalities about mastering his Thread and sharpening his mind for the greater glory of Rojenhold. One night she became so frustrated that she demanded specifics about the nature of Tumdown's lessons. But Ben responded to her entreaties with sullen silences and averted gazes until Wynston intervened. "Stop badgering the boy," he said firmly—though his eyes once again refused to meet hers.

Yet Malkyn still might have been able to forge on, burying her gathering sense of doom under a frenzy of housecleaning, gardening, and school lessons, if not for Wynk. The leopard had always been a relatively rare sight for Malkyn. In the fourteen months since Ben's familiar had first arrived, she guessed that she saw the creature no more than every week or so. She supposed that it spent the rest of its days and nights roaming the woods that surrounded the Thystle home—or going wherever it was that familiars went when they were not with their compeers. But after Tumdown's lessons began, she did not see Wynk for more than three weeks.

The creature finally reappeared on a sunny but crisp afternoon marked by a breeze that carried a strong hint of the fast-approaching fall. Ben and Tumdown were inside, behind that closed door. The carriage and its driver were far down the path that ran past their cottage, tucked away under a piece of shade. So Malkyn and Rowan were alone in the garden, gathering beans for supper.

Malkyn and Rowan had almost worked their way to the end of the last row when she paused, suddenly certain that she was being watched. She looked up from where she was kneeling amid the rows to find Wynk sitting at the far end of the garden. It was the first time she had ever seen Wynk without Ben around.

Rowan kept picking beans, oblivious to the presence of the big cat, even as his mother stood to face the beast. Wynk remained as motionless as a statue, but her shining eyes bore into Malkyn's face with an intensity that made her feel as if the earth was shifting underneath her feet. Transfixed, she forced herself to return the familiar's gaze. And as the seconds passed she felt a great sorrow well up in her. For it seemed to her that the leopard's eyes were full of baleful accusation. How can you let them do this? those eyes seemed to say. How can you pick beans while that woman is inside your home, curdling the soul of your eldest son?

"What's wrong, mother?"

Malkyn looked down at Rowan's upturned face, which appeared more deeply etched with worry every day. The daily visitations by Tumdown troubled him, and Ben no longer read to him or played with him after dinner. His childhood innocence was vanishing in front of her eyes, spilling out of him like water from a cracked gourd.

"Nothing, sweetheart," Malkyn said, pasting on a tight smile. "Keep picking. You're doing a fine job." Rowan smiled uncertainly and returned his attention to the beans. Whereupon she turned back to Wynk . . . only to find that the beast was gone.

14

An Unexpected Encounter

Tabytha nudged her horse forward slowly, her eyes pinned on the rider ahead. He was tucked up against a thin ribbon of larches that ran through the middle of the valley, their needles just beginning to turn gold with the coming fall. His head was bent down intently over a map unscrolled across his lap. As she drew ever closer, she felt her pulse quicken. Who was this stranger that had Nomad so stirred up?

She briefly glanced into the woods to her left. Somewhere on the other side Traejon was circling around to the north. He intended to press on another fifty yards or so to a break in the trees, cut across to this side of the wood, and approach the rider from there. Tabytha, meanwhile, had positioned herself to block him from turning tail and fleeing south.

At first, the maneuvering had struck her as needlessly cautious. The two of them had crossed paths with a handful of other travelers over the previous three days, and they'd never resorted to such trickery. But when Traejon observed that none of those other travelers had caught the falcon's attention as this one had, she had to admit he had a point.

A moment later, Tabytha saw Traejon emerge out of the woods some distance beyond the mysterious rider. He turned toward them, keeping his horse and the extra mount trailing behind him at a relaxed walk. Tabytha, meanwhile, continued to close in from the south. She was only about thirty yards away from the stranger herself now, and she could see that although the rider was small of frame, he sat his horse comfortably, as if the saddle were a second home.

At that moment the mystery rider's mount raised its head from the grass on which it had been grazing and snorted, ears twitching as it caught sight of Traejon and his horses. The rider followed his horse's gaze an instant later, and Tabytha could see his shoulders stiffen at the sight of the shadow. He half-turned his horse toward Tabytha and as he did so, the hood of his cloak fell back to his shoulders. Tabytha blinked in surprise. The rider was a girl, not a boy. And a pretty one at that, despite the windblown state of her long dark hair and the faded laborer's clothes she sported. As the girl finished turning her horse away from Traejon's approach she spotted Tabytha. Their eyes locked for an instant, and Tabytha saw both fear and anger in the girl's expression.

Blocked from fleeing north or south, the rider pointed her horse toward the eastern end of the valley, where grassy slopes gave way to dense forest. Whoever she was, she wasn't going to submit meekly. She intended to make a run for it. "Wait!" Tabytha called. "We mean no harm!"

The girl glared at her, then dug her heels into her horse's flanks. But just as the steed bolted away from the line of larches, the gyrfalcon flew past the girl's head and landed in a tree behind her. The rider reined her horse in with a yelp of surprise and turned it about, then peered up into the tree. She was still staring up at the bird as if mesmerized when Traejon and Tabytha slowly walked their horses up on either side of her.

The girl's demeanor had completely changed. Where a moment before she appeared determined to race through the mountains until her mount collapsed under her, she now sat her horse easily. A dazed half-smile played about her lips as she stared up at the big gyrfalcon, which returned her gaze steadily.

Strange.

Tab glanced over to Traejon to gauge his reaction, only to find the shadow studying the girl intently, as if she had just alighted out of the sky herself.

"Nomad, you raggedy old bird," the girl said to the falcon. "I've missed you more than I can say. It's good to see you." She turned then to Traejon. "I remember you. From a year or so ago, isn't that right?"

"Almost two years ago now," Traejon said with a nod and a friendly smile. "Traejon Frost, at your service. It is very good to see you again, Your Highness."

Your Highness? Tabytha felt a wave of shock roll over her. "Wait, what?"

Traejon gestured to Tabytha. "Your Highness, this is Tabytha Fyncloud. She is a cadet in Tydewater's Shadow Guard. Tabytha, say hello to Princess Jessalyn Suntold."

"River and Sea, we actually found her?" Tabytha's mouth dropped open in stunned wonderment for a moment. The princess was alive! It seemed impossible to believe. Truly, the entire kingdom would rejoice when they heard the news! Then it hit her in a sudden rush that she was still gaping open-mouthed at the heir to the Fyngrean throne. "It is an honor, Your Highness," she stammered, bowing elaborately in her saddle.

Jess smiled faintly and nodded her head in acknowledgement, then turned her gaze back to Traejon. "And what can you tell me of my father and events in Kylden? Have you and Nomad been out here ever since . . . that night?"

"We have. After the gargoyle's attack King Owyn mobilized much of the kingdom into search parties. As part of that effort, he sent Nomad and some of Fyngree's other winged familiars deep into assorted wilderness areas—the sort of areas where kidnappers might find refuge."

Jess frowned. "Tonight will be ten nights since you departed, then. That's too long," she said.

"Too long?" Tabytha asked, puzzled.

"Too long for my father to be separated from his familiar," she said with a trace of impatience. "He does not possess the constitution of his younger days. And yet here Nomad is, hundreds of miles from home. She should return immediately."

"Wait, what?" Tabytha exclaimed again. She looked up wide-eyed at the falcon, who gazed back down at her, unblinking. Then she turned to Traejon. "The falcon's compeer is *Owyn Suntold*?" she said dazedly. "And you're her *shadow*?"

"You didn't know?" Jessalyn said lightly, but Tabytha heard a note of reserve enter her voice. And a sudden glimmer of apprehension in her eyes.

Tab felt her face flush. She reminded herself that she had nothing to feel guilty about, but clearly, the revelation that Tab had been unaware of Nomad's importance disturbed Jessalyn. The princess had undoubtedly assumed that Tab was a proven colleague of Traejon's. Someone who, despite her standing as a mere cadet, had been entrusted by her father with the secret of his familiar's identity. But now

Jessalyn realized that she had been wrong to make such an assumption—and that she knew nothing about the stranger standing before her now. Tab could practically see the gears turning in the princess's mind as she worked to make sense of the situation.

"My orders were to seek you out for twelve days before pointing my compass back to Kylden, Your Highness," Traejon said in what struck Tab as a clear effort to change the subject back to the falcon. "And Nomad has left me behind a time or two in the past when occasion arose. She can make it back to Kylden Hall from these mountains in less than three days of flight. Surely your father can withstand another few days' absence from his familiar."

"I suppose," Jess said grudgingly. "But I'd still feel better if she began her journey back tonight. It was foolish of him to draw so deeply from his powers. He should know better. Fyngree needs a Throneholder at full fighting strength during such dark days."

"He was a grieving father who wanted his daughter back, Your Highness," Traejon responded. "And truth be told, the terms of that order underwent considerable negotiation before Nomad and I departed. Captain Treadlow and I had to implore your father to allow us to turn around after twelve days. Under his *original* command, Nomad and I were not to return until you were found."

†††

Since it was clear to all three of them that further discussion was in order, they dismounted and set their horses to graze, then appropriated a fallen log for a spot of lunch. As they passed around food from their saddlebags, Traejon and Tab told the princess about the massive search that the

Throneholder had launched after her disappearance, and about King Owyn's order to reinforce Fyngrean garrisons along the border with Rojenhold.

At first, Tabytha was so flustered by the knowledge that she was sharing cheese and bread with King Owyn's daughter—and that said daughter was watching her every move with a suspicious glint in her eye—that she stammered out every sentence in a self-conscious rush. But she gradually regained her composure, aided in no small measure by a slow thaw in the princess's expression after Traejon explained how the two of them had come to be traveling together. As well as Jess's subsequent request that they call her by her given name rather than as "your highness" or other forms of royal address. Without those constant reminders of the princess's exalted station fluttering around in the air, it became a little easier to pretend that she was not actually conversing with the heir to the Fyngrean throne.

Then it was Jessalyn's turn. As she launched into her tale of the attack at Muncenmast's shop and her subsequent flight from Kylden, Tab initially found the princess's manner to be almost strangely nonchalant. As if she was accustomed to telling such harrowing and bloody tales. An old hand when it came to recounting political skullduggery, gargoyle attacks, and midnight rides through moonwashed lands. Could that be true? Tab found herself wondering. Was Jessalyn some sort of veteran adventuress, despite her youth and pampered upbringing?

But midway through her account, Jessalyn's air of cool self-possession fell apart. When Jessalyn began to speak of finding her printer friend's broken body in the aftermath of the gargoyle's attack, her voice faltered and her eyes blurred with tears. A moment later she began weeping in earnest, and Tab felt her own throat knot up in sympathy.

In many ways, she supposed that the princess had been born under a lucky star. Certainly she was a comely girl. Even ten days wandering in the wilderness had not appreciably dulled the shine of her handsome features. And somehow, the drab, mismatched clothing she had appropriated from farmboys and milkmaids during her travels still showed her slim figure to advantage. Tab was not envious by nature, but as she watched Traejon hang on every word of Jess's tale, she could not help but feel a little pang at the princess's stubbornly durable charms. Indeed, Jessalyn's presence made her keenly aware of how long it had been since she herself had bathed—or even drawn a brush through her hair.

And Jess had been given much more than mere beauty. She also was heir to the throne of Fyngree, with all the attendant luxuries and power that accompany that position. And given her bloodlines, she was almost certainly a caster of at least moderate aptitude. Her familiar was probably watching over them even now from some perch in the surrounding crags. She and Traejon had been fortunate that Jess's first instinct when they had first closed in on her had been to flee rather than fight.

Nonetheless, Jess's sudden outburst of tears reminded Tab of all that she'd been through. And of the towering fear she must be feeling for her father. And of how unprepared she must have been for any of this, no matter how powerful her Thread. Was it really so surprising to find that the shield of composure wielded by the princess was parchment-thin? As Tab watched Jessalyn's shoulders shake with her sobbing, she felt the tiny claws of resentment and envy that had been seeking footholds in her heart fall away. Fortune may have smiled on Jess for the first seventeen years of her life. But she must have spent a good portion of the past ten nights feeling utterly forsaken and alone.

After another minute or so of crying, Jess wiped roughly at her cheeks. "Please forgive me," she said shakily, her voice so quiet that it was almost as if she were talking to herself. "I guess I haven't spoken to anyone about all this . . ."

"It's all right," Tab said quietly, infusing her voice with all the sincerity she could muster. She lightly placed one hand on the princess's shoulder. Jess turned and looked up at Tab with a startled expression, and for an instant Tab wondered uneasily if she had overstepped. But after a moment a grateful smile spread across the princess's face, and she began to blink away her tears.

The princess took another minute to compose herself, then resumed her account. From that point forward, Jessalyn told her story simply and without pretense. She even included a few self-deprecating jests about the toll that her travels had taken on her perpetually growling stomach and saddle-numbed bottom. And though her determination to defend her father still shone through, she acknowledged to Tab and Traejon that since leaving Kylden, there had been moments when she had felt not unlike a leaf caught in the grip of some relentless current that was carrying her toward a roaring horizon line wreathed in mist and shadow.

Tab greeted the arrival of this new, more genuine and approachable version of the princess with no small measure of relief. But not with any great surprise. She might have armies sworn to protect her. And she might well be able to bend the elements to her will with her Thread. But once you've dissolved into tears in front of a couple of strangers, Tab mused, there wasn't much point in behaving as if you've got everything under control.

After Jessalyn was done, she grabbed a skin of water at her side and washed down the last of her lunch. "And so," she said, setting the skin down and brushing dust off her thighs with an air of "I'm-done-here" finality, "I'm off for the Widow's Torch. If I can only find the blasted thing. I confess that I was a little lost when you found me. It is hard to navigate through these mountains. One wrong turn and you have to backtrack for hours."

Traejon studied her impassively for a moment. "I can't permit that, Your Highness," he said finally. "The Throneholder sent me to find you, and I've done that. You need to return with me to Kylden. That is King Owyn's wish, and I will obey it. And so must you."

"And how do you propose to do that, shadow?" Jess said lightly, though her expression betrayed her displeasure with the idea that Traejon was somehow in charge. "Do you intend to bind me like a stack of kindling and throw me over your saddle?"

"If necessary."

"I think you forget to whom you speak," Jessalyn said, and now there was no mistaking the anger in her voice. "And you must think a great deal of your abilities if you think you can overpower a caster of the Suntold line."

Traejon said nothing to that, but he locked eyes with Jess and his gaze did not waver. Tabytha looked back and forth between them with mounting anxiety. This was an unwelcome turn of events. Did *every* meal Traejon shared with renewed acquaintances end in disharmony? The silent staredown between Traejon and Jess ticked by, with neither shadow nor princess displaying any inclination to back down. Until Jessalyn finally sighed and dropped her eyes.

"Look, Traejon," she said, trying another tack. "What is your mission? Why were you given those rings on your left hand? Why do you spend weeks and months riding through the wilderness of Fyngree? Why do you spend your life fording rivers, crossing valleys, tromping through marshlands, and shivering under the stars?"

"My mission is to protect and defend Nomad."

"No, it's not. Your *mission*, the oath you took as a shadow to the Throneholder, is to protect and defend my *father*. Nomad is merely a vessel that contains a part of my father's, I don't even know what to call it, his life essence or whatever. It is my *father* that you are sworn to protect. And the message in that Tiding Horn asserted that King Owyn, the monarch to whom you have sworn your allegiance, is in grave danger. And that message said that there's a fellow named Gydeon who can tell us about the forces conspiring to push my father off his throne. And that Gydeon—whoever he is—may still be waiting for Percy at the Widow's Torch. And while I admit that these mountain passes and ridges have me a little turned around, I know that I'm close. Probably less than a half-day's ride from where we sit."

Traejon sat stonily, the fire in his fierce green eyes banked for the moment. He looked away to where Nomad was perched. She gave a desultory shake of her wings as she returned his gaze, then turned and stared with unblinking eyes out over the valley.

"This isn't a lark, Traejon," Jess continued quietly. "I'm trying to save my father's life and kingdom. And as Nomad's shadow, you shouldn't just be *willing* to accompany me to the Widow's Torch. You should be *demanding* to go with me."

Traejon stood with a sigh and looked out over the mountains arrayed before them. Then he turned back to where Jess and Tabytha sat. "Very well," he said finally. "But if this Gydeon fellow lost his nerve and ran off, we immediately return to Kylden. Agreed?"

"Agreed. And no matter what we find, we send No-mad back to my father tonight." Jess laughed in relief, pushing a loose tendril of hair back behind her right ear. "Whew! I was worried for a moment that I was going to have to turn you into a toad!"

Traejon smiled and offered his hand to help the princess to her feet. Tabytha relaxed as well, grateful that the spiraling tension between them had subsided. Once Jess was standing, though, Tabytha saw the two of them exchange a look that seemed freighted with significance. It was the look, Tabytha thought, of two people who shared a secret.

15

The Widow's Torch

Traejon pointed to a great slab of rock that jutted out into the valley like the prow of a warship. "The Torch is just ahead, around and to the left," he shouted over the rising roar of the still-unseen falls.

Jess peered up at the surrounding peaks. Unlike the more spacious southern reaches of the range, where the mountains were set far apart by broad carpets of grass and forest that connected to one another via wide natural thoroughfares, this northerly section felt cramped and gloomy. Here the peaks gathered together tightly like the concertinaed folds of a smithy's bellows, blocking out sunlight for all but a few hours of the midday.

The rising tumult of sound added to Jess's sense that she was entering an alien world. Off to their right flowed the upper reaches of the Gryndstone. Even here, only a few miles from its headwaters at Fireflynt Lake, the river's volume was significant. It galloped over its boulder-strewn bed as if it were competing with all the other rivers of Tempyst to be first to the sea. And yet, the cacophony of the rapids was nearly drowned out by the full-throated roar of the Widow's Torch, looming around the corner like a storm on a chain.

A moment later they rounded the bend and Jess could not help but gasp. Here, within the narrow canyon in which the Widow's Torch was housed, the waterfall's thunder was overwhelming. Her nose, meanwhile, was overwhelmed by the musty odor emanating from the groves of evergreens crowded around the base of the cataracts and the moss-encrusted flanks of the sheer mountainsides surrounding them.

But it was the sight of the Widow's Torch at the far end of the canyon that truly took her breath away. She estimated that the top of the waterfall was at least 1500 feet above their heads. For much of the drop the falls appeared as a massive column of pulsing white and gray water. In its lower reaches, though, the waterfall was largely hidden behind a tremendous corona of spray created by its plunging impact with a great foamy pool of water cradled deep in the canyon bedrock. The walls of the violently churning pool, worn to a smooth gloss over millennia, channeled the resulting spray upward, further heightening the torch-like appearance of the frothy mist at the base of the falls. At one end of the great stone pool, meanwhile, a rushing torrent that seemed equal parts air and water boiled through a rupture in the stone. From there the newborn Gryndstone River shook off its manes of white foam, then proceeded at a steady gallop down the valley.

They rode across the grassy canyon floor toward the Torch. As they neared the roaring falls, Jess felt a cold film of spray settle over her hands and face, as if she were riding through an early spring shower. Tearing her gaze from the waterfall, she glanced over at her new traveling companions.

Tabytha's expression was an awestruck one. Absently steering her nervous horse through the long grass to the grove at the base of the falls, the cadet was taking her surroundings in with an almost child-like wonder that made Jess feel a little better about her own overwhelmed senses. And she found Tab's very presence to be a comfort as well. Jess had been furious with herself when she had broken down crying in front of Tab and Traejon earlier in the day. But Tab's gentle kindness had been an unexpected balm, and when she had looked into the cadet's eyes, Jess had seen that there had been nothing calculating or condescending about the gesture. It had been a pure expression of concern for someone in pain.

Traejon, on the other hand, was making her terribly anxious. The shadow had known right where the Widow's Torch was located—a benefit of a long-ago deployment at a garrison in the southern reaches of the these mountains, he said. As they neared the canyon in which the cataract could be found, though, he had stopped, removed his cloak, and stuffed it in the saddlebag of his extra mount. When he saw the question in Jess's eyes, he said "gets in the way some-times" and tapped the quiver of throwing knives strapped tightly to his side. Traejon winked as he said it, as if to imply that he knew he was being over-cautious. But his low-key preparation for a possible battle had been a sobering remind-er to Jess that the Torch could be harboring enemies as easily as friends. And his attention now was not on the towering, howling waterfall, but on the pine grove and the surrounding ridges and promontories.

Jess understood his wariness, for a skilled archer could wreak carnage on them from any of those positions. So although Traejon's expression was calm and Nomad patrolled the skies above, Jess sensed the coiled energy that fairly thrummed through the shadow's body as he rode beside her. And Traejon's battle-readiness was doing nothing to soothe the already considerable turmoil of her own thoughts. What if this was an elaborate trap for Percy into which they were falling? What if this Gydeon told of a plot that they were helpless to stop? Or what if no one was here at all? Jess thought that she might just curl up at the base of the waterfall and stay there forever in the face of such crushing disappointment.

When they approached to within fifty feet of the outer fringe of the grove, Traejon suddenly stopped his horse in its tracks. He remained motionless, staring intently at a particularly murky pool of shadows under the trees. Jess and Tabytha halted as well, though Jess saw nothing out of the ordinary under the boughs. She exchanged a momentary glance of puzzlement with Tab, but then Jess sensed a flicker of movement at the edge of the trees.

A tall man in a gray cloak stepped out of the shadows. Or rather, the shadows shrank away from his form. It was so strange, Jess thought. The man did not so much step out of the gloom as cast off the surrounding dark like a second cloak.

There was not much doubt that this man carried the Thread.

As she studied the stranger, though, relief flooded through her. The Tiding Horn had instructed Percy to seek a man with a "great blade" of a nose, and this fellow certainly qualified. He sported a nose so narrow and long that it reminded her of the gnomon of a sundial. This *had* to be Gydeon.

Her heart pounding in her chest, Jess shouted out a question that was instantly lost in the roar of sound swirling around them. The stranger frowned and brought a small rectangular bottle out of the folds of his cloak. It appeared to be stuffed with tufts of cotton, yet it was stoppered with cork. The man tugged the cork free and waved a hand over the bottle, and over the course of the next five seconds or so the thundering of the cataract dimmed, as if the wizard had moved the entire waterfall to a neighboring mountain. Jess recognized it as some sort of sound-dampening enchantment, and a fragment of free-floating memory suddenly flashed across her consciousness; her father had once teased her that during her childhood, he liked to use a variation of this spell when she was being particularly whiny or demanding.

"There," the man said. "That's better." He nodded at all three of them, his gaze lingering on Traejon for an extra heartbeat of time.

"Are you Gydeon?" Jess asked.

"I am, Your Highness," he said, bowing formally. The lines on his face suggested a man of middle years, but he still boasted a thick shock of dark hair that was only starting to go gray. And although his limbs were on the spindly side, the trousers, shirt, and coat in which they were clad were of fine quality. "Gydeon Gloomwater is my full name, and I am honored to make your acquaintance again."

"Again? Forgive me but—"

"I'm sure you don't recall, but we actually met several years ago. I am an instructor at the Acaderum in Tapwyll's Cross. I was introduced to you and the Throneholder himself at the gala celebrating the dedication of our new library and archives four summers past."

Jess's face lit up. "One of my favorite places in all of Fyngree. Such a beautiful city and campus. And the gardens! I daresay they are the finest in the entire kingdom. I briefly entertained the thought of studying at the Acaderum, but my father thought that my presence would be too much of a distraction to the faculty and other students." Her smile faded. "And there were security concerns as well, of course . . . "

"A shame. Well, the university is still there should you and your father reconsider."

"I do-"

Traejon coughed and shifted in his saddle, and Jess realized with embarrassment that she had allowed herself to be sidetracked. Traejon was right. There were much more urgent matters to discuss.

"You do not seem surprised that we have come in Percy's stead," she said.

Gydeon's expression darkened. "I know of Percy Muncenmast's fate. The shops and taverns of Fyngree have been bubbling with news and speculation about the events that brought you here for days now. It is not difficult for an unassuming traveler to acquire information. And even accounting for exaggeration and rumormongering, the essential facts of his demise were not in dispute. As for your identity, well . . . my friend here has a talent for surveillance." A tiny brown owl, no more than seven inches tall, glided in out of nowhere and alighted on the man's left shoulder. A flitting owl, the smallest species of owl in all of Tempyst. Jess had never been this close to one before. Its brown quilling was laced in white and black at the tips, and its round eyes were of such a blazing orange-yellow hue that they looked as if they had been painted on its head. "This is Vyx," Gydeon said.

Jess blinked in surprise. It was exceedingly rare for a caster to voluntarily reveal the identity of his or her familiar, even to friends of long standing. Instantly she understood that Gydeon's gesture was designed to reassure them of his loyalty to the Throneholder. "It's a pleasure to meet you both," she said warmly. "And please. Call me Jessalyn. Or even better, Jess. It feels odd to be addressed so formally when I smell of the stables and wear a boy's boots."

"Very well. Jess it is," Gydeon said, a faint note of amusement in his voice. Then he turned his gaze to Traejon. "Your eyesight is keen. Do you carry the Thread as well? Or do one of those rings fortify you against spells of concealment?"

"Neither," Traejon said easily. "Just suspicious of dark woods in general. Or perhaps you need to brush up on that particular spell a little." Jess glanced over at the shadow. The young warrior was sitting casually, but she could tell that he remained ready to spring into action at any moment.

She turned back to Gydeon, whose face had stiffened at Traejon's not-so-veiled insult. "How long have you been waiting here at the Widow's Torch?" she asked brightly.

"I arrived only yesterday," Gydeon replied. "My journey was a long one, and even with my abilities, progress was slow. Fyngree is filled with riders of unknown purpose and loyalties these days, and Vyx is not equipped to travel long distances, unlike some of her larger brethren." Gydeon reached up and stroked the owl's side affectionately with one long-fingered hand. "When I first learned of Percy's death I considered abandoning my travels and returning home. But while I suspect that there's not a tavern drunk in all of Fyngree who doesn't have an *opinion* about what befell you back in Kylden, in reality your whereabouts remained a mystery. And so I pressed on, nurturing a hope that you might have borne witness to Bryscoe's message. And that you might somehow find your way here. I am relieved to find that I was not a fool to harbor such hopes."

"I am touched by both your faith and dedication," Jess said, dismounting from her horse. Traejon and Tabytha looked at each other and the shadow nodded almost imperceptibly. They dismounted as well, and Jess could feel them move to either side of her.

At that moment Nomad came swooping out of the sky and alighted in a nearby tree no more than thirty feet from where they stood. Vyx and Nomad immediately commenced staring at each other with an unblinking intensity that captured the attention of them all.

Jess had seen this phenomenon before on a few occasions in Kylden Hall. When familiars came within close proximity to each other, they seemed to recognize each other as creatures not wholly of this world. And during such events, they often fell to staring at one another for long periods. Jess didn't think that familiars entered into these encounters for the purposes of preening or intimidation, though. The only times that Jess had ever heard of familiars attacking one another were when their respective casters were at odds. No, in most instances familiars were content to just stare at one another—evidently for the simple reason that they found their counterparts to be endlessly fascinating.

"How long have you known we were coming?" Traejon asked, his eyes turning from Nomad back to Vyx and her compeer.

"I learned of your approach a few hours ago. I've been sending Vyx on regular reconnaissance missions since our arrival. She spotted you from a stand of trees in the last valley through which you passed, and when she returned and I laid my hand upon her, I saw that the princess was part of your company. Of course, I don't know you or her"—he nodded in Tabytha's direction—"from a marsh goblin. So I thought it wise to remain concealed as you approached."

Gydeon turned back to the princess, implicitly dismissing Traejon. "Now then—"

At that moment a screech split the air above their heads. They all looked up as Nomad flew away, beating her wings furiously as she wheeled up toward a rocky rift in the mountainside to Jess's left. She followed the bird's flight . . . until her gaze was snared by movement midway down the mountain.

Several large wolves were scrambling down through a rocky scar in the mountain's otherwise sheer face, springing from slab to slab with fearsome purpose. Jess felt the blood drain from her face, felt her heart spasm in fear. She turned to Traejon, only to find that he was looking back down the narrow valley from which they had come. Following his gaze, she saw another, even larger pack of wolves sprinting toward them through the gap between the churning river and the prow-like outcrop that had marked their final turn to the Torch. They were a few hundred yards away but closing fast, gray and white and black streaks sprinting through the tall grass.

The realization hit her like a hammer blow; with the roaring river on one side of them and the cliff walls on the other, they were trapped here at the base of the Widow's Torch with no possible route of escape.

Traejon leaped at Gydeon, a glittering dagger appearing as if by magic in his right fist. "You bastard," he hissed, grabbing the wizard's shirt with his left hand and pressing the blade of the dagger against his neck. "Call the wolves off or I'll turn your neck into a fountain for them to drink from."

Gydeon's eyes filled with fear and shock, and Jess knew that his expression was no ruse. The man standing before them was a terrified professor, not a deceitful sorcerer. She leaped forward and placed a hand on Traejon's arm. "They are not his to command!" she shouted. "His familiar is an owl! Only a wolf familiar can bend fellow wolves to its will!"

Traejon turned to look at her, and she quailed for a moment at the fury burning in his eyes. But somehow she kept her gaze from falling away. "Trust me on this, Traejon," she said. "He is not the enemy here." Traejon's eyes bore into her for another instant, and then he nodded, released Gydeon, and sprinted for the horses. Tabytha had already grabbed their reins to keep them from bolting, but they were kicking and rearing in fear, their nostrils swimming with the scent of the fast-approaching wolves.

"Spellbound wolves will focus on Jess, and they'll sacrifice themselves to bring her horse down!" he shouted to Tabytha as he pulled his cloak from a saddlebag and grabbed Jess's stolen crossbow and a bolt from her gear. "Even if the fall doesn't kill her, they'll be on her in an instant. We'll make our stand here. Ready your bow, focus on the ones in the rocks. Let the horses fend for themselves, the wolves will probably ignore them anyway."

Tabytha dropped the reins and the horses promptly scattered. She fitted an arrow in her bow and turned to the mountainside, where the wolves on the rocks—eight of them by Jess's count—had nearly descended to the canyon floor. Jess watched, paralyzed, as Tabytha raised her bow. A moment later she loosed her arrow. It sliced through the air until it buried itself in the hindquarters of the lead wolf. The beast collapsed in the rocks as the others poured on past.

Then Traejon was back at the side of Jess and Gydeon, who still looked stunned by the sudden turn of events. Gone was his vaguely aloof and aristocratic bearing; he looked almost as scared and bewildered as she felt.

"Do you know how to use this?" Traejon asked Jess, shoving the loaded crossbow at her.

Jess looked dumbly down at it, as if she'd never seen a contraption of its like before. "I, I've practiced with it a little—"

"If you can hit something, take a shot. But don't bother reloading, you won't have time." Traejon looked over to the mountainside, where the first wolves had reached the bottom, then back down along the river to the second pack. The lead wolves from that larger group were less than a hundred yards away now, almost within bow range. He shoved his cloak and a dagger, hilt-first, toward Jess. She looked up at him uncomprehendingly. "Wrap my cloak around your left arm, you can use it as a shield. If one gets to you, stab for their eyes or their underbelly, below the rib cage."

Jess managed to nod, even as her expression went slack with fear. She knew she looked terrified, but she felt helpless to do anything about it. It was as if some sorcerer had frozen her facial muscles. Traejon patted her shoulder. "You're going to be fine," he said calmly, locking eyes with her. Then he unslung the bow off his back and pulled an arrow from his quiver. "Gydeon," he called over to the wizard. "Can you assist Tabytha?"

"What? Uh, yes, I know of several enchan—"

"Good, help her." Traejon raised his bow, pulled the string back to his cheek, and sighted down the shaft of the arrow.

Gydeon gestured in Jess's direction, his expression one of mystification. "Can't the princess—"

"She's threadbare," Traejon said tersely as he tracked a lean black wolf at the head of the pack.

Gydeon's mouth worked soundlessly for a moment, his shocked eyes turning to Jess. "But the falcon . . ."

"Get to it, professor," said Traejon at the same instant that he released his arrow. Jess watched it sing across the valley and plant itself deep in the chest of the bounding black wolf about sixty yards away. He then fired three more times in quick succession, each arrow sending a wolf somersault-ing into the high grass.

Gydeon ran to Tabytha's side, Vyx sailing off his shoulder into the dark interior of the grove. As he ran he tried to tuck the vial back into his cloak, but the item tumbled out of his hand and shattered on a rock at his feet. Instantly, the roar of the Widow's Torch swept back over them all in a tre-mendous wave. Jess felt almost as if she had been physically thrown into the sound, so sudden and disorienting was its return. She saw Tabytha bring another wolf down with a well-placed shot just as the beast completed its descent, and a thought suddenly struck her like a thunderbolt.

"Look for the wolf familiar!" she shouted, trying to make herself heard above the tumult of the Torch. "It has to be somewhere nearby to control these packs! If you can kill it, the wolves will scatter—and the caster who threatens us will fall as well!"

Both Tabytha and Traejon nodded their heads once in acknowledgment, but Gydeon continued staring at the half-dozen wolves rushing forward from the rocks. His hands moved furiously in the air as if he were polishing an invisible table. The three lead wolves from that pack were only thirty feet away when they all simultaneously plunged into the ground up to their chests. The beasts snarled and snapped as they pawed frantically at the ground, trying to find purchase to pull themselves out of the suddenly soupy turf. Mean-while, Tabytha dropped her bow and unsheathed her sword to confront the remaining three wolves that had eluded Gydeon's spell.

Jess turned back to the river, where the lead wolves from the larger second pack were on the verge of washing over them as well. She could see their shining eyes and the way their lips curled back from their fangs in bloodlust. She fired her crossbow at a wolf bounding in from the left, groaned as the bolt sailed harmlessly over its head. "The cloak!" Traejon reminded her as he sent another arrow through a wolf's skull, then dropped his bow and drew his sword from the scabbard hanging from his back. Jess flung the crossbow aside and began frantically wrapping Traejon's cloak around her left forearm.

And then the wolves were on them.

The world around Jess dissolved into a twisting chaos of sharp teeth, slashing swords, and acrobatic contortions by wolf and warrior alike, all of it punctuated by spectacular eruptions of blood and gore. The cyclone of violence around her moved so swiftly that she could only absorb fragments: Tabytha cutting down a leaping wolf just before it landed on Gydeon's exposed back; the wizard scrubbing away at his invisible table, sweat pouring down his face as those three wolves sank ever deeper into the quicksand of grass he'd conjured; Traejon wheeling left and right, hurling daggers that found their mark again and again even as his sword flashed and carved, trailing crimson behind it like a comet's tail.

And Jess cowering behind them all, her heart shuddering with terror and helplessness as the sound of the Widow's Torch pounded in her ears.

And then one wolf leaped through a tiny crease between Traejon and Tabytha, its slavering jaws yawning open to rip out her throat. She cried out and blindly thrust her left arm before her, felt the wolf's jaws clamp down on it like a vice. The weight of the wolf slammed her to the ground, and Traejon's dagger spilled from her right hand. As the wolf wrenched its mouth back and forth in an effort to shred the cloak wrapped around her arm, its eyes locked on those of Jess for an instant. Her blood ran cold as she gazed into the wolf's eyes, for they burned with an implacable desire to rend her limb from limb. I'm going to die here, she thought, terror crashing through her mind like a blind, raging giant. An instant later, though, the wolf sprang away with a howl, flinging droplets of blood from its ruined right eye as Nomad wheeled back up into the heavens with dripping talons. Jess scrabbled back to her feet as Traejon turned and finished the wounded beast off.

Jess looked around frantically, her left arm upraised to defend herself from further attack. And then she slowly lowered her arm.

It was over.

The bodies of wolves littered the valley. They were scattered here and there in the rocks and down along the river, then piled up in a rough circle around where they stood. She stared dazedly at the other three. The faces and bodies of Traejon and Tabytha were streaked with blood, gore, and mud, but they otherwise looked mostly intact, if terribly weary. Gydeon looked less well, though his garments were not so sullied; his visage was gray and haggard, and it appeared that he might collapse from exhaustion at any moment.

Gydeon raised his eyes to meet hers, and he mustered a watery smile. But though she labored to return his smile, she found herself quite unable to do so. Instead, she felt her thoughts tumbling into darkness. How could she have missed so badly with the crossbow, she thought miserably. Truly pathetic. And then she felt her skin grow cold as she recalled how close that wolf had come to ripping her throat out . . .

Jess felt a nudge on her arm. "Look!" Traejon shouted. He was pointing to an opening high up in the rocks, from where the first pack of wolves had descended. She followed where he was pointing, then stiffened. A solitary wolf of black and gray was looking down on them. Even from this distance, Jess could see that the wolf was enormous. She watched the wolf silently for a moment before the beast rose and padded at a leisurely trot up the ridge away from them.

When the wolf disappeared over the rim, Traejon turned to Jess and the others. "Everyone all right? Any injuries that need immediate tending?" Jess shook her head slowly, as if the motion itself might deepen the exhaustion now descending over her. How was she still alive? How were any of them still alive? Traejon looked at the shredded remains of the cloak still wrapped around Jess's arm. "You owe me a new cloak," he said, a small smile dancing on his lips.

This time Jess managed to paste a semblance of a smile on her face, even though she felt as if she might throw up at any moment.

"Any idea where our horses went?" she heard Tabytha say from somewhere behind her.

Gydeon gestured half-heartedly toward the grove. "My mount is still tied up at the back of the woods. The others fled down the valley."

"All right," said Traejon. "Let's go find 'em. And then we can talk about what just happened."

Traejon collected his throwing knives from the cooling bodies of various wolves as Tabytha gathered the bows and quivers and crossbow out of the beaten and bloody grass. Then the four of them began trudging out of the canyon and into the broader valley as Nomad and Vyx flew overhead, Gydeon walking his nervous but otherwise serviceable horse behind him. And so they left the Widow's Torch behind, leaving only the ghosts of the wolves to hear the waterfall as it roared on and on and on.

16

Nomad

Nomad streaked through the mountains, wings pumping steadily as she slalomed past peaks and ledges toward the open lands to the west. After leaving the canyon holding the great waterfall, the Daughter and the One Who Follows had called her in close. They had spoken to her of wolves and treachery and journeys to come in a matter-of-fact tone, as if they were dictating a note of correspondence. And then they had closed with instructions for her to return to Kylden Hall—and her compeer's side—with all due haste.

Nomad had taken flight immediately, her entire being suffused with a feeling that, had it been housed in the heart of a human, would have approximated relief. For the last few days she had felt the tug of her compeer's fading vitality. More than once she had nearly peeled away from the riders below and set course for his hand, so strong was the instinct to reunite with him.

But the love that the King held for the Daughter coursed through Nomad's being as well. And so the gyrfalcon had forged on deeper into the mountains, black eyes continually scanning the wilderness below—first for signs of the

Daughter and then, after she had been found, for anyone or anything that posed a potential threat to her.

Now, though, Nomad was free. Free to return home and pour her restorative magical essence into the King's dwindling cup. Free to watch him return to life like a mountain meadow after a long winter's nap. And so she sailed through the dimming sky like a sleek and slender galley ship, her wings beating with the same rhythm as the long oars that propelled such vessels across the sea. She streaked past the ice-and-snow encrusted crags of the upper peaks, pushed past the black caves that pockmarked the faces of some of the mountains, soared above the darkening valley floors.

She burst out of the last palisades of the mountains just as the sun was setting. The last of it glowed on the far horizon like the light under a closed door. But the moon was up, and in the dusky half-light she could see woods and plains laid out before her. And far off to the south, the great glittering river that ran all the way to her compeer's home.

But she failed to see the gargoyle pinned like a bat to the side of the mountain behind her. And she did not notice when the beast released its great claws from the rocks and took flight, its leathery gray wings closing the distance between them with each passing second.

17

Pruning the Tree

Malkyn had just set breakfast out on the table when the pre-dawn quiet was shattered by a frantic pounding on their door. She looked over to Wynston, a question in her eyes, but her husband ignored her and continued shoveling bacon onto his plate. She then glanced at Ben and Rowan. The knock had pulled both of them out of their usual early morning grogginess. They sat there at the table, staring silently at one another. Was it Glynt? Tumdown? Or perhaps some new blight upon their house?

Doing her best to ignore her racing pulse, Malkyn walked over and opened the door. To her great relief she found that it was only one of their neighbors, Prylla Overbeek, huddled under a cloak with a glowing lantern in one hand. An instant later, though, Malkyn noticed that Prylla's face was streaked with tears.

"Prylla, what's wrong?"

"Please, Malkyn," she said beseechingly, her eyes rolling like those of a panicked horse. "Tell me where they've taken him. Tell me he'll return home soon. Raven and Crow, what am I going to do?"

"What?" Malkyn said, alarmed. "What are you talking about? Is it Roland of whom you speak? One of your sons? What happened?"

"They came for him not two hours ago! Roland. They broke our door down and carried him off without a word. Our oldest, Caleb, tried to step in and . . . . They beat him badly, Malkyn. His left eye is swollen shut, and I think he has a broken nose."

"That's awful! Oh I'm so sorry, Prylla! Who was it? Was it . . . "

"The Faithful Shield? Aye," Prylla said, choking back tears. "I'm never going to see Roland again, am I?"

Malkyn's mind was swamped by visions of the terrified farmer being carried off into the night, his family helpless to save him. "Do you . . . do you have any idea why they came? What might have prompted his arrest?"

At this the panic in Prylla's eyes vanished, replaced by smoldering rage. "Why don't you ask your husband that question?" she said, her mouth curling in contempt as she spat out the words.

"What?"

"Roland gets along just fine with everyone else in the valley," Prylla said accusingly. "The only problems he's ever had with anyone have been with Wynston, who has never given anyone in this valley a fair price for their grain."

Malkyn blinked, flustered by the sudden turn in the conversation. "Wynston doesn't have anything to do with this, Prylla."

"No?" Prylla choked out a bitter laugh. "Come now, Malkyn. Everyone knows that your family has ties to the Faithful Shield now. We're not blind to the comings and goings at your home."

Malkyn fell silent as she considered the implications of Prylla's words.

"Wynston Thystle!" Prylla called out, attempting to shoulder past Malkyn into the house. "You tell them to give me back my husband!"

Malkyn felt a presence behind her. She half-turned and found Wynston at the door, his face ruddy with—what?—vexation? Embarrassment? Shame? Malkyn felt a stab in her heart at how unfamiliar her husband had come to seem to her. The comforting conviction that she knew Wynston, a belief that she had acquired over the course of seventeen peaceful if taciturn years of marriage, had dwindled considerably over these last few wretched weeks. She had begun to see the Faithful Shield's sudden intrusion into her family's life as a crucible of sorts. A test of strength that had dissolved the carefully crafted masks that she and Wynston showed to the world and illuminated their deepest, truest selves with a clear and unsparing light. Malkyn was not sure what that light might be revealing about her. But she knew that in Wynston's case, the light had not been kind.

"I know nothing of Roland's circumstances," said Wynston in a low voice. "Go home, Prylla, and quit making a spectacle of yourself."

"You miserable man," said Prylla. "Is a little extra silver that important to you, Wynston? Or do you simply like wielding the power that comes with your new associations? Tell me, Wynston, I'd really like to know. Do you feel like more of a man these days?"

"This is nonsense. I had nothing to do with Roland's arrest, and know nothing of his affairs. Perhaps news of his deceitful character finally reached the ears of Stormheel. I'm sure I'm not the only man he's tried to cheat over the years."

Malkyn gasped at her husband's callous words. At the same instant, Prylla stepped forward and slapped Wynston hard across the face. "How dare you. Do we look like we grow fat off Roland's bartering?" She gestured down at her faded and fraying clothing. "We raise wheat on land that is two parts clay for one part soil! Roland has no choice but to bargain for every penny. He has four children to feed!"

"And a shrew of a wife as well," Wynston snarled, rubbing the cheek where she had struck him. "Get back to your home, Prylla. Perhaps the Faithful Shield only means to question him about some matter pertaining to the security and welfare of Rojenhold. Fyngree's agents are everywhere, you know."

"He's no spy for Fyngree! He's a simple farmer! Who would accuse him of . . ." Prylla's mouth snapped shut, her eyes widening in dawning horror as they searched Wynston's face.

"Go home, Prylla," Wynston repeated stonily. "I know nothing of your husband's affairs. Or his whereabouts." He reached over and took hold of the door, using his arm to crowd Malkyn out of the doorway and back into the interior of the house at the same time. Then he slowly but firmly shut the door in Prylla's anguished face.

Malkyn and Wynston turned to their sons, both of whom were staring up at them, their forgotten breakfasts congealing on their plates. Rowan was on the verge of tears again—a much more common occurrence these days—but Ben's expression was harder to read. Was there a hint of anger swirling in those eyes? And if so, with whom was he angry? Prylla Overbeek? His father? Her?

"Eat up, boys," Wynston snapped, taking his seat. "We have a busy day ahead of us."

Malkyn shuffled over to the table in a daze, her thoughts a chaotic jumble. She caught movement out of the corner of her eye and looked out the window. In the wan light of the approaching sunrise, she could see the dim form of Prylla Overbeek retreating down the lane back to her home, her lantern swinging loosely in one hand. Even from this distance, Malkyn could see her shoulders heaving with sobs.

"Wynston?" she said. Her voice sounded faint to her, as if it was reaching her ears from a great distance.

He kept eating, giving no indication that he had heard her.

"Wynston?" she said again in the same small voice.

Her husband sighed heavily. "Sit down and eat, Malkyn. Put Prylla's delusions out of your head. Roland will probably be returned before sundown, none the worse for wear."

"You know that's not what happens to people taken away by the Faithful Shield," she said.

"Well there's nothing I can do about it."

"You could put in an inquiry with Captain Glynt, ask him about Roland's arrest. This must be a mistake."

Wynston set his fork down and glared at her. "I'll do no such thing," he said. "Overbeek's affairs are none of my business. If he's innocent of wrongdoing, he'll be fine."

Malkyn raked a hand through her hair, staring at him in disbelief. "How can you say that?" she said wonderingly after a moment. "Have you forgotten Selwyn Wayland already?" Wynston was silent, but his mouth set in a grim line at her mention of the name.

Selwyn had been one of their best friends back in Hanken. A wine seller who loved to eat, drink, laugh, and debate, Selwyn lived in a modest but comfortable room above his shop. Several years back, when Ben was just a young boy and Rowan had yet to be born, Selwyn's apartment had been a beacon of color and excitement for them, a respite from the sweat and grain dust of the mill. Sitting around Selwyn's long table with a half-dozen of Hanken's other young shop owners and artisans, they would gather once a month or so to laugh and argue about love and religion and work and friendship deep into the night. And the irrepressible Selwyn would preside over it all like a benevolent monarch, pouring wine, quoting lines of poetry, bellowing with laughter, and gently mocking his guests when their passion spilled over into self-importance.

The conversations never veered into outright criticism of King Whytewender or a particular government policy—they all knew that informants were the lifeblood of the Faithful Shield, whether in the capital or smaller towns like Hanken. They all knew not to cross that line. But they had still felt daring and full of life on those evenings. Bolder than their meek and mild neighbors at any rate. Malkyn still recalled one night when they were walking home late from Selwyn's shop, Ben sleeping in Wynston's arms, and she compared their little group to a cluster of fireflies aglow in the otherwise black Rojenholdean night.

And then one morning they discovered that they had all misjudged where the line was. Selwyn was gone, his shop ransacked. Rumors flew about town that the Faithful Shield had taken him away in the deep of the night, as was their practice. They never heard from him again. Or from any of the other men and women who had joined them for Selwyn's revelries. None of them disappeared in the same manner as Selwyn. But after his disappearance, they studiously avoided looking at one another when they crossed paths. Before long those dear friends came to seem like apparitions from a dimly remembered dream.

"Selwyn would not approve of your words," Malkyn said now, placing her hand gently on her husband's forearm. He shook it off furiously, his face going crimson.

"Selwyn is dead. He can't approve or disapprove of anything these days," Wynston leaned toward her, his eyes locking on hers. "Wouldn't you rather be on this side of things? Where Ben and Rowan are safe? Where we can set a fair price for wheat and not have farmers like Overbeek gnaw away at it until our profit is gone? Where we know that we can sleep through the night in peace?"

"Raven and Crow," Malkyn said in a tone of wonderment. "Are you sleeping through the night? I know I'm not. Not with Glynt or Tumdown descending on our home every day and our neighbors trembling at the sight of us. I haven't had a good night's sleep in weeks. And you, Wynston? Don't forget that we share the same bed. I know you've been having nightmares. Bad ones. I've heard you cry out in the night."

"Shut up, Malkyn," he hissed. "You behave as if I have a choice in this matter. When the Faithful Shield calls, you answer."

"And what of Roland Overbeek? Did the Faithful Shield call on you regarding him? Or did *you* call on *them?*"

"They're pruning the tree," said Ben from the other end of the table. Malkyn and Wynston exchanged a surprised look, then turned to their eldest son. It had been two days since Ben had spoken to them. Malkyn regarded him now as a horseman would a spooked horse. She didn't want to make a move that would send him galloping into the darkness again.

"Pruning the tree?" Malkyn asked cautiously. "What do you mean, Ben?"

"That's what Professor Tumdown calls it," he said, looking back and forth from one parent to the other as if he was a tutor explaining a simple rule of grammar or arithmetic. "For Rojenhold to grow straight and true and strong, it has to be vigilant about pruning diseased and damaged branches and roots from its body. Some limbs are just too small and brittle and withered, and they suck up nourishment that would otherwise go to the stronger parts of the tree. And if we keep pruning the tree, someday it will be long and straight and dense enough to reap and carve into a great spear. A spear capable of piercing the armor of Fyngree and stilling its foul heart."

Malkyn stared at her son, horror rising like bile in her chest.

"That's what they want me and Wynk for," Ben said in a matter-of-fact voice, though his eyes shone with tears. "To help them prune the tree."

18

Gone

Owyn watched as the courier withdrew from the doorway and Pynch shut the door. He turned back into the king's private chambers, a gleaming Tiding Horn in his hand, and brought it to where Owyn sat slumped before the room's massive fireplace. The fire cast a warm coppery glow over the king's garments, staff, and crown, but its light could not disguise the lassitude in his eyes and face. Indeed, Owyn could feel the life slipping out of his body with each passing hour.

He saw now that it had been a mistake to expend so much energy on the Tiding Horn messages and pilgrimage spells in the hours following Jessalyn's disappearance. As a younger man, he would have recovered from that expenditure of magical labor in a matter of hours. This time, he didn't think he'd ever regained full strength—and he never would if Nomad did not return soon. Another week without the restorative touch of his familiar and he would be forced to use his last reserves to conjure a shielding spell over his entire chambers and submit to the dark waters of oblivion. The latter enchantment would leave him in a deep, almost death-like sleep. But it would also extend his life—hopefully long enough for Nomad to return to him.

"A Tiding Horn from General Splyntbell, Your Highness," said Pynch as he placed the wood box on a small table at Owyn's side. His tone was formal, and it still carried the peevish note that had laced the high votary's remarks of the last few days.

It had not taken long for Pynch to recognize that Owyn was not being entirely forthcoming with him about the contents of Jessalyn's letter. To be sure, Owyn had informed his chief counselor that his daughter was alive and well. He also informed Pynch that Jess had urged him to bolster Fyngree 's defenses against possible attack from Rojenhold, and to extend additional protections to the kingdom's witches and wizards. But Owyn had been vague about Jessalyn's whereabouts—and he had been silent about her warning that Whytewender's agents roamed Kylden Hall. He felt guilty about keeping Pynch in the dark. But his daughter had urged him to "trust no one," and he had taken that warning to heart.

Owyn touched the rune-etched lid of the box, and within seconds it dissolved and a dense, misty light began to issue forth. The mist then resolved itself into the face of Grayfus Splyntbell, high commander of all Fyngree's armies. Splyntbell's countenance, framed by a silvery widow's peak on top and a thick goatee of similar hue on his square jaw, was as stoic as ever.

"Your Highness," the general rumbled, "I extend greetings to you from High Sentinel Tremeny of Tydewater, whose army joined my forces west of Fireflynt Lake last night. The high sentinel kindly prepared this Tiding Horn for my use.

"Our infantry is some distance behind me, but they will be entering the Loaf by the end of the day tomorrow, and my officers will have them in place along Tucker's Front in two weeks' time. I'm taking our combined cavalry on ahead, and I anticipate reaching our garrisons along the Front by the end of the week. Meanwhile, the garrisons have already received some reinforcements from Tapwyll's Cross, with more on the way. Valyedon reports that it is mustering several companies as well, but Lady Tusk's troops won't reach Tucker's Front until the end of the month."

Splyntbell looked down for a moment as if consulting notes. "The border with Rojenhold remains open to trade at the moment, but we're stopping every rider and wagon that comes across to ensure as best we can that they have legitimate business in Fyngree. We're checking those seeking to enter *into* Rojenhold as well to make sure that no wildlife is being smuggled in. Elsewhere, naval forces are on high alert in Tydewater and Emrych, as are the lighthouse watches of Siren Island and up and down the coastline of Skellus Bay. If Whytewender's warships stray below the Rumdrop Islands, we're ready for them."

The general sniffed. "As we anticipated, Rojenhold has bolstered its defenses on its side of the Green Road. Whytewender has sent several emissaries who insist that he is only doing so to defend Rojenhold from possible aggression on our side. They also say that despite our 'provocations,' Whytewender has faith that tensions will subside once Fyngree understands that bearing false witness against Rojenhold serves the interest of neither kingdom."

Splyntbell spat off to the side. "Not that I believe that baldheaded bastard. Just letting you know what I'm hearing, Your Highness. I'm sending more detailed reports via regular courier for you to review, but that's how the main current is flowing." The general's face then broke into a rough but broad smile. "And finally, Majesty, we were enormously relieved to hear that Princess Jessalyn is alive and well and recovering nicely from her ordeal. The news of her deliverance has spread across the army like wildfire, lifting the spirits of every Fyngrean soldier. Truly, it is an omen of which Stormheel should take heed."

Splyntbell inclined his head slightly, and a moment later the image disappeared. Owyn turned his attention to Pynch. "Summon Treadlow and Sevenshade to my chambers first thing tomorrow morning. I want to hear about their progress in reaching known casters across Fyngree."

"I'll inform them of your wishes. I know they have been urging all known witches and wizards to keep their familiars close at hand, if only for the next few days. Even those traveling to Tucker's Front. And High Sentinel Grandyse has opened his castle in Talonoux to all casters seeking safety in numbers."

"Good, good."

Pynch coughed. "But what of the casters who are *not* known to us, my liege? Those who conceal the existence of their Threads? Are they to remain in the dark about this alleged threat? And the general population, too? They grow anxious, Your Highness. Our armies are being ordered north and they glean the reasons only dimly, especially since being reassured that the princess is safe."

"And what would you have me tell them, Marston?" Owyn snapped, giving vent to his own frustrations. "We have nothing but a handful of disappearances, a berserk gargoyle, and the cryptic warnings of my daughter to go on. Bolstering our border defenses is a sensible course of action and I make no apology for it. But Whytewender has not invaded our lands. I need more information before I issue such a warning. Specifics about the manner of threat our casters face and the steps they can take to protect themselves. Otherwise, I will just sow fear—the kind of fear that has people barring their doors to friend and foe alike."

"As you wish, Majesty," said Pynch.

Owyn sighed, then plunged ahead with the question that had been on his lips all day—even though he knew the answer. "Still no sign of Nomad or Frost?"

"No, Your Highness," said Pynch, and Owyn could hear a softening in his advisor's stiff tone. "But a description of Frost is being distributed to all wardens' outposts and garrisons, as well as to Splyntbell's scouts."

Owyn grunted. Now that he knew that Jess was alive and well—if frustratingly hidden from sight—he found himself able to spare a thought or two for his absent familiar. And his thoughts were troubled. It was true that Nomad and her shadow had been instructed to continue their search until this very night—the twelfth since Jess's disappearance. Depending on where and when their searching had taken them, it could take Nomad two or even three days to return. He understood that. But without any explanation, his right shoulder had begun aching with a dull throbbing intensity the previous evening. And all day today he had found himself dogged by a vaguely claustrophobic feeling. The sort of feeling, he imagined, that might coil around you if you found yourself trapped in dark, cramped quarters.

Like a cage.

Owyn closed his eyes and herded his thoughts to a more comforting scenario. Frost and Nomad had been sent in the direction of the Marching Mountains, and Owyn knew from Warden Brasse that his daughter had maps of that region in her possession. Was it possible that they had found Jessalyn? Might that account for Nomad's extended absence? The yearning to give voice to such a hope was so great that he felt it might crack him open.

A knock on the door interrupted his reverie. Pynch walked over and opened the door, murmured a greeting, then stood aside as Rodyk Stonewyck entered the room. Owyn's eyes widened. The portly Stonewyck usually carried himself with a sort of irrepressible good cheer that Owyn found refreshing. He had spent more than one night tossing back goblets of wine with the gregarious caster, who loved nothing more than to talk about his beloved prize pigs and reminisce about his youthful misadventures. A little talk about swine went a long way, granted. But most of the other lords of Fyngree were so consumed by political intrigue, romantic trysts, or the state of their mask-and-shadow networks that his occasional evenings with Stonewyck always felt like a balm.

Now, though, Stonewyck's ruddy features had an unhealthy sheen to them, as if he was in the grip of some terrible fever. And his usual rolling gait was gone, replaced by a sort of halting shuffle as he made his way deeper into Owyn's chambers.

"Lord Stonewyck!" Owyn cried, forcing himself out of his chair to greet his guest. "Are you unwell?"

Stonewyck bowed, then swiped a trembling hand across his forehead. "Thank you for seeing me, Majesty. I—please accept my apologies for disturbing you, Your Highness. I know that you have many affairs of state to attend to."

"Nonsense. I'm never too busy to see an old friend. Please, take a seat at the fire next to me. Can we get you something to drink? A glass of wine or brandy? Or tea, perhaps?"

"Thank you." Stonewyck collapsed into a sumptuously upholstered sofa positioned at right angles from Owyn's own seat. "Tea. A cup of tea sounds wonderful."

Pynch poured a cup and brought it to the caster. Owyn exchanged a troubled glance with the high votary as

Stonewyck brought the cup to his lips with trembling hands. He had never seen the man so pasty-faced and out of sorts.

"Now what is this about?" Owyn asked as he returned to his chair. "I'll not speak false to you, Rodyk, I'm alarmed to see you in such a state."

Stonewyck sighed and stared into the fire. Owyn could see the reflection of the flames dancing in his sad dark eyes.

"It's Kuff, Your Highness," Stonewyck said. "My familiar. She's been gone two weeks now. She's never been gone that long before."

Owyn felt goosebumps sprout up and down his arms, but he kept his voice calm. "Two weeks, you say? I understand your concern, of course. But ravens are contrary creatures, Rodyk—"

Stonewyck shook his head violently. "Not my Kuff," he said mournfully. "She's as true as they come, Majesty. Comes back like clockwork every three days. Even when I was a young man, her sojourns never exceeded a week's span."

"Perhaps she's injured somewhere," suggested Pynch. "Does any part of your person feel especially sore? Any unexplainable bruising?"

"No. But she's gone." Stonewyck turned back to the fire. "She's gone, and so soon will I be. I received your warning, Owyn. All the casters I know in the southern Loaf have heard it. They're either fleeing to the shelter of Talonoux with their familiars or striking out for Tucker's Front. I thought of making my way to the Front myself. . . . But what effect will I have on our soldiers' spirits if I reach their side, only to be struck down by whatever invisible hand holds Kuff in its grasp?"

"Come now, Rodyk," Owyn said gently. "Kuff still lives. Your presence here before us is proof of that. I'll grant you that it's possible that she is in the hands of Whytewender—or whoever it is that has been foolish enough to threaten our casters. But if that is so, she might yet be rescued, and your Thread preserved. How much longer do you have?"

"Before her absence kills me? I don't know. Another week, maybe? I'm not as young as I once was, and my powers are not so great."

"You must keep your spirits up, Rodyk," Owyn urged. "A week is a long time, and I can assist—"

Stonewyck gasped, and his gaze suddenly floated off into the shadows. "Kuff?" he whispered after a moment, as if he'd heard the beating of distant wings. Owyn straightened and watched him with narrowed eyes, chilled by the bewildered, mournful aspect of his friend's voice.

Then Stonewyck suddenly bucked and writhed in his seat, his hands fluttering toward his back as if an invisible sword had been thrust through the back of the sofa and into his spine. He spilled forward onto the hard stones of the hearth, limbs thrashing in agony for a moment before falling still.

Owyn knelt down at the side of the caster and looked into Stonewyck's sightless eyes. After a long moment he turned to Pynch, grief and fury warring for primacy on his haggard features. "Summon the printers on Wyndlass Row," he said, his voice ragged with emotion. "And prepare our riders. You're right, Pynch. There are hidden casters out there who have no inkling that evil stalks our lands. They need to know. Everyone needs to know."

19

Charnel House

Faxon Glynt stepped outside, closing the heavy iron gate behind him, and surveyed the rows of tall pines that trailed behind Stormheel Keep like a dark green bridal train. Here, next to the broad, moss-encrusted stone walls of the castle, the rows extended only a few hundred feet. With each step away from the keep, though, the manicured forest widened and deepened until it finally terminated at a long, graceful curve in the Monument River. And squarely woven into the center of the forest's hem, at a stop overlooking a section of frothing rapids, sat a black diamond—the royal mausoleum of the Whytewender line.

As Glynt entered the woods, rust-colored pine needles crunching under his boots, he struggled to contain his excitement. True, the massive charnel house was a place of silence. A repository for the moldering bones of dozens of King Whytewender's ancestors. But though it stank of death and decay and rat droppings, Glynt had come to regard the place as a birthplace of sorts. To him, the building heralded a new age across Tempyst. An age of luxury and pleasure and abundance for himself and other members of the king's inner circle. And an age of privation and terror for anyone who had ever displeased or defied Glynt. The latter list was already a long one, and he added to it every day, methodically mining his memories for old slights and indignities. Glynt grinned to himself as he thought of the amusements that awaited him in the weeks to come.

But then the image of his father came unbidden to his mind, as it so often did, and his smile faded as quickly as it had arrived. Glynt was not an indecisive man. But whenever he thought of his father, he could never decide what he would do with him when that fast-approaching day of retribution arrived. Flay the man's skin off his bones, glorying in every shriek of agony? Or provide him with a seat next to him at the banquet table, so that he could bask in his father's mealy flatteries and squirming gestures of reconciliation? Glynt supposed that he would not know what selection to make until he saw his father's face.

Long after the muffled roar of the Monument reached his ears, the charnel house finally came into view. Glynt tightened his grip on the handle of the small, canvas-covered cage that swung at his right side as he approached the long building, then mounted the broad stone steps. At the top of the stairs waited a pair of arched iron-banded doors set deep in the mausoleum's massive stone front. Hewn of dragon oak, each door featured an intricate carving of a parade of rearing gryphons. Given the incredible density and hardness of the wood, the carvings must have taken months to complete.

Glynt knocked firmly on the doors, and a moment later they glided open as if weightless. He stepped inside and the doors closed behind him again. A man and a woman stood inside, standing on either side of a raised tomb at the center of the vast chamber. Both of their figures were bathed in coppery light from a lantern perched on one corner of the tomb. Glynt bowed to the man. "Greetings, my liege," he said, his voice echoing off the high shadowed ceiling and cold stone walls.

"Hello, captain," said Thylus Whytewender. The king wore garments of the finest leather and fabrics, all cut to accentuate his tall, lean form. And the small gemstones braided into his dark beard and the rings on his hands shone in the flickering light. But as usual, his gleaming bald head was unadorned by any crown.

Some whispered that King Thylus let the crown of Rojenhold gather dust because his skin erupted in lesions and sores whenever it came into contact with silver or gold. Others said that he had taken a vow forsaking *all* crowns until his dominion extended over all of Tempyst—not just its bleak northeastern quadrant. Glynt did not know the truth of the matter, but he preferred the latter explanation. It smacked of the sort of obsession that he could understand.

Glynt glanced to the woman on the other side of the tomb as he straightened. "Lady Tumdown. A pleasure as always."

Dendra Tumdown inclined her head to him. "Captain," she said, her tone betraying a hint of prim distaste. Glynt smiled to himself. Tumdown was an able enough headmistress for those Faithful Shield recruits that carried the Thread. But she was an acolyte of order and structure, and Glynt knew that she disliked the raw scent of entropy that sometimes wafted off his person.

Glynt placed the covered cage on the tomb as he made a quick survey of the mausoleum's cavernous interior. Nothing had changed since his last visit. The room itself had the rough dimensions of a great stone coffin, as if built for some leviathan of ancient times. At regular intervals along the long left wall, relief carvings depicted gryphons, bears, eagles, trolls, wolves, and other bygone familiars of the royal

Whytewender line. On the right, a total of sixty crypts—Glynt had counted—lined the wall in three stacked rows, like honeycombs from some enormous hive.

The entrances to the crypts were shrouded in black—all except the bottom one at the far end of the hall. A sliver of *that* crypt's far wall could be seen; it glowed with the light of a lantern or torch set deeper in the crypt's interior. As Glynt watched, the glow on the wall flickered, the light blocked for just an instant by movement from within. He felt a thrill run up his spine at the sight, though he kept his face impassive.

Glynt turned back to Whytewender, whose attention was fixed on the covered cage that Glynt he had set upon the tomb. After a moment or two, though, Whytewender blinked slowly and shifted his gaze to Glynt.

"Dendra was just telling me that the instruction is going smoothly with young Ben Thystle these days."

"Indeed?" Glynt said, raising the eyebrow over his one good eye. "Not unexpected, Your Highness. The boy's powers are considerable, but they terrify him. And he and his parents are quite . . . malleable. "

"That's certainly true of the boy and his father," agreed Tumdown. "The father, in fact, seems quite comfortable with their altered circumstances now."

Glynt grinned at the memories of his last several meetings with Wynston Thystle. "Tis true. That miller is a cur of a man. I don't know how his wife ever convinced him to flee Hanken in the first place. Probably leaned on his instinct for self-preservation. He's got that in spades."

Tumdown frowned. "Yes, he's useful. I'm not as sanguine as Faxon about the mother, though. She's offered no overt resistance to my tutoring sessions. But I see a look in her eyes sometimes. . . . I don't want to dispose of her unnecessarily. That would set back my efforts with her son. But I'm keeping an eye on her. And in another few weeks he'll be ready for formal induction."

"So you continue to counsel grooming the boy for the Faithful Shield, then?" asked Whytewender. The king made a vague gesture toward the glowing crypt at the back. "There are other uses for his familiar, you know."

"I beg your patience, sire," said Tumdown. "The boy has not yet displayed the requisite ardor for our cause, but he's talented. And he's taken to the alchemical arts quickly. The exercises are doing their work. His resistance is parchment-thin now and smoking at the edges. A few more pieces of wood on the fire and he'll be ours to forge into whatever weapon you desire. And as you've noted yourself, sparing *some* loyal casters from harvesting will aid us not only in the war, but in governing the Fyngrean territories once they are flying under your colors."

"Very well," Whytewender said. He turned to Glynt. "And I assume that the whereabouts of Jessalyn Suntold remains a mystery?" he said icily.

Glynt grimaced. "For the moment. King Owyn has publicly announced that the princess is alive and safe. But does he speak truly? None of our spies in Kylden—indeed, anywhere in Fyngree—have seen her since the night she vanished. And Owyn knows that word of her demise would cast a pall over Fyngree at a time when his people are already unsettled."

"I think she yet lives, Your Highness," Tumdown declared. "And that she might well have heard whatever message that damned goose carried. Even as we speak, she might be roaming the countryside somewhere, acting on that information."

Glynt's lips peeled back from his teeth in an unpleasant grin. "Steady now. Jessalyn Suntold is a spoiled little girl who to all appearances remains a threadbare. Every message borne to us from Kylden has asserted that the magic of the Suntold line has run dry with her. What harm can she possibly do, even if she is skipping through the meadows of Fyngree as you suggest?"

"A fair amount, if King Owyn's efforts have somehow stirred her Thread to life during these last weeks," Tumdown countered.

"Then why would she have not intervened when that pamphleteer friend of hers was getting his head caved in? If she was present in Muncenmast's shop when the goose arrived, as we suspect? No, she remains as threadbare as the day she was born. Still, I'll grant you that she might yet be alive. It's possible that the girl managed to slip out of the shop when Esolat was occupied with her guards. But what then? All indications are that she simply fled into the night in hysterics. Where she either managed to drown herself in the Whetstone or spent the past two weeks shivering and mewling in someone's hayloft."

He turned to Whytewender, who had remained silent throughout his entire exchange with Tumdown. "Just the same, Your Highness, our agents in Kylden Hall and elsewhere in Fyngree are keeping their ears to the ground," he said reassuringly. "If she *has* been found, we'll know soon enough. Of greater interest to me this evening, though, are reports that the Throneholder's own familiar is overdue."

"That *is* interesting," said Whytewender thoughtfully. "I initially thought that Jessalyn's presence at the printer's shop that night was damned bad luck but it's turning out to be the best—"

A chuckle floated to their ears from the far end of the mausoleum, and all three of them fell silent. The low laughter trailed away into a brief spate of muttering, followed by the sound of pages being slowly turned. Glynt stole a brief glance at Tumdown, whose gaze was directed resolutely down at the tomb around which they stood. She's terrified, Glynt thought. The realization filled him with a mix of dark glee and heightened apprehension.

Whytewender smiled tightly. "Keep me apprised on that score, yes? Let's move on. Tell me about developments along the border."

"All unfolding as you anticipated. We have three winged familiars flying daily reconnaissance missions over Twenty Night Canyon and the Jailer's Key, as well as the surrounding lands. Their compeers confirm that our forces are in position, and that Fyngree's lines swell with each passing day."

"Good. We will depart for the border at the end of the week. Prepare a caravan with all the necessary precautions."

"Yes, Your Highness."

Whytewender nodded down at the cage. "Will you have any more gifts for us before we depart?"

"Doubtful. The border remains open for now. But Fyngrean sentries are searching everyone seeking to enter Rojenhold, so we are unable to smuggle anything in overland. Even the southern passes into the Speartips are being patrolled now. And none of the winged familiars at our disposal are capable of carrying such cargo for any distance. It's not how it was even a few weeks ago, when we could pluck familiars like apples from an orchard." Glynt smiled. "But once we break through their lines, who knows what Faeros and your other agents will have waiting for you."

"Faeros knows your needs," agreed Tumdown. "He'll have some tasty morsels waiting. Perhaps even that little owl you sent him in search of."

Whytewender smiled faintly, though his eyes retained their cold, almost metallic cast. "Once Fyngree is ours we'll have no need to limit ourselves to such a monastic diet. Owyn Suntold's entire kingdom will be our banquet table."

"Yes, Your Highness," Glynt and Tumdown murmured in unison.

"Hmmm. All this talk of conquest has me restless now." Whytewender nodded down at the cage. "So how about another preview of events to come? A little appetizer to sate my hunger for the evening."

The king turned and looked to the far recesses of the charnel house, where the light from the glowing crypt flickered and danced. Despite himself, Glynt felt the muscles in his body tense up, as if bracing for immersion in a cold lake.

"Teryk?" the king called, his voice ringing across the cavernous space. "Please join us."

Glynt suppressed an involuntary shiver as a tall, cloaked figure emerged from the glowing crypt at the far end of the mausoleum. Backlit by the flames from the far braziers, the figure was little more than a black silhouette. As Teryk moved toward them, footfalls echoing, Glynt saw how the gloom trailed in ribbons behind him, as if snagged on cruel thorns. And how his cloak blended seamlessly into the pooled darkness, as if it had been cut from the same material as the night itself.

Teryk entered the trembling halo of light cast by the lantern, his face still hidden in the shadows of his hood. But Glynt could see the faint golden glow of his eyes smoldering within.

"How has your reading been going, Teryk?" asked Whytewender, his voice studiously casual.

The figure slowly lifted his hands to his hood and pushed it off his head, revealing a boy of sixteen or seventeen years, with dark hair that cascaded down to bony shoulders and a pointed jaw free of facial hair. The boy's features might have been handsome were it not for the faint, puckered scars that crossed his cheeks and the shadows that lurked in his sunken eye sockets. But it was the eyes that mesmerized. Devoid of pupils and irises, they glowed like ovals of yellow stained glass at sunset.

"How do fish respond when the shadow of the bear falls over them?" Teryk asked in an unearthly voice that seemed to shimmer in the air. Glynt felt himself sway as a vivid memory rolled over him like a black wave. A memory of being caught above tree line in the Speartips as a massive storm boiled over the peaks, casting shards of lightning all around him. He felt the same charge of electricity in the air now, in this charnel house, as he had felt on that long-ago afternoon.

"The sleek and fat fish—the old ones—they dive deep to hide under the logs and the roots of the rivergrass. But the little ones, they dart to and fro, seeking to escape, seeking sunlight." Teryk cocked his head, as if he was hearing distant voices. *"And some are finding light in the west. Isn't that nice? That they can still feel the sun on their scales? That they can still rise and pluck insects off the surface like good little fish, even as the bear gobbles up all the other fish—the fat ones that went deep and the little ones that swam in the wrong direction?"*

"Son—"

"But even those smart little fish cannot hide from the bear forever, can they? Because the bear is always hungry—he can't help himself, father, he's a bear!" Teryk's features twisted into a grotesque parody of a smile.

"That's right, Teryk," Whytewender said evenly. "And we've brought you a nice big fish today."

Teryk said nothing to this, but he turned his otherworldly gaze to the canvas-covered cage sitting on the tomb.

Whytewender nodded, and Glynt pulled the cover off, revealing a sturdy metal cage. A raven lay listlessly at the bottom, one dark wing beating weakly against the bars.

The boy's golden eyes were riveted on the raven. *"Thank you,"* he breathed.

Glynt swallowed hard. "Tis my pleasure, milord," he said, doing his best to ignore how even *talking* to this magic-blasted scarecrow of a boy made his skin turn clammy and cold.

As Teryk placed his hands on the cage, Glynt backed away until he stood next to Tumdown at the far edge of the lantern light. He stole a glance at the king, who was watching his son intently.

Teryk unlatched the door of the cage and placed one hand around the bird's neck, then removed it from the cage. Gently but firmly, he laid the bird face up on the surface of the tomb, spreading her wings open with care. He looked up for a moment at his father, his eyes blank and glowing, before bending his head down low over the prone raven. Then he dug his sharp fingernails into Kuff's chest until she broke open in a cloud of sparkling golden mist. . . .

. . . that Teryk inhaled deeply until there was nothing left.

20

Crossroads

Traejon rolled over, opened one eye to the early morning gray, and beheld a sight that brought him to instant wakefulness. Tabytha was kneeling by a small, crackling fire, pouring what looked like coffee into two dented tin cups. He watched her carefully set the blackened pot on a flat stone at the edge of the flames and pick up both tins. Then she looked over and saw him watching her. She broke into one of her bright-as-the-sun smiles and extended one of the cups in his direction, gently moving it back and forth as if coaxing a timid dog to her side with a treat.

"If that doesn't hold coffee, then truly your cruelty knows no bounds," he said, rising to join her by the fire. As he settled in next to her, he ran a hand through his hair and took a look around the small grassy clearing where they had made camp the night before. Small copses of mixed birch, larch, and fir sprouted amid craggy slopes, all of it set against a backdrop of sloping mountain walls.

As Traejon took stock of his surroundings in the early light, he recalled the chaotic events of the day before. After their departure from the Widow's Torch, they had managed to collect his two horses and Tabytha's ride in fairly short order. But of Jess's horse they had found no sign until Traejon spotted its body bobbing in a tangle of fallen trees and branches in a bend in the Gryndstone. His guess was that when the wolves attacked it panicked and plunged into the river, only to be overcome by its surging waters.

Traejon had dreaded informing Jess of his grim discovery. The princess had endured much since the night she fled Kylden, and the battle at the waterfall had left her with a kind of glassy-eyed aspect. And though he managed to retrieve her saddlebags from the corpse, he wondered if the death of the horse—who had served Jess well since her flight from Kylden—might be one blow too many. But she had received his news expressionlessly, then silently accepted his offer of his second mount.

After completing the task of gathering the horses, Traejon and Jess had sent Nomad back to King Owyn. The decision to do so had not been an easy one. Watching the falcon disappear around a curve in the darkening mountains, he had felt a stab of apprehension at the knowledge that she was now on her own, unprotected in a land suddenly swimming with treachery. But there was no help for it, the king needed her back at his side.

The four of them had then ridden until dusk before stopping. They had washed up at the edge of a stream, eaten in near-silence, and laid out their bedrolls, all of them trudging about with the unspoken understanding that Gydeon's tale could wait for the next day. Traejon and Tabytha agreed to split the watch so that the professor and Jess could sleep through the night. They were still sleeping, he saw now, their huddled forms tucked up amid a stand of birches. Good. They needed it. He would give them another half hour before rousing them.

Traejon accepted one of the cups from Tabytha and took a sip. "Ah," he murmured in appreciation, closing his eyes. Then he opened them and smiled. "You're my hero."

Tabytha laughed, dimples popping out in her cheeks. "I was *dying* for coffee the last half of my watch," she said in a conspiratorial half-whisper. "But I didn't want to wake anyone. I exercised my iron willpower until the horizon began brightening. It was a feat of amazing self-control."

"Very impressive," Traejon agreed solemnly. He took another sip from the steaming cup, stealing a glance over at Tab as he did so. It felt strange sitting here next to her. The pull of the empty wilderness was strong even now. It was safer out there, where the rivers and forests dreamed of clouds and wind and silent padding creatures with pelts that shone with rain. Where no one trafficked in dreams of waterlogged corpses or crying widows or fathers wiping blood from their knuckles.

And yet it felt good to be sitting here next to Tab, watching the morning sun chase the shadows off the faces of the surrounding mountains. Enjoying her nearness. Feeling a stray lock of her hair brush against his arm as she leaned over to refill her cup. He had almost forgotten how it could be. To feel comforted by the presence of another.

But all he said was, "Thanks for pulling an extra shift."

Tab poked at the fire. "It wasn't so bad. I love watching the world come awake. I've always been an early riser, ever since I was a wee one. And my parents taught me that if I was going to insist on being the first one up, the least I could do is have coffee ready for the lazy folk who insist on slumbering till dawn. Or in your case," she grinned, "till well past."

Traejon's expression changed to one of mock outrage. "Hey, it's not *that* late."

They smiled at one another, then settled into a companionable silence broken only by the morning's songbirds.

"You were pretty calm yesterday, Tab," Traejon said after a time as he bent to refill his cup.

"I don't know about *that*," she said, rolling her eyes. "I thought I was going to pee my pants when I first saw those wolves pouring down the mountain. And I wouldn't have been able to hold my side without Gydeon's help."

"He performed well," Traejon agreed. "I was wrong to be so suspicious of him. But I'm still at a loss as to how that wolf knew to look for us at the Torch. Gydeon must have been followed. His powers of concealment aside, he's still a professor. He comes to us from a world of classroom lecterns and library shelves, not masks and shadows. We're fortunate it only cost us a horse."

"It was a close thing," she allowed, leaning forward once more to give the campfire a stir. As she did so, though, Traejon glimpsed the smallest suggestion of a wince cross her face. "Uh oh," he said. "What's that about?"

Tabytha looked at him, a trace of apology in her eyes. "I know I should have mentioned it yesterday. But I really wanted to get Jess away from that waterfall. Before then she had carried herself with such confidence . . . I sometimes forget that she's not accustomed to this sort of thing. Not that I am. And it's not *that* bad." She turned her side to Traejon and pulled the side of her torn shirt up a few inches. Underneath lay a blood-soaked piece of cloth that she must have taken from her saddlebags.

Although Traejon pulled the makeshift bandage off as gently as possible, the fabric had adhered to the wound at several points. But Tabytha remained stoic about it, taking occasional drinks of coffee as he peeled it off. Traejon tossed the bandage into the campfire and looked at the wound more closely. "Ouch," he said mildly. "That's going to need a few stitches. You're fortunate the wolf clamped on your hipbone. Could have been much worse."

Tabytha sighed. "I don't feel fortunate."

"Hold on. Let me get my kit."

A minute later Traejon returned, and over the next half-hour he disinfected the wound with a small bottle of vinegar and stitched her up. They conversed about this and that as he worked, murmuring and laughing quietly so as to not disturb Jess and Gydeon. And Traejon even found himself lingering over the last stitch or two so as to make the task last a little longer.

"That feels better," Tabytha said after he had finally finished up. She lightly patted the fresh bandage under her shirt. "Thank you."

Traejon placed a couple more pieces of wood on the fire. "My pleasure."

Tabytha crossed her forearms over her knees. "So tell me: Does it feel strange to be sitting here as the Throneholder's falcon flies back to Kylden?" she asked.

"Very," he admitted. "Nomad's left me behind a time or two in the past when she's returned to Kylden Hall. But even then I trailed behind her, trying to keep up as best I could. Nothing to be done for it this time around, but it's hard not to feel that I'm neglecting my duties somehow. She'll be all right, though. By tomorrow she'll be sitting on the Throneholder's arm again." Traejon smirked. "And she'll be giving him an eyeful, won't she? When King Owyn sees what happened at the Widow's Torch yesterday, I don't know whether he'll reward us for saving his daughter or kill us for allowing her to go there in the first place."

†††

The morning chill kept them huddled around the fire as they ate—more dark bread slathered with honey—and Traejon took stock of his other two traveling companions. Gydeon sported dark bags under his eyes, and his hair was disheveled and corkscrewed. But Traejon thought that the professor looked refreshed, even invigorated, now that he had a good night's sleep under his belt. In between bites of honey-dipped bread, in fact, he exuberantly recounted every moment of the previous day's battle to a faintly amused Tabytha. Gone was the haughty professor who had greeted them yesterday. In his place was a man who fairly glowed with satisfaction at having proved his mettle in battle. It was more than just relief at being alive; it was the pride that stems from acting courageously even when nearly paralyzed with fear. Traejon did not begrudge him any of it; the professor had reason to be proud.

The dark clouds had not lifted from Jess's brow, however. Though she partook of the coffee and bread around the campfire, she remained subdued, rarely speaking. It was hard for Traejon to discern the precise source of the princess's melancholy, but it troubled him—not least because he had no idea how it might color her response to whatever information Gydeon had brought with him. Well, he thought, we might as well find out.

"So professor," he said as the others polished off the last of the bread and honey. "We stand at a crossroads of sorts this morning. To the west lies Kylden, where King Owyn awaits the return of his daughter. To the south lies Tydewater, where Tabytha has family to see and a scoundrel's ears to box. And to the north. . . . Well, we don't really know what lies to the north. But evidently you have a story for us. And perhaps after we've heard it we'll have the wisdom to know which path out of the mountains each of us should take. Either way, let's hear it. Because—" Traejon pointed back deeper into the mountains, "—we don't know whether that wolf's compeer is hours or days away."

Gydeon nodded, somberness returning to his features. "Quite right." He turned to Jess, then glanced at Tabytha and Traejon in turn. "As is usually the case with these things, I think it would be best for me to start at the beginning.

"The man who sent the Tiding Horn to Percy was a friend of mine named Bryscoe Rygaard," he said. "He's not himself a caster, but as you'll see, he's keeping company these days with at least a caster or two capable of such spells."

"Who—"

Gydeon held up his hand. "Please, Tabytha. I'll be happy to answer any of your questions when I'm done. Now then. Bryscoe is a spice merchant based out of Tapwyll's Cross, and a prosperous one at that. Lovely estate, fine office on the square, all the trappings. But it wasn't always so. He grew up in Kylden, son of a drunk father and a defeated mother with four little mouths to feed. It didn't take long for Bryscoe's schooling to fall by the wayside so that he could contribute a few scraps of food to the family table. But when Bryscoe was about ten years old, he and his parents moved into a dingy flat that was just three doors down from the shop of Kylden's finest pamphleteer."

Jess smiled at the allusion to her friend. "Percy," she breathed fondly.

"I don't know exactly how the two of them met," continued Gydeon. "But within a year of his family's move, Bryscoe was running errands for Muncenmast by day—and receiving schooling in reading, writing, and other subjects from him in the evenings. Bryscoe told me that by the time he was ready to chart his own course in the world, Muncenmast had given him all the tools he needed to go anywhere in Fyngree and build a successful life for himself." Gydeon smiled at Jess. "Your friend was generous with both his time and talents, Jessalyn. I regret that I never had the honor of meeting him."

"Thank you," Jess said, swallowing hard.

Gydeon cleared his throat. "Eventually Bryscoe established himself as a spice trader, with a regular route that took him through the cities and towns of the northern Loaf all the way up to Valyedon. He also built a nice little side-business in exotic herbs and paraphernalia that he sold to a select group of healers and apothecaries and casters such as myself. And so he thrived.

"But the spice trade makes vagabonds of merchants, and Bryscoe was no exception. Especially because he never found a partner or lieutenant he trusted to safely navigate the dangers of the spice trade, from blackhearted highwaymen to deceitful buyers and sellers. So he continued to ride the circuit himself, a handful of guards in tow to keep an eye on his goods.

"Bryscoe's life proceeded along its usual contours until about four months ago." Gydeon paused as Vyx fluttered down and landed on his right shoulder. Traejon thought that it was almost as if the familiar had come down from the trees just to listen to this part of Gydeon's tale. For all he knew, maybe she had.

"Bryscoe told me once that the first portents of trouble he discerned reminded him of distant peals of thunder. Peals to which he paid little heed. Until black clouds veined with lightning began rolling over the horizon, that is. The first rumble came when Bryscoe called on a witch named Prudy Beltwheel at her estate on Lake Almygen. Her Thread was modest, but she was of noble birth, so she could afford to indulge her taste for expensive spices as well as arcane spell-casting ingredients. Bryscoe said that she was one of his best clients. When he arrived at her gates, though, he found her servants in frightened disarray. They reported that her familiar, a marten, had vanished more than three weeks earlier—and that Beltwheel herself had died just that morning, twisting at her breakfast table in sudden agony."

Traejon looked over at Tab and Jess and saw by their pale aspects that they fully understood the implication. Beltwheel's Thread had been snapped—violently.

"Over the next two months, four more casters on Bryscoe's trade route died or disappeared," Gydeon continued. "One of them, a fellow who lived east of Treffentown, must have put up a fight. Whoever his assailants were, they burned his home to the ground."

"Treffentown?" Traejon said, thinking back to his last conversation with Fyfe Treadlow deep in the bowels of Kylden Hall. "I think I might have heard something about that one."

"Yes? Well his was the only home that showed any signs of struggle. The other three just vanished or died in their sleep. None of them were particularly powerful or politically connected. Moderate spellcasting abilities at most. No one whose demise would attract attention all the way down in Kylden.

"It was at that point that Bryscoe came to me. In part he came to warn me to keep a close eye on Vyx. But I think he also just wanted to talk to someone about his growing suspicion that all of these casters were victims of the same unseen hand. Bryscoe hoped that I would dismiss his speculation as foolishness. No such luck. To the contrary, as a caster myself I think I was even more alarmed than he. Despite our shared forebodings, however, we did not really know how to proceed. And then—" Gydeon reached up and began gently stroking the side of Vyx's body with one long finger, "—my familiar disappeared."

Tabytha gasped involuntarily, and Gydeon turned to her with a humorless smile. "Exactly. Vyx doesn't usually leave my side for more than a day, and she's usually only gone for a matter of a few hours. She doesn't possess the wanderlust or constitution to explore distant lands as more powerful familiars are wont to do. It's one of the underappreciated benefits of being threaded to a familiar of modest strength. I've never even hired a shadow such as yourself to watch after her, Frost. It always seemed unnecessary, given her limited forays afield.

"In any case, I'm sure that you can appreciate that Vyx's disappearance caused me no small amount of anxiety. And Bryscoe was no help in that regard, either. Several times I caught him looking at me as if he expected me to keel over dead at any moment. I came to expect the same thing. During Vyx's absence, though, I began having a strange dream. On three consecutive nights I was visited in my sleep by a young girl in a deep wood. She was smiling and beckoning me to join her. It wasn't a nightmare by any means, but the timing of this recurring visitation further unnerved me. I wondered more than once if the lass was calling me to the Far Shore.

"And then Vyx returned a week later." Gydeon smiled crookedly, his lined face lighting up at the memory. "I felt like a man who'd been fitted with a hangman's noose, only to receive a pardon at the last moment. I've never felt such relief."

"I guess so," said Tabytha, shaking her head in wonderment.

"But when she alighted on my shoulder and I touched her, her travels of the previous week poured through my mind like a spring flood. She'd flown all the way to the Matchstyck Forest, well over a hundred miles from Tapwyll's Cross."

Gydeon's sharp features relaxed as he recalled the images that had come to him through his Thread with the owl. "I watched through Vyx's eyes as she flew through vast corridors of dragon oaks, their leaves green with high summer, until she arrived at a ruined estate of some sort. The main building looked long-abandoned, but it had a sort of faded grandeur to it all the same. Vyx entered, and after a few minutes of flitting around in the gloom, she came out into what looked to be a grand banquet hall from some bygone age.

"And there, standing among the ruins, were fifteen people or so. All ages, genders, and bloodlines, gathered in a semi-circle. And about half of them had familiars by their sides." Gydeon shook his head at the memory. "It was astonishing. You could just tell that the creatures were magical in nature. How else to explain a goose and a lynx placidly sitting no more than three feet away from one another?"

Traejon exchanged a glance with Tabytha at the mention of the goose. She looked as dumbstruck as he felt at Gydeon's revelations. He turned to Jess, but she did not look his way. The princess's focus was wholly on the professor, who rubbed a hand over his face. He looked bone-weary now, as if the memories of what Vyx had seen were slamming into him all over again.

"Everyone in the half-circle of people and compeers was facing a girl, dark of skin and hair. A girl I instantly recognized as the one who had appeared in my dreams. She was young, no more than fourteen or fifteen years of age, I'd guess. At one point someone addressed her as Lylah. And then a young woman stepped forward out of the circle, and as I—Vyx—watched, this woman warned Lylah that Kylden Hall has been infiltrated by agents of Whytewender."

Traejon exchanged a wordless look with Tab. This was a disquieting tale, indeed, one that confirmed all of Jessalyn's worst fears.

"But that wasn't the worst of it," Gydeon said, stroking his beard in agitation. "The young woman also asserted that King Thylus has unearthed some dark piece of magic dating back to the age of Elves. Magic powerful enough to destroy any caster opposed to Rojenhold."

Gydeon turned to Jess. "It was this declaration that convinced Bryscoe to try to contact your friend Percy, Jessalyn. We now knew that the Throneholder's inner circle was riddled with traitorous scoundrels. We did not know where to turn or who to trust. Approaching High Sentinel Tusk up in Valyedon seemed unwise, given her perpetual quarrels with Kylden Hall. And sending a message directly to King Owyn seemed a fool's errand; we knew that protective castings around your father's castle would prevent any familiar from reaching him directly. So we decided to avoid government channels altogether and contact Bryscoe's old pamphleteer friend. The thought being that if Percy revealed the truth, then all of Fyngree—including King Owyn himself—would know of the threat. At which point measures could be taken to root out Rojenhold's agents and defend Fyngree's imperiled casters."

"But it all went for naught when the gargoyle slew Percy that night," said Tabytha.

"Yes."

"Not all for naught," said Traejon, meeting each of their eyes in turn. "It sounds to me like a visit to the Matchstycks is in order."

21

The Familiar's Shadow

Traejon brought the spyglass down and handed it to Tabytha. "Take a look," he said. Tabytha brought the glass up, stepping forward from the forest's edge where she had been standing with Jess and Gydeon.

As Tab scanned the broad green valley below, Jess studied the back of her head, a slow buzz of resentment burning through her. Little wonder that Tab had chosen the soldier's life, she thought spitefully as she studied Tab's broad-shouldered back and tangled hair. She clearly wasn't going to make her mark in the world by virtue of her feminine gifts.

Then Jess ran a hand through her hair, which was more than a little greasy itself, and chided herself. She knew that she should not chew on such bitter cloves of consolation. Was it Tab's fault that Traejon now looked to her first for counsel? It was grossly unfair to blame that on the cadet, who had been nothing but kind to her ever since they met. But Jess found it difficult to keep such ugly sentiments at bay these days. They kept leaking in, poisoning her thoughts and leaving her more miserable with each passing hour.

Not that she had withdrawn entirely from their company. Jess's pride wouldn't allow for that. She still pitched in with camp chores, and she forced herself to join the others around the fire each night. But she found herself unable to partake in their wide-ranging conversations or return the encouraging smiles they sent her way. For her thoughts always returned to the Widow's Torch, where those murderous wolves had exposed her for the pretender that she truly was.

Until the events at the waterfall, Jess had almost managed to convince herself that she was a brave and determined young woman. One who had cast off her cloistered childhood to make her way in the world. Who didn't require the Thread to thrive in that world. And who was fully capable of saving her father from the dark forces gathering around his throne. But now she saw the folly of those beliefs. She had been utterly helpless against the wolves. Unable to contribute to their party's defense in any way. Useless to her father and kingdom. If not for Traejon, Tab, and Gydeon, those wolves would have torn her limb from limb.

So what was she doing out here, stumbling through the wilderness? Perhaps it would be better for everyone if she just went home. Cocoon herself in the smooth compliancy of her servants and the envious stares of the ladies at court and the memory-dulling capacities of the royal wine cellar. Savor the silken garments and glittering jewels that were her birthright. And leave the kingdom-saving to warriors like Traejon and Tab. Men and women whose minds did not go blank with terror when confronted with danger.

"Here, Jess."

Jess blinked and looked down. Tab was holding the spyglass out to her, a look of encouragement on her face. Or was that an expression of pity? Pushing the thought away, Jess took up the glass and peered down the valley, halfheartedly trying to assume a posture of interest.

Far below them, a long column of cavalry was moving at a steady canter. Hundreds of riders strong, it wound through the grassy valley floor like an enormous blue serpent, weapons and helmets and the barding of the warhorses gleaming like scales in the afternoon sunlight.

"They are moving at a fast clip," she heard Tab say. "To Tucker's Front?"

"No doubt," Traejon said. "General Splyntbell is leading them."

Jess turned the glass to study the leading edge of the column. "You can see that from here?" she asked doubtfully as she handed the glass to Gydeon. How could Traejon identify anyone from such a distance?

"It's him," said Traejon simply. "Jess, I'd like to ride down to Splyntbell. Learn what's transpired in our absence, and apprise him of what we've learned and where we're going. He can send word to your father, and arrange for a company of soldiers from Valyedon to meet us when we reach the Matchstycks. Wouldn't hurt to replenish our food stores and obtain fresh horses as well."

Jess felt his gaze on her, and she forced herself to respond. "Do you need a letter of introduction?" Jess asked tonelessly, gesturing to her horse's saddlebags, which still contained her inkpot, paper, quills, candles, and matrix. "The seal will speak to my note's authenticity."

"That won't be necessary," Traejon said. He patted the breast of his shirt. "My oathstone will prove my standing. Splyntbell will recognize its worth."

Jess nodded in understanding and Traejon turned to go. As he mounted his horse, though, she felt a niggling thought bob to the surface of her mind. A vestige from a time that seemed irretrievably lost now—that brief flurry of hours after they had joined together, when she had still felt confident in her beliefs and abilities. "Perhaps you should request additional riders to accompany us," she offered. Her voice sounded strange and scratchy to her, like the creaking door of a long-abandoned room. "We have many miles yet to travel to reach the Matchstycks, and we know not what threats lie ahead."

"I'd counsel against that, Jess," said Traejon. "We've made good time in the three days since we left the Marching Mountains behind. And if we maintain this same pace, we should pass out of the Loaf's northern districts and into the foothills of the southern Speartips in another day. And from there tis less than a week's ride to the outskirts of the Matchstycks. Where Bryscoe Rygaard and the mysterious Lylah await." He smiled. "We hope. And with them, the answers to many of the questions swirling around all of our minds. Adding to our party, though, might slow us down."

The shadow tilted his head theatrically, bringing Jess's attention to the cawing of several crows in the woods behind them. "And Rojenholdean spies are almost certainly patrolling our skies and woodlands. Humans or familiars, they could be anywhere, and our journey is a clandestine one. The smaller our party, the less likely we are to draw their attention."

Jess nodded and turned away, face burning at Traejon's dismissive rejection of her suggestion. Who was she fooling? Traejon didn't need advice from a threadbare princess whose thighs still throbbed after a day of riding. And who was almost as likely to put a crossbow bolt through her own foot as an approaching enemy. She drifted away from the others, fully aware that her disillusionment was blurring into bitter self-pity but unable to muster enough will to care.

As Traejon departed, Tabytha pulled the last of their cheese and bread out of her saddlebags and called Jess and Gydeon over. After lunch, with the professor settling in for a nap and Tab turning to some minor gear repairs, Jess went to her saddlebags. She hauled out Brystlebrow's *Chronicles of the Bolde Temple*, the book that she had borrowed from Percy what already seemed like a lifetime ago, and wandered over to take a seat on a slab of dark rock at the edge of the woods. Bathed in afternoon sunshine, the rock offered a warm perch from which to observe the broad valley below.

Jess settled on the rock and began paging listlessly through the book. Back in those first feverish nights of flight from Kylden, she had occasionally read passages from it before falling asleep. Other times she just held it to her chest, running her fingers over its rough leather cover. The book had both comforted her and set her ablaze with the desire to avenge Percy's death. Today, though, the tome did not have that effect on her. Today it was just an old book.

"May I join you?"

Startled out of her bleak reverie, Jess looked up to see Tab standing before her. Wonderful, she thought morosely. Has the soldier decided that the two of them should be fast friends now? The notion was a demoralizing one. The last thing she needed was a session of interminable chatter with a woman whose every word and gesture now struck Jess as the embodiment of cool self-possession and competence—virtues that she now recognized as ones of which she had only a very meager supply.

But even as these thoughts flashed through Jess's mind, she knew that she couldn't just tell Tab to go find someone else to bother. She owed the young soldier her life.

"Of course," said Jess, after the briefest hesitation. Tabytha took a seat next to her, and for a moment they both just looked out over the valley to the horizon. Then Tab turned to her with a smile.

"So," she said, "tell me about these oathstones of which you and Traejon spoke. I've never heard of such objects, and judging by the look on his face, neither has Gydeon."

Jess opened her mouth to respond, and Tab hastily held up a hand. "I understand if you are not at liberty to discuss them. I was just curious."

"No, it's all right," said Jess. It wasn't, really. She still didn't feel like conversing with Tab. But at least oathstones were a subject that she could speak about with some authority. "Oathstones are items of considerable power, crafted by castings that have been passed down through many generations of Throneholders," Jess said. "They're useful in monitoring the loyalty of those to whom they are given. But they are exceedingly rare because they are a lot of trouble to make. Each one has to be personalized to its intended recipient and invested with sufficient power to last the lifetime of its creator. This can entail many decades, even taking into account that witches or wizards capable of executing such a spell aren't able to do so until they are in their casting prime."

Tabytha nodded. "Does your father make extensive use of them?"

"Not as much as I'd like," Jess admitted. "But crafting an oathstone involves hours of exhausting and dangerous incantations. In addition, the ritual requires the presence—and a not inconsiderable amount of the blood—of the person for whom the oathstone is intended. And asking longtime friends, colleagues, or attendants to submit to the oathstone ritual is a tricky business. Such a request—which is not really a request, of course—might be interpreted as a sign of distrust."

"Which it is, I suppose."

Jess hesitated. "On some occasions it would be, yes. Do you recall that note I left for my father at the Warden's Outpost? I considered urging him to prepare oathstones for High Votary Pynch and a few others at Kylden Hall. The keep's master falconer, for example, and the head chamberlain responsible for the upkeep of father's quarters. But I knew that he would be loath to question the loyalty of such longtime members of his staff in so brazen a fashion—it would be a tremendous insult. And to be honest, father's age gave me pause as well. I was concerned that carrying out even one oathstone ritual would take too great a toll on him."

"So who carries them?"

"To *my* knowledge? Only a select group of people. Individuals whose loyalty is absolutely vital. Nomad has had four shadows over the decades since father's Thread awakened, Traejon being the latest. I know that all three of his predecessors carried oathstones during their period of service, then on into retirement. The shadow responsible for my mother's familiar also had one, though he relinquished it after she died. And I'm sure that Splyntbell and a handful of other military leaders carry them, as well as the high sentinels of our major city-provinces."

"How do they function? What do they look like?"

"Are you familiar with sounding weights? The devices that mariners use to measure the depth of the seas through which they pass?" Jess turned to Tabytha then, and despite herself she felt herself warming to the lesson.

"Sure."

"Well, each oathstone has the long, cylindrical appearance of a small sounding weight, though the runes etched along their lengths betray their true nature. My father could have selected any item. But he told me once that he liked the symbolism of using a sounding weight as a way to gauge the depth of loyalty of those who served him."

Tabytha raised her eyebrows. "That's quite clever, actually."

"I always thought so." Jess gestured down into the valley. "When Traejon meets Splyntbell, he'll take out his oathstone and present it for inspection. He'll then press it over his heart and recite a pledge of loyalty to my father. And when he is done, the runes of the oathstone will glow a brilliant blue in affirmation that his words are true."

"And if they are not?" Tabytha asked after a moment's hesitation.

"Then the sounding weight will vanish and rematerialize inside his heart, killing him where he stands."

Jess saw the blood drain from Tab's face. "That's horrible," she said, turning her face back to the sun-soaked vale into which Traejon had disappeared.

"You must know that no harm will come to Traejon," Jess said hastily. "His loyalty to my father is unquestioned."

"No . . . I know that. But the whole ritual sounds, I don't know . . . slavish."

"Slavish?" Jess said, an ember of indignation flaring to life in her mind. "How so?"

"How are these oathstones different than what Whytewender practices up in Rojenhold?" said Tab. "Stormheel secures allegiance through fear. Is this really any different? What if someone who enters into this covenant genuinely comes to feel that the interests of the Throneholder and Fyngree no longer align? If he or she comes to feel that the king has gone mad or become cruel to his people? Or that the health and happiness of Fyngree necessitate the corona-tion of a new Throneholder? What happens to such a person when they speak the pledge?"

Jess was quiet, and she felt her face cloud over with doubt. "I don't know," she said finally. "I never considered that."

Silence descended over them as Jess mulled the troubling turn that their conversation had taken. She had always viewed oathstones as an unalloyed good. As righteous instruments of defense against treason and treachery. Could what Tab claimed be true? That in the wrong hands, they might be employed as weapons of cruel subjugation?

Tabytha finally broke the silence. "My apologies, Your Highness. I spoke out of turn."

Jess turned and looked into Tab's eyes. And felt a shiver of shame at the unkind thoughts she had directed at Tab since the Widow's Torch. For she saw now that Tab had not engaged her in conversation in order to curry favor. Rather, she had done so in an effort to draw Jess out of the dark well of despondency into which she had flung herself these past three days. And though it wasn't that easy, she could at least have the grace to appreciate the gesture.

Jess patted Tabytha's arm reassuringly. "Please, no apologies. People rarely speak so forthrightly to me, Tab, and it's always driven me mad. I can't very well complain when someone speaks to me in the manner I've always claimed I've wanted."

Tabytha smiled wanly in return, but Jess recognized that their discussion of the oathstone still cast a pall over Tab's thoughts. "The rings Traejon wears on his left hand, on the other hand, are more . . . benign."

"I *knew* it," Tab said, as if some longstanding suspicion had been confirmed. "Can you tell me their purposes?"

"Not specifically. But they were gifts from my father. Many shadows of powerful familiars receive them. They have their limitations—spells of alchemy always do. But typically, they provide the people to whom they are bound with certain abilities deemed to be of particular value in carrying out their unique duties. Such as to see through warding spells placed over secret passageways and rooms. Most often, though, they are defensive in nature. They provide protection against castings that seek passage into their innermost thoughts. Or spells that would otherwise enable a caster to decipher his location, even across great distances. Or castings that might turn his own clothing or weapons against him. That's a good one to have. No one wants to die from one's own knife."

Tab shook her head in wonder. "I had no idea. Maybe he'll let me try one on."

Jess shook her head. "Sorry, they only work for him. And he couldn't remove them anyway. They're welded to his skin."

"River and Sea."

"But that doesn't mean he might not bestow another ring on you one of these days."

"What? I –I don't—"

Jess grinned at her suddenly flustered expression, and as she did so she felt something lighten in her chest. "Oh come now," she chided playfully, "I've seen how you two look at one another."

Tab's freckled face turned crimson. "You're mad. I don't know what you're talking about."

"Come on, Tabytha. Admit it. You fancy him—and not just a little."

Tab was silent for a moment. Then a hint of a shy smile crept across her features, and she stole a glance at Jess. "He is sort of handsome, isn't he?"

Jess snorted. "I'm threadbare, not blind. And he's covered in sweat and grime and the dust of the road at the moment. Just imagine him all cleaned up!"

"Oh stop it," said Tabytha, who was nonetheless now grinning herself. "Traejon could choose virtually anyone in the kingdom," she said. Then Tab sighed and gestured down at her dirty and wrinkled clothing. "And when he does, he's likely to pursue someone who is not perpetually caked in trail dust herself."

"I have the clear impression that Traejon would not mind taking a washcloth to you and determining what lies beneath."

Tabytha gaped at her, quite unable to muster a response.

Jess leaned forward conspiratorially. "Tab, I know when someone's smitten."

"Well . . . I suppose I could endure his attentions if it came to that."

Jess caught a flash of movement in the valley below. "Here he comes now. And he's bringing company."

There were five riders, all of whom sat their mounts with an ease that marked them as experienced horsemen. Jess recognized Traejon at the front, deep in conversation with a burly rider at his side. The presence of the other riders was a bit of a puzzle, but she supposed that their purpose would be explained soon enough.

They both watched the progress of the riders for a moment, then Jess cleared her throat. "Tabytha?"

"Yes?"

"What do you know of him? Traejon, I mean. Where does he hail from? Does he have family?"

Tab sighed and ran a hand through her hair. "I don't know much about him," she admitted finally. "We spent several days together before we found you, and during that time I must have recounted virtually every moment of my childhood. I talk when I'm nervous. But whenever I asked him anything about his past he deflected my questions. He was quite skilled at it, really. I didn't take heed of his evasions for some time. All I know is what you know: his appearance suggests he has some Koah blood in him; he knows how to handle blade and bow; and his dreams are not always peaceful ones, to judge by the way he groans in his sleep."

"Yes, he's disturbed me more than once with his muttering. But there's something else about him as well. His eyesight is—"

Tabytha locked eyes with Jess. "You've noticed that too? He doesn't bring attention to it but his vision is almost eerily sharp."

"Perhaps he owes that to one of those rings. . ."

"Perhaps. But here's another thing." Tab paused, then cocked her head quizzically at Jess. "How old would you guess he is?"

"I don't know. Young for a shadow. I'd guess perhaps four and twenty years, but that would mean he would have been in his teens when my father appointed him as Nomad's shadow, and I can't imagine him doing that. So late twenties?"

"I would have guessed something similar. But he's older than that. Considerably older, perhaps."

"Why do you say that?"

"Because when I was telling him about my childhood in Tydewater, he mentioned that he'd once spent a night gambling at the Toad's Tongue, one of our city's more notorious gaming dens."

"So?"

"So the Toad's Tongue burned down thirteen years ago. And while my understanding is that the Toad's ownership didn't run a very tight ship, I don't think they allowed children at their tables."

"Feather and Foam. Perhaps it's his Koah blood that accounts for his youthful appearance. The lack of facial hair and all."

Tab shrugged, though her brow remained furrowed in thought. "I don't know. Maybe."

The two of them fell silent as they watched Traejon and the other riders make their way up the hillside.

Tab cleared her throat. "So perhaps you will prove more forthcoming than Traejon on another matter."

"Hmmm," said Jess noncommittally.

"May I ask what has been troubling you? Ever since we left the Widow's Torch you've been . . . difficult to reach. Until our conversation today I'd almost become convinced that the spirited princess Traejon and I first encountered was a trick of my memory."

Jess sighed heavily. "I know. I've been behaving abominably."

"No, you haven't," said Tabytha, pushing a windswept lock of hair out of her face. "It's just that your aspect since then has been so . . . sorrowful, and none of us really understand why."

Jess shifted on the rock until she was facing Tabytha, whose features were arranged in an expression of genuine concern. And just like that, Jess felt the frustration, anger, and sorrow of the last several years boil over. "The past few years at Kylden Hall have been . . . difficult," she said. "My father is convinced that as a threadbare, I will not be able to hold the throne once he is gone. So he's forced me to submit to a parade of indignities that have been by turns ridiculous and humiliating. All meant to awaken the slumbering Thread within me."

"I'm sorry."

"Not your fault," she said brusquely, even as she felt her eyes sting at those miserable memories. "I told myself that father was underestimating not only me, but the kingdom over which he ruled. And even after the gargoyle's attack, I convinced myself that I had the necessary steel in my spine. Perhaps not all of Fyngree was loyal to the Suntold line. What of it? I was not one of those pallid, vapid creatures who spend all their energies strutting around at court in order to gather admirers like bouquets. Who spends half their waking hours worrying over which dress will present their breasts to their best advantage. My sense of self has never rested on my ability to attract young noblemen or old lechers."

Jess looked away for a moment, studying the approaching riders. Traejon and his new companions were midway up the escarpment now. "And when I ventured out in the wild alone, foraging for food and evading pursuers and finding shelter for myself, I felt . . . well, proud of myself, to be honest. I was tired and cold and frightened, yes. But I was *doing* it. Forging my own path, taking action to defend my father's realm, and doing it without the Thread or an escort of soldiers."

Jess shook her head in dismay at how completely she'd fooled herself. "There were times out there that I half-wished that Nomad would find me. Just so that she'd fly back to Kylden Hall and my father would lay his hands on her and he would *see*. He would *see* that I was brave and strong and capable of taking care of myself. And of ruling Fyngree. Without virtue of a familiar or the sheltering arm of a husband from some venerable casting family."

"You had ample reason to be proud, Jess," said Tabytha. "I was stunned to find you so deep in the mountains. It seemed inconceivable to me that you were even alive. That you were not only alive but thriving."

"Yes, well, I was feeling my oats then."

"So what changed? Was it something that Gydeon said?"

Jess looked down at her hands. It was almost as if she could feel the shadow of her nonexistent familiar looming over her, chuckling with malign glee at her unrequited longing for his touch. "It was the wolf attack at the Widow's Torch. I was just so *helpless*. As you and Traejon and Gydeon fought those wolves, I just cowered behind your backs, so riddled with terror that I thought I might faint—or throw up." Jess shook her head in bitter self-recrimination. "The one crossbow bolt I fired missed so badly that I might as well have fired it into the waterfall."

Tabytha looked genuinely baffled. "But . . . you're not a soldier, Jess. Or a caster. What could you have done?"

"That's my *point*, Tab," growled Jess. "I couldn't do *anything*. I can contribute no spells to ward off our enemies. I'm unable to wield a sword or bow with any skill. And I'm not even armed with any rings such as the ones that Traejon wears. Father thought that they might interfere with his efforts to awaken the Thread in me. After the Widow's Torch I realized that my father was right: I can't possibly hold the throne after he's gone. I'm like a fawn in a forest full of panthers. I'll be utterly at the mercy of the kingdom's casters and high sentinels, men and women who command respect and loyalty. My only hope is to agree to some politically advantageous marriage with someone possessing some of the talents I lack. And if such a union takes place, the reins of the kingdom will pass over to my husband anyway. I might officially be the Throneholder, but everyone will know where the true power resides. I'll be naught but a figurehead."

Tabytha stared incredulously at Jess. "Let me see if I understand you correctly," she said, and Jess was surprised to hear real anger in her voice. "You travel through the country-side without detection for two weeks, managing to send correspondence to your father as you go, even though half the kingdom is looking for you. No entourage, no military escort, and roaming through unfamiliar wilderness. You are able to do so in part because although you are threadbare, you still possess considerable knowledge of the alchemical arts. And in part because you are both clever and brave—assets that are prized in any ruler.

"In the meantime"—Tabytha pointed to the northern end of the valley below, where the last of the cavalry had dis-appeared—"the cities of Fyngree move as one to meet a possible threat from Rojenhold, their actions proving once again their deep devotion to the Suntold line—of which you are a part, are you not? And yet you are prepared to cast aside all of that because you did not perform like a seasoned warri-or the first time you faced combat? Well, all I have to say is that you certainly set high standards for yourself."

Jess stared at Tab for a moment, torn between an urge to snarl an angry retort and an equally strong impulse to embrace her. Thoroughly unsettled, Jess decided on a crook-ed smirk. "You're taking full advantage of my 'I prefer when people are honest with me' declaration, aren't you?"

Tab's cheeks colored again, but she did not look away. "I'm testing the boundaries of that policy."

"Well, I appreciate your perspective—bluntly impart-ed though it was. Perhaps I am being too hard on myself. I'll think on all you've said." Jess paused, then raised a finger. "In any event, I would be in your debt if you would provide me with some instruction on the use of that crossbow. For any future encounters with bloodthirsty hordes of wolves."

Tabytha grinned. "I'd be happy to."

Traejon arrived a moment later, trailing four riders and three fresh mounts behind him. Jess was happy to see the horses, all of which looked strong and fast.

"You look comfortable," Traejon observed as he looked down on them from his saddle.

"We are," said Tabytha brightly.

"Were your ears burning?" asked Jess with exaggerated innocence.

Traejon looked at them uncomprehendingly for a moment before a slow smile spread across his face. "A little, now that you mention it," he said, his sea-green eyes lingering on Tab for an extra heartbeat.

Traejon motioned the riders forward and introduced them one by one. Leanly built and garbed in the clothing of scouts and woodsmen, they looked to Jess like able navigators of Fyngree's rivers and forests. Young, though. Only one of them, a burly sargeant named Noxon Straw, looked to have more than a few years of military service under his belt.

Once the introductions were concluded, Traejon turned to Jess. "By the time I reached Splyntbell, I decided that you were right about the wisdom of securing a few more swords for the next stage of our journey, Jess. I remain a little concerned that adding to our party may slow us down or draw undue attention, but the general assured me that these scouts know their craft."

"Excellent," Jess said mildly, as if Traejon's decision to accept her counsel was of no great consequence. But as Gydeon strolled up to greet the new arrivals, she could not help but share a secret smile of vindication with Tab.

22

Oblivion

King Owyn turned away from the bustling city below him to study the two men standing at the far end of the balcony. "So all the preparations have been made?"

"They have, your Majesty," said Pynch, his eyes briefly alighting on the king's right arm hanging limply at his side. Owyn's face drew down into a scowl at his counselor's grave expression, but he said nothing. Over the last few days the pain in his shoulder had failed to subside. To the contrary, it now throbbed as if it had been pierced by a hot poker, and he could no longer lift his arm to his chest without a grimace of pain.

To Owyn, the pain was a relentless reminder of Nomad's continued absence—and of the grim likelihood that his familiar was no longer soaring the skies above Fyngree. But where was she then? Crippled at the bottom of some dark canyon? Beating tattered wings against an iron cage? None of the alternatives he could conjure offered any succor for his tormented thoughts.

"And steps have been taken to inform Rynelle Tremeny of my decision?" he asked.

"Yes," said Pynch. "We sent riders to intercept Tremeny north of the Marching Mountains. I know that will take longer than if you had conjured a Tiding Horn to convey your message. But you must husband your strength, Majesty, and our riders should reach her by the end of the week. And once she has received your orders, the high sentinel will return to Tydewater immediately."

"Tis a pity that we were not able to reach General Splyntbell with word of your impending plans until yesterday," rumbled Sevenshade. "If only our message had arrived a day earlier, the princess would already be on her way back to Kylden—and to you, Your Majesty."

Owyn glanced at the bearded falconer. Brundy had spent the last few weeks dashing from one end of the Gilded Coast to the other in service to the crown, but he looked as sturdy and well-rested as ever. Owyn felt a surge of gratitude toward the falconer—and Pynch too. Both men were taciturn by nature, but they had been steadfast and true over these last few weeks, and Owyn felt a twinge of shame that he had ever doubted them. If there were indeed agents of Whytewender roaming through his castle, surely they wore the masks of other men.

Owyn shuffled back to the railing of the balcony, which jutted out from his private chambers like a great stone disc half-buried in the citadel's western wall. He looked down at the city sprawled before him—his city—as it prepared for the coming evening.

The sun was nearly at the horizon now, its slanting rays washing the slender towers that dotted the city's skyline in molten gold. Proud symbols of Fyngree's foremost casting houses, the towers pierced the sky at widely spaced intervals, like tent stakes holding up a canvas of cloud. Oh to have been alive when those towers were being built! To see the great stone blocks that constituted the bones of those spires as they floated upward through the air, like leaves being borne aloft by campfire heat. To watch the wizards and witches far below as they chanted and gestured, their necks craning up to the heavens, until each massive block gently settled into its place. That would have been a grand time to be alive. To watch a young city spring up around you in a matter of weeks, like flowers in springtime. To *feel* that first generation of casters fill the lungs of Kylden with magic.

Owyn shifted his gaze to the streets below, watched as lantern lights sprouted in Kylden's shops and homes. Even from his high vantage point he could hear the faint cries and shouts of the drovers and merchants as they scurried to conclude their business for the day. Then he raised his watery eyes back to the cloud-marbled sky above, and beyond the city walls to the shimmering pelt of the Amaranthine Sea.

Owyn rubbed at his eyes. "And Splyntbell feels that even his swiftest riders cannot catch up to them?"

"Not with Frost setting the pace," said Pynch. "And he had a day's head start, as well as fresh mounts. No, our best bet to reach the princess now is to intercept them on their travels westward. I've sent messages to several mayors and constables along their most probable routes westward. And if Frost and the princess steer clear of those villages, we can still reach them at the entrance to the Matchstyck Forest, their stated destination. Tremeny has been instructed to send a Tiding Horn to the Tusk twins. The Tusks will see to it that when Frost and the princess reach Rucker's Mill, they heed your order to return to Kylden immediately."

"And the Tusks will send along a detachment to accompany the princess on her journey back here," added Sevenshade.

Owyn nodded but kept his back to the men as he scanned the horizon.

"Are you all right, Your Majesty?" asked Pynch.

The king pivoted from the balcony, absently rubbing his right shoulder. "No. I really am not. And as much as I would like to continue to stand vigil, we both know that's not possible, don't we?" He limped across the balcony to the vaulted entrance to his chambers, the high votary and the falconer trailing behind. When he reached the archway he turned and placed his left hand atop the falconer's shoulder. "Master Sevenshade. You have been a good and faithful servant to me and I thank you. If Nomad remains lost and my days are indeed nearing their end, I beseech you to serve my daughter with the same constancy you have provided me."

Sevenshade bowed his head. "Of course, Your Majesty."

Owyn then turned to Pynch. "Marston, you have been at my side for even longer than Brundy here. What has it been, twenty-two years now?"

"Twenty-four years, Your Majesty."

"Twenty-four years. And throughout that time your wise and selfless counsel has helped chart a peaceful and prosperous course for Fyngree." He stepped close and pulled Pynch into a rough embrace. Owyn could feel the high votary stiffen momentarily in instinctive distaste at the physical contact. But then he felt Pynch's left hand clumsily pat his once-strong shoulder. Owyn held the embrace for a moment longer before releasing him.

"And you've been a good friend as well," Owyn said, locking eyes with Pynch. "I've not always heeded your counsel. But I think that speaks more to my stubbornness than any shortcomings on your part. I've been an imperfect vessel for the dreams and aspirations of our people at times."

"You have been a great king," protested the high votary. His tone was irritable, but Owyn recognized with something like wonderment that Pynch—sour old Pynch—almost seemed to be fighting to control his own emotions. "A glittering jewel in the Suntold firmament, Your Majesty. And you shall be for years to come."

"Hush now," said Owyn with a faint smile. "You are getting softhearted in your old age." Owyn coughed and gestured into his interior chambers. "You gentlemen know the way out. If you'll excuse me, I seem to have run out of reasons to tarry any longer. I have an enchantment to prepare."

Pynch and Sevenshade bowed and left him on the balcony. A moment later he heard the door to his chambers open, then softly close. He was alone.

Owyn left the balcony, closed the doors behind him, and entered his chambers, his footsteps echoing faintly in the high rafters. He went to a long table crowded with the materials he needed and spent the next several minutes measuring ingredients and sprinkling them into an upturned turtle shell. Once the shell was ready, he drew a deep breath and launched into the incantation necessary to cast an invisible shield over his chambers. A shield that only Nomad or Jess could enter. Midway through the spell, though, he felt a spasm of panic shudder through his body. His limbs felt heavy and sodden, his tongue thick and sluggish against his teeth. Had he waited too long?

As the half-woven spell wavered and trembled, despair skulked toward his heart like a jackal in the night. But with a desperate heave of effort he beat the panic down and continued on, slicing the air over the shell with his shrieking right arm at the necessary intervals, muttering ancient words that gushed out of him like water from a hidden spring.

And then it was done.

Owyn sagged against the table, wiping a shaking hand across his sweating face. He looked to his bed at the other side of the room. It looked a million miles away in his wasted state. But he could feel a faint shimmer of magic pulsating through the chamber's walls and windows.

The king took a few minutes to gather himself, then staggered over to his bed. He stared vacantly into the dark recesses of the room for a time before finally turning to the goblet sitting at his bedside table. He had prepared the potion ahead of time, fully aware that once he had cast the warding, he might not have the focus or dexterity to mix the potion correctly.

Owyn picked up the goblet and watched pensively as the light from the fireplace danced over the surface of the liquid within. He raised the cup to his lips and quaffed its contents down in several long swallows. He expected it to burn his throat, to leave a bitter aftertaste in his mouth. But though the drink was of an almost syrupy consistency, it had virtually no taste at all. Vaguely disappointed, he placed the empty goblet back on the table. Then he lay himself on the bedspread, closed his eyes, and waited for the spell of oblivion to pull him down.

23

A Many-Braided River

Malkyn's heart trembled in her chest as she watched her husband steer their flour-laden wagon down the lane in the meager dawn light. Wynston's run up to Stormheel would keep him away for three days. She wouldn't have that full allotment of time to steal away with Ben and Rowan. Tumdown would turn up later that same afternoon, as she always did for her tutorials with her oldest son. But she had eight or nine hours before the witch would appear on their doorstep, and she intended to make the most of it. And if they were very lucky, Tumdown might attribute their absence to a last-minute decision to make the journey up to Stormheel a family affair. That might buy them another day's head start—possibly even two.

Turning from the window, she moved swiftly and quietly through the house so that she did not disturb Rowan's sleep. She had spent the last days crafting and culling mental checklists of all that they would need, so she proceeded now with no wasted motion. In less than an hour she had crammed four satchels and packs with hoarded food, clothing, medicine, maps, furs, gloves, boots, and other tools for the journey ahead.

Malkyn set the stuffed packs by the door and took one last look around, hands on her hips. Her tired eyes lingered here and there. To the silent hearth that had provided warmth and light to their family since their arrival. To the old rocking chair that had listened to her sing countless lullabies to her boys during their earliest years. To the modest but neatly arranged shelf of well-worn, well-loved books on the other side of the room. Then she sighed, opened the door, and walked purposefully to the gristmill next door.

When she entered the mill's dim interior, it took her a moment to locate Ben in the gloom. With a kind of absent-minded irritation she realized that he had not even lit a lantern to see by. But then she heard the scuffing of a broom on the far side of the millstone that filled the center of the room. She walked around the tall millstone, then stopped. Ben was working with illumination after all. A small cluster of what looked like fireflies hovered about a foot above the face of the broom in Ben's hands, casting dim golden light over the rough-hewn floor he was sweeping.

"Ben?" she said quietly.

Ben turned to his mother, his expression unreadable in the gloom.

"Hold on," she said, and made a move toward one of the dark lanterns hanging from the ceiling. Just as she reached up to take it off its hook, though, the lantern blazed to life.

Malkyn turned back to her son. "Very good," she said encouragingly. "Your casting becomes stronger by the day, Ben."

He shrugged. "It's a simple spell. Professor Tumdown showed me."

"You would have gained the spell on your own, you know. She's not giving you casting abilities you wouldn't otherwise have. She's just—pushing you along. Isn't that right?"

Ben shrugged again, turning his eyes down to the broom in his hands. "I guess." Ben reached over and plucked a small glass vial off the millstone. Inside it, a single firefly was flitting about, bouncing off the walls of its little prison. Ben unstopped the small cork at its top and the firefly escaped. Instantly, the cloud of lights orbiting the head of his broom vanished. "What do you want, mother? Father left me a lot of work."

Malkyn swallowed hard, her thoughts a hopeless tangle. She had rehearsed this conversation countless times in her mind over the last few days. Now that the moment had arrived, though, the words had vanished. She felt her resolve waver, her gaze wandering aimlessly around the mill. But then her eyes returned to her son's face, and the unhappiness she saw there reminded her of the stakes.

"Ben, I can no longer abide what's happening in our home."

"I don't walk to talk about this, mother," Ben said, turning away.

"No? Well, you don't have that luxury anymore," said Malkyn with such steel in her voice that Ben's head snapped back around to her. "You're a man now, whether you like it or not. Whether you're ready or not. So stop behaving like some poor beast with its leg caught in a trap. Some dumb, helpless creature that has decided to lie down in resignation and wait for the warden to come and deliver the killing blow. We *both* need to cast off that delusion."

Ben's cheeks flushed at her cutting words, but he did not look away. Malkyn's heart gladdened at the sight. He might not have liked her scolding, but it had brought him—if only for a moment—out of the haunted netherworld in which he'd been wandering since Glynt had first shown up at their doorstep. For the first time in weeks Malkyn felt that her son was fully present before her.

"Ben, that trap has not yet closed around your leg. We can still leave. We *need* to leave. But we need to do so while your father is away. You, me, and Rowan. It is—"

"What are you talking about? Go where?"

"*Away.* From here. Someplace where Glynt and Tumdown can't find us. Someplace where your casting gifts won't be corrupted into some debased weapon for King Thylus to wield as he pleases."

Ben studied her carefully, his expression alert but wary. "You want to leave father behind. Abandon him."

Malkyn felt tears rising and shook her head angrily so as to ward them off. "Your father," she said slowly, "has already abandoned *us.* In spirit if not in body. He doesn't see it, Ben, but he's given you to them. As far as he's concerned, you're the property of the Faithful Shield now, to do with as they wish. As are the rest of us. And once the Faithful Shield's manacles bind your wrists, they never leave. They never dissolve or unlock. They just tighten with each passing day."

Ben's brow furrowed. "Professor Tumdown says that a true Rojenholdean's greatest allegiance is to Thylus Whytewender and the throne on which he sits. All else is secondary to Rojenhold's glory. Even family. Even *parents.* Rojenhold first, Rojenhold always. She warned me that not everyone understands that. Which is why the Faithful Shield is so vital to our survival."

"*Survival?*" Malkyn said, her voice dripping with scorn. "Whose survival? Yours? Rowan's? Or Whytewender's? Ben, war is coming. Everyone can see it. All across Rojenhold, towns and villages are being emptied of men and women of fighting age. Even boys and girls—some only a little older than yourself—are being conscripted and sent to the border. Prylla Overbeek lost her two oldest sons to the front just the other day. All because the king's envy of Fyngree's wealth has finally gotten the better of him."

"That's blasphemy," Ben said instantly, and Malkyn was suddenly, crazily, reminded of how the bells of Stormheel rang out every night at midnight to commemorate the alleged hour of Whytewender's birth. Ben's objection had the same rote mindlessness as those pealing bells.

Malkyn stared at her son for a long moment, so furious with him that she didn't trust herself to speak. But as she looked into his eyes, a realization struck her like a thunderbolt. Although her son was parroting the vile propaganda fed to him by Tumdown and Glynt, his voice lacked passion or conviction. It was as if he was offering up each twisted pillar that held Whytewender's kingdom aloft, presenting them before her to see whether she had the strength to knock them down.

"Is it blasphemy to criticize a king?" she challenged. "You don't believe that, Ben. I know you don't believe that. Don't swallow that poison. One blasphemes gods, not monarchs. Especially not ones who rule by sowing fear and resentment and suspicion."

Ben's eyes widened at her treasonous words, and now she could see the turmoil boiling behind those mild gray eyes.

"Oh Ben," she said, reaching out and placing a hand over his heart. "My kind and gentle son. Do you remember how the river braids just north of Stormheel, before it enters the sea?"

Ben glanced down at the hand on his chest. He said nothing, but he did not push her hand away.

"And do you remember your father's conversation with those fishermen? How they told him that one of the braids offers clear passage to the ocean? But how the other braids are false ones, ending in desolate marsh or impenetrable thickets of deadfall? The Faithful Shield is a false braid, Ben. As false as they come. There's power there, I grant you. And potential riches, too, I suppose. Even a chimera of security. That's what your father tells himself. But if you ride down that braid it will leave your soul in tatters, caught on the bleached and broken limbs of innocent men, women, and children. Is that the future you want for yourself?"

Ben reached up and gently removed her hand from his chest. He stepped away, then made a slow circuit around the millstone at the center of the room, his expression pensive. When he had circled back to her, he raised his head. "What about father?" he said again, and she felt her spirits rise. For she knew what he meant.

"Circumstances change," she said. "Rivers in flood cut new paths to the sea. I don't know what Tempyst will look like when this is all over. Gods help us if Whytewender triumphs and conquers Fyngree. We'll spend the rest of our lives running, Ben. But I pray that doesn't come to pass—and that the gods will favor us with a better world. One in which you can someday be reunited with your father."

"Where would we go?" Ben asked. "The border will be heavily guarded, all the way from the Span to the coast. Between the army and the familiars patrolling our lands, we'll never get across. And Rowan won't survive a full winter in the Speartips. My spellwork can't sustain us through that."

"I know." Malkyn took a deep breath and let it out. "We will go west—"

"West?" Ben breathed, his gaze sharpening suddenly. Malkyn paused, watching her son closely. There was something there in his eyes. A flash of something, like a barely glimpsed movement deep in the woods. She waited for a moment, but he said no more.

"Yes," she continued. "We'll go west to Valyedon. But rather than forge a path through the Speartips, we'll go north first. And reach Valyedon via the Puzzle."

Ben stared at her. "We'll never make it," he said after a moment.

"We will," she said emphatically. Ben was listening to her now. He was ready to be convinced. She just needed to find the words.

"I've already packed food and clothing for the journey, and your casting powers can help keep the cold at bay. Your father left us Ajax and Blackeye, and what we lose in speed we gain in endurance. They are strong horses with thick coats. And winter has not yet arrived. I'll grant that the Puzzle will be impassable in another six weeks. But we are leaving for the Puzzle today, and we can be at its outskirts in a week, I wager. And once we're in, if we can find the Keyhole, we can make our way south through the mountains until we're on Fyngrean land."

"Finding the Keyhole is no sure thing, not even with Wynk," he countered. "And just reaching it might well require weeks of travel through the Puzzle. And what of the crevasses hidden beneath the snow? They stretch on for hundreds of miles, or so they say."

Malkyn thrilled at her son's words, laced as they were with doubt. His words were skeptical but not hostile. They were the questions of someone seeking reassurance that her plan of deliverance had at least some prospect—however dim—for success.

"Wynk will guide us through," she said with more confidence than she felt. "She'd be able to pick her way past the hidden crevasses, wouldn't she?"

Ben's eyes took on a faraway cast, as if he was imagining his familiar padding across the Puzzle's icy wastes. "She could do it," he said finally. "But we would have to follow her path exactly. One false move and the abyss awaits."

Ben ran a hand through his hair, pacing now. Malkyn could tell that despite his fears and doubts, he was warming to her scheme. "Glynt will give chase," he pointed out. "And as you admit, our horses are slow."

"That is the other reason we chart a course through the Puzzle. The Faithful Shield will look for us at the border and its approaches. And they'll scour the streets of Strovenstaff and Stormheel—and every house and stable in between. And they'll send familiars and soldiers into the Speartips. But they won't even consider the Puzzle, especially since we'll have Rowan with us. Their reaction will be as yours was—that setting course across the Puzzle is insane!" Malkyn laughed suddenly, and her laughter was so genuine that a hint of a smile crossed Ben's face. "By the time they realize their error—if they ever do—we'll be too far in for them to overtake us. Because they'll have to navigate the same icefields that we've already passed through."

Ben studied her face intently. "Do you really believe we could make it?" he said, hopefulness and doubt warring for primacy with every word.

"I don't know," Malkyn said honestly. "Perhaps not. But I think Faxon Glynt underestimates what a mother will do to protect her children." She paused. "And I think he underestimates you, Ben."

24

Shelter from the Storm

Traejon watched as Gydeon gently stroked Vyx's bedraggled wings, staring all the while into the small owl's shining eyes. Vyx had been absent since early this morning, so her return had prompted a great sigh of relief from the caster. Traejon well understood Gydeon's feelings; it had to be difficult for the professor to send the creature off scouting every morning, knowing that familiars were under siege all across Fyngree.

As he waited for Gydeon's report, Traejon took a look around at his other companions huddled with him under the dripping boughs of the great cedar. Their faces were resolutely stoic, although he knew they were cold and tired. The last two days had been miserable, marked as they were by heavy rain, high winds, and recurring spasms of lightning and thunder that mangled the nerves of their horses. Even now, with the rain dwindling to a cold mist, the wind continued to snap their cloaks like flags.

Traejon caught the eye of Noxon Straw, who was hunkered down in the lee of the other riders. He had somehow managed to light his pipe in the storm. Straw grinned through the pipe stem clenched between his teeth and waved sardonically, smoke billowing out of his nostrils like a chimney. Traejon offered an amused half-wave in return, which had the effect of widening Straw's smile. As far as Traejon could tell, there were few things in this world that didn't elicit such a reaction from the slope-shouldered sergeant. Most infants exited their mothers' wombs in a torrent of red-faced squalling. He thought it more likely that Straw had entered this world with a roar of laughter.

When Traejon had accepted Straw and the other three scouts into their company ten days ago, he had done so with mixed feelings. The benefit of adding a few swords was undeniable, and Splyntbell had assured him that all four men were accomplished wilderness trekkers of proven loyalty to the Throneholder. Still, distrust was a river that ran deep and fast in Traejon, and he had spent the first two days after their arrival watching them closely.

On the morning of their third day together, though, Straw had sidled up to Traejon and given him a playful nudge. "They're good boys, Frost. You've got nothing to worry about. Max and Borys just keep to themselves because they're bashful. The princess and Tab have them thoroughly spooked. And Stefron over there? He comes from one of Talonoux's most prominent families. His parents would kill him if he even thought about betraying King Owyn."

Traejon had given the sergeant a considering look. "And you, Straw?"

"Me?" he asked, stroking one of his bushy sideburns as if he had never considered the question before. "Well, I'm a scoundrel and a degenerate according to my wives. The first three, anyway. But I'm not *that* kind of scoundrel and degenerate. And I hate Rojenholdeans even more than I hate last call."

The conversation had been a mildly reassuring one. But it wasn't until they made camp that night that Traejon truly began to appreciate Straw's presence. Straw had unexpectedly unpacked a fiddle from his gear and brought it to the campfire. He then spent the next two hours regaling them all with spirited versions of several tavern standards, each song stitched to the next with rueful tales of personal misadventure. He also tossed in a few clever, improvised songs—one that imagined Max and Borys's secret lives of debauchery, another that gently teased Jess about her small stature, and a third recounting the diabolical lengths to which Traejon and Tabytha would resort to ensure that they sat next to one another at mealtime.

At several points Straw had the entire company howling with laughter. By the time they finally turned in, Traejon's cheeks were sore from grinning so much. But as Traejon watched everyone settle in to sleep, he reflected that there was more to Straw than met the eye. The sergeant played the part of an irreverent man of simple and prodigious appetites. But it was not lost on Traejon that in the space of a few hours, Straw had torn down the lingering reserve between the scouts and Traejon's party and made them a much more unified company. That unity would not only buoy everyone's spirits, it might also make them fight harder for one another down the line if the need arose. And that was no small thing.

The ensuing days had thrown fresh wood on the fires of friendship that had been kindled by Straw that night. In this effort they had been aided by day after day of fine autumn weather. As their party passed through the rolling fields and shining lakes of the Loaf into the forested foothills of the Speartips, they repeatedly came upon vistas that seemed conjured just to remind them all of their love for Fyngree—and the importance of preserving it from harm.

The pleasing scenery and good weather had kept everyone in fine fettle, even with long hours of riding. And the nights had been just as fine, a succession of crisp, clear evenings perfectly crafted for cooking, conversation, and sound slumber.

So when bruise-colored clouds finally moved in and the sound of distant thunder reached his ears, Traejon had given a mental shrug. It had been a tremendous run of good weather, no sense in getting greedy. A few hours of riding in the rain never hurt anyone.

That had been two days ago.

Traejon watched now as Max and Stefron, who had been placed in the rear guard for the day, appeared around a bend in the road and joined the main group. As Tabytha informed them about the owl's return, Traejon studied Gydeon and his familiar with rising impatience. How long was the caster going to make them sit here?

As if catching a whiff of Traejon's thoughts, Gydeon raised his hand and Vyx flew off into the woods. The wizard turned to the group. "The road is empty of other travelers, and Vyx did not sense fellow familiars among the wildlife she encountered," said Gydeon, raising his voice to be heard above the wind. "So our path remains clear."

"Well that's something at least," said Tabytha from the depths of her hooded cloak.

"But that's not all," said Gydeon with a smile. "There's an inn not three miles distant. And a fine one, by the looks of it, at least for these hinterlands."

As one, the entire group swiveled to face Traejon. He tried to maintain a facade of stony contemplation for a moment, but their expressions were so full of childlike hopeful-ness that he was unable to keep a straight face. "Well," he said with a smile, "I guess that's up to Jess, since we'll be paying for the rooms from Fyngree's treasury."

Everyone turned to Jess, who frowned and tapped her finger against her chin, as if she had just been presented with a difficult riddle to decipher. But she proved just as un-able to maintain any pretense of indecision. "Hmmm. Well, I *suppose* . . . " she began slowly, a mischievous grin playing around her lips, and the entire party erupted into relieved cheers.

They quickly resumed their journey, everyone sitting a little straighter in their saddles at the prospect of securing shelter from the storm. As they made their way, everyone ex-citedly jabbered about how they intended to spend the evening. Jess and Tabytha agreed that a change of clothing and—dare they dream of it?—a warm bath were their first orders of business. Noxon and Gydeon debated whether the inn might offer ales from any of the region's better brewmas-ters. Even Max chimed in with a description of his dream meal: lamb chops, apple-cider braised cabbage, and fresh-baked bread with honey and jam.

When the inn finally came into view, its appearance did nothing to dampen the group's spirits. Tucked above the curving road midway up a wooded hillside on the right, it sat on the western edge of a bluff overlooking a frothing creek swollen with rain. The inn's first-story facade featured two large round windows in the front and a row of smaller round windows along the right side. Its second story held several of the small spherical windows as well. Every window was inlaid with intricately curved muntins that were silhouetted to fine effect by warm lantern light within.

As they crossed a small stone bridge that provided passage over the roaring creek, Traejon noted other details as well. A steeply pitched but well-maintained slate roof that spilled rainwater to the ground in virtual sheets. Amid the second-story windows, the faint outline of an oddly placed door, its outside face framed and painted to blend in with the surrounding wall, that opened out onto nothing but the boulder-strewn ravine below. A sturdy-looking stable off to the left of the main house. And a faded sign by the roadside, swinging back and forth in the wind, that announced the name of the establishment: The Penny Whystle.

Their party left their mounts at the front porch and opened the main doorway in a clatter of boisterous conversation and stomping feet. As they did so, a smallish, white-haired older man bustled out from behind a long bar counter that stretched along the right side of the room.

"Welcome, welcome!" the man exclaimed with a friendly smile as he wiped his hands on his apron. Paunchy with a curly white beard, he reminded Traejon of someone's twinkle-eyed grandfather. "Welcome to the Penny Whystle. I'm so glad you found us! My name is Elston Gunn, and I'm the proprietor of this modest public house."

"Traejon," he said, shaking Gunn's extended hand. "We're glad to have found you as well."

Traejon casually scanned the main room. To the left stood a magnificent stone fireplace that held a crackling fire. Several members of the party brushed past him to warm themselves before it, casting wet cloaks, jackets, and gear off their shoulders as they went. Otherwise the room featured the usual pub trappings—an old but well-oiled bar backed by casks of wine, ale, and whiskey, a handful of spittoons and hissing lanterns, and half a dozen long, rough-hewn tables with benches. All in all, it was an inviting room.

"Devilish traveling conditions out there," offered Gunn, who appeared delighted at the unexpected windfall of customers. Traejon absently wondered just how badly they were about to be gouged for the pleasure of a hot meal and a dry night. Both the Penny Whystle and its owner appeared relatively prosperous, despite the fact that the inn was located on a lightly traveled road in one of Fyngree's least populated provinces. The man must charge premium prices for his rooms, taking full advantage of those travelers who did come his way.

But the price Gunn quoted for his rooms was surprisingly reasonable, even with the price of baths included. After Traejon made payment the innkeeper called out a couple of names and two servants promptly entered the tavern area. One entered from a swinging door that must have housed the kitchen, to judge from the enticing smells wafting forth from within. The other came down the staircase at the room's far left. Gunn instructed the man from the kitchen, a bearded giant named Tarantyn, to tend to their horses. He then turned to the other servant, a short fellow named Vyne whose bulbous eyes and wide mouth gave him an unfortunate toad-like aspect. The innkeeper instructed him to heat water for baths before assisting Tarantyn down at the stables.

As the servants departed, Gunn briskly fulfilled drink orders. He then disappeared into the kitchen—but not before declaring that the feast to come would satiate even the most ravenous of hungers. This announcement triggered a considerable uproar of hooting and clapping led by a stein-swinging Noxon, who pronounced the Penny Whystle to be his favorite tavern in all of Fyngree.

The only one who didn't join in the revelry was Tabytha, who had picked the short straw in a drawing to see who would have to leave the warm confines of the inn and take the first shift of sentry duty outside. Sticking her tongue out at her companions, she glumly marched to the front door and stepped out into the dusky light.

Once she departed, Traejon and the others dragged themselves away from the fire to take their gear upstairs and clean up for dinner. Jess claimed the first room closest to the stairs for herself and Tabytha, while Noxon and Stefron took the next room. Max and Borys hauled their gear into the room at the end of the hallway, leaving Traejon with Gydeon—the worst snorer in the bunch—in room number three.

Traejon breathed a silent growl. Even if the princess's safety was not paramount, he recognized that arithmetic and appearances necessitated that Tabytha stay with Jess. But he sensed that sleep would come slowly to him that night. There was Gydeon's roof-raising snoring to contend with, for one. Far more maddening, though, was the knowledge that Traejon would have to bank his fast-growing desire for Tab—a freshly bathed Tab who would be sleeping only two doors away—until another time. Two doors away? She might as well be in Stormheel.

At least the rooms looked well-kept, he noted grudgingly. Glancing in every doorway on his way to his own room, he saw that all appeared to be furnished with two sturdy-looking quilted beds, a straight-backed chair, a wash basin and water pitcher, a small lantern, and a mirror. A small round window graced the outer wall of each room as well, letting in natural light. The rooms even contained thick braided rugs that covered the span between the beds and the door. Clean in appearance if a little musty smelling, every room promised cozy sanctuary from the rain pattering against the inn's roof and windows.

Yet as Traejon and Gydeon set their gear out to dry and began changing into dry clothing for the evening, the shadow could not shake a niggling suspicion that something was off.

He couldn't point to anything, really. Gunn seemed affable and competent, the inn's accommodations were pleasant but not so ostentatious as to seem out of place in this remote corner of Fyngree, and getting out of the weather for the night would refresh both the humans and horses in their party.

So why this whisper of apprehension tickling at the back of his mind?

Traejon paused in the act of unbuckling the knife sheath on his left arm. He looked thoughtfully into the distance for a moment. Gydeon was behind him, midway through an extended soliloquy about the architectural bloodlines of the inn's round windows. But Traejon pushed the caster's voice to the far margins of his consciousness and began replaying every moment since they had first caught sight of the inn.

And then he had it.

Traejon left the room and stepped into the dimly lit hallway. He looked down to the far end, where the door that he had barely detected from the outside was located. From the inside the door looked perfectly ordinary. One would never guess that it opened out onto nothing but air. Had Gunn or some previous owner once intended to build a balcony out there?

Still standing outside his room, he turned his gaze the other way, toward the stairs that led down to the tavern area. The entire length of the hallway floor was covered by a faded green runner filigreed with black along its borders. Every few feet the carpet was marked by a faint line of collected lint and dirt. As if the runner was usually rolled up and had only recently been unrolled.

Traejon strolled down to the mysterious door at the end of the hallway. He felt along the doorframe and ran his hand over the surface of the door itself before trying the handle. It was locked. That made sense. Gunn wouldn't want any of his guests drunkenly stepping out into the abyss. Nonetheless, the vague sense of foreboding remained.

He looked down at his feet. Or more precisely, at the carpet upon which his feet were planted. The runner ended only two inches or so before the door. In the gap between the door and the runner, a narrow strip of wooden floor was visible. Traejon squatted down on his haunches and studied the bare floor. Its surface was marred by a set of rough, shallow grooves set about three feet apart. Like wagon ruts in miniature.

Traejon frowned, his eyes once again traveling all the way down the length of the hall to the top of the stairs. He reached down and began rolling up the carpet, stopping only after he had passed the doorways into the room that he shared with Gydeon and the one into which the brothers were settling. Studying the floor, he could see that the odd grooves in the wood not only extended the length of the hallway, they also sprouted fainter lines that curled into both of the rooms. He glanced in at the floor of his room. Now that he was looking for it, he could see that the grooves disappeared under the big rug.

Curious.

Traejon kicked the rolled-up runner back into place, then strode into his room. Gydeon was stripped to his waist, his pale back gleaming in the lantern light as he washed in the basin. "Going out for a minute," Traejon said briskly, snatching his bow and quiver off the peg from which he had hung them. "Don't drink all the ale."

"No promises," said Gydeon as he rubbed soap out of his eyes.

Traejon casually descended the stairs and looked around. Noxon and Max had already returned to the crackling hearth, the sergeant armed with his fiddle. He was warming his fingers on the strings, plucking away happily as Max looked on. No one else was in the room.

Quietly making his way to the front door, Traejon slipped out into the gloaming, his eyes searching for Tabytha. He spotted her leaning against the base of a large oak in the front yard, a good vantage point from which to watch the road below.

Tabytha smiled at him as he walked over to join her. "My shift can't be over yet, but I'm happy for the company. The rain and wind are finally dying down. It's not so bad out here."

Traejon looked down at her, and her smile faded. "But this isn't a social call, is it?" she said after a moment.

"I wish it was, Tab. You have no idea."

"Perhaps I do," she said softly.

Traejon felt an almost overwhelming impulse to toss his bow aside and take Tabytha into his arms. But then he recalled that odd second-story door opening out into the void, and the grooves in the floor. And how the inn had already been awash in savory smells when they arrived. As if the innkeeper had been expecting them.

"Are the servants still in the stable?" he asked.

"Yes," she said, her eyes searching his face for some clue to his troubled aspect.

"Come on," he said, moving to leave the shelter of the tree, but she placed a hand on one forearm to stop him.

"What is it?"

Traejon paused, searching for words to articulate the uneasiness he felt. "I do not think I like this place," he said finally.

Tabytha looked at him for a moment, then nodded. "All right," she said. They glided across the darkening yard until they were outside the stable. Keeping to the shadows, they crept along the walls until they were at the open entranceway. They could hear horses nickering and moving about, as well as human footfalls on the floorboards. Ducking down low, they peered around the corner and into the lamplit interior.

Tarantyn and Vyne were at the far end of the stable. They were carrying out their chores, but in the most desultory fashion, as if they had no more responsibilities for the evening. Tarantyn was tossing occasional pitchforks of hay into the stalls, but he was taking long pauses in between loads to converse with Vyne, who was leisurely rubbing down Max's horse. Apparently they had every expectation that Gunn could handle drinks and dinner for his guests by himself.

Traejon tapped her on the shoulder and they withdrew.

"What's going on, Traejon?"

"I'm not sure yet. Maybe nothing. But I don't think so." He trotted down the slope to the road, Tabytha following close behind. Once there, he led her down the forested corridor until they reached the stone bridge they had crossed earlier that afternoon. Traejon stopped and looked up at the darkening silhouette of the inn, its rows of round windows spilling light into the evening like some otherworldly lantern.

"Can you see the door?" he asked, raising his voice to be heard over the storm-swollen creek pounding under their feet.

"The what?"

He pointed. "The door on the second floor that opens up over the ravine."

Tabytha dutifully surveyed the upper reaches of the inn, but Traejon could see the puzzlement on her face. "Well it's up there," he said, "and I'm going to find out what lies below it."

Traejon studied the upper ramparts of the ravine, which was wholly cloaked in black. The west side of the gorge next to the inn was a sheer cliff. But the east side offered a more gradual slope down to the creek. "Follow me," he said, sprinting off the bridge and up the wooded hillside to the right. He could sense Tabytha's bewilderment as she scrambled up into the forest behind him but there was no help for it.

Traejon stopped climbing when he was roughly at the same height as the first floor of the inn across the way. Tabytha joined him a moment later, rubbing a knee that she had bashed against a fallen tree. They looked across the open gorge into the row of windows running the length of the main tavern room. The distance was considerable—nearly forty yards—but framed in one of the windows he could see Noxon sawing away on his fiddle, a big smile on his face. And two windows over stood Gunn, leaning against the bar and nodding his head lightly to the music, which they could faintly hear now that they had moved farther above the creek.

Traejon felt his sense of urgency slip a notch. The scene within the inn was hardly one to provoke alarm. But then he looked down into the inky blackness of the gorge and his eyes narrowed.

"Wait here," he said.

"What? It's pitch-black down there, and we don't have a lanter—"

Without another word Traejon dropped down the slope and into the darkness, leaving Tabytha sputtering in surprise and—he was fairly certain—irritation. No time to worry about that now, he thought, as he made his way nimbly down amid the boulders and disintegrating logs. A moment later he was at the bottom, peering across the foaming water to a pile of rocks on the other side, directly below the door high above. He felt his heart quicken as his eyes roamed over the debris, but he had to be sure. Traejon pushed back up the slope until he found a semblance of a ledge, then vaulted across the raging creek, landing squarely amid the rocks.

As he scrabbled for purchase among the loose debris, the icy waters of the rushing creek slammed into his legs and nearly carried him off. But Traejon dragged himself higher up the mound and began shoving rocks and splintered tree limbs aside until he found one of the rocks that had caught his eye from above. He pulled it out of the froth and brought it up with both hands. It was a stone all right.

A stone carved into the perfect likeness of a screaming man's head.

†††

The cockatrice watched the young soldier through the window, her obsidian eyes following the man's right arm as it carried the razor back and forth across the soapy surface of his jaw. Despite her nearly three-foot height, the creature's slender, serpentine body and closely folded wings enabled her to stand comfortably on the outside sill.

The beast turned her head and clamped her beak on the rusted nail that had been hammered into the outside of the window frame. Easing the unlatched window open, the cockatrice slipped through the opening and hopped down on the bed beneath, wings briefly opening to slow her descent. The creature stared at the soldier's back, waiting.

It didn't take long.

When Borys felt the cool air wafting in from the window he turned, his right arm poised midway up to his face. His gaze snapped onto the creature standing on his bed, onto the black eyes studying him so coldly. In an instant Borys saw what manner of beast had descended on him. He saw her leathery wings, and the way that the talons sprouting from the ends of her two spindly, gnarled legs sank into the quilt. He saw the gleaming, blood-red scales that adorned the cockatrice's body. And the misshapen rooster's head into which those horrible eyes were set.

But even as his expression stretched into a rictus of horror, Borys felt his pulse slow, as if the blood in his veins had been turned to molasses. Borys felt his limbs hardening, felt the sludge coursing through his body, infiltrating every corner of his being. An involuntary gasp of agony rose through him. But by the time it reached his frozen mouth and rigid tongue he was already dead, each chamber of his heart transmuted into cold granite.

The cockatrice spread her wings and glided off the bed to the door. She hovered in the air, twisting her beak to grasp the handle, then opened the door and floated out to land in the hallway. She turned toward the three doors standing between her and the stairs. Bobbing her head in a gentle barnyard rooster rhythm, the cockatrice walked down the hallway to the next door. The creature stood for a moment in front of the door, then used her terrible beak to tap at the door three times.

A moment later Gydeon opened the door. He looked down.

And a moment after that, a small owl flitting about in the woods a few hundred yards away evaporated in a shower of glittering sparks.

✝✝✝

As Traejon regained the top of the slope, Tabytha strode forward to meet him.

"What are you *doing?*" she hissed. "How—"

Traejon shoved the stone head into her hands. "Look."

Tabytha looked at him doubtfully, then turned her gaze down to the rock in her hands. "What's this?" she said, turning it this way and that in her hands, squinting in the dark. Then she stopped as the trailing remnants of the storm clouds parted overhead, bathing the stone in watery moonlight. Traejon saw her entire body stiffen as she recognized what she held.

"There's more down there," Traejon said. "Hands, arms, torsos, legs. You name it."

"But what . . . "

Traejon turned to the inn across the gorge and studied its glowing lights. "Gunn's a wizard," he said grimly, and the truth of it made the hair on the back of his neck stand up. "A bad one. With a cockatrice as a familiar."

"Raven and Crow," Tabytha said in a voice thick with dread. She shifted her gaze to the bank of windows across the way. "We have to get back and warn everyone."

Traejon unslung his bow and drew an arrow out of his quiver. "No time. The cockatrice could be in there right now." Traejon stalked the edge of the bluff, staring across the ravine into the inn's windows. There was Noxon, still sitting at the edge of the hearth, sawing away at his fiddle. But no one else was visible. Traejon began moving further up the hill, his gaze locked on the windows of the inn. The innkeeper had been there just a moment ago . . .

Tabytha sensed his intention and walked alongside him, an arrow nocked on her own bow. "Tis a long shot from here, Traejon," she said quietly as her own gaze jumped from window to window.

"But if we make it we take Gunn out. And without the element of surprise we can't beat him."

Traejon halted. Gunn was visible in the very last window. He was standing at the bar with a faint smile on his face. Only Gunn's head and chest were visible in the platter-sized window. But those were the parts he wanted.

"There he is," he said, pointing. "Tab, we need to shoot together."

"What? Why?"

"When the first arrow hits the window, the shattering glass and wood will alter the arrow's flight. It might still put him down. But it might not. And if it doesn't, he'll duck out of the way and start casting before I can launch a second arrow, and we'll all be doomed. We can't give him time to react."

Tabytha released a shuddering breath and wiped her free hand on her pants. "All right."

Side by side, the two of them set their stances, brought their bows up, and drew their strings back to their cheeks. "Say 'now' when you release," Traejon said with considerably more calm than he felt. "My arrow will follow an instant later."

Traejon waited, the shaft of his arrow sighted directly on the juncture of Gunn's neck and chest. He could hear the wind rustling in the forest behind them. And the creek raging through the gorge below. And even an occasional faint note from Noxon's fiddle as it drifted out into the night from an open window somewhere. But those sounds meant nothing to him now. His entire being was focused on the task at hand.

†††

Eyes glittering, the cockatrice flew out of the third room and landed lightly in the carpeted hallway. Behind her, the petrified form of Stefron stood in the shadows, one arm extended for a sword that he would never reach.

The creature bobbed her way down to the last door, the one closest to the stairs. The door was slightly ajar. The cockatrice paused for a moment, then pushed the door open. The creature glided around the room, thorny serpent's tail twitching, as she studied the girl sleeping on the bed below. Then the cockatrice alighted on the bed next to Jessalyn's thigh.

When Jess did not stir, the cockatrice cocked her head and leaned in close to her face, its razor-sharp beak hovering mere inches from Jess's closed eyes. The beast spread her wings wide, as if she meant to smother her. Then the beast reared back, stuck out one foot . . . and sank her long talons into the meat of Jess's leg.

†††

"Now!"

The two arrows streaked across the dark ravine, Tabytha's no more than five feet ahead of the one released by Traejon. Tabytha's arrow hit the window's right quadrant and blew it out in a spray of glass and wood. The path thus cleared, Traejon's arrow slammed into the base of Gunn's throat an instant later.

The impact of Traejon's arrow hurled the caster's upper body backward over the bar. Gunn clutched frantically at the shaft, his hands slippery with the blood pumping out of his neck. Noxon and Max leaped out of their seats by the hearth to come to the aid of the innkeeper. But by the time they reached him his hands were still and his eyes were wide and sightless. The only thing moving was the blood coursing out of his throat.

† † †

"Ow!" Jess exclaimed, her eyes snapping open in pain. She bolted upright in bed and grabbed for her thigh, her gaze darting around the dimly lit bedroom. She saw a strange, vaporous cloud of twinkling lights hovering above her bed for just an instant. And then it was gone, leaving naught but a faint afterimage. Then even the ghostly echoes of light disappeared. Jess slowly sank back onto the mattress, an expression of bewilderment spreading across her face as she looked around the empty room.

25

What a World

J ess rubbed her sore thigh as she pushed herself to a sitting position at the edge of the bed. She had not intended to fall asleep before dinner. After washing her face and changing into dry clothing, though, she had felt the accumulated weight of weeks of arduous travel roll over her like a heavy tide. And the bed had looked *so* inviting.

Jess had told herself that she would just steal a quick catnap. As soon as she had laid herself down on the bed, though, she had known she was lost. She luxuriated in its softness, a far cry from the cold hard ground that had been her mattress for the last several weeks. And as she lay there, smiling to herself in pleasure, the sound of Noxon Straw's fiddle had wafted up through the floorboards. The music had become a lullaby, and before she knew it she had fallen into a deep and dreamless slumber.

Until that strange sharp pain in her leg had jolted her awake, that is. Jess touched her thigh again, her fingers coming up dabbed with blood. Smoke and Ash, she thought blearily. Had a shard of glass or piece of sharp metal somehow become tangled in the threads of the quilt? She studied the top of the bed, passing her hand tentatively over its surface.

Then a great crashing sound from downstairs reached her ears, followed by angry shouting and the sound of breaking furniture. The clamor chased the last of the sleep-fog from her mind. Springing from the bed, Jess grabbed her crossbow and a couple of bolts, opened the door, and sprinted for the landing overlooking the tavern hall below.

Where she beheld a chaos of murderous struggle.

On the far side of the room, over by the great hearth, Noxon was desperately fending off Vyne, who was armed with a long pitchfork, its tongs crusted black with rust and dried dung. Noxon's sole means of defense was a small fireplace poker that he was brandishing like a sword. She watched in dismay as the sergeant barely parried a deadly lunge from his foe. Retreating steadily backwards, Noxon nearly lost his footing on the splintered remains of his shattered fiddle.

Closer to the stairs, amid the long dining tables, the larger of the servants—Tarantyn—was stalking the unarmed Max with a long, single-bladed axe. In some distant recess of her mind, Jess recognized that the axe was intended for splitting wood rather than war. But it still had the capacity to spill Max's brains, especially in the hands of the massive hireling.

As Tarantyn swung the axe in a great roundhouse motion, Max raised a chair to shield himself from the blow. The axe sank deep into the chair seat, nearly splitting it in two. Max pulled at the chair, trying to wrench the axe handle out of his attacker's grip. But the giant tugged back, heavily muscled shoulders bunching under his shirt, and as Max stumbled forward, Tarantyn directed a vicious kick squarely into his belly. Max collapsed at the feet of the servant, who began methodically working the axe blade loose from the chair.

Terror galloped through Jess' heart as she gazed down into the hall. Where were Tabytha, Traejon, and the others? And where was the innkeeper? Who was going to keep Noxon and Max from death at the hands of these suddenly berserk servants?

Jess looked down at the crossbow and bolts she held in her trembling hands. Fear clogging her throat, she frantically worked to fit one of the bolts in the bow's grooved tiller. Risking a glance below, her eyes alighted on Tarantyn, who had finally worked the axe blade loose. He tossed the remains of the chair to the side and looked down at the prostrate Max, a dark grin of pure bloodlust on his face.

Jess dropped the crossbow from her hand, sick with the knowledge that she'd never be able to load and cock it in time to save Max. She stepped forward and pulled herself to a standing position atop the bannister, bolts gripped like daggers in both of her sweat-soaked hands. Then, hardly believing that she was doing it, her heart thudding so hard she thought it would surely burst, she launched herself off the railing at the man below.

She landed on Tarantyn just as he was beginning a mighty overhead swing intended to split Max's head open. The bolt in her left hand fell harmlessly from her fingers as she crashed into the big man's upraised left arm. But the bolt in her right arm somehow found its mark, plunging into the meaty back of his shoulder like an ice pick.

Roaring with pain, Tarantyn twisted as he completed his swing. The blade of his axe buried itself in the floor no more than an inch from Max's face. Jess, meanwhile, was hurled from the giant's back. She spun in the air until she landed heavily against the side of one of the long oaken tables, her right arm cracking like a piece of kindling against a table leg. An incredible explosion of pain flared up her arm, and for a moment she thought she was going to black out.

"You bitch!" Tarantyn bellowed in disbelief, turning his neck to regard the shaft of the crossbow bolt jutting out of his shoulder. "Oh, you're going to pay for that, little girl," he snarled. He bashed Max in the side of the head with one heavy work boot, then strode around the long table toward Jess. He hefted the axe purposefully as he walked, like a logger calculating the number of cords contained in a tree standing before him. Jess scrabbled backward on her butt as the giant approached, her injured right arm cradled against her chest.

Tarantyn caressed the handle of his axe as he loomed over her. "You're a beauty, darling, that's plain to see. Even if you are wearing the clothing of a stable boy. Now ordinarily I'd help myself to your charms before sending you on your way to the Far Shore. But we must be off. So I'll just have to split you with this axe instead."

Tarantyn raised the axe over his head, his features rupturing into an expectant grin. Jess recognized that he assumed that she would beg or scream or shut her eyes tight against the coming blow. But instead she felt a strange sort of peace settle over her, calming her frenzied thoughts. She looked steadily into his eyes. If this was to be her end, so be it. She'd not spend her last moments of life with her head bowed to this man.

Tarantyn faltered in mid-swing when he saw the defiance blazing forth from her eyes. He looked at her blankly for a moment, as if uncertain how to proceed. Then uttering a low, angry oath, he regathered himself to deliver the killing blow.

At that instant Tabytha and Traejon burst through the front door, bows at the ready. Tarantyn pivoted to meet this new threat, only to have two arrows pound into the center of his chest simultaneously. The impact sent him staggering backwards, his knees nearly buckling. The giant's mouth worked soundlessly as he dropped the axe, his disbelieving gaze moving from the archers down to Jess. Then his eyes glazed over and his lifeless husk collapsed to the floor next to Jess.

Jess turned her attention back to Tabytha and Traejon just in time to watch the shadow seize the handle of one of the throwing knives strapped to his left side. Traejon sent the blade hurtling across the room in one smooth backhanded motion. The knife buried itself in the belly of Vyne, who dropped his pitchfork. A second knife sprouted in his stomach a second later, this one from the sheath strapped to Traejon's right forearm. Vyne doubled over in agony, then sagged against the bar counter. And with that a strange silence descended over the tavern hall, broken only by Vyne's low panting as he slid to the floor, ineffectually pawing at the handles of the blades lodged in his gut.

She was still alive. It seemed impossible, but somehow she was still alive. Jess rose to her feet with a grimace of pain and began making her way over to Tabytha, who had notched another arrow in her bow. As Jess shuffled forward she finally noticed the innkeeper's prone form behind the bar—and the pool of blood slowly expanding out from underneath him.

Well, that explains Gunn's absence during the fighting, Jess thought. Had he been slain by his own servants, or had he been a participant in the treacherous assault on Noxon and Max? And where were Gydeon and the other two scouts? Surely they couldn't have slept through all this racket. . . .

As Jess reached Tab's side, Traejon wordlessly brushed past them both. Taking the stairs three at a time, he disappeared down the upstairs hallway as Noxon walked over to Max, who was trying to regain his feet. Jess and Tabytha rushed over to help, and between the three of them they got the young scout off the floor.

Max still looked a little green from Tarantyn's kick in the stomach, and his right eye was swollen nearly shut. But on the whole, his injuries looked less severe than she had feared.

Noxon grinned and lightly patted Max's shoulder with one hand. "There you go, son. None the worse for wear, right?"

Max nodded, then winced in pain and brought his hand up to his battered face.

Noxon turned to Tabytha, who had walked over to the other side of the room to stand guard over Vyne. "What was *that* all about, Tab?" he called. "One minute I'm playing 'Blackbird's Lament' for Max here, the next you and Frost are killing our host. I assume it was you two, at any rate, based on the sudden uncongeniality of Gunn's servants. If you didn't like your rooms, you could have just said so."

Tabytha was silent for a moment. "Traejon will return shortly," she said finally, nodding in the direction of the stairs. "We'll talk about it then."

That seemed to satisfy Noxon, who turned back to Max. But Jess kept her eyes on Tabytha until she returned her gaze. Tabytha's expression was grim, and Jess felt a cold tendril of uneasiness coil around her heart. She looked to the top of the stairs, suddenly very anxious to see the faces of Gydeon, Borys, and Stefron.

Noxon, meanwhile, had begun strolling around the wreckage of the room. "Would have been a nice little tavern brawl were it not for the barnyard implements," he commented to no one in particular. "That wasn't very sporting at all."

Then he glanced sideways at Jess, an expression of amusement playing around his eyes. "You're a lucky fellow, Max. It's not every day that you get your life saved by a princess."

"Me?" Jess stammered. "It was Tab and Traejon-"

Noxon waved his hand dismissively. "Yes, they made a dramatic entrance with their bows and their throwing knives and such. All very impressive. But it was you who delayed that big lummox until they arrived." A big grin spread across Noxon's face. "I'll confess that I was pretty occupied, but I still saw you throw yourself off those stairs, Your Highness. Begging your pardon but you looked like a flying squirrel up there. A mad flying squirrel. With fangs," he added with a wink.

Jess felt warmth rising up in her cheeks. Somewhat unmanned by the jolt of pleasure she received from hearing the sergeant's praise, she nonetheless managed to roll her eyes. "It wouldn't have been necessary if I could load a crossbow in a timely fashion," she protested, then shrugged nonchalantly. "I guess I just didn't feel like taking the stairs to join the fun," she said, a smile of her own now playing around her mouth.

Noxon laughed appreciatively, but Max studied her with his one good eye. "Is that true?" he asked dazedly. He went back down on one knee and inclined his head. "Thank you, Your Highness. Truly, my life is pledged to you."

Jess looked down at the top of Max's head, embarrassed all over again. Back at Kylden Hall, she and her father had received pronouncements of fealty on a near-daily basis. But those declarations had a rote quality to them. Draped in ceremonial pieties, those pallid declarations did not stir her blood. They were just a familiar, vaguely pleasurable part of the daily fabric of her life, not unlike the way that the hairbrush felt when Gwyn pulled it through her hair every morning.

But this oath from Max, delivered on bended knee in a voice trembling with emotion? Given by a fellow member of this traveling party, which she had grown to like and respect and trust so much? This was an oath with some weight to it. It was like the difference between *hearing* stories about the majesty of the Marching Mountains and actually *feeling* the cool air in the shadows of its mountainsides and *seeing* its forested sides sway in response to the zephyrs swirling about its peaks.

"Thank you, Max," she said softly, touching his shoulder to bid him rise. "But I know you would do the same for me."

The youthful scout rose slowly, eyes shining. "Of that you should have no dou—" He stopped when he saw that her eyes had shifted past him, to the top of the stairs.

Where Traejon was leaning against the top of the bannister with both hands, his head hung low.

Max followed her gaze, then wordlessly raced upstairs, leaving the rest of them in a semi-circle standing around Vyne. They looked down on the servant in bleak silence as they listened to Max's footfalls pound down the hallway, then his muffled cry of anguish upon beholding the stone statue that had once been his brother.

Max's cry seemed to pull Traejon out of the stunned trance into which they had all fallen. He turned to Jess, Tab, and Noxon. "Gunn's familiar was a cockatrice," he said in a stricken voice. "It got the others before we could lay the wizard low."

Jess heard Tab gasp, and her own hands flew to her mouth—but not in time to stop the groan that escaped her lips. Gydeon, Borys, and Stefron? All dead? She stared at Traejon, as if he might somehow help her find her footing in this sudden hurricane of grief roaring across her mind.

But Traejon's attention was elsewhere now. He knelt down on one knee before Vyne, who had finally managed to pull the daggers out of his stomach. They lay there next to him, black hilts and gleaming blades smeared with viscous mementos from his insides. Traejon took the knives in one hand and began methodically cleaning them on the trousers of the fallen man, his eyes never leaving Vyne's face.

When he was done he tossed the blades up on the bar above Vyne's head. Then he smiled at the wounded man, though his green eyes shone hard and cold. "So. Where does Gunn keep it?"

Vyne's lips peeled back in an angry grin, revealing a mouthful of yellow and rotted teeth. "Where does Gunn keep what?" he snarled.

"The money and other assorted valuables from the travelers that you and your late master have murdered over the years," Traejon said. His voice was almost preternaturally serene, but Jess could feel the urge to commit violence radiating from him, like a corona of heat from a blacksmith's forge.

"You couldn't just leave it behind, could you?" Traejon continued. "Even when you saw that Gunn was dead. The thought of possibly losing all that plunder was too much for you. And it just never occurred to you or your similarly witless friend"—he nodded over at Tarantyn—"to vanish now and skulk back later to retrieve it."

"I don't know what you're going on about, mate," said Vyne through gritted teeth, shifting against the side of the bar as a fresh ripple of pain rolled over him. "I'm just a working fellow who earns an honest day's wages. If Gunn was up to more nefarious goings-on . . . well, I know nothing about such things."

Traejon nodded his head quietly for a moment, as if considering Vyne's words. Then his fist shot out in a blur, hammering into the center of Vyne's chest a few inches above his wounds. The workman's face collapsed in agony, his heels drumming against the floor.

Traejon's blow was so sudden that Jess jumped in surprise, and she heard Tab make a vague sound of protest. But Traejon did not appear to hear. He kept his eyes on Vyne until the man's thrashing subsided, then leaned in close. "You're a death beetle," he said levelly. "A parasite who feeds on the scraps tossed his way by his master. Nothing more."

Vyne stared at him for a moment, his sweat-slickened face betraying both the fear and hatred now coursing through his veins. Then he twisted his head to look up at Jess. "Are you really King Owyn's daughter?"

Jess looked down on him. She felt as if a magnifying glass had been inserted between herself and the wretch on the floor. Every pore, scratch, whisker, and bruise on his awful face seemed visible to her. "I am," she said, her voice sounding very far away.

Vyne swore, shaking his head slowly as he looked at his boots. Then he cranked his head up toward her again, his eyes gleaming with crude calculation. "You can heal me then? Spare me? If I tell you what I know of this place?"

Jess felt the gaze of the others turn to her. "I can," she said, shifting on her feet so that she could casually drop the angle at which she was holding her throbbing arm. Vyne had not yet taken heed of her injury—and the fact that she had not yet healed herself. She intended to keep it that way.

The hireling sighed heavily. "All right," he said, his eyes darting to Traejon and back. "Keep this foam-eater away from me and I'll tell you how it all worked. But I want your pledge that you'll use your castings to tend my wounds. And that I'll then be free to go. I never killed anyone. It was always Gunn."

She cast her gaze around the room a moment, waiting for someone else to speak. But no one said a word. "I pledge it," she said quietly, feeling all the while as if a part of her was floating away into the night.

And so Vyne told them about the cache under the kitchen floorboards. And of how Gunn's familiar would steal into the rooms of visitors and send them to the Far Shore entombed in stone. And of how he and Tarantyn would climb the stairs and peel the jewelry and clothing off their motionless forms, then break their heavy bodies into pieces and cart them out of the rooms and down the hallway and to the door that opened up over the ravine. And of how they would dump the shattered bodies of the men, women, and children into the rushing water below. And of how Gunn would caper and laugh afterwards, his fingers gleaming with rings plucked from the freshly murdered. And of how they sold the horses of Gunn's victims to Tarantyn's older brother, a stable owner who plied his trade in a small village fifteen miles to the west.

And when Jess thought he was finally done, Noxon asked Vyne how long Gunn and his cockatrice had maintained their inn of horrors. And Vyne said that he didn't really know. But that he had been a servant at the Penny Whystle for thirteen years.

Jess turned away then. What a world, she thought dismally. Is this my inheritance? This brutal, selfish world, peopled with men such as this? Is this the kingdom that my father will leave me?

Traejon stood up and walked around to the back of the bar. He pulled a bottle of whiskey off the shelf and leisurely poured it over the knives that he had used on Vyne, turning them over once twice thrice by the tips of their slender blades, like filets of trout over an open flame.

When Traejon was satisfied as to the daggers' cleanliness, he sheathed them and turned to Jess and the others. "Let's gather up our gear from upstairs and retrieve Max," he said, then gestured toward the kitchen door. "I'll find their cache. I doubt that it's all that well-hidden. Gunn thought that it would never end."

Jess fell in behind Noxon and Tabytha as they left the bar and began picking their way through the shambles of the hall to the stairs.

"Your Highness!" called Vyne from the floor, his hoarse voice laced with an undercurrent of panic. "Your pledge! You promised to heal me!"

Noxon and Tabytha continued up the stairs, but Jess turned at the base and looked back at Vyne. He was panting like a winded dog as he labored to stanch the continuing flow of blood into his lap.

"Sorry, *mate*," she said in a voice of dark triumph that she scarcely recognized. "Did I not tell you? I'm threadbare."

Then she turned on her heel and made her way up the stairs, Vyne's curses falling off her shoulders like blackened leaves from a poisoned tree.

26

Teeth or Meat?

Faxon Glynt stepped out of Whytewender's tent and let the folds of the heavy canvas drop down behind him. Adjusting the patch that masked his ruined right eye, he surveyed the vast army encampment before him. Campfires and lanterns burned away into the far distance, draping slivers of light on shadowy soldiers, horses, chariots, and tents. Interspersed among the tents and campfires, hulking catapults and ballistae towered over the camp like altars abandoned by some ancient brotherhood of giants.

Inhaling deeply of the night air's pungent blend of smoke, sweat, grease, and horseflesh, Glynt began strolling through the camp. The king had been in fine spirits tonight. Who could blame him? Already confident that Fyngree was staggering to its demise, Whytewender had taken delivery of a Tiding Horn from Kylden earlier that afternoon with momentous news: The Throneholder was on his deathbed.

True, the enchantment under which King Owyn had placed himself protected him from virtually all direct threats. But his familiar remained lost, and as Whytewender explained it to him, Suntold's spell of oblivion was merely delaying his demise. The sands passing through the throat of the hourglass of his mortality may have slowed, but they had not halted altogether. Those grains were still slipping away, and one day soon Suntold's withered, papery heart would fall silent at last.

And in the meantime? Well, Owyn Suntold could not stem the coming tide of death and devastation from his bed-chambers. And even Glynt had come to believe that the generals and soldiers and casters gathered here under the oxblood and black banners of Rojenhold were ready. They were poised to sweep forward like the finest theatrical troupe, confidently striding across the stage to hit their marks and deliver their lines with voices cruel and strong. And when they were done, their audience—the people of Fyngree—would cry out and bow their heads in miserable acknowledgement of the masterful performance they had witnessed.

Glynt snorted to himself. His escalating anticipation of the coming battle was a strange sensation for him. By instinct he was an unbeliever and pessimist, perpetually braced for disappointment. He had come by that stance honestly, for he had spent most of his life locked behind bars of scuttled ambition and unrequited coveting. For more wealth. More women. More power. Especially more power.

Granted, there had been moments of pleasure and triumph over the years. The satisfaction that accompanied a well-executed robbery or swindle. Half-remembered nights of debauchery fueled by blood-dappled coins. The way his blood always sang when he looked down on eyes shining with terror—or freshly glazed over in death.

But those moments had always been so fleeting. They failed to compensate for the long days, months, and years of grinding struggle. Petty thefts and robberies that barely covered the cost of a flagon of ale and a lice-infested boardinghouse room. Alliances with fellow thieves and murderers of truly breathtaking stupidity. Months of frantic flight from Fyngree's constables, wardens, and soldiers through desolate lands and horrid weather. And a ruined eye, memento of his long years as a highwayman, that made even the leather-thighed whores of Talonoux shudder and turn away.

All of those humiliations had taken their toll so much that Glynt had even begun doubting himself. Perhaps he was not just unlucky. Was he truly teeth, as he had always told himself? Or was he meat, like all the other grasping fools and cowards around him?

And then everything had changed.

Glynt's deliverance had come seven years ago, when he had been forced to forsake the land of his birth for Rojenhold. At that point he had been in Fyngree's army for several years, living under an assumed name. He had joined the military reluctantly, desperate to evade the growing number of bounty hunters and constables on his trail. But he had thrived there, for even in the Throneholder's army he had found pockets of greed and avarice that provided fertile ground for graft.

Moving up through the ranks on the strength of well-crafted lies and the blackmail of a superior officer with both a wife and a wandering eye, he had even managed to devise a profitable scheme to part veterans from their pensions. But the operation had run aground after some crusading pamphleteer down in Kylden revealed it to the world. Glynt had barely escaped the soldiers sent to put him in manacles. They chased him all the way into the Speartips, where he nearly died before finally emerging on the other side, in the realm of King Whytewender.

Glynt had feared that he would be apprehended and executed as a spy. Stormheel took a notoriously dim view of footloose men who roamed its lands without their papers in order. But he managed to secure forged documents with the last of the stolen pension funds, and in a matter of weeks he had burrowed deep into the anonymous ranks of the Rojenholdean military.

And then the most unexpected thing happened. In Whytewender's dark and glittering kingdom, Glynt finally found a place—and a monarch—who recognized the value of his particular gifts. Whytewender had sifted through the dross of humanity gurgling around his feet and seen the hard steel of Glynt's soul. He had bent down and picked Glynt up and washed the filth off until he gleamed like a fresh-polished sword. And then he had set him loose to help cleave the world into the shape that the king desired.

It was not exactly gratitude that Glynt felt toward Whytewender. He recognized that the king would cast him back into the shadows if his usefulness ever faded. Nonetheless, Whytewender had provided him with a home in the Faithful Shield and set him loose to indulge appetites that he had never previously been able to fully slake. And to gorge on some that he had never even known existed. Glynt would never forget that.

And Glynt respected Whytewender's deft hand as a ruler. The king kept his boot so firmly on the throat of his people that they remained completely docile and *exquisitely* pliable. Yet he never cut off the air to their windpipes to the point that they became incapable of carrying out his wishes. Truly he possessed a rare talent.

He was teeth, through and through.

As Glynt wound his way past the tents and campfires, he glanced to the north. Teryk's big black carriage sat at the far edge of the encampment, surrounded by a dozen or so members of the Faithful Shield. To Glynt the cavernous carriage resembled some otherworldly creature squatting in the night. The lantern glow from its pulled-down shades reminded him of Teryk's own alien eyes, and the carriage's body of dark wood and iron gleamed like the scales of some great lizard. Even the twisting gryphons frozen along its flanks curled like swollen veins along its musculature.

Getting the prince to the border had been an arduous affair. The problem had not been with Teryk—to the contrary, the boy had been eager to leave Stormheel. Every horse that they attempted to harness to Teryk's carriage, however, went frothing mad with fear.

Whytewender had finally devised a complex spell to place on the harnesses of a team of horses. The enchantment calmed the horses and enabled them to carry out their appointed task. But by the end of the journey the horses were falling apart. Rearing, kicking, and snapping at the air incessantly, they behaved as if phantoms were perpetually pinching and stabbing at their sides. Glynt had watched the horses' escalating frenzy with great interest. It was clear that continued exposure to Teryk had gradually overwhelmed even his father's spell. Unable to sleep, eat, or even drink, they had finally been put down on Whytewender's orders.

Leaving Teryk's carriage behind, Glynt made his way to one of the gargantuan tents that dotted the sprawling camp. Stretched into taut, swooping shapes by dozens of poles and guy lines, the tents were merely ugly during the day. But at night, when lantern and campfire light turned their wind-rippled sides into shifting mosaics of light and shadow, they took on a more mysterious and forbidding aspect.

Glynt stepped inside and let the tumult of sights and sounds wash over him. From one end of the tent to the other, veteran soldiers were drilling freshly conscripted recruits on the basics of military movements and hand-to-hand combat. Glynt could see the weariness etched on the sweating faces of the conscripts—and on some of them, utter exhaustion.

It *was* stifling in the tent. Its canvas skin trapped the heat generated by all these laboring bodies, and guards lined the walls every few feet to make certain that no flaps were turned up to let in even the smallest breath of cool night air. The risk that some Fyngrean familiar might fly through camp and catch a glimpse of the preparations within was simply too great. So with every tent flap battened down tight, the air inside was a fetid stew of sweat, stale breath, and churned-up grass and mud.

But it was not just the heat that was bowing the backs of the men and women before him. Beneath their mail and helmets, Glynt could see that few of them were of prime fighting age. A far greater number either carried gray in their thinning hair or stumbled about on the coltish legs of teens.

Glynt moved slowly around the perimeter of the great tent. At one point he paused to watch two weary recruits drag the limp body of a third recruit off to the side of their cramped square of training ground. They dropped the body at the feet of a waiting sergeant, who promptly began thudding heavy kicks into the fallen recruit to make sure that she was not feigning unconsciousness. Glynt moved on after a moment, only to stop again at a sight in the middle distance--an unconscious older man who had been crucified on one of the tent's tall central poles. Stripped of mail and clothing, the man had been nailed several feet off the ground so that his head and upper torso were visible above the churning, clanking mass of humanity swaying at his feet. He bobbed there like a buoy in rough seas, stripes of blood running down his arms and face. Wonder what *that* fellow did, Glynt thought idly.

He had nearly completed his circuit of the tent when he saw a boy, sweating and panting as he hacked with a wooden sword at another boy of similar size. Had the boy's hair been a little shorter and his nose a little less prominent, he could have passed for Ben Thystle.

Glynt felt his jubilant mood darken. In the grand scheme of things Thystle was just a callow boy, with casting abilities that were years away from full maturity. But it rankled to have so underestimated Thystle's mother—who almost surely was responsible for the boy's mysterious disappearance—and to know that their defiance had thus far gone unpunished. Torturing and killing the boy's father had served as a modest salve on his burning fury. But that had only dampened the worst of the sting; he could still feel the dull throb of the abscess beneath.

No matter. Ben and his mother would eventually be found. If they were still in Rojenhold, they would be discovered within a matter of days—either by the Faithful Shield or by the retinue of casters that Whytewender had spared from Teryk's hunger. Their winged, furred, and clawed familiars were stalking the skies, forests, and streets of Rojenhold with single-minded purpose, their wild senses alert for any sign of the Thystles.

And if Malkyn Thystle and her sons had somehow slipped into Fyngree? Well, Whytewender would hold sway over those lands soon enough. And when he did, Glynt would not rest until Ben Thystle and his mother lay broken and bloody at his feet—and that big cat was laid out on Teryk's feasting table.

He worked his way back to the tent entrance and drifted out again into the night. Angling south now, away from the cramped core of the camp and through its outer circles, his ears filled with the distant roar and boom of the sea. The ramparts of the rocky coastline that girded Rojenhold's eastern flank were no more than a few hundred yards distant. But although those cliffs offered a spectacular view of the moonlight-dappled Uncrossable Sea, he continued walking south until he stood at the edge of another cliff.

Glynt gazed across the great black emptiness of the gorge to the other side, where the campfires of the gathered Fyngrean forces flickered like fallen stars.

He was standing at the edge of Twenty Night Canyon—so named because according to legend, one could fall from its edge for twenty days and twenty nights without hitting bottom. Two miles long, a half-mile deep, and more than twice that distance wide for much of its length, this black gash in the earth's flesh demarcated the lands of Rojenhold and Fyngree along the easternmost edge of the continent. Only two pathways existed to circumvent the gorge, and neither were conducive to invasion.

Two miles inland from the coast lay the Pauper's Way, a narrow, boulder-strewn strip of gristly, wheel-busting land that ran between the eastern walls of the Speartips and the scree-covered western beginnings of the gorge. Both kingdoms maintained small posts at their respective ends of the Way, but Glynt knew that assignments to either gatehouse were regarded as death knells for the careers of officers so stationed. The plum assignments were two miles to the west, at the edge of the Uncrossable Sea. For there stood the Span, the most spectacular relic of the bygone Age of Elves in all of Tempyst.

Glynt studied the bridge, following its great gleaming arc from the stone gatehouse at Rojenhold's side across the wide gorge to its terminus on Fyngrean land, at a gatehouse of even more imposing stature. Wide enough to fit two dozen wagons side-by-side, the Span was still imbued with ancient elvish magic after all these years. The bridge gave off a faint lime-green glow in the darkness, like a comet's tail frozen into stone by some dark cockatrice peering down from the heavens.

Although a trickle of black market trade seeped through the Speartips from time to time, the Span had been the sole artery of *official* commerce between the two kingdoms for generations. For better than three hundred years, in fact. Ever since the legendary Tucker Suntold had chased the last battered remnants of Rojenhold's invading army out of Fyngree and across the bridge like a fire-wielding shepherd harrying a hungry bear back into its den.

Until a few short weeks ago the Span had crawled with wagons and riders and carriages, most of them hauling the Loaf's bounty to the hungry villages and cities of Rojenhold. But now the Span stood empty of travelers, its deserted expanse home to naught but shining moonlight and ghostly shimmers of sea spray.

Owyn Suntold and his high sentinels preferred to frame the Span as an instrument of mutually beneficial commerce between kingdoms, at least in their public pronouncements. Carefully avoiding allusions to its past and present military significance, they called it the Green Road in diplomatic missives with Rojenhold. But in Stormheel and Strovenstaff, Whytewender's pamphleteers called it the Jailer's Key.

Glynt's impression was that until recently, the people of Rojenhold had actually paid little heed to those broadsides. They were careful not to give public voice to their views, but most of them saw Whytewender's bitter condemnations of the Jailer's Key as nothing more than impotent grousing from a frustrated tyrant.

But in the last few weeks, as food supplies in the streets and barracks of Rojenhold had steadily dwindled, that black characterization of the Span as an instrument of repression had taken root in the hearts of a growing number of Whytewender's subjects. After all, winter was fast approaching, their pantries were growing bare, and wagons loaded with the Loaf's bounty remained parked on the Fyngrean side of the gorge. They might as well have been at the bottom of the sea.

Glynt smirked. It was astounding how quickly the prospect of starvation could change attitudes. Now the people of Rojenhold were rattling the bars as well, their hands sweaty with fear and anger. Their growing anxiety had even eased acceptance of Whytewender's conscription orders. To be sure, there had been pockets of sullen resentment against the order. Even a few suicidal acts of defiance. But for the most part, the bewildered and fearful citizenry swallowed the explanations offered by Whytewender and his minions.

They said that conscription was a necessary response to Fyngree's provocations.

They said that the real enemy was Owyn Suntold, who had embarked on a cruel campaign of starvation against Rojenhold for offenses that were solely the product of a feverish, deteriorating mind.

They said that the time to finally end Fyngree's miserly grip on the natural riches of the continent was nigh.

And the people of Rojenhold believed these words. Or at least they convinced themselves that they believed them. Because the alternative was to admit that they were willing to stand passively by as their sons and daughters were sacrificed to a war that was being orchestrated to satisfy their king's appetite for empire. And who wanted to believe that of themselves?

Glynt turned away from the canyon's edge and made his way back into the thick of the camp. Winding his way to his own tent, he could feel the low buzz of nervous energy wafting off the soldiers around him. He savored the sensation, which was thrumming through his own bones as well. There was nothing quite like the feel of a military encampment preparing for battle.

Glynt entered his tent and made his way to his cot, laying his sword on a low table. He turned the lantern wick down low and laid himself down with a heavy sigh. But though he knew he should get some sleep, his one good eye kept staring up into the darkness.

The years of preparation and rehearsal were almost at an end. Everyone had memorized their lines and cues. In six days, when the Gryphon's Eye finally rose into the heavens, it would all begin. Opening night. And they were going to bring down the house.

27

Clay in the Kiln

After Vyne revealed the Penny Whystle's blood-soaked history, Traejon and Max tied him to one of the tavern hall's thick oaken tables while Tabytha bandaged Jess's broken arm and Noxon's pierced side. Tabytha then joined the men in wrestling the heavy stone corpses of Gydeon, Borys, and Stefron down the stairs and out the inn's front door. Grunting and sweating, they buried them at the edge of the forest by lantern light, using shovels and spades retrieved from the stable.

Tabytha felt a kind of numb, distant relief that the interment of their friends went quickly. The ground was soft from the previous days' rain, and there was no need to carve out the graves to their customary depth. Wild animals would not be digging up these remains. But the task had been a heartbreaking one. Max had withdrawn into hollow-eyed silence, and they all found it difficult to bury their companions with those horrified, disbelieving expressions forever etched on their faces.

When the burials were complete, they hauled three chests of treasure out from beneath the kitchen floorboards. No one quite knew what to do with it all. Just leaving it was out of the question. But burying it all deep in the forest seemed a poor and even disrespectful alternative. The lockets and circlets and rings and necklaces and silver snuffboxes they found in the boxes had once been gifts between loved ones, tokens of affection and accomplishment, heirlooms of family history and pride. They deserved deliverance from the blood-soaked place into which they had fallen.

Finally, Tabytha suggested that they pack the treasure up and distribute it among worthy orphanages and almshouses in the surrounding territory. The ravenous Gunn and his bloodthirsty help had destroyed countless families over the years. At the very least, they could see to it that the riches of their victims went to easing the lives of the parentless and the impoverished.

The wisdom of her suggestion had been evident to them all. They quickly distributed the spoils among the horses, including three sturdy mounts in the stable that belonged to Gunn and his men—horses that had almost certainly once been the property of previous visitors to the Penny Whystle.

After the horses were packed, Traejon left them by the massive oak at the inn's approach and disappeared into the Penny Whystle once more. A moment later he reappeared, dragging Vyne out of the building by his hair. He dumped the moaning, bleeding man in the dirt at the base of the front step, then vanished inside again. A moment later Tabytha and the others heard the crash of breaking lanterns, and the light blazing forth from the inn's windows assumed a brighter intensity.

Traejon's silhouette appeared in the doorway, another lantern swinging by his side. He made his way down the steps, crossed over the yard to the open doors of the stable, and hurled the lantern inside, where Tabytha heard it shatter against a wall or beam. Seconds later, she saw flames race across the straw-strewn floor. He's burning it all down, Tab realized. Every floorboard and table and stall. She tried to muster up some grim satisfaction at the prospect of seeing the inn and stable incinerated before her eyes. But she found her heart to be so swollen with sorrow that it had no room for anything else.

So she felt nothing as she watched the flames consume the two buildings. The stable collapsed first. Fed by bed after bed of dry straw, it blossomed into a brilliant orange-yellow torch within a matter of minutes. The inferno basted Tabytha and her companions in a fierce, bleak light that sent their shadows shooting behind them like long ribbons of night.

The inn's death was more drawn out. It grunted and roared in the night, like a live thing seeking to smother the fire in its gut from sheer force of will. But finally its round windows exploded one by one by one from the heat trapped within, releasing great ropes of gray and black smoke that churned up into the night as if drawn upward by unseen hands. The fire drank up the night air rushing in through the broken windows, and moments later flames punched through the collapsing slate roof.

They departed then, ignoring the steady stream of pleas—then curses—that came from Vyne's crumpled form. They had spared him from outright execution. But between the deep, organ-puncturing wounds in his gut, their unspoken agreement to not leave him a horse or weapon, and the fact that the only sources of food and shelter for miles around were burning to the ground before their eyes, Tabytha guessed that the man would not live to see another sunset.

She was not gladdened by that knowledge. It was no small thing to leave a man—even a wretch such as Vyne—to bleed out alone in the wilderness. But as they made their way down the moonwashed road and Vyne's cries grew fainter behind them, she found that she was not assailed by doubt about the fate to which they had consigned him. She remained numb to it all.

The awful, endless night dragged on. They pushed westward down the lonely road, the clop of hooves echoing into the dark wood surrounding them. Tabytha felt exhaustion fall over her like a heavy veil, and she knew the others felt the same. But Traejon wouldn't let them stop. Not until they reached the village where Tarantyn's brother kept his stable.

About an hour before sunrise, they came across a wide, hardpacked trail branching off the main road. They peered down the rough road, which descended into a small valley clogged with small buildings and corrals. A few lantern lights trembled here and there as shopkeepers and craftsmen went about early-morning tasks.

"Wait here," Traejon said. "I won't be long."

Tabytha and the others watched him silently as he disappeared down the village road. Tab glanced over at Jess, wondering if she might try to stop him. But the princess just turned away and stared vacantly into the surrounding woods. So they dismounted and let the horses graze, looking past each other with haunted eyes. They stroked the necks of the horses and refilled their water skins from a nearby stream and watched the night shapes gradually give way to gray, fog-shrouded forest.

About two hours after he had steered his mount down into the dark vale, Traejon reappeared on the main road. A curtain of low fog swirled around his form in the early morning light, the mist obscuring his horse's cannons and fetlocks so that it appeared as if they were fording a shallow, frothing river. The shadow rode above the heavy brume, however, and Tabytha could see his face clearly as he drew close. Though his features were carefully composed, his sea-green eyes gleamed as if a storm raged behind them. "It's done," he said curtly, to everyone and no one. Then he dismounted, set his horse to graze with the others, and turned in Tab's direction.

As he walked over to join her, however, Tabytha realized with a sickening rush of clarity that she did not wish to be in his company. When the shadow had reappeared, she had told herself that Tarantyn's brother fully deserved the sentence that Traejon had imposed and carried out. But she was not at all sure she believed that. And every time she thought of his interrogation of Vyne—of how he had struck the helpless man—she felt a fresh shiver of misery shoot through her insides.

In the weeks since she had first met him up in the Whetstone Highlands, Tabytha's attraction to Traejon had grown at a speed that she had found dizzying, even disorienting—but she had savored every moment of it nonetheless. His considerable physical attributes aside, she liked the steady manner with which he carried himself and led their party. He was decisive without being autocratic, and was careful to treat Jess as the group's nominal leader even though everyone looked to him for everything from campsite selection to the nightwatch schedule. He was amusing too, in a droll sort of fashion, and conversant on a wide range of subjects, from fine works of literature to canoe design.

And the glint of hunger in Traejon's eyes when they settled on her never failed to set her heart to racing. The mutual desire between them had become an exquisite, steadily escalating blend of pleasure and frustration these past weeks. A dance with an ever-spiraling tempo that left her short of breath and unable to do more than pick at her food. And for Tabytha at least, her yearning for Traejon's touch had become an almost physical ache. As if her mind and heart and loins harbored some caged beast that was pacing back and forth, desperate to be free.

But here on this fog-shrouded roadway, Traejon no longer felt like a man she wanted to laugh with or lie with or begin a family with—the latter a possibility, however dim, that she had begun to secretly ponder during these last days and nights. The man standing next to her now had donned the mask of some dark avenging angel, alien and unreachable. The idea of building a life with Traejon suddenly seemed as strange and foolish as announcing one's betrothal to the stars or the thunder or the river.

With a sting of self-reproach, she realized now that in many respects, Traejon was as much of a mystery to her now as he had been the first night they met. Traejon's striking appearance suggested a measure of Koah blood somewhere in his ancestry, but she still knew nothing of his family, and next to nothing about the life preceding his current employment as shadow to the Throneholder.

And where had he learned to fight as he did? It was true that Tabytha had never set foot in Kylden, Treffentown, Consadus, or any of Fyngree's other western cities. Nonetheless, she had grown up in a military family. She had attended archery competitions as a child and excelled in them as a young woman, holding her own against bowmen from all around Tydewater and even as far as Talonoux. But she had never seen anyone as talented with a bow as Traejon. And his bladework, whether with sword or dagger, was just as astonishing.

If Tab was honest with herself, she would have to admit that his capabilities in combat had been reassuring at first. She took pride in her bow and riding skills, but she knew in her heart that she felt safer in his presence. But no longer. Now his almost supernatural dexterity with blade and bow carried a disquieting undercurrent.

Perhaps she would not feel that way if it were not for the fact that his powers of sight were, if anything, even more disconcerting than his prowess as a fighter. She had known from the very first night she met Traejon that his eyesight was exceptionally keen. But she could no longer deceive herself about the extent of his abilities in that realm.

Traejon could see in the dark.

Even among people gifted with the Thread, night sight was said to be a rare thing. But Traejon had it. She could feel the truth of that in her bones.

So was Traejon a secret caster then? A man both mask and shadow, engaged in his own inscrutable game for his own unknowable purposes? Or some manner of assassin trained in the bloody arts of war? And if none of those . . . what then?

Tabytha blinked away a sudden urge to cry. She no longer felt like a young woman falling in love. She felt like someone who had been on the verge of diving into a clear blue lake, only to realize at the last moment that heavy clouds had scoured the shimmer off the water. And that she could see nothing beneath the gray of the once-beckoning surface.

". . . do we do now?"

Tabytha emerged from her unhappy reverie, dimly aware that the silence among them had finally broken.

"What do you mean?" asked Jessalyn, her eyes locked on Noxon.

He cleared his throat. "I mean that without Gydeon's familiar, we have lost our guide. None of us knows where we are going, or how to get there."

"What are you suggesting, sergeant?" Jess said. "That we give up? Retreat? With the future of Fyngree still hanging in the balance?"

Noxon reddened. "I'm not counseling any such thing. But blundering around in these woods and mountains without any clear destination will not aid your father. I'm as fond of relying on good fortune as the next man, but if we don't know where to look for this Bryscoe Rygaard fella or that mysterious girl of whom Gydeon spoke, we may never find them. If they are even still in there."

"Noxon has a point, Jess," said Traejon. His voice was mild again, familiar. But to Tabytha it sounded strangely off-pitch. Like a good impersonation of a voice that she had once known and welcomed.

"We're less than a week south of Valyedon at the moment," Traejon continued. "High Sentinel Tusk and her brother will surely have news of the state of affairs with Rojenhold. As well as of your father's recent actions. Perhaps King Owyn is on his way to Tucker's Front himself. When it comes to events taking place in the wider world, we've been traveling blind for several days now."

"Or perhaps your father has discovered the identity of Whytewender's agent, the one behind this caster killing spree about which you've told us." Noxon surveyed the surrounding forest, squinting against the sun as it rose over the tree line. "I've heard tell that Thrynjack Brymborne lives here on the edge of the Speartips. Old Mad Jack himself, scrawny as a half-starved coyote but a good deal more dangerous. Spends his nights traipsing around the forest half-naked, eating sparrows and frogs and cackling at the moon. We don't necessarily want to blunder around blindly until we run into him or whatever dark familiar he commands."

Jess stood silently for a moment, her gaze moving back and forth between the two men towering before her. "No," she said, and Tabytha could hear the iron in the princess's voice. "We're not going to Valyedon." Jess gestured down the road before them. "We are nearly to the eastern outskirts of the Matchstycks now. And I'm convinced that we need to reach this Lylah and the casters that have flocked to her if we're to understand what manner of threat we face."

She turned to Traejon. "You already made arrangements with Splyntbell for the Tusks to send a company to meet us at Rucker's Mill. Surely that company will have news of any recent developments regarding my father or the borderlands."

"That's true," he acknowledged. "But we still don't know where to look for this Lylah, or for Gydeon's friend, and the Matchstyck Valley is large. Even with the assistance of whoever the Tusks send along, that's a lot of land to cover. Assuming they even want to be found. If they don't . . . well, even a group of minor casters could cobble together a fairly strong web of spells to prevent us from detecting their presence."

"It won't come to that," said Tabytha, speaking for the first time. She looked over at Jess. "And Jess knows it."

Tabytha turned to Traejon. "You'd have already thought of this, Traejon, if you weren't so blinded by your executioner's hood." Traejon's eyes widened in surprise at the jab, then narrowed in displeasure. A cold shiver of unhappiness blew through her at the sight, but she forced herself to continue.

"We've been assuming that we need to find people who do not want to be found," she said. "But that's not true, is it, Jess? At least when they are confident that the people seeking them are not intent on slitting their throats or absconding with their familiars."

Jess nodded. "That's right. Our quest is just and our motives are pure, and we have carried ourselves accordingly throughout our travels."

"All true," said Tabytha. She locked eyes with Traejon. "Do you really believe that Bryscoe Rygaard and these casters we are pursuing are unaware of our motives—or our progress—at this point? With all of the familiars that they have at their disposal to track us? They've probably been watching us for several days now, sending familiars out in shifts to keep an eye on us."

Traejon and Noxon stood silently, assessing her words. Even Max seemed to have emerged from his fog of grief to consider them.

"I'm not sure about that," Noxon said. "If one of their familiars saw us enter the Penny Whystle, why wouldn't it sound some sort of alarm on our behalf?"

"Because they wouldn't be any more aware of Gunn's true nature than we were," Jess said. "From all appearances it was nothing more than a well-maintained inn on a seldom-traveled roadway. No, we're going to forge on. We will enter the Matchstycks. Because Tab's right. We don't need to worry about finding them. They're going to find us."

†††

Tabytha watched as Traejon approached her guard post at the edge of a line of towering pines, a cup cradled in his gloved hands.

"Some tea?" he asked quietly. "To help keep the chill off."

Tabytha hesitated, then nodded. "Thank you," she said curtly, reaching up from her seated position to take the steaming cup from his hand.

She took a slow sip, her gaze passing over their sleeping travel companions arrayed around the campfire. She felt Traejon standing silently beside her and knew he was waiting for an invitation to take a seat beside her. But the prospect of conversation with him was exhausting. They had ridden all day, stopping only shortly before dusk, when the Matchstycks had appeared on the horizon. Now, nearly two days since she had last slept, all she wanted to do was finish her guard shift, crawl under her cloak, and escape into a deep and dreamless sleep.

"May I join you, Tab?" he asked finally. "For a moment? Then I'll leave you to it."

Tabytha smothered a sigh. Well at least she was too tired to cry. "If you wish," she said tonelessly.

Traejon sat down beside her and laid his forearms over drawn-up knees. They quietly watched the fire for a few minutes, Tab's mind roiling at his closeness. Even now, after everything had gone dark and sour in her heart, Tabytha could still feel the pull of the man. She swallowed hard.

"I know not how it is that I can see so well in the dark," Traejon said abruptly, without any preamble. "It's an utter mystery to me. When I first realized that other people— my parents, my brother—were unable to see in the dark, I was stunned." He mustered a wan smile. "How could anyone live like that, I wondered, always bumping into furniture and stubbing their toes in the night?"

Tabytha set the cup down by her side, her eyes studying the fire as she considered his words. She remained sad and angry and wary. But she also recognized an olive branch when she saw one.

"So you possessed the ability even as a young child?" she said after a long moment.

"As far back as I can remember. It has nothing to do with being Threaded or cursed—I don't think. Sometimes I wonder if I just . . . I don't know . . . put a piece of magic in my mouth when I was an infant or something. You know as well as I do that strands of magic poke out of this land in the oddest places."

"That's true enough," Tabytha said neutrally.

"I know. It's not much of an explanation. But I've seen strange things in my travels over this world, Tab. Things that I can't account for as the handiwork of any witch or wizard. A lone horse that I swear was made entirely of fire galloping silently across a darkling plain at midnight. A human skull the size of a small shed half-buried in one of the dunes of the Crimson Desert. A long-forgotten well deep in the Gilded Hills that smelled of saltwater and echoed with the sounds of the ocean. So I don't know. Nightsight has just always been part of who I am."

"And your parents knew?"

"My mother knew of my ability early on. But she never spoke of it. She taught me to treat it as a secret, something to be hidden away. Hidden away from the other islanders. But hidden from father, too. I never really understood that. But he suspected, I think."

Tabytha brushed a stray lock away from her face. "Tell me more," she said, a hint of challenge in her tone. "About your family."

Traejon smiled faintly. "My mother was a seamstress for a sailmaker. She taught me and my brother to read and write by candlelight, after her work was done each day. She would hover over us late into the night, murmuring encouragement. Like a mourning dove. Her voice was soft like that.

I don't know when she slept. But she was pretty and kind. And she kept a clean house. I remember that."

"And your father?"

Traejon turned his face back to the campfire and sighed in the manner of a man preparing to take up a heavy burden. "My father was a cooper by trade. He kept a small shop on Ram Island, where we lived. One of the Tomorrows' inner islands. But he only brought in a modest income from that. He was a fine cooper when he felt like being one. He just didn't feel like being one very often."

"How did your mother end up with him?"

"I don't know, really. He was a mainlander, but I'm sure he didn't come to the Tomorrows out of some abiding affection for the Koah. He often fumed about being surrounded by foam-eaters, even after taking a Koah bride and bringing two half-Koah sons into the world. He liked to tell us that the blood we got from him was our only hope. The only thing capable of lifting us out of the world of net fishing and pearl diving that surrounded us. How did he end up all the way out there? I suppose he washed up there during one of his periodic flights from the law."

"What—"

"I'll get to that. As far as how my mother and father came together, I never heard any details. But I imagine it was the same old story that's played out a million times before. Maiden meets a man who seems to be one thing. She falls in love. And he turns out to be another thing entirely." He turned to her then, searching her face until their eyes met, and Tabytha could tell that he did not want her to look away.

"People say follow your heart," Traejon said. "But that's not always sound counsel, is it? Because sometimes your heart loses its way. One day the road it's on is wide and finely graded and promises passage through warm and fertile lands. And the next you wake up and find that the cobblestones are broken. And thorns and nettles are crowding the path. And the warm breeze that once caressed your face is now a cold, cutting wind that leaves your eyes red and watering. But you look behind you and the forest has closed in and you don't have the faintest idea of how to get back to that sun-soaked road. I think that's what happened to her."

He sees the doubts that have wormed into my thoughts, Tab realized with a start. Her fears that the man that she'd been falling in love with was an illusion. Or worse, a trap. Yet he was not ridiculing the notion, or denouncing her. No, he was acknowledging it as a creature of real power—and one given life by his own actions. And in that moment of understanding, Tab felt the rickety barriers of indifference that she had so recently erected around her heart begin to weaken.

Yet all she said was, "It must have been very hard for her."

"For a while. And then it wasn't. She vanished when I was eight years old. I woke up one morning and she was gone."

"Gone?"

"Just . . . gone. Father said she abandoned us, ran off to Talonoux or Tydewater in search of a better life. Then he forbade my brother and me from ever speaking of her again. But as I grew older I heard rumors of other possibilities. That my mother had taken a lover, a mariner from one of the ships that regularly stopped in the islands. And that it was this mysterious sailor who convinced her to leave the Tomorrows. Others said that my father discovered their trysts, murdered them both, weighted their bodies with stones, and sank them in the sea. And others accepted his rendition of events. Given what they knew about his temper and his indifference to honest work, it wasn't absurd to think that she might have just run off. Though people who knew my mother best said she never would have left without her sons."

"What did you and your brother think?"

Traejon ran his hand through his hair. "We didn't have too much time to think about it either way. The bottom line was, she was no longer there. And my father kept us pretty busy after she disappeared."

"Thunder and Thorn," Tab said softly. She tried to imagine waking up as a youngster and having your mother suddenly erased from your life—and to have neighbors whisper that your own father had sent her to a watery grave. "It must have been terrible, to lose your mother so."

"It wasn't easy. Because that left us alone with a man whose true passions were robbery and smuggling and stealing. Really, anything that involved preying on other people. That's what got his blood going. Not making casks and barrels."

Traejon shifted in his seat. "Father always used to ask my brother and me: Are you teeth or meat? Are you predator or prey? To him, you could separate everyone into those two categories.

"Well, he sure as hell saw himself as teeth. And after our mother disappeared, he had free rein to make sure that we were teeth, too. And the sharper the better. So the books went in the fire and the knives and lockpicking tools came out. We became bandits and smugglers in training. Assets to someday replace the loose assortment of cretins and backstabbers that our father had always been forced to rely on for his schemes. And so he drilled us in the arts of fighting and thievery, drawing upon his early years in the Fyngrean army as well as lessons learned from his years as a criminal. Hour after hour, day after day."

Tab swallowed hard. What a nightmare. "Oh Traejon. I'm so sorry. I had no idea."

"How could you?" Traejon managed a wintry half-smile. "I haven't been very forthcoming about my past. I know that."

"People have all sorts of reasons to keep silent about their histories. Legitimate reasons. It needn't be seen as a black mark against them."

"No. But a darkness has fallen between us. And it seems to me that some light is called for." Traejon nodded slightly to himself. "So. By the time I was twelve he was hauling us all across Fyngree for one score or another. He even took us down into the Black Marsh, where he bartered with goblins for bloodweed, balestone, and other poisonous plants to sell on the black market. That's when I first learned to recognize goblin sign. We were like pieces of clay in some unholy kiln, Tab. But when *we* came out of the fire, we were all jagged barbs and sharp edges."

Traejon grabbed a stick off the ground next to him and began breaking pieces off and tossing them into the fire. "And my edges were razor-sharp, Tab. He recognized early on that I had a certain . . . facility with weapons, and that I was faster and stronger than my brother Faxon, even though he was five years older. Father began to belittle Faxon's abilities, using my skills like a whip across his back. He would make us fight, then mock Faxon when I beat him. Said he'd never be anything but a foam-eater, and that at least with me, he'd managed to thin the Koah blood that ran in my veins. Once in a while I tried to throw a match, but he could always tell. He'd beat us both when I did that. Father intended the humiliations as a spur in Faxon's side. A tool for goading him to higher performance. But there was cruelty there, too. He'd spend entire days addressing Faxon as 'meat.' He liked watching my brother's face when he said that.

"My relationship with my brother finally withered under the strain. After a while . . . well, Faxon came to hate me. But somewhere along the way he did figure out a way to gain favor with our father. He could not match my strength or speed or eyesight, or my talent with bow or blade. But he far surpassed me in his capacity to view anyone who crossed his field of vision as a potential victim." Traejon's voice was so quiet now that Tab could barely hear it over the sounds of the crackling fire.

"As Faxon's cruelty and greed blossomed, he became our father's favorite. I just couldn't match his appetite for preying on others for profit or pleasure. It was quite a reversal of fortunes for the two of us. The two of them came to see me as weak, as someone who was squandering his talents. It drove father mad. I think on some level he simply couldn't understand a worldview that wasn't as feral as his own."

A grim smile creased Traejon's face. "So they vowed to toughen me up," he said. "They devised . . . tests. Some of which I passed, I'm ashamed to say. And then came a day. . . . We were camped on the Mastyff River, south of Parsca. My father and brother came to me with a heavy canvas sack. The bottom of the sack sagged with several heavy stones--and some manner of creature frantically clawing at the fabric, trying to escape."

"Father handed me the sack—" Traejon stopped and looked away into the darkness. Tabytha watched him helplessly. A part of her wanted to tell him that he could stop, that he did not have to say any more. But she remained quiet, for she felt as if she was bearing witness to a great purging, a vomiting up of rancid poison that had been steaming in Traejon's soul for years.

"Father told me to throw it in the river," Traejon resumed, his voice rough now with emotion. "And so I did. I walked over to the riverbank and pitched it out over the water and watched it sink beneath the waves. My father slapped my back in congratulations, and I heard my brother laughing. And later that afternoon father insisted that we take a ride into a nearby village. The streets were full of people crying. Turned out that the local constable, a young fellow with a fine wife and a couple of small children, had fallen down dead on the street a few hours earlier. When they tried to revive him, they found his lungs full of water. As if he had somehow drowned in the middle of the village square."

Tab watched the firelight play over Traejon's troubled countenance. "It wasn't your fault," she said softly. "You couldn't have known."

"Ah, but I did," he said, his voice dripping with self-loathing. "I didn't know the identity of the caster that father was targeting. But somewhere deep inside my heart I knew that I was snapping someone's Thread when I threw that sack in the river. I was just too weak to defy him. And even if it had just been an ordinary raccoon or cat or whatnot, a creature not invested with any particular magical qualities . . . what kind of man snuffs out an innocent life in such a manner?

"I left one week later, after we had returned home. I was fourteen. I snuck away under cover of darkness and never looked back. Spent about two months running until I was sure that they were not on my trail. Took my mother's maiden name and left my old one by the side of the road. That was seventeen years ago. And that was the last time I saw them. But at times I still feel their presence."

"Like when you strike a dying man? Or slip into the home of a sleepy stable owner to send him to the Far Shore?

Neither of those men were your father, Traejon. Or your brother."

Traejon stared at her for a moment, then bowed his head in a way that made his eyes disappear into the firelight-shadowed hollows of his face. Tabytha felt a pang of regret at her words. But what did he want from her? Absolution for his sins? Words of comfort? An empty promise that there would come a day when the ghosts of his father and brother would trouble him no more?

And then she understood. He wasn't seeking any of those things. He just wanted to be *known*. To have someone else in the world who knew the waters in which he'd swum. Who understood how cold and black those waters had been. And how he'd spent so many years submerged below the surface of that icy sea that he thought his lungs would burst. He wanted her to know everything. Even if it meant that she might leave him to swim alone.

"Do you know I've never been back?" Traejon said after a long moment. "To our home, or to any part of the Tomorrow Islands?"

"Your work as a shadow never took you there?"

"No. I've followed Nomad over virtually every corner of Tempyst, from the dunes of the Crimson Desert to the Speartips. But never back to the Tomorrows. Sometimes it almost feels like she knows. Like she's sparing me."

"And you enjoy being a shadow."

Traejon nodded. "I do. It gets lonely at times. I never realized how lonely until a few weeks ago," he said meaningfully, glancing at her. "But after the Throneholder asked me to watch over Nomad, I felt like I'd finally found my place in the world. To be given an opportunity to safeguard King Owyn's own familiar, so many years after that day on the Mastyff..."

He's doing penance, Tabytha realized with a jolt. Traejon sees his service as a shadow as atonement for the innocent blood that had stained his hands during his youth.

Traejon looked over at Tabytha, his eyes coming out of the darkness to shine in the night. "Whew," he said with forced lightness. "Got a little more than you bargained for, didn't you?"

Tabytha didn't say anything. But she smiled and put one hand on his forearm and gave it a gentle squeeze. And that, she saw as she watched his expression loosen with relief, was enough.

28

Into the Matchstycks

As Traejon gazed out from the fringe of the forest onto the derelict buildings below, he felt an unexpected twinge of melancholy. He had known what to expect at Rucker's Mill. Still, the forlorn scene was jarring.

Until a few years ago, the giant mill below them had been a frenetic beehive of human activity. Armed with massive sawblades and complex gears drenched in various enchantments to deal with the spectacularly strong and dense wood of dragon oak, the mill had converted dragon oak timber into beams and planks for over a century. It also had provided steady work to hundreds of men and women over the years, and attracted hardy logging outfits that spent their days bringing timber out of the Matchstycks and their nights carousing in the taverns, brothels, and gambling dens that dotted the streets.

Rucker's Mill had supported reputable craftsmen and merchants as well, including some of Fyngree's finest wood carvers. Men and women who earned a good living turning slabs of iron-hard dragon oak into more aesthetically pleasing forms—doors and chairs inlaid with exquisitely rendered symbols and mosaics, or majestically curving roof beams to gird the banquet rooms and bedchambers of Fyngree's wealthiest families. Some craftsmen even turned the flesh of dragon oak into battle shields and maces that were the equal of steel in strength—and a good deal lighter. Indeed, the bow across Traejon's own back was testament to the skill of the town's weapon makers. Made from a particularly dark vein of dragon oak grain, it was the strongest bow Traejon had ever wielded. And yet the woman from whom he'd purchased the bow had treated it—or enchanted it—in some way that gave the weapon the supple pliability of a much softer wood.

But all that was gone now. The mill itself sat silent as a tombstone, its hulking waterwheel motionless where it stood, half-submerged in the river. The surrounding streets and shops were silent as well, emptied of villagers by the opening not ten years ago of a new sawmill twenty miles to the north at Shepherd Falls, where the river ran deeper and stronger. The new operation was owned by a cabal of Valyedon merchants rumored to be closely connected to the Tusks. And they had wasted little time in neutralizing Rucker's Mill. Within weeks of the opening of the mill at Shepherd Falls, timber outfits that continued to sell their dragon oak harvest to Rucker's Mill began to receive ominous visitations from the Tusks' taxmen. It did not take long for them to get the message.

It had been an understated, bloodless little execution, reflected Traejon. The Tusks and their accomplices did not resort to torching Rucker's Mill or threatening the families of the logging crews. No sense in attracting unwanted attention from Kylden Hall. Not when you could just quietly set up a vice and squeeze.

A shame, though.

"No cavalry here from Valyedon to greet us," observed Tabytha.

Tab's voice pulled him out of his reverie about the ghost town before them—and reminded him again about how much things had changed over the last two days. That night at the Penny Whystle, when the full scale of Gunn's treachery had been revealed, he had descended into a black fury so deep and absolute that he thought he might never find his way out. He had become so lost in its depths, in fact, that when he felt that familiar plague ship of dark memories stir to life in response to the evening's blood and carnage, he did nothing to stop it. To the contrary, he welcomed it . . . then spent the next several hours adding cargo to its hold. Such as the cracking sound his fist made when he punched the chest of the helpless Vyne. And the way the inn went up in flames, the bodies of Gunn and Tarantyn still inside. And the look of fear that rose in the eyes of Tarantyn's brother when he looked up to see Traejon standing in the doorway of his stable.

Traejon told himself that he was merely meting out justice. That he was a scythe of righteous retribution, and that his victims deserved everything that came their way. But some black, pulsing part of his soul enjoyed every moment. Gloried in it, even. Until he bent down to retrieve his dagger from the cooling body of Tarantyn's brother. He felt the rage drain out of his body like an ebbing tide, leaving only the bleak knowledge that he would always be his father's son. For it was his father who had forged the scythe—and first baptized its blade in blood.

But the worst was yet to come. When he returned from the stable owner's home to Tab and the others, he had seen the look in Tab's eyes. A blend of fear and pity that cut him like nothing had ever cut him before. There was no place to hide from that withering look. And he had known in that instant that if he did not find some way of coming to terms with his past, he would spend the rest of his life doing nothing but guarding against the plague ship's approach—or being lashed to its mast.

So Traejon decided on a different course.

Rather than burn the ship down yet again, only to see it resurrect itself, he would throw open the doors of the hold and see what effect fresh air and sunlight might have on its dank contents.

It had not been easy sharing so many long-buried, festering memories with Tab around the campfire that night. At times the ache of misery and shame had been almost too much to bear. But he had gone to sleep afterwards feeling like someone who had just broken the surface after escaping from some cramped, black chamber at the bottom of the sea. And he had awoken the following morning feeling the same way. And the sense of well-being had grown throughout these past two days, fortified by the welcome return of Tabytha's warm smile. Would he ever be fully rid of the awful memories of his childhood? Of what he had seen and done in thrall to his father? Of the hatred that radiated from his brother every time their eyes met? He doubted it. But it had been a long time since the ship that had haunted him for so many years had drifted so far out at sea.

"This is an unwelcome development," said Jess. "What do you make of it?"

"Hard to say."

Traejon looked at the princess, whose broken left arm was now hidden in a sling under her cloak. Despite the injury, her face fairly glowed in anticipation of exploring the valley before them. Which was no surprise, he reflected. Jess might never possess the skills of a warrior, but he had come to realize that she had the heart of one. As well as a truly impressive capacity for mulish willfulness. It was a potent combination, all in all. And although he had no idea what the Matchstycks held in store for them, he knew that Jess would never relent until she found the answers she sought. She would look behind every tree in that forest until Lylah and Bryscoe were found, the Blazing be damned.

"I'm not sure why no one awaits us," he admitted. "But it could be that the familiar sent by General Splyntbell never reached Valyedon. If the familiar was intercepted, the Tusks never received instructions to divert soldiers here."

Jessalyn nodded. "That would explain it."

"Or," said Noxon as he took a long pull on his pipe, "this mystery girl whom we seek came here—either alone or with some of her minions—and did away with them." He saw the look of irritation flash across Jessalyn's face and raised his hands appeasingly. "I'm not saying that's what's occurred, Your Highness, just raising the possibility."

"Stop calling me your highness," said Jessalyn grouchily. "Out here it's Jess. I don't know why you can't re-member that."

Noxon bowed his head in solemn acknowledgment of her scolding, then winked merrily at Traejon. The shadow fought down a smirk. The relationship that had evolved be-tween the pipe-chomping sergeant and the princess was a curious one. They clearly respected one another. But just as clearly, Noxon enjoyed poking at her. From Traejon's per-spective, teasing nobility seemed like a somewhat dangerous pastime with which to while away the hours on the trail. This was not your usual royal jaunt through the countryside, however. And he sensed that Jess often enjoyed their banter.

But perhaps not all the time.

"Is it possible that the detachment awaits us at the new mill?" speculated Max.

"That could be," said Tabytha. "Is it possible that Valyedon is operating under the misapprehension that we meant to meet at Shepherd Falls?"

"I don't think so," said Traejon. "I was specific about the meeting place and Splyntbell understood why. The new mill may now be the nexus of the province's dragon oak trade, but Rucker's Mill remains the natural entranceway into the Matchstycks."

"I don't wish to delay any longer," said Jess. "We've traveled so long and so far to reach this point." She turned to look at each of them in turn. "And I still believe that when we enter, we'll receive guidance to help us find our way."

Traejon nodded. "I think so too." The others murmured assent. And with that they made their way down the hillside and into the abandoned village.

They passed through at a leisurely pace, the hooves of their horses echoing against crumbling stone walls and slate roofs. Some of the windows in the buildings remained intact, reflecting passing riders and scudding gray clouds. Others were already empty of glass, and they yawned blackly like a skull's sockets. Like every village Traejon had ever encountered that had been hollowed out of its human heartbeat, Rucker's Mill was a dispiriting and desolate place.

Soon the arched stone bridge that would carry them over the Bloodstone and into the Matchstyck Valley came into view. Thin stands of aspen and cottonwood were arrayed along either side of the bridge's broad entranceway, obscuring the river and the land beyond. But when they guided their horses onto the bridge and began making their way up its length, the valley beyond began to reveal itself. And when they reached the bridge's crest, they stopped as one to take in the breathtaking view before them.

Shaped like a shallow, ridged bowl, the broad valley was carpeted with dragon oaks. Densely packed together at the valley bottom, they gradually thinned out along the valley's rocky flanks. But virtually every dragon oak in view, whether standing like a lonely sentry along the valley's uppermost pavilions or tangled together among its sisters, was topped by a broad, thick canopy of vibrant crimson, gold, and orange leaves.

Traejon could see no other manner of tree in the valley itself. No pines or firs. No birches. No ash or aspen or maple. For how could any such trees survive in a world where its neighbors spontaneously burst into flame every autumn, showering the air with leaves of hungry fire? The only exception was a skein of evergreens perched along the highest reaches of the valley's walls. Separated from the dragon oaks below by bands of rock, the pines formed a deep green crown around the valley's rim.

The forest before them was hardly bereft of other vegetation, however. Vast seas of high flaxen-colored grass rippled in the shadows of the dragon oaks, further imbuing the valley with a sense of ceaseless, ocean-like movement. For a moment, in fact, the entire scene reminded Traejon of a vast fleet of brilliantly colored ships cresting gentle sea swells. The grasses would burn this fall, like everything else in the valley. But next spring the grass would return, stalks poking through the ash like blonde beard stubble. And by midsummer, when the canopies of the dragon leaves were full once more, the grasses would be back as well.

Max finally broke the spell that seemed to have fallen over them. "It is even more beautiful than I imagined it would be."

The others murmured their agreement. But after a moment Jessalyn nudged her horse forward. "Time for a closer look," she said, clopping her way down the far side of the stone bridge. Traejon and the others fell behind her. Together they crossed the modest plain that sat between the abandoned town and the beginnings of the Matchstycks, then followed an overgrown logging trail into the forest itself.

They made steady progress, moving on and off old logging trails without difficulty. Since the dragon oaks incinerated virtually everything on the forest floor each fall, there was naught but the high grass to impede their progress. And while they occasionally encountered trees that were ablaze in roaring fire—and even one or two tall cinder-blackened trees that had completed their Blazing for the year—most of the forest looked a week or two away from erupting.

As they ventured ever deeper into the woods, though, their progress took on a certain aimless quality. With no fixed destination in mind, they were in essence simply wandering. Traejon supposed that they might, by happenstance, eventually come upon the ruined manor house they sought. But that's not what they were doing. They were announcing their presence. And in so doing, hoping that their pilgrimage would be acknowledged with guide or guidepost. And if it was not? Or if this mysterious Lylah chose to use her Thread to conceal herself and her brood of casters from their eyes? Then eventually he would have to insist that they depart the Matchstycks, before they all burned to a crisp. Traejon sighed to himself. That would *not* elicit a positive response from Jess. Maybe before this was all said and done, he actually *would* have to tie her up and throw her over his saddle like a bundle of kindling. As he entertained that unpleasant notion, he felt his first ever twinge of gladness that the princess was threadbare.

As the sun dipped behind the western slope, they happened upon a small clearing in the forest where loggers had removed several dozen trees some years before. A few dragon oak saplings peeked above the high grass here and there, but they had not yet reached the age of combustion. It was a good camping spot.

Traejon stopped them there for the night, and everyone quickly turned to one chore or another. As they went about their business, swallows darted in and out of the surrounding forest, gobbling insects. Deep in the thick grass, meanwhile, mice and chipmunks scampered about.

"I'm surprised to see so much wildlife here," said Max, his gaze following a small hawk as it flew across the darkening sky above. "How do they survive the Blazing each year?"

"Because the Blazing doesn't strike every tree simultaneously," said Jess. "Some dragon oaks blaze days or even weeks before others, and for some reason one tree's leaves are unaffected by those of another. So a valley-wide forest fire never takes place. And they only burn for a short time—"

"No more than a day or two, so they say," said Noxon.

"—before exhausting themselves," finished Jess.

"A dragon oak also gives off a faint aroma of sulphur in the moments before it erupts," added Traejon. "The creatures hereabouts must have learned that."

"And why is it that dragon oaks only grow here? Is it the sea air wafting off the Amaranthine? Something in the soil? An enchantment left over from the Age of Elves?" asked Max.

"No one knows," admitted Jess. "My father made several attempts to grow dragon oaks in other parts of Fyngree, as did my grandfather. But none were successful."

"And I've not heard tell of any dragon oak in Rojenhold," said Tabytha.

Jess shook her head. "No, they can't grow them there, and believe me they have tried. Whytewender hates having to trade with us to obtain it, he's always complaining about the price."

Tabytha looked at the forest wreathed around them. "I wonder how long this would exist if it ever came into Whytewender's possession. A decade, perhaps?"

"If that," said Jess with conviction. "He's not a fool, so he'd keep a few sections intact for future harvests. But most of this? Gone. You'd see mills appear up and down the Bloodstone. And they'd cut day and night for years. The Tusk twins are the same way. Ever since the mill opened at Shepherd Falls, they've been petitioning for a fourfold increase in the annual timber harvest. "

"How have those requests been received?" asked Tabytha.

Jess grinned. "About how you'd expect. Father approved a small increase—he likes a dragon oak throne chair as much as the next monarch—but as you can see, most of the forest remains undisturbed. Because every chair he sits in doesn't have to be carved from dragon oak."

✝ ✝ ✝

Traejon awoke to birdsong early the next morning. He rose and looked around him in the low light, nodding silently to Max, who had taken the night's last guard shift. Wandering over to the forest's edge to relieve himself, he caught a faint whiff of burning leaves and wood in the air. He looked to the sky, where several thin tendrils of smoke spiraled upward in the distance. A few more dragon oaks had gone ablaze in the night. Another week and they would be going up all around them. All the more reason to leave the Matchstycks if Lylah did not reveal herself soon.

As Traejon returned to their camp, a slight movement on the other side of the clearing flickered across his vision. Without breaking stride he positioned his head so that he could watch the area out of the corner of his eye.

There in the shadows, tucked away on a high branch several feet deep in the forest, perched a tall condor, great black wings folded over its long gray body like a heavy cloak. A short, dagger-like beak protruded out of its blood-red, skinless head, which in turn sat atop a neck ringed with a frill of crimson plumage. But the most arresting aspect of the bird was its dead black eyes, which were shifting back and forth between Traejon and their camp.

Then the condor's gaze locked squarely on Traejon, and a moment later the bird straightened, as if it realized that it had been detected. The creature's wings stirred and an instant later the bird wheeled up and away, deeper into the forest's depths.

Traejon marched into the center of the camp, chilled to the bone. And though everyone was already in some stage of wakefulness, he told them to make haste. "We're being followed," he said in response to their questioning expressions. "And I'm not certain that everyone roaming through this forest is our friend."

Spurred by his brief account of the condor's visitation, they briskly packed their horses and set off again in short order. Occasionally they came across other paths cut into the forest by loggers, and they followed those for a time. But they always ended up cutting back into the tall grass, as if they sensed as one that the manor they sought would not lie at the end of any logging trail.

As they roamed deeper into the forest, Traejon sensed the mood of the party darken almost imperceptibly. It was not just his sighting of the familiar that morning—and he had no doubt that the condor *was* a caster's familiar. The forest itself had taken on a more threatening aspect. The smells of sulphur and smoke drifted across their path more frequently now, and on several occasions dragon oaks erupted into flames less than one hundred yards from their location. By noon they were moving through a faint haze of smoke.

Tabytha rode up beside him. "I'm starting to get a bad feeling about this," she said mildly.

Traejon glanced back at the rest of the party. Noxon seemed oblivious to the smoke—perhaps because of the prodigious amounts of smoke that he was generating himself with his ever-present pipe. But the strain was evident on the faces of Max and especially Jess, whose horse had become skittish under the deteriorating conditions. Tab was right. They couldn't go on like this.

"Should we head for higher ground?" he asked. "The smoke won't be as bad up there in the wind, and there won't be as many trees poised to ignite in our faces."

"You won't get any complaints from me. But what if we select the wrong side of the valley? If we head for one slope and Bryscoe and Lylah are on the other, we might never reach these ruins we're looking for before the entire valley is in flames. The dragon oaks may only go up one at a time, but at the height of the Blazing entire sections of the Matchstycks could be burning at the same time."

Traejon smiled with a confidence that he did not feel. "Well, let's make certain that we guess correctly then. I don't think we have any choice, Tab. And if we choose the correct side of the valley, we might yet stumble upon them without aid. Think about it: why would anyone place a manor or hunting lodge deep in the valley, where the forest transforms into a fiery death trap for a week or so every year? It would be madness. No, it would be placed somewhere on the valley's flanks, where the dragon oaks are more sparse."

"That makes sense. But it still doesn't help us determine whether to steer a course to the southern end of the valley"—she pointed to their left—"or the northern slope."

"Perhaps this visitor can help us with that decision," called Jess from behind them. Traejon and Tab turned as one to see Jess, Max, and Noxon all smiling widely. Jess gestured with her chin to the left, and when they turned in their saddles to follow where she indicated, Traejon felt his spirits lift instantly.

For perched atop a nearby rock was a small gray goose, her ebony eyes gleaming through the smoky haze.

2 9

Into the Puzzle

I t was so much worse than she had imagined.

Holding up a gloved hand to shield her face from stinging pellets of icy snow, Malkyn looked down on the boys where they huddled together in the dark under piles of furs, the light from the braziers flickering across their sleep-slackened features. How much longer would they be able to go on before they succumbed to the cold, hunger, and exhaustion that dogged their every step? She looked up and imagined how they must look from the ice-shrouded cliffs to the south. Like dark specks of flotsam on a vast white sea of ice and snow.

She settled herself next to her sons, being careful not to block them from the braziers' life-sustaining heat. Closing her eyes, she waited for sleep to deliver her from the dull ache in her bones, the punishing, lacerating wind, and the gnawing hunger in her gut, if only for a few brief hours. But though the icy wall against which they huddled gave them some meager shelter from the wind, it still howled across the surrounding wasteland at a keening pitch that clutched at her mind. And as she listened to the wind scream on and on, the question came unbidden as it always did: how had it come to this?

The first leg of their flight, to the southeastern outskirts of the Puzzle, had gone as well as Malkyn could have
possibly hoped. Within an hour of concluding their conversation in the gristmill, she and Ben had packed Ajax and
Blackeye up, tossed Rowan over Blackeye's back, and set out.

Rowan had been confused and uneasy about the dis-
ruption to his usual routine, but Ben had stepped in and
quickly secured his cooperation. Speaking to his little brother
in a voice of gentle affection that Malkyn had not heard in
weeks, Ben enthusiastically described the coming journey as
an "adventure" that would take the three of them to exciting
new places. Within a matter of minutes Ben's reassurances
had done their work. Rowan spent much of the first hour of
their flight excitedly pointing out natural landmarks, birds,
and small wildlife that crossed their path.

They had traveled no more than ten miles when
Wynk suddenly appeared out of the forest to their right. The
arrival of the leopard triggered a squeal of delight from Rowan, who had not seen his brother's familiar in weeks. It also
lifted the spirits of Malkyn. Wynk was a reminder that Ben
possessed casting abilities that, even in their early stages of
development, could still protect them from many threats.
And Malkyn could hardly imagine a bodyguard better suited
to ward off attackers.

Wynk spent virtually no time actually traveling with
them, of course. If she was seen she would draw unwanted
attention to the rest of them. And if word reached Tumdown
or Glynt that a snow leopard was prowling the eastern foothills of the Speartips, the Faithful Shield would descend on
the region with vengeance in its eyes and steel in its hands.
Besides, Blackeye and Ajax were not fond of her—to put it

mildly. Familiar or not, she looked like a leopard, moved like a leopard, and smelled like a leopard.

So Wynk traveled with them at a distance, keeping to deeper sections of forest and high ridges overlooking the valleys through which they passed. Every once in a while, though, Wynk would swing close enough to them that Malkyn or Rowan would catch a glimpse of her form. She knew that Wynk could accompany them without revealing herself if she so chose, so it felt almost as if the leopard's appearances were meant to comfort them as they marched deeper and deeper into the unknown.

Keeping to remote wooded pathways and empty fields and grasslands, they pressed steadily northwest, almost imperceptibly gaining elevation as they went. Occasionally they were forced to hide themselves away when farmers or riders came into view, but such encounters were rare. Much of the land through which they traveled seemed strangely emptied of people. Malkyn supposed that the local folk were either already defending the border, hiding out from the conscription orders of the Faithful Shield, or—in the case of the elderly, the infirm, and those with small children—scrambling to prepare for the coming winter without benefit of their most able-bodied family members.

By the third day they settled into an ambitious but manageable routine that steadily added to the number of miles between themselves and the world they had left behind. At dawn's light Malkyn would prepare a quick breakfast, doling out the more perishable food first, while Ben saddled Blackeye and Ajax for the day. Ben would then walk off a short distance until Wynk joined him. Malkyn would watch her son stroke the leopard's head, absorbing all the sights and sounds and smells that the familiar had accumulated during the night as she stood watch over their camp. Wynk would then bound away into the woods as the brawny work horses carried them steadily north and west, ever deeper into the stone-girded foothills of the Speartips.

Malkyn and Ben took turns riding with Rowan, passing the time by telling stories, singing songs, or playing rhyming games. Ben even began conjuring simple castings to entertain Rowan. One day Ben made all the buttons in Rowan's vest button and unbutton themselves as the boy looked down at himself in goggle-eyed wonder. The next day Ben even managed to animate a few pieces of sticks, bark, and tall grass into a rough semblance of a human form. Then, as Rowan sang his favorite nursery rhyme over and over, Ben added his own voice, spilling strange words out into the crisp fall air while simultaneously gesturing to direct the stick figure in an elaborate, spirited dance. The figure romped from the base of Ajax's long, broad neck all the way up the crown of his head, then executed a series of spinning pirouettes right between the horse's big brown ears.

The whole display sent Rowan into paroxysms of joy. When the "fairy," as Rowan called it, finally hopped off the horse's neck and strolled into the folds of Ben's coat, the boy pleaded so fervently for a repeat performance that Ben obliged—and agreed to arrange daily appearances by the fairy. Whereupon Rowan promptly began offering suggestions of musical accompaniment for the next day's performance.

These interactions between her sons filled Malkyn's heart with such gladness that they briefly dispersed the fear that otherwise followed her around like a second shadow. Rowan spoke several times a day about how he missed his father, but the recurring glimpses of his brother's old attentive and playful personality made for a potent salve. The expression on her youngest son's face when he looked to Ben now was one of such deep love and admiration that Rowan almost seemed to glow in his brother's company.

Despite Ben's attentiveness to his younger brother,however, Malkyn saw that the wounds that had cut him so deeply these last weeks would be slow to heal. Perhaps they never would be. Ben still fell into long silences, especially in the evening. During those times Malkyn was certain that her oldest son's thoughts were tangled up in memories of Tumdown's mysterious lessons, Glynt's mien of sinister glee, and his father's twisted justifications for relinquishing his son to the Faithful Shield.

The boy needed to eat more, too. He had always been on the slim side, but there was a faintly hollow-cheeked aspect to him now that Malkyn found disquieting. And the circumstances of their current situation—always on the move, always conscious of the need to husband their food supplies for their upcoming trek over the desolate Puzzle—made it impossible to fatten him up.

Despite all that, though, it seemed to her that the fog into which Ben had been pulled by Glynt and Tumdown receded a little more each day. The boy took good care of the horses and helped out with other camp chores without complaint. He also smiled with greater frequency, even as the air became colder and the grasslands gave way to stunted dwarf pines and hulking slabs of snow-sprayed rock—and then to cold pavilions of granite entirely denuded of trees and vegetation. He even laughed out loud once in response to Rowan's philosophical musings about the advantages and disadvantages of having the entire wilderness as a chamber pot.

And one night, camped high in a boulder-studded pass that would deliver them to the outskirts of the Puzzle the next day, Ben told her about a dream. A dream that Ben said had first come to him in mid-summer, just before Glynt darkened their doorstep for the first time, and which had returned several times since.

Ben spoke haltingly, and at first his gaze wandered aimlessly. To his little brother's sleeping form. To the dancing flames of the campfire. To the cold black star-pocked heavens above. Anywhere but to her own attentive face.

But once he got started Ben's reticence faded. His voice strengthened, and he looked directly into his mother's eyes as he spoke. He told her that he kept dreaming of a crumbling manor house in the wilderness—and of a girl within, with eyes that shone out of her dark face with the same warmth as a crackling hearth on a snowy mid-winter's eve. She spoke not a word, but Ben sensed that the girl was somewhere in the west, between the Speartips and the sea.

The house in which the girl stood was tucked deep in a great wood of fiery dragon oaks, and their canopies were ablaze, lighting up the night like the world's largest torches. The flames were not threatening, though. To the contrary, the burning leaves that separated from each tree's core of flame transformed into whorls of fiery color as they floated up into the heavens. In Ben's dream, the roaring light cast by the forest was a benediction, a promise of refuge.

Refuge from what? Malkyn had asked after a moment. Whytewender? Glynt? The Faithful Shield? Ben said he wasn't sure. But that sometimes his dream also hinted at something awful that lay beyond the horizon in the east. Some long-slumbering colossus coiled at the bottom of a cold, frothing river. Some great beast in its earliest stages of wakefulness, eyelids slowly opening and closing in growing awareness of the hunger roiling its vast and pitiless belly.

They had entered the Puzzle the following morning.

Upon reaching the edge of the vast icefield Wynk abandoned her practice of keeping a goodly distance between herself and the horses. No one lived in this gods-forsaken world of desolation, so there was little danger that she would be seen by anyone who might report her to Stormheel. More importantly, Malkyn and Ben knew that they could not possibly negotiate through the Puzzle's unstable, towering seracs and snow-hidden crevasses unless they followed her path precisely. And that meant keeping close behind her. The horses would just have to become accustomed to her presence.

The first few hours in the Puzzle had been uneventful but torturously slow. On two occasions Wynk had stopped in her tracks, then doubled back and made wide detours around smooth blankets of glittering ice and snow that, to Malkyn's eyes, looked no different than the rest of their frozen surroundings.

The withering cold, slow pace, and bleak sameness of the land around them, meanwhile, triggered a bout of extended complaining from Rowan. The whining did not stop until Malkyn, her apprehension about the difficulty of their passage rising by the minute, scolded him sharply. Rowan went silent, burrowing even deeper into the furs draped about his little form. For the next several hours all Malkyn could see were great clouds of the boy's breath pulsing through a small opening in his furs.

They lurched forward throughout the day, battling through snow squalls that rose up and tapered off again with the same abruptness. In some open stretches, the relentless wind had scoured the land to such an icy sheen that no snow could find purchase. Other times, though, the heavy snow piled up to the point that it reached the bellies of the massive horses. And whereas Wynk's big paws served as virtual snowshoes, keeping the comparatively light cat above the worst of the snow, the horses had no choice but to plow through the drifts, their great legs ponderously churning forward as Malkyn and Ben urged them on quietly. She and Ben thus took turns in the lead so that neither horse would have to shoulder the burden of constantly breaking trail.

"What is the nature of the enchantment on this land?" asked Ben wearily during one of their stops, his breath spooling out in ragged puffs of white. "Little more than a week ago we slept among woodlands of pine, and the only white on the land was the morning frost. Yet now we travel as if through a block of snow-crusted ice."

"No one really knows," Malkyn said. "Some say that it's nothing more than an accident of geography. That the Speartips trap the cold and snow pouring out of the north in some mysterious fashion. That the mountains lock it in like some sort of monstrous icehouse. That's what Whytewender has always claimed." She sighed heavily as she looked at the bleak canvas of glittering white surrounding them. "But I'm sure you've heard other stories. Everyone has. That this land once experienced the march of the seasons like anywhere else. Until the elves that once lived here departed. Leaving behind an enduring spell that would prevent humankind from ever finding the cities and treasures they left behind."

"What do you think?" he asked.

Malkyn almost didn't answer. Until she decided that Ben had heard enough lies in his young life. "I don't know," she said slowly, her gaze settling on the pile of furs under which Rowan was sleeping. "I had hoped that Whytewender was being truthful for once. But does this *feel* natural to you? Like this snow and cold and ice are nothing but a natural phenomenon? Because it doesn't feel that way to me. It feels to me like a warning to turn back."

Ben turned and looked at her. "Is that what you want to do?" he asked carefully.

Malkyn searched her son's eyes for some clue as to how he wanted her to answer that question. But he just looked at her steadily. She shook her head. "No. There's no turning back now."

As their first day in the Puzzle had drawn to a close, Malkyn's gaze had turned to the cool orange disk hovering on the western horizon. Its dying light was much too thin and watery to warm her face in advance of the numbing darkness to come. She had endured many cold winter nights in Rojenhold. But at the end of every one of those evenings, she had been able to warm herself in front of a crackling hearth. The cold out here—it was so implacably brutal. She could not even imagine how bad it would be in the Puzzle in a few months, when winter descended on this land in earnest.

And the distance . . . it seemed so insurmountable, especially given the day's slow pace. The snowy plain spread out before them looked endless, and the towering mountains to their left promised no safe harbor. In fact, the sheer flanks of the Speartips seemed to Malkyn to be an almost malevolent force conspiring against her and her sons. Not only were these northern walls of the range impassable—with the possible exception of the Keyhole, which lay who knows how many days or weeks ahead—but their stone palisades were partially responsible for the icefield's soul-crushing conditions. The mountains trapped the flaying winds that slammed across the ice from the north and west and east, turning them back onto the Puzzle in violent gales that toppled seracs and reshaped snowdrifts up and down the coast. Had the elves incorporated the mountains into their spell, like a potter uses the clay at hand? Did it matter?

She was still peering over at those frozen mountains when the bottom suddenly fell out of her world.

Malkyn had been riding Blackeye, following no more than thirty feet behind the path that Wynk was taking. Ben and Rowan had been just behind her on Ajax. She only took her eyes off the leopard's route for a moment to study the shadows at the mountain's base for possible campsites. She never noticed as Blackeye strayed a few feet to the left of Wynk's path.

But it was enough. Suddenly the horse was pitching forward and down, as if stumbling through a trap door. The horse's descent stopped momentarily, snow midway up Malkyn's legs. She stared dumbly at the reins in her gloved hands and the back of the horse's head, paralyzed with a kind of buzzing terror. Then she heard Ben's voice piercing the crystalline air.

"Jump away!" he screamed. "To the right!"

Malkyn scrabbled madly to her right as Blackeye grunted, writhed, and jerked below her. She threw herself off the horse, arms and upper torso landing on a slab of hard ice, just as the last of the snow bridge holding Blackeye collapsed. She felt the horse fall away beneath her, then her legs dangling in empty air as Rowan screamed and screamed from atop Ajax's back.

Her heart pounding in terror, Malkyn desperately clutched for purchase on the icy surface, only to feel herself sinking backward into the void. Inch by inch she could feel herself slipping away, and her mind dissolved into a black sea of gibbering thoughts about an eternity spent entombed in ice and darkness.

And then Ben's hands were on her wrists, pulling and heaving upward with frantic urgency. For a moment Malkyn thought that her weight would take them both down. But instead he slowly dragged her out of the gash in the ice until she collapsed in the snow. He looked at her for a long second, panting heavily, before slogging back to Ajax, who stood unmoving with Rowan wailing on his back.

Malkyn lay there, her heart still galloping in her chest,as Ben murmured words of consolation to Rowan, whose cries trailed off into sniffles and hiccups. She heard Wynk pad up to her side, the familiar's breathing heavy but steady and strong. But the sounds around her paled in comparison to her sense of sight. For she found herself quite unable to take her eyes off the opening in the earth that had devoured Blackeye.

✝✝✝

That had been four days ago.

Malkyn rose to a sitting position, shaking her blanket to free it of the carapace of snow and ice that had crusted over it during the long night. The tiny particles of ice sparkled in the light cast by the sliver of sun on the eastern horizon. The braziers had gone out sometime in the predawn hours and the cold felt like a living thing, intent on turning her blood to sludge. Shivering, she reached over to where her eldest son still lay sleeping. "Ben," she whispered, nudging at his shoulder. "Wake up. The braziers have gone out."

Ben stirred and looked around him blearily before his gaze settled on the empty braziers sitting between them. He cursed quietly, then reached into the folds of his coat and sprinkled what looked like bits of dried leaves and slivers of blackened rock into the braziers. She watched as he began motioning with his hands, listened as strange words flitted past her ears—then vanished from her mind before she could commit even a syllable to memory. The metal bowls blazed back to life after a few minutes, and Malkyn sighed in gratitude as she felt the heat wash over her.

Ben burrowed back under his furs, but she raised no objection. Did it really matter if the boys slept for another half hour? Besides, that would give her more time to work up the will to push herself away from the braziers and rifle through their supplies for breakfast.

The options were limited. Blackeye had taken about two-thirds of their food into the crevasse with him, as well as his portion of the feed for the horses. And much of what was left required thawing by the braziers before it could be eaten. The only saving grace was that Ajax, not Blackeye, had been carrying their braziers and snowshoes. And that the conditions were so terrible that they had not lost much in the way of furs or clothing—they were already wearing everything that they had brought with them to ward off the cold.

Malkyn looked over at the immense form of Ajax, who was sleeping heavily in the lee of a serac that had toppled on its side, the last of their blankets thrown over his bulk. Gentle Ajax, who even now was sharing the heat from his great body with the small boy tucked along the crook of his long, shaggy neck. Sweet Ajax, who loved apples and having his flanks rubbed with a good hard-bristled brush and who never nipped at a soul in twenty-odd years of life as a working horse. Good old Ajax . . . who at this rate would probably be dead from exhaustion in another three or four days.

Malkyn blinked back sudden tears, then wiped savagely at her eyes with one furred glove. River and Sea, she thought miserably. What have I done?

30

Sanctuary

When the dark stone walls of the manor finally came into view, Jess's heart surged with a great confusion of emotions. Relief that their long, arduous, and at times sorrow-filled quest was finally at an end. Vindication, since their journey was apparently concluding in triumph. But most of all, she felt a thrill of anticipation at the prospect of meeting and talking with the people waiting within. After all these weeks, she would finally have the answers to the questions that had bedeviled her since she had fled Kylden.

The manor itself was tucked midway up the western side of a gently sloping ridge that ran from tree line to valley floor. A few immature dragon oaks could be seen around the manor's outer walls, but for the most part the approaches to the ruins were clear of trees. The forest was much more sparse here along the valley's rockier ramparts, and Jess saw that at some point in the distant past, the land immediately surrounding the manor house and its outbuildings had been cleared.

Jess studied the building more closely as they approached. Squat and vaguely triangular in shape, the manor was crowned by a heavy slate roof and its black-grey walls were pocked at regular intervals with tall window wells. The building's closest point was blunted at its end with an expanse of stone wall, at the center of which stood a large, arched gateway that stood open to the elements. Whatever manner of gate or door had once filled the space, it had long since been removed or crumbled into dust. The other two points of the triangular manor, meanwhile, were marked by large towers. But only the one on the left remained intact. The spire on the right had partially crumbled in on itself like a rotted tooth, leaving a ragged cave-like hole in the manor's side. Jess could see other indications of the manor's long-forgotten status as well. The roof was dotted with missing tiles and even outright holes, and few of the window wells still held any glass.

Drawn to movement off to the right, she spotted more than a dozen horses grazing in a small paddock encircled by a crumbling but still existent stone wall. Adjacent to the paddock stood the graying carcasses of what must have been the estate's stable and carriage house. And there, tucked away against one of the crumbling walls she spotted an incongruous sight: a fine wagon painted in hues of black, silver, and gold. A couple of the doors along its flanks were partially open, revealing a cask, an apothecary cabinet, and a basket heaped with vegetables.

Jess glanced back down from whence they had come, out over the vast forest. From this vantage point she could see how the Matchstycks' brilliant foliage was punctuated with smoking torches of fire. And how here and there the blackened tips of dragon oaks that had already burnt themselves out marred the colorful canopy, like burns in a hearthside rug. The sound of the distant flames washed over her with a sort of steady relentless noise, like distant surf.

"Welcome!"

Jess turned to the booming voice. She immediately recognized the man walking toward them as Bryscoe Rygaard, the spice merchant who had spoken to Percy through the Tiding Horn six weeks past. Raven and Crow, had it really only been such a short time ago? It sometimes seemed that the gargoyle's attack had taken place in another life, so event-filled had been the intervening weeks.

As Rygaard approached, the gray goose that had guided them throughout the afternoon glided over their heads toward the manor. She landed near the gateway at the feet of a thickset man with a corona of curly brown hair and a beard to match. The man crouched down on his heels to stroke the goose's head, then turned and disappeared inside. Jess watched as the goose fell in step and waddled in behind the man, giving a low honk that sounded for all the world like an expression of satisfaction at a task well done.

Jess studied Rygaard. He wore a soft gray coat of fine cloth over a white tunic of similar quality, and the padding in his midsection indicated that the spice trade had been good to him over the years. Nonetheless, he didn't approach them with the haughty air that sometimes afflicted members of Fyngree's merchant class. Instead, Rygaard's wide grin and shambling gait indicated that he was both happy and relieved to receive them.

Rygaard bowed as Jess and her companions brought their horses to a halt. "Greetings, Your Highness. My name is Bryscoe Rygaard. It is my great honor to welcome you and your stalwart friends to the Sanctuary."

Jessalyn smiled and nodded her head in acknowledgement of his greeting. "Thank you for sending the goose, Master Rygaard," she said after introducing the merchant to her fellow riders. "Her guidance was most welcome."

"I am sorry that I could not prevail upon Clay to send her earlier, Your Highness. Ever since Willow's near-capture by the gargoyle in Kylden, he has not permitted her to roam beyond the Matchstycks. That experience left him quite shaken, I'm afraid."

"I understand. Even so, the goose's assistance came at an opportune time, and for that we are all grateful."

Rygaard bowed his head again, but when he returned his gaze to Jess his expression was troubled.

"I see that Gydeon is not with you," he said slowly. He gestured obliquely behind him. "And I've heard reports that he was not with you at Rucker's Mill, either. Does he do the Throneholder's work elsewhere?"

Jess's smile disappeared. "Gydeon was carried to the Far Shore several days ago, as we traveled through the foothills of the Speartips," she said with all the gentleness she could muster. "I'm sorry. We all miss him terribly. He was a fine and true companion."

Rygaard looked away over the smoking forest, sorrow clouding his face. "I am sorry to hear it," he said finally. "He was a good friend. As was Percy Muncenmast. I learned of Percy's death a few weeks ago, on my last supply run into Tapwyll's Cross. The streets and taverns were awash with speculation that the gargoyle's attack was a prelude to war with Rojenhold."

Jess felt her eyes sting at the mention of the kindly pamphleteer, and sympathy for the merchant standing before her welled up in her heart. The poor man. In the space of a few weeks he's lost both his best friend and a man who had treated him like his own son.

"Please," Rygaard said, clearing his throat. "Come in and join us. Everyone is anxious to see you. And we'll see to your horses as well. They look as weary as their owners."

Jess nodded gratefully, then carefully dismounted so as not to bang her broken arm against her horse's flank. "Your Highness!" exclaimed Bryscoe. He stepped forward, his features breaking into an alarmed expression. "You're injured!"

"She broke it several days ago," Traejon said casually as he swung off his own horse. "The injury has proven too severe for her to execute a healing spell on herself. The damage extends up into her hand, limiting her ability to make the necessary gestures. Perhaps someone here . . . ?"

"Of course. We have two, maybe three casters capable of such healing. And Lylah as well."

Jess smiled, both at Rygaard's reassuring words and at the shadow's quick evasion to mask her threadbare condition. She fell in step with the merchant, the rest of the party falling in behind the two of them.

"And this is . . . what did you call it? The Sanctuary?"

"Well, that's what they've come to name it, Your Highness. From what I've been able to glean, this was a summer retreat for Valyedon's high sentinels of yesteryear. But it must have lost favor over the course of time. As you can see, generations have passed since any effort has been devoted to its upkeep. But it has suited the needs of its present inhabitants quite nicely. There is a small stream above the manor that is suitable for bathing, and we have prepared food for your arrival."

"Thank you, Master Rygaard."

"If it pleases Your Highness, call me Bryscoe."

"Only if you call her Jessalyn!" interjected Noxon with a grin as he rambled along behind them.

Jess saw Bryscoe's mouth open in surprise at Noxon's words. His reaction reminded her that outside the world of their little traveling party, addressing the Throneholder's daughter in such a manner would be seen as scandalously insolent. And perhaps it was again, now that she was going to be walking once more among a greater number of her father's subjects. But she just could not muster enough interest in the issue to scold the sergeant.

So she rolled her eyes instead. "As you can see, Bryscoe, I may not have my royal diadem or attendants with me. But I could not bear to undertake my sojourn without a court fool."

Upon entering the manor, Bryscoe briskly ushered them through a cavernous room that included a massive staircase of polished stone and the dangling stalks of old chandeliers. From there they entered a drawing room made warm by a crackling hearth fire and the excited smiles of the people assembled within.

Some bowed or curtsied to Jess with tears glistening in their eyes, others with grasping hands, shy smiles, and warm words of welcome. Whatever form their greetings took, however, the scent of desperation woven throughout their expressions of happiness and relief was so strong that even Noxon seemed moved. The perpetually talkative sergeant fell into an uncharacteristically deep silence as the refugees gathered around Jess and told her of the homes, lives, and people they had left behind in their flight. And when one young girl burst into tears upon being introduced, he blinked furiously and began fumbling in his vest for his tobacco and pipe.

Jess counted twenty-one Sanctuary residents in all, ranging in age from a small child of no more than three years to an aged elder who must have been nearing her eightieth year. In between were seven or eight young people milling on the doorstep of adulthood, including a solemn, dark-eyed beauty that Bryscoe introduced as Cady. There were also a like number of men and women ranging in their thirties and forties—including Clay Clattermoon, the caster with the goose.

After introductions had been completed, attention turned to Jess's broken arm. A spirited debate quickly broke out among the Sanctuary's residents as to which caster most deserved the honor of healing her. As Jess watched their good-natured banter, she could feel herself being lifted up by their cresting mood of jubilation. These people had had so little to celebrate these past months. Little wonder that their arrival would prompt such an outpouring of laughter and revelry.

In the end, it was decided that since Clattermoon's familiar had guided Jess and her party to the Sanctuary, he should have the honor of healing her broken arm. The bushy-haired Clattermoon stepped forward as the rest of the crowd showered him with cheers and good-natured ribbing. But when he raised his hands over her outstretched arm and the ancient words of magic began tumbling out of his mouth like diamonds spilling from a purse, everyone fell silent.

Jess watched him intently as he worked, his voice forming unfamiliar words that instantly fell away from her memory, his hands carving runes into the air. She felt a growing tingle of warmth radiating up and down her forearm, then an abrupt escalation of heat that, had it lasted even an instant longer, would have registered in her mind as pain.

And then all of that was gone, and she was flexing her arm and fingers with a big smile on her face. The crowd erupted in a fresh wave of cheers, and several of them stepped forward to give Clattermoon hearty backslaps.

Clattermoon blushed at the hullabaloo, but he was clearly pleased. He leaned in close, his face red with exertion and pride. "Good as new, Your Highness?" he asked confidently, though Jess could hear the thirst for affirmation hidden in his rumbly voice.

"Good as new!" she agreed, favoring him with a wide grin. Because it was.

31

Cady's Story

After Jess and the others washed up and changed, they joined the rest of the Sanctuary residents for a simple but filling supper. Afterwards, Bryscoe asked them to join him and the pretty young woman that he had previously introduced as Cady for a private counsel.

As they made their way deeper into the manor house, they passed a lynx lying atop an old table, lazily sunning itself in the slanting rays of the declining sun. Jess could not help but marvel at the sight. It was exceedingly strange to see familiars unmasked in such fashion. Apparently the casters gathered here felt that among fellow fugitives, there was no point in concealing the identities of the beasts to which they were Threaded.

Their stroll ended in a large room banked with empty windows that provided views of both the gaudily colored roof of the forest and the pale peaks of the Speartips on the northeastern horizon. Tattered sun-bleached tapestries hung from the walls of the chamber, and its stone floor was littered with grit, bird droppings, and ash that the winds had carried through the window wells over the years. But here and there within the room sat chairs and benches of dragon oak that appeared as sturdy as if they had been built yesterday.

After they seated themselves in a rough semi-circle, Jess explained to Bryscoe and Cady how the Tiding Horn had been delivered to Muncenmast's print shop that fateful summer night. She then briefly recounted the series of events that had brought her company together and led them into the Matchstycks—including the nightmarish evening at the Penny Whystle when Gydeon, Borys, and Stefron had been lost.

"Your turn now," said Jess after she was finished.

Bryscoe stroked his ginger-colored beard.   "Hmm, yes. Where to begin."

"First," said Traejon, "can you tell us whether any of the casters assembled here is threaded to a condor?" Jess turned to look at the shadow. Traejon had been quiet since their arrival. She sensed that out of respect for her, he had been careful not to give any indication of his unspoken leadership role these past weeks. Now, though, he was leaning forward in his seat, those deep green eyes of his alive with questions. Good. Traejon knew the cloak-and-dagger world of spies better than she ever would.

"A condor? That would be a powerful familiar indeed, Master Frost. No. The casters here are mostly threaded to lynx and badger and creatures of similar ilk. Familiars of not inconsequential power, but nothing quite so formidable as a condor. Except for Lylah. Her familiar remains a mystery to me." Bryscoe smiled. "But Lylah Rendsong's familiar is no condor, I can tell you that."

"We haven't met her yet."

"She's off in the woods somewhere. For all I know she's with her familiar as we speak."

"Is that safe?" asked Jess. "With the forest beginning to blaze all around us and unknown enemies prowling across Fyngree?"

Bryscoe shrugged. "Perhaps not. But Lylah did not ask permission. Fear not, your high—Jessalyn. She'll probably be along soon. Though I shouldn't issue predictions where Lylah is concerned. One never knows. She's not much for keeping us abreast of her plans."

"Gydeon said that you knew many of the casters here in the north country," said Traejon. "Any of them that might be thus threaded? What about Aleyda Tusk?"

Bryscoe raised his eyebrows. "High Sentinel Tusk? Tis possible. But she guards the identity of her familiar just as jealously as the sentinels of the southern provinces do. Why do you ask?"

"A condor familiar was following us in the valley below," said Traejon.

"Are you sure it was a caster's familiar? Tis true that such birds rarely stray from the Speartips, but—"

Noxon chuckled and took his pipe out from between his teeth. "Trust me, brother. If Frost says the creature was someone's familiar, you can wager your last piece of silver that's exactly what it was."

"Perhaps it was threaded to a caster loyal to neither Kylden or Stormheel," offered Max. "We all have heard tell of witches and wizards who have withdrawn entirely from the world outside their doors. Perhaps it was the familiar of such a caster, sent only to monitor the passage of nearby travelers."

Traejon nodded reluctantly, but Jess could tell that he was unswayed. "Perhaps." He turned back to Bryscoe. "Can you tell us how this lonely corner of the Matchstycks came to be peopled with so many casters?"

Bryscoe looked to the young woman at his side. "I think Cady can explain that better than I."

Jess followed the merchant's gaze. Cady was a striking lass of about twenty years, shapely of figure and pale of skin, with large brown eyes that shone in the slanting light of the declining sun. But Jess could see that the past weeks had been hard on her. The dark shadows under her eyes bespoke many sleepless nights, and the nails on her hands had been chewed to the quick.

Cady glanced around nervously at Jess and her companions. "They were led here by their dreams, Your Highness," she said quietly. "All of them, including my younger sister. Emmalyn. She's the one who burst into tears upon your arrival. I'm sorry about that. She is threaded to Revel. He's the lynx that we passed earlier."

"You do not possess the Thread yourself?" asked Jess.

"No, Your Highness."

Jess sighed inwardly at Cady's formal address. She supposed that now that she was no longer wandering through the Fyngrean wilderness, she would just have to get used to royal salutations again.

"We only have eight casters here," explained Bryscoe. "The others are family members. Fathers, mothers, siblings. Wives and husbands and children."

Jess nodded her understanding. "Tell us of these dreams that came to your sister and the others."

Cady's brow furrowed. "I can only tell you what Emmalyn and the other casters have shared with us. They all tell of being drawn here by the same recurring dream. Some began having them in the spring, others more recently. Some of them report disturbing elements to these dreams, such as fleeting glimpses of some terrifying beast rising in the east. But all of them report dreaming of this place"—she gestured around them—"and of Lylah. And Emmalyn and the others all report that when their dreams shift to the Sanctuary, they feel a sense of safety and well-being."

"How did you find your way here?"

"Emmalyn and I were led here by Revel," said Cady. "The other casters report the same. They followed their familiars."

"And where do all these casters hail from?" asked Traejon, looking from Cady to Bryscoe.

"Everyone here is from the more northern districts of Fyngree—or from Stormheel, in the case of Cady and Emmalyn," said Bryscoe. "The caster who traveled the furthest to reach us came from the banks of the Whetstone River. Dayna Bossory and her husband maintained a carpentry business there with her two brothers. A few miles upstream of Wenlas Grove. Almost two months ago now, they were set upon by raiders in the deep of the night. A score or more of them, and at least one or two of them were casters. Dayna narrowly escaped thanks to her own casting abilities, but she could not save her husband and brothers from the marauders. Poor woman. She was the last caster to arrive here. She came in a week ago, half-starved, riddled with lice, and wracked with guilt about the death of her family. Dayna insists that if she had only heeded her dreams and convinced them to come here, they would be alive today."

"I know the place," said Traejon, a distant, pained look of remembrance flickering in his eyes. "Nomad took me there, no more than a day or two after the raiders struck. Just before the gargoyle's attack on your pamphleteer friend, Jess."

"Why are there no sojourners here from the more southern districts?" wondered Tabytha. "Kylden, Tydewater, and Talonoux are the greatest cities of Fyngree, with the highest number of casters. Why does this Sanctuary of yours not harbor people from any of those cities?"

"Perhaps those who dreamed of Lylah from those cities felt there was sufficient safety in their numbers," said Max.

"Or the greater distance involved in making such a journey convinced them to make the best of things at home," said Noxon. "Especially once the trumpets of war began sounding across Kylden."

"Or perhaps casters down in the southern districts were not visited by such dreams," said Jess, her expression thoughtful. Her father had never mentioned such visions, nor had she sensed any stirrings of unease among the handful of casters at court this past spring and summer. "Could it be that the range of the message from Lylah only extended so far?"

"That could be, Your Highness," agreed Cady. "Emmalyn always described her night visions of Lylah as if they were signal fires. Like a beacon in the night promising safe harbor to ships lost at sea."

"But even the strongest beacons can only be seen from a certain distance," said Traejon. "And the same goes for those darker elements of the dream radiating out from the east. It may be that even as these dreams began insinuating themselves into the sleep of the casters of Valyedon and Treffentown and Stormheel, the slumber of witches and wizards down in Kylden and Tydewater remained untroubled."

"What does Lylah herself say of these dreams?" asked Jess.

Cady and Bryscoe exchanged a look. "Nothing at all," said Bryscoe. "She insists that she has no role in their creation."

"Lylah becomes agitated whenever we bring the issue up with her," added Cady. "Emmalyn thinks that our accounts of the dream frighten her."

Bryscoe shifted in his seat. "There's something else you should know about Lylah before she returns from her wanderings. She's a mute."

"What?" Noxon exclaimed, his eyes widening incredulously. Jess glanced over to Traejon, who looked as stunned by this revelation as she felt. The ability to give voice to the ancient words of magic was essential to any casting of which she had ever heard. Wizards and witches had to be able to both speak the words that opened the gateways of magic for use *and* execute the hand gestures that set the desired spell in motion. The two aspects worked together like lock and key. How could Lylah possibly launch spells without being able to speak?

Bryscoe shrugged his shoulders, smiling a little at the shocked expressions on their faces. "I don't understand it either, but she is unable to talk. It is no deception, I'm sure of it."

He looked to Cady for affirmation, and she nodded her head in agreement. "She carries around chalk and a tablet of slate on which to write," she added.

"Well I for one can't wait to meet this girl," declared Noxon. "I just wish she was closer to my age. A female caster who can't talk? I've been looking for a woman like that my whole life."

"Hush, Noxon," said Jess absently. "Cady? I'd like you to tell us now about how you and your sister came to be here. And about what you know of spies in my father's government. As the only people here from Rojenhold, you and your sister must have been the wellspring of Gydeon's claim that traitors roam Kylden Hall." Jess looked over at Bryscoe. "It was your tale, in fact, that finally convinced Bryscoe and Gydeon to send that Tiding Horn to Percy if I'm not mistaken."

Cady nodded and squared her shoulders. "Both Emmalyn and I lived and worked in Stormheel Keep, just like our mother, who worked as a scullery maid. She died when I was eleven and Emmalyn but three, but mother's friends among the staff saw to it that we weren't hauled off to one of Stormheel's orphanages to starve. So we grew up in Stormheel Hall. In servants' quarters tucked away in the far corner of the bailey, adjacent to the castle itself."

"Did you often see King Whytewender or Prince Faeros while carrying out your duties?" asked Jess.

Cady tucked a loose tendril of hair behind her left ear. "No. Or not for many years, I should say. When I was young I only worked in the kitchen. I wasn't a server, so I never had cause to stray into the castle's great dining hall or any of the private chambers. And in Stormheel Hall, a girl quickly learns not to stray where she does not belong. Not if she wants to see the next sunrise."

"Are the Whytewenders and their minions really such monsters that they would prey on young girls in such a manner?" asked Max, his face suddenly ashen.

Cady blinked. "You misunderstand me, Master Tugg. The risk in wandering off or becoming lost is not of being seized and ravaged. The risk is of being detained by the Faithful Shield as an assassin or spy. I lost two friends in such a manner during my years in Stormheel Hall."

"They would treat even children so?" gasped Jess, her mind recoiling in horror.

"Youths of tender age can become powerful casters," reminded Traejon. "Once they are Threaded, even the most timid boy or girl can bloom overnight into a force to be reckoned with. Several of the casters here in this sanctuary have seen no more than thirteen or fourteen years, and from what we've heard of Lylah, she is little older than that herself."

Jess felt a hot wave of anger roll over her. "Don't make excuses for them," she said. "It's despicable. There are other ways to protect one's throne."

"I'm not defending the practice, Jess," protested Traejon. "I'm just explaining it. Yes, it's cruel and heartless. But it does protect Whytewender. And its existence heightens the atmosphere of menace that he cultivates to maintain his grip on power in Rojenhold. It's not a portrait of perversion. It's a disciplined policy of ruthlessness. There's a difference. And we need to heed it, for it speaks to the manner of threat we face."

Jess glared at Traejon for a moment, then sighed and slumped back in her seat, shaking her head.

Bryscoe coughed lightly. "Please, Cady. Resume your story."

Cady looked questioningly at Jess, who waved her hand in a vague gesture of consent. "Well, as I said, I spent much of my youth working in the kitchen. But about fifteen months ago a position opened among the servers. And I was chosen to fill it." Cady gave a trembling sort of laugh. "I was terrified. We'd all heard tales of servants who had been imprisoned or executed for being clumsy or inattentive at Whytewender's table. But it was fine. At least for a while. The king and the prince were often absent from Stormheel Hall. And when they did take meals there, they generally paid little heed to the lowly servants fluttering silently about them.

"As the months passed, however, Faeros began calling on me more than any of the other servants. To refill his goblet and otherwise tend to him at the table. And whereas he was sometimes gruff and impatient with the others, he always smiled at me."

Cady stopped for a moment, swallowing hard. "I . . . I became his lover. Secretly, of course. King Thylus would have been unhappy to find his son regularly consorting with someone of such low station. But Faeros changed my duties. He whisked me out of the dining hall and made me one of his personal attendants so that he could send for me under any pretext."

"Did he . . . . What is he like?" asked Tabytha.

Cady's eyes grew distant as she considered the question. "He was boastful. Vain. Privileged. Not particularly self-aware. But he was attentive, too. Even charming, in his way. I think Faeros loved me. Or he thought he did at any rate. And he wanted to believe that I was falling in love with him as well. He would make a special point of showing how much he trusted our bond. That's what he called it. Our *bond*. One night his familiar came to him while I was in his chambers and he did not send me away. As you know, Your Highness, that is no small thing."

"No, it's not."

"What was his familiar, Cady?" asked Traejon.

Cady's expression froze, and Jess sensed that she wished that she had not mentioned the prince's familiar.

"Cady." Jess said. "We have to know this."

Cady nodded unhappily. "A great wolf with a brindle coat of gray and black," she said finally. "He called her Black-bell."

Jess felt her mind unspool away to the Widow's Torch, and to the grim battle for survival they had waged against the wolf packs there. Those packs had been led by a huge brindle wolf. A familiar, it would seem, threaded to Prince Faeros himself.

"Did you love him?" she heard Tabytha ask, and Jess forced herself to push aside those harrowing memories and return to the present.

"No," Cady said firmly. "But I couldn't very well spurn Faeros's affections. There was never any question of resisting him. My own life aside, I had Emmalyn to think of."

Cady paused, a sad smile hovering on her lips. "If I'm honest, though, there was a part of me that took some pleasure in it. There were evenings, lying there in his arms on sheets of the finest linen, wine and fruit and cheeses and other delicious foods within arm's reach. . . . It was nice, not having to share a straw mattress with Emmalyn. And I felt valued when I was with him. In the light of day I knew that he would eventually discard me for some caster with noble bloodlines, and I cursed myself for a fool. But when darkness fell and he sent for me, I could almost convince myself that it might not end."

The room was dimming now in the day's last light, and Bryscoe lit a lantern atop a nearby table. The stark light filled the hollows of Cady's drawn features and revealed anew the frayed and worn state of her garments.

Jess leaned forward in her chair. "Cady, how was it that you and your sister decided to flee Rojenhold? And how did you manage to get out?"

Cady sighed again. "It all began last winter, when Emmalyn became Threaded," she began. "She woke up one morning and there Revel was, staring at her from the foot of the bed."

"How did Emmalyn react?" asked Tabytha.

Cady gave a short, bitter laugh. "How do you think? She was terrified. It's not like it is down here in Fyngree. In Rojenhold, all commoners gifted with the Thread are snapped up for service in the Faithful Shield, and they don't make exceptions for twelve-year-old girls. Revel's arrival felt like a death sentence." Cady ran both hands through her tangled hair, her eyes skipping like a stone from face to face around her. "So we decided to hide her Thread. Mother's old friends didn't want to see her taken away, either. It was difficult. But Emmalyn instructed Revel to stay away for weeks at a time, even though his extended absences made her sick. And on the few occasions when Revel did visit, he always managed to elude the guards to reach her bedside. Still, we knew that it was only a matter of time until we were discovered.

"And then Emmalyn began having her dreams. She told me that a young girl in a faraway place—*this* place as it turned out—was calling to her. Promising her refuge. And that some awful beast was stirring in Rojenhold, slowly blinking away the crust from hundreds of years of sleep. Emmalyn begged for me to take her from Stormheel. She promised me that a new and better life awaited us if we were brave enough to seek it. And she said that if we did not run, the beast in her nightmares would find her and fill the night with her screams."

Cady's eyes filled with tears, and Jess waited quietly. What an awful burden to carry, she thought. To know that your sister's life rests in your hands. And that both staying put and taking flight held terrible dangers.

Cady wiped her cheeks and tried to smile, but it was a quavering, unnatural thing, and she quickly abandoned the attempt. "I'm sorry, Your Highness. It was a difficult time."

Jess offered a sympathetic smile. "Take your time."

"Thank you." Cady heaved a great sigh and squared her shoulders as she wiped the last of her tears from her face. "I decided that Faeros was our only hope," she said after a moment. "He could provide us with the resources to escape into Fyngree, beyond the reach of the Faithful Shield. I even determined that I would vow to return to Stormheel—to him—if he would just help me deliver my sister to safety. So one evening I went to Faeros. I told him that Emmalyn had been gifted with the Thread. But before I could even ask for his help, he told me that I needed to take my sister away immediately."

Cady's countenance had a haunted aspect to it now, and Jess recognized that she was finally coming to the crux of it. The revelations that had led to the gray goose's visit to Percy's print shop and everything that followed.

"Faeros arranged for Emmalyn and me to join a small trading caravan that he was taking across the Span and into Fyngree. This was in the late spring, when the Span was still open to trade and the monarchs of Fyngree and Rojenhold had not yet begun shaking their spears at one another." Cady stopped guiltily, glancing at Jess to see if she had taken offense. But Jess just looked at her expectantly, and after a moment Cady resumed.

"Faeros traveled with false papers as well, disguising himself as a trader in fine wines and spirits. I didn't understand that at first—until I learned that he intended to smuggle both Blackbell and Revel across in a couple of the casks. Once we crossed over, he provided Emmalyn and me with fresh horses and supplies, released Revel into our care, and sent us on our way."

Noxon cocked his head. "He didn't wish to know where you were going?"

Jess heard the skepticism in his voice, but Cady did not flinch. "All he said was that we should flee far from the borderlands. He didn't say where—I think he knew we already had a destination in mind, however hazy—just somewhere wild and remote, unmarked by road or field. And wait there. Until it was all over and we could be reunited. He said that he would be better able to protect both myself and my sister then."

"Until what was all over?" asked Tabytha.

"Why, the war of course."

Jess sat back in her seat, exchanging looks with both Tabytha and Traejon. Tabytha's features were pinched with worry, her arms folded tightly under her breasts. Traejon's expression was far more tranquil. But his right hand was fidgeting absently with the dagger hilts sheathed at his side.

"Was it from Faeros that you learned that King Whytewender had agents in my father's castle?" Jess asked.

"And among Fyngree's armies and even among his Wardens," said Cady. "Some nights he would drink too much. He usually gossiped about inconsequential things. Scandals simmering around Rojenhold's more prominent families, that sort of thing. The names meant nothing to me, and his accounts of their petty campaigns of seduction and betrayal were tedious. But I smiled and laughed at his stories, as I knew I must.

"One night, though, the wine loosened his tongue more than usual. And that evening he talked of weightier things. At first he only made a few coy remarks about how in a few short months, the stiff neck of Fyngree would finally be forced to bend before his father's sword. But as the hour grew late and he kept refilling his goblet, he told me more and more."

Cady leaned forward, her eyes gleaming in the lantern light. "Your Highness, Faeros said that his father had set a trap for King Owyn many years ago, and that the trap was almost ready to be sprung. He claimed his father had unearthed a terrible weapon from the Elvish Islands, and that this weapon had finally been honed to an edge sharp enough to cut down every witch and wizard in Fyngree. And he avowed that agents loyal to Whytewender had been planted all across Fyngree over the years. Agents poised to emerge when the time was right."

Jess felt a cold chill in her bones at Cady's words. From the first moment that she had heard Bryscoe's warning echo through Percy's printing shop, she had somehow sensed the truth of it. Yet a small part of her had always held out hope that when her journey finally was at an end, she would make the happy discovery that it had all been a misunderstanding. Or that the threat had been exaggerated. But she knew that she could no longer cling to such fantasies. It was time to release that final wisp of hope and acknowledge that the months ahead were going to run red with blood.

"Did Faeros mention the names of any of these spies?" asked Traejon.

"No." Cady drew in her breath, her eyes searching Jess's face. "But Faeros said that the ranks of spies included your father's most trusted falconer. And that this falconer was a caster. A powerful one. Threaded to a gargoyle."

Jess felt her mind go numb for a moment, then draw down into a black undertow of horror and fury. Brundy Sevenshade was an agent of Stormheel.

And his familiar had snuffed out Percy's life.

32

The Endless Empty

Ben looked down numbly at Ajax's motionless form, his gaze drifting up and down the length of the once-powerful horse. The animal's broad, heavily muscled flanks were still now but for the rippling patterns that the wind made in his short-haired hide. Snowflakes rained down at a slant, melting as they settled onto the horse's warm body and his large marble-like eyes. But they would not melt for long. Ajax's body would cool quickly out here in this frozen hell. By this time tomorrow, the horse would be concealed under a shroud of snow and ice, where he would remain for ... how long? Did it ever get warm enough for flesh to decompose out here in the Puzzle? Or did the few people and beasts who met their end out here remain preserved in coffins of ice for all eternity?

Ben tried to muster up some sadness at the thought. But no spark of emotion spiraled up out of the blackened, burned-out remains of his mind and heart. There seemed to be no tinder left. He felt as shriveled and blackened in spirit as his frostbitten fingers, toes, and nose had become in flesh.

He slowly turned his head to look at his mother and younger brother, his neck creaking like a rust-clotted weathervane. His mother's face, framed as it always was these days deep in an oval ring of heavy furs, was speckled with frostbite at her cheeks and the tip of her nose. She was gazing expressionlessly over Ajax's body to the north and west, where the Puzzle ran on and on, its white mirror-like surface broken only by distant seracs that jutted out of the ice like monstrous sharks' fins.

Blinking away thin coatings of frost that had formed on his eyelashes, Ben looked down to the bundles at her mother's feet. After Ajax had drawn his last, shuddering breath, she had moved quickly to consolidate their most essential belongings into packs that the two of them could carry. Malkyn had worked silently, tossing aside virtually anything that was not primarily intended for warmth. His mother made only three exceptions. One was for a small jar of honey, most of which had already been sacrificed to their lips in a doomed effort to keep them from breaking into dry, cracked ruins. The second was for a small pot for melting snow to make drinking water. And the third was for the meager supply of meat that Wynk had managed to bring them.

Ever since Blackeye had been lost, Ben had sent Wynk out to find food for them. And twice she had returned from the edge of the Speartips with small game in her jaws— once bringing in a lean white hare, the other time a small mountain goat. His mother had cooked these gifts over the braziers with a strained air of celebration, as if trying to convince herself and her sons that these bounties, modest though they were, amounted to good omens.

But they weren't, of course. That supplemental meat had dwindled quickly, despite rationing that had left Ben's stomach perpetually clenched with hunger. Another day or two, and even the last of the stringy goat meat would be gone.

The hunger, though, felt like an afterthought compared to the ever-present cold. Day after day it did its cruel work, robbing them of their strength with an implacable power that felt increasingly useless to resist. Their furs and braziers seemed more inadequate for the task with each passing hour. It was like fighting off a broadsword-wielding highwayman with a butter knife.

"Time to go, Ben," Malkyn said tonelessly, shifting Rowan from her left hip to her right so that she could hoist up the smaller of the packs from the ground. The boy lolled bonelessly against his mother's shoulder, unresponsive to any of her manhandling. Rowan had fallen asleep again, Ben noted dully. Sleeping was about all that his brother did now. Even Ajax's death had not been enough to rouse the boy out of his cold-induced stupor. Rowan had looked at Ben expressionlessly when he told his little brother that the beloved horse would not rise again. Then he had just closed his eyes and burrowed back into his mother's furs.

He thought about trying to light one of the braziers. Maybe the warmth and the flickering light would revive Rowan, at least a little. But his fingers had become so afflicted with frostbite that he could barely move them in the sequence necessary to put the fire casting in motion.

His mother cleared her throat. "Time to go, son."

Ben turned to look at her, and she quickly dropped her gaze to hide the hopelessness in her eyes. She turned abruptly and began walking west, following the trail through the snow cut by Wynk, who was watching them silently from a few yards ahead.

"Mother."

Malkyn stopped and half-turned toward him, keeping her back to the wind. "What?"

Ben gestured weakly down at the horse. "We should. . . . There's meat here."

Malkyn remained motionless for a long minute, then tramped back to Ben and the fallen horse. "Take Rowan with you," she said, handing him the boy. "Go over to where Wynk waits. Keep your brother facing away from me. Give me fifteen minutes. We won't be able to carry that much." And with that she reached down and took out a long knife sheathed in one of her heavy boots.

Ben stared at her as she bent to her haunches with a groan and began her bloody work. "Go on," she said without looking up. Some time later—Ben couldn't say whether it had been fifteen minutes or two hours—Malkyn rose from the carcass and made her way over to them. Her gloves, sleeves, and boots were sodden with blood, and one corner of her pack now left a steady drip drip drip of red on the ice and snow. She halted in front of him and took Rowan out of his arms, then brushed past him down the trail left by Wynk.

Ben sighed heavily, his breath chugging like chimney smoke out of the recesses of his furs, and fell into step behind his mother. Plodding forward, pushing leaden legs through the heavy snow, he kept his eyes on his mother as she dragged herself forward.

He knew that he should find the strength to carry Rowan, or at least exchange packs with his mother. But he felt a bilious geyser of resentment well up in his heart at the thought of doing so. Smoke and Ash, he was so *tired*. More exhausted and miserable than he had ever been in his life. All he wanted to do was to go back and curl up next to Ajax and close his eyes. His chapped lips compressed in a tight line. *She* was the one responsible for their plight. *She* was the one who had dragged them out here into this graveyard of ice, snow, and shrieking wind. *She* was the one who had promised him that they could find the Keyhole and deliver him from the slave collar that Glynt and Tumdown were fitting for his neck.

And it was *her* prattling on about free will and fresh starts that had half-convinced Ben that there was something worth heeding in those strange visions of his about that girl beckoning to him in the West.

She could just keep carrying Rowan as far as he was concerned.

He shook his head angrily at how foolish he had been. Once he had agreed to his mother's proposed plan of escape from Rojenhold, he had felt a soaring, anticipatory joy well up within him. Though fear of Glynt and King Whytewender continued to stalk him, he had allowed himself to actually believe that he might someday meet that girl floating through his dreams. Perhaps he really *was* meant to be more than an instrument of war and oppression. Perhaps his Thread was a gift that could deliver him and his family to a brighter and more prosperous life. Not an anchor that would drag them all into the cold black deep.

Ben thought back to those first quietly euphoric days of flight through the empty fields and highlands of Rojenhold. Mornings full of sunlight and birdsong as he fit tack over the broad backs of Ajax and Blackeye for the hours of travel ahead. Days of doing magic tricks for Rowan and listening to his mother tell stories and sing songs to his brother. Stopping at sun-dappled streams to replenish their waterskins and scrub their scalps and faces with deliciously bracing water, Wynk flashing through the woods along the banks. Evenings around the crackling campfire in which he gave himself over to fantasies of a new and better life.

Ben smiled bitterly to himself as he trudged forward, making the fissures in his lips crack open anew. At first he didn't even notice. But when he licked his lips and the coppery taste of his own blood filled his mouth, he blinked and stopped in his tracks.

It was true that they were going to die out here. There was no denying it any longer. He would go to the Far Shore without ever hearing his little brother's infectious laugh again. Or without ever tasting a girl's kiss. Or feeling the embrace of children of his own. And it was true that since his father would likely never know what happened to them, they had sentenced him to a special kind of mourning, a gray limbo without pyres or gravestones.

But as he tasted his own warm blood lingering on his tongue, Ben felt the shock of another realization. That for a handful of wondrous days, his mother had given him hope. She had given him a reason to look forward to rising in the morning, to savor the rushing current of his pulse and the tidal ebb and flow of his lungs. She had pulled him out of a place where his soul would have continued to harden into stone—or broken outright. In a way those halcyon days out in the world between the gristmill and the Puzzle had been a gift of sorts as well.

From a mother who had nothing else to give.

Ben lifted his head and turned his eyes to the sun, pinned low on the western horizon ahead of them. All light and no warmth, it shone down on them as though it hovered on the other side of a thick pane of leaded glass. And yet when the sun forsook them in a few hours and night spilled over the Puzzle, the temperature would plummet yet further.

So tonight would probably mark the end of their journey.

Ben returned his gaze to the slowly receding back of his mother. She was plowing onward to the west, drawing on gods knew what reserves to put one snowshoe-shod foot in front of the other. He sighed and flexed his fingers in his half-frozen gloves. He did not want to die. But at least he would make the crossing armed with some fine memories. And with the knowledge that his mother had loved her sons enough to fight her way to the very edge of the world in search of a better, prouder existence for them.

He hoped that his mother felt a measure of peace at that. At the realization that she had done her best.

"Give him to me, mother," Ben croaked suddenly, urgently. "My turn."

For a moment he thought that she would just keep walking, as if he was already naught but a ghost haunting this ice-rimmed land. But then she stopped and slowly turned. And when their eyes met he smiled, even though his lips cracked and broke apart anew.

†††

When Malkyn fell three times in the space of five minutes, they knew they could go no further. Using the very last of their strength, Ben and his mother dug a deeper hole in the lee of a great frozen wave of snow.

As they finished, Wynk loped off in the direction of the Speartips to the south. Ben watched her go, then turned and pondered the sun, a faint orange bruise at the edge of the horizon. Even if Wynk found the Keyhole, they no longer had the strength to reach it. This shallow cave would be their final resting place.

He looked over at his mother, who had patiently extricated Rowan's head out of its cocoon of furs so she could feed him the last of the goat meat. Ben grabbed the three small braziers and one by one managed to coax them to fiery life a final time. When he was done he stuffed a chunk of thick ice into their water-melting pot and placed it atop the nearest brazier, then sat back against the hardpacked snow, pulling his gloves back on over his blackening fingers.

"There we go," he said, crossing his arms over his chest to hide the shaking of his hands. "That will warm things up a bit. I can cook up a little of the . . . other meat in a few minutes."

Malkyn smiled in acknowledgement, but he could see that she was not fooled by his tone. When they had first started out on this journey he could light all three braziers in an instant. This evening it had taken him the better part of twenty minutes—and the last brazier alone had taken him at least ten minutes to light.

His mother slowly slid over until she was next to him, inserting Rowan between the two of them as she went.

"You want some water, mother?" he asked, taking the pot of water off the brazier and sticking it in the snow to cool for a moment.

"Thanks, yes."

He passed it her way. "Drink it all. I'll melt more."

Malkyn finished off the pot's contents, then stuffed the pot full of snow and shards of ice before handing it back to Ben. He took it and put it back on the nearest brazier, his eyes brushing briefly over his mother's haggard features. She looked dead already but for her eyes, which glistened as they watched the firelight. Out of nowhere he found himself wondering who would die first, Rowan or his mother, and he bit back a sob.

His mother didn't appear to notice. They sat quietly for several minutes, listening to the wind howl and watching as the last sliver of light from the sun disappeared below the ice.

"We used to call this the Endless Empty," his mother said quietly, her voice just audible above the wind swirling around them.

"What? The Puzzle, you mean?"

"Yes. The village where I grew up was about as far west as you can go in Rojenhold and not yet set foot in the Puzzle. Wyndom. You've heard me tell of it?"

"I think so. Once or twice."

"Both my parents—your grandparents—lived and died there. I always meant to take you to the meadow where they used to graze our goats and sheep. I'm sorry we never did that. It's a beautiful spot, Ben."

Ben stared into the flames of the braziers. "Perhaps you can take me there after this is all over."

Malkyn smiled. "Perhaps," she said, her words just reaching his ears before the wind took them spinning down the desolate waste. "I'd like that. Now where was I? Oh yes. Military expeditions hailing from Stormheel would occasionally launch into the Puzzle from Wyndom when I was a child. They never said what they were looking for, but that didn't stop my parents and the other villagers from speculating. Another route into the southern Speartips? A well-marked route to the fabled Keyhole itself? Elvish gold and silver buried under the ice and snow? None of us ever knew. But they were astoundingly well-supplied. And horses, dogs, sleds— they tried all manner of transport."

"Did any ever return?" Ben asked, taking a sip of meltwater from the pot.

"Oh sure. After a week or two weeks or four weeks they'd return—some of them, at any rate. And before they left to go back home to Stormheel they'd spend a night or two in Wyndom's taverns, raising toasts to fallen members of their party and going on and on about how empty and endless this all was." She weakly lifted an arm and gestured into the darkness. "Endless and empty. Empty and endless. After a while we just adopted it as our own name for the Puzzle. The Endless Empty."

"And yet their failures did not discourage you from mounting your own expedition with your own sons, thirty years later," Ben observed, a final flare of bitterness edging into his voice despite his best efforts.

"No," she said simply. Malkyn looked down at Rowan between them and gently stroked the fur hood covering his head. Then she turned her gaze to Ben. "Because we were already in the Endless Empty, Ben. It just took us some time to realize it. And all things being equal," she added, "I'd rather die in this Endless Empty than that one."

"So you've given up hope," Ben said, his heart a roiling confusion of anger, misery, and love.

"Not for you and Rowan." His mother said. "I want you to take Rowan and go on without me in the morning."

"What?"

"That will be more food for the two of you, and three braziers can more easily warm two bodies. And I'm slowing you down now, son. I can barely walk."

Ben stared at her, tears pooling in his eyes.

"I-I can't do that," he said, and he could hear the quaver in his voice. "I won't do that. I'm not leaving you here."

"And we can outfit Rowan in some of my furs, get some of that wretched clothing off of him," his mother said, as if she hadn't heard his protests. "And I know that Wynk wouldn't accept Rowan on her back before, but maybe if he's sleeping all the time—"

"That won't matter to Wynk. She just can't do it. She may be my familiar, but she's still a wild animal. It's hard to explain, but being forced to submit to such bondage would drive her to distraction. She'd end up at the bottom of a crevasse and take Rowan with her."

Malkyn frowned. "Well, nonetheless, you need to leave me here, son."

Ben started to interrupt again, but she shut him down with a fierce glare. "You need to listen! The Keyhole may be no more than a day or two away. If you can find the entrance, keep traveling south, to lower elevations. Keep to the wider valleys. You may find someone who can help you somewhere in the mountains. And if you do, perhaps they can send back aid for me as well. But for now, my son . . . I can go no further."

Ben shook his head furiously, hot tears carving runnels down the frosted plains of his cheeks. "Mother . . . Please."

His mother brushed a fur-clad arm over her own shining eyes. "Ben, you have to understand—"

Wynk suddenly appeared around the corner of the shallow snow cave. Ice was caked on her muzzle and her whiskers glistened silver in the light cast by the braziers.

Ben felt his spirits plunge yet again. He had expected the big cat to be out hunting all night. Had she somehow sensed the anguish in his heart and returned to check on him? He took off one glove so that he could stroke the head of the great leopard.

And that's when he understood why Wynk had returned so soon.

His mind flooded with the sights and sounds of Wynk's most recent excursion. He felt himself running and bounding and swerving to avoid hidden crevasses, his body gliding over the ice like a ghost as the mountains drew near. And then he saw it, coming out of the Speartips straight toward him: the silhouette of a hulking figure atop a giant sled streaking across the snow. At the back of the sled, glowing lanterns swung back and forth on swaying poles, casting moving circles of yellow light on the ice and snow as the sled churned forward.

And at the front of the sled, a team of eight wolves in harness, their eyes and teeth gleaming in the moonlight of the Endless Empty.

33

Gryphon's Eye

As Marston Pynch made his way through Kylden Hall's gardens, he kept his eyes on the dimly lit cobblestoned pathway unwinding at his feet. Several years earlier he had tripped on the lip of a misaligned brick on this very path and broken his hip. And while King Owyn had mended the bone within an hour of his fall, Pynch still remembered how he had lain sprawled in a bed of peonies, grunting and sweating with pain, until the Throneholder had knelt down by his side.

The high votary paused on the path and looked to the far end of the garden to gauge his progress. There, past the garden's pavilions of flowering bushes and decorative trees, patches of the Menagerie's broad stone walls could be glimpsed, flakes of embedded mica glittering in the day's dying light. Pynch turned his head back down to the cobblestones and resumed his slow progress.

Three weeks had passed since King Owyn had cordoned himself away from the outside world and placed himself under an enchantment of oblivion. And three weeks with no news of Nomad—a silence that Pynch now viewed as an almost certain indication that the gyrfalcon was in Whytewender's possession.

He didn't know why Whytewender had yet to kill the familiar. Was he just drawing out the Throneholder's torment in order to flaunt the power he possessed over him? That didn't make sense. If humiliation was Whytewender's intent, he'd be sending taunting Tiding Horns on a daily basis. And if he saw the familiar as leverage, wouldn't he be actively seeking to extort land and riches and power from King Owyn in return for the bird's safe return? Instead, Whytewender and his emissaries had withdrawn into stony silence, even as their armies along Tucker's Front buzzed with war preparations.

So what was his play?

Soon it wouldn't matter, of course. The casters and scholars that Pynch had consulted on the issue all agreed that Owyn's oblivion spell only had the capacity to extend his life for another week or so. Then King Owyn would expire once and for all, as surely as a man starved of air or food. And where would Fyngree be then?

Pynch feared the answer, especially since Princess Jessalyn's whereabouts remained a mystery. Was she dead? Captured? Or was she somewhere in Fyngree's north country, operating even now under Traejon Frost's protection? There was no way of knowing.

Not that the people of Fyngree were panic-stricken, exactly. True, their monarch had not been seen for days, and his daughter had been absent even longer. And the warnings issued to the general populace after Stonewyck's demise had unsettled casters and threadbares alike. No one relished the thought of familiar-stalking agents of Rojenhold in their midst.

Yet still and all, Fyngree was long accustomed to its status as Tempyst's dominant kingdom. And though the warning—crafted by Pynch himself—had conveyed troubling news, it had also projected serene confidence that the unknown malefactors would soon be identified and apprehended. And so there remained a widespread assumption among Fyngreans—and especially its vast majority of threadbare citizens—that while an outbreak of war would result in a wasteful deluge of blood and tears, it was Rojenhold that would shed the bulk of both of those precious bodily fluids.

Pynch wished that he shared that confidence.

It was hard for him to put his finger on the source of his unease, exactly. Fyngree's military advantage was clear: the combined size of the armies pledged to King Owyn significantly exceeded what Rojenhold could possibly throw together; Fyngree still enjoyed an advantage over Rojenhold in both the number and capabilities of known witches and wizards, despite the recent spate of mysterious caster deaths and disappearances and Owyn's unavailability; and perhaps most important of all, Rojenhold was incapable of feeding itself long-term without the benefit of shipments from the Loaf. Especially since he could see no evidence of Rojenholdean hording in Fyngree's trading ledgers. Sooner or later the prospect of presiding over a starving kingdom would surely force King Thylus to seek peace.

So what was the source of the apprehension that had burrowed into his heart like a carrion beetle? Perhaps it was because King Whytewender and his army seemed oddly content with the current state of affairs. Two days after the Throneholder had shut himself up in his citadel, Rojenhold had abruptly ended all diplomatic talks. And since that time Whytewender and his generals had turned away every Fyngrean emissary.

It was as if Whytewender was biding his time. Waiting for something.

Passing out of the garden, Pynch reached the Menagerie's iron gate—the lone opening in the wall on the building's entire first floor. Through the barred gate he could see an expanse of green grass and several widely spaced birches and maples, their leaves just beginning to turn. And carrying faintly on the evening breeze, a low murmur of animal and bird noises.

Pynch pulled a small key out of a pocket and waved it over the gate lock. He heard a clicking sound as the lock's heavy gears moved in response, and a moment later the heavy gate swung open.

Pynch stepped through the gateway and strolled alone out into the open grass as the gate closed behind him. Why had he come here? No real pressing reason, he had to confess. But his offices and chambers back at the castle had felt suffocating to him all day, and by the time he had finished his supper he thought to pay a visit to Brundy, who had just returned from several days of traveling. Check to make certain that no rider or messenger bird had returned from up north with word of Jessalyn's whereabouts. Perhaps even ruminate about other strategies for locating the princess or Nomad.

Pynch stopped in the middle of the great circle of green and looked around. Oversized lanterns and braziers were ranged about the amphitheatre-like space at regular intervals, but none were lit despite the gathering gloom. All about the inner wall stood great cages housing all manner of beasts. Weasels and ocelots. Wolves and bears. Even a couple of bone-white trolls pacing back and forth in their cages, their stumpy, serrated horns gleaming softly in the dusky light. Most of the creatures around him were asleep, but a few returned his gaze, their eyes unblinking.

He craned his head to take in the massive dome that crowned the paddock. It featured a dozen great curving columns of iron that united with one another a good five stories above, the space between each column alternating between open air and great panes of blue glass. Through one of the open spaces he could see the full moon, a pale orange ghost pinned against the fast-darkening sky.

Was the Menagerie always this empty at this time of the evening? Were there no trainers about at all? Perhaps Brundy and his assistants were working with the birds instead. Pynch resumed walking through the bestiary, his focus now on the dark archway at the far side of the paddock.

Pynch entered the cool, dark passageway that led to the Menagerie's aviary section, his footfalls echoing loudly on the stone floor, then emerged into another great circle of green space and towering columns. Were it not for the creatures that lined its walls, the aviary could almost have been the twin of the bestiary through which he had just passed. It featured the same assortment of enormous cages curving around its walls, the same array of unlit braziers and lanterns, the same smattering of widely spaced trees, the same vaulted roof of air and painted glass. But in these cages perched falcons and hawks and owls and pelicans. He felt their eyes tracking him as he moved deeper into the circle, and for an instant he felt like an exposed mouse in an open meadow.

Pynch had just reached a circle of cork-topped pedestals at the center of the paddock when a lantern flared to life at the far end of the green. That had to be Brundy. He released his breath in a great sigh, and it was only then that he realized that he had been holding it. River and Sea, he thought shakily. This place is eerie at twilight.

The high votary shuffled toward the light, and a moment later Brundy Sevenshade came into view. The big falconer sat at the edge of a circle of light cast by the lantern, which hung from a post that had been hammered into the side of a maple. He was lounging in a stuffed high-backed chair, the fabric faded with age. At Brundy's side was a table that held a tall goblet and two bottles of dark wine. One looked empty, and it appeared that the big man had just broken the seal on the other one. The whole scene struck Pynch as strangely incongruous, as if Sevenshade and the furniture had just materialized from some distant parlor room.

Brundy smiled lazily at Pynch as the old man entered the circle of light. "Master Pynch," he said. "What an unexpected pleasure."

Pynch inclined his head in acknowledgement, even as his eyes narrowed in disapproval. He had never seen Brundy drink before, not even at King Owyn's table, let alone to excess. This was a disappointing discovery, given the circumstances.

"Master Brundy," he said. "Taking a respite from your training duties, I see."

Brundy's smile expanded into a broad grin that made his teeth gleam in the lantern light. "And why should I not? It's not as if the Throneholder will be calling me to the castle anytime soon, is it?"

Pynch's scowl deepened. "Watch your tongue, falconer."

Brundy gestured expansively to the cages behind him. "And my friends here?" he continued as if he hadn't heard the counselor. "They don't mind."

Pynch was dumbfounded. This behavior was completely unlike Brundy, whose sole interest over these many years had been in developing the finest masks in Fyngree.

The falconer had always spurned anything that interfered with that obsession, whether it was getting drunk or chasing women or indulging in games of chance. King Owyn had once joked that if they cut Brundy open they'd find nothing but jesses and leashes for veins.

"Besides, my friends and I are celebrating, and we haven't had much to celebrate around here lately, have we?" said Brundy. "What with King Owyn's abandonment of his duties and Princess Jessalyn's abandonment of her people?"

Pynch stared at Brundy, his mind reeling at the man's casual condemnation of the Throneholder and his daughter. What manner of madness was this? Sevenshade was behaving almost as if under some glamour, though the falconer's eyes betrayed no tell-tale glaze to them. To the contrary, they shone clear and diamond hard.

So where did that leave him? Pynch was accustomed to following certain routines and conventions with the men and women with whom he regularly crossed paths. He saw his interactions with them as dances of sorts, with each person moving in choreographed harmony with the other.

Most of the dances were tedious affairs, to be sure. Like the rote greetings Pynch exchanged with the guards and servants each morning. Or the endless rounds of maneuvering with assorted high sentinels, merchants, and casters over the same few things. Wealth. Power. Status. Respect. After all these decades, Pynch knew those joyless steps by heart.

But this dance of the falconer's tonight. . . . It was full of strange spins and swayings that made Pynch feel dizzy and leadfooted. He didn't know where to put his feet or how to move his arms. It was as if the falconer was suddenly stepping to some strange and alien music playing at a pitch beyond Pynch's hearing.

"You're celebrating?" Pynch said numbly.

"Oh yes. Have you noticed the moon tonight, Master Pynch?"

Pynch looked up into the heavens at the orange disc that hovered there, its color deepening as the sun dropped further below the horizon.

"It's full."

"That's right. Beautiful, isn't it? Do you know what Rojenholdeans call the last full moon of the fall? Their harvest moon? They call it the Gryphon's Eye. It holds great symbolic meaning for them. They regard it as a promise. An augury. Of the day when a caster threaded to one of the great beasts from the Age of Elves will rise, conquer Fyngree, and place all of Tempyst back under the dominion of Stormheel."

Pynch remained silent, even as he felt a dark tendril of foreboding take form and curl around his heart.

"You hear that and think it a comforting fable, yes? A thin, moth-eaten cloak for shivering Rojenholdeans to pull around their shoulders as they wait for King Owyn to dole out his miserly allotments of food, clothing, iron, and wood? I used to think that too."

"But not anymore."

Brundy tilted his head speculatively at the high votary, his eyes shining orange in the lamplight. "Can I ask you a question, Pynch?" he said.

"What is it?"

"How has it felt to do the bidding of that doddering old fool up there, year after year after year?"

Pynch felt the blood drain out of his face. "The only fool around here is you. I was willing to overlook this"—he waved at the bottles on the table, his hand trembling with anger—"indiscretion. But such expressions of insolence toward King Owyn cannot go unanswered. You will have much to answer for in the morning, Sevenshade."

Brundy laughed, the noise booming across the cavernous paddock. "*I* have much to answer for? We'll see about that. Though I would have to agree with you about one thing; my circumstances will look much different come the morrow." The falconer grinned again, his teeth splitting open his bearded face like a white blister.

Pynch smiled thinly in return. The falconer was spouting nonsense now. Little wonder that he usually avoided spirits. Evidently they turned his brain to gruel.

"I'm serious, Pynch. Does it ever bother you? Gently but firmly guiding the king away from some dimwitted decision or another? The Thread business with the princess, for instance. Don't misunderstand me. The ordeals that Owyn has put his daughter through on that score have been entertaining. But not for you, I daresay." The falconer shook his head wonderingly. "Doesn't it wear on you, always holding your tongue? Always playing the role of the patient advisor? Doesn't that mask get heavy?"

"If that's what you think, then you don't know me at all."

Brundy took a sip from his goblet, smacking his lips afterwards in exaggerated appreciation. "Hmm, that's good. Of course, we all carry around masks of one sort or another. I know I do. I've been carrying one around for the better part of twenty years. But tonight, I can finally cast that mask aside."

And with that Brundy pulled a dagger out of a sheath at his side, raised the blade to his left forearm, and sliced deeply into the flesh, his eyes watching the old man's face all the while. Pynch watched in horror as blood poured out of the wound, quickly coating the falconer's arm in a deep crimson glaze. The falconer has gone mad, Pynch thought. Could he be under some foul enchantment after all?

Brundy smiled at Pynch's stricken expression and tossed the blood-soaked dagger onto the table. Then he murmured a few half-heard syllables, his hands slicing the air in patterns that sent droplets of blood spraying around him. At which point Pynch felt an icy fissure of fear crack open along his spine. For the ugly wound in the falconer's arm was closing fast, the gushing blood slowing to a trickle and then stopping altogether.

Brundy Sevenshade was a caster. A very strong one.

Pynch retreated out of the lantern's circle of light and into the darkness, his blood roaring in his ears. He turned and ran gimpily for the archway at the far end of the paddock, doing his best to ignore the protests from his knees and the rising panic in his mind.

He had just passed the pedestals at the center of the green when light burst across the aviary in a flood, as if a levee holding it back had broken open. Pynch stumbled to a halt as the birds fluttered and screeched in their cages. Blinking and squinting, he looked around him. Every lantern and brazier in the circle was ablaze.

Pynch turned back in the direction of Brundy. And as he did, he saw three slumped bodies that had been hidden by the earlier gloom. Piled in a heap in the shadow of an empty cage, each body clad in the jacket of an assistant trainer.

"Them?" asked Brundy, following his gaze. "I dropped my mask for them earlier this evening. They didn't like what they saw. Pity. The girl in particular had real potential as a falconer. Oh well. Everyone has to die sometime." The falconer began walking toward him. "You too."

Pynch staggered away, terror clogging his throat. But he'd taken no more than three or four steps when he sensed movement to his right. He raised his head just in time to see a flash of glowing eyes, massive claws, and flapping wings.

Then the gargoyle slammed into him, breaking his right arm and several of his ribs as she drove him into the ground.

Enveloped as he was in a black cloud of pain, Pynch hardly noticed when the gargoyle lifted him into the air. They spiraled upwards slowly, his body caught in the beast's grip like a rabbit in the talons of a great owl. He opened his eyes groggily, blinking away a ribbon of blood from his forehead. The gargoyle was carrying him toward one of the openings in the dome.

"Farewell, Master Pynch!" called Brundy from far below. "Of all the people in Kylden Hall, I think I'll remember you most fondly! You didn't like anyone around here either!"

And then the gargoyle passed through the opening and set a course for the open ocean to the west.

Pynch groaned as the night air rushed past his ears, felt his stomach lurch with each rise and fall of the gargoyle's great wings. They reached the water's edge in a matter of a few minutes, but still the gargoyle did not slow. She kept flying westward, high above the moonlit swells, until they were several miles off the coastline. Only then did the creature release him.

The last thing Pynch saw before he hit the water was the Gryphon's Eye, bobbing like a hellish apple in a pool of black water.

34

A River in Winter

Tabytha recognized that Jess had been crushed by the revelation that King Owyn's falconer was a traitor. Her expression was one of utter shock and sorrow, and for a moment Tabytha feared that Jess would crumple under the force of the blow. But then the dazed cast of the princess's eyes cleared and her mouth set in a thin line of anger.

"We must ride for Kylden tonight," she declared. "And ask Lylah or Clay to send a Tiding Horn of warning about Brundy." Jess turned to Traejon. "We can send it to Pynch or Captain Treadlow. They may be traitors as well for all we know, but we'll have to take that chance."

Bryscoe stepped forward, one hand raised. "Your father is safe," the spice trader said quickly. "King Owyn has erected a powerful ward around his chambers at Kylden Hall."

"What? How do you know that?"

"Lylah told me. Three days ago."

"But how does she know?"

"No idea. But she was clear on the subject."

For a moment, this information seemed to mollify Jess. For one thing, it proved that as of a few days ago at least, the king still lived. And as long as that spell remained in place and the Throneholder drew breath, no one but his familiar—not this traitorous Sevenshade or his gargoyle, not Rojenhold's most bloodthirsty warriors, not even Thylus Whytewender himself—could enter.

Just as Jess was about to return to her seat, though, her eyes widened again. "But—But to take such a step . . ."

Bryscoe pulled a hand across his beard. "Your Highness, a rumor has spread across much of Fyngree that King Owyn's familiar, whatever she is, has been lost. Captured by Whytewender's forces most likely. They say that the Throneholder can do naught but husband his energies in hopes that his familiar might somehow be rescued from her captors before he is called to the Far Shore."

Tabytha glanced sideways over at Traejon, who was standing at the fringe of the lantern light. The shadow's body remained perfectly still, but she saw a look of utter dismay flash across his face before his features hardened into a stony mask. Smoke and Ash. If Nomad truly had been seized during her return from the Widow's Torch to Kylden Hall, Traejon would never forgive himself.

"Well, these are hardly the tidings I was hoping for, but at least we are not flying blind anymore," Jess said tightly, and Tab was heartened to see that though the princess's face was flushed and her eyes dark and exhausted, there was no tremble in her voice. "None of us has the luxury of indulging our fears and regrets tonight. There will be plenty of time for tears later, if it comes to that. For now . . . we need to devise a plan." Jess looked up through the hole in the roof to the night sky. "But to be honest, I'm not in the best condition to consider such plans at the moment. I'm so tired I can barely stand."

"You're not alone on that score, Jess," agreed Noxon. He stood, stretched his arms, and yawned widely, peeking around with one eye to see if anyone else would follow suit. "This is one soldier who will have a much clearer head on the morrow, after a good night's sleep."

"For once we agree, Noxon," said Jess.

Recognizing a cue when they heard one, Bryscoe and Cady promptly explained that the manor's library had been appropriated as a common sleeping area by the refugees. When they offered to find more private lodgings for the night for Jess, she quickly waved them off, saying that the library sounded grand. But when Bryscoe suggested that Jess might benefit from a light sleeping spell from Clattermoon or one of the other assembled casters, the princess's tired eyes lit up. Tabytha approved. A sleeping spell was likely the only way to soothe Jess's feverish mind and permit her a peaceful night's slumber.

Cady escorted Jess, Max, and Noxon out of the chamber. Just before disappearing through the doorway, Noxon stopped to wave back mockingly at Tabytha, Bryscoe, and Traejon. "No disturbing our snoring when you're done here. I need my beauty sleep."

"That's an understatement," said Traejon.

Noxon laughed, then turned and trotted out the doorway to catch up with the others. As the echo of their footfalls receded, Bryscoe leaned back in his chair. "The princess seems . . . frayed," he observed in a carefully neutral voice.

"She has good reason, don't you think?" snapped Tabytha, determined to nip any criticism of Jess in the bud. "Consider how the past two months have gone for her. She's been terrorized by a gargoyle, hounded through the wilderness by soldiers and treasure seekers, attacked by wolves and an evil caster and his henchmen, watched several friends die, endured weeks of cold, hunger, and mind-numbing weariness in the saddle, and dodged an entire forest full of trees capable of burning one alive at a moment's notice. All to find at journey's end that her father's kingdom is indeed riddled with enemies—and that the most treacherous and dangerous one of all sometimes eats at his table. Not to mention that her father's familiar is missing and presumably in the possession of Fyngree's greatest enemy."

Tabytha leaned forward in her seat, her eyes boring into Bryscoe's own. "All things considered, Master Rygaard, I'd say she's holding up remarkably well."

"I understand your concern," added Traejon. "But if you had traveled with us these past weeks . . . . You underestimate her, Bryscoe. She's young, it's true. And she's been hard on herself at times. But she's borne up well, all things considered."

"I'm pleased to hear it," Bryscoe said.

"Despite the fact that she's threadbare," said Traejon. "But you know that already, don't you?"

Bryscoe looked at the shadow for a long moment, then slowly nodded. "I think Clattermoon suspects too. Possibly Dayna and one or two of the others as well. I'm not a caster. But I've spent enough time catering to wizards and witches to learn a few things. And one of them is that in most cases, a broken arm is not a severe enough injury to prevent spellcasting. A couple broken fingers or a mauled hand? Sure. But not a broken arm. And if she possessed a Thread of any potency, she wouldn't need Clay to prepare a sleeping spell for her. She'd just do it herself."

"You don't seem particularly surprised."

Bryscoe gave them a long, considering look, then stood up from his chair. "I'm not," he said as he began to pace back and forth in front of them. "Because during my time here in the Sanctuary I've made some observations that have led me to reassess my—all of our—assumptions about the Thread."

Tabytha exchanged a look with Traejon. "Well, that's an intriguing little thing to say."

Bryscoe smiled and stopped his pacing to grip the back of a chair. "Bear with me now," he said. "The witches and wizards of Tempyst are usually from families of noble birth, correct? To be sure, one occasionally hears of a caster—sometimes even a powerful one—of common blood. But those are the exceptions, yes? Ever since the Age of Elves, the great majority of Tempyst's most formidable casters, whether they swear allegiance to Kylden or Stormheel, have had aristocratic blood running through their veins. That's why generations of Suntolds and Whytewenders have ruled Fyngree and Rojenhold. And why so many of the high sentinels that preside over the provinces can trace their bloodlines back to ancestors who fulfilled the same roles."

Tabytha nodded. "The Thread is typically passed on without interruption within our ruling families, yes. There are exceptions, of course. Jess being one, to her great distress."

"And exceptions exist on the other side of that coin as well," said Bryscoe. "Commoners with casting abilities. Cady's sister Emmalyn, for example. But how do you regard such oddities? What does *everyone across Tempyst* think of such peculiar exceptions?"

"The Thread works in mysterious ways," summarized Traejon. "Magic is by its very nature a strange and unknowable force. Sometimes it bestows the Thread—or withholds it—without rhyme or reason."

"Precisely," Bryscoe said, pointing at the shadow in agreement. "But what if there *is* a rhyme or reason to it. Just not one that we've ever perceived before." He pointed to the doorway. "Seven casters are sleeping in yonder library right now. They all hail from different points of the compass. And none of them are of noble birth. Two are from moderately affluent families with a modest history of casting, the rest are ordinary working folk. Commoners whose parents toiled as bakers or farmers or farriers or chandlers."

"That's . . . odd," acknowledged Tabytha.

"At first glance, yes," said Bryscoe. "But they all share something in common. Something that I never would have heeded had they not all gathered together in one place and told their stories to one another. They all either grew up—or are the progeny of parents who grew up—as servants, soldiers, or staff in one of the great fortresses of Tempyst. Kylden Hall. Stormheel Hall. Tydewater Keep. The House of Clouds in Talonoux. Valyedon's White Palace."

Tabytha absorbed this information. "Are you sure?" she said with a glance over at Traejon, who was studying Bryscoe pensively.

"As you've already heard, Emmalyn was born at Stormheel Hall," Bryscoe said, using his left index finger to tick the tips of each finger on his right hand. "Lylah's father served for many years as captain of the guard at Valyedon. Dayna Bossory's parents tended the grounds at Kylden Hall. Clay Clattermoon grew up in the shadow of Tydewater Keep. His mother was the chief farrier in the stables of Domhnall Tremeny, Rynelle's father."

"So what does it all mean?" asked Tabytha after Bryscoe had accounted for every caster in the Sanctuary.

Bryscoe's eyes gleamed in the lamplight. "What if being gifted with the Thread is not a matter of bloodlines? What if it is a matter of place, of location? What if the only reason that certain families boast generation after generation of casters is that they live in the right place? Locations that are such natural reservoirs of magic that *other* children born there occasionally receive the Thread as well?"

Tabytha stared at Bryscoe, her mind buzzing at the ramifications of his theory. "So the Thread is not so much a birthright as a case of being born in the right place at the right time?"

"Or perhaps of being *conceived* in the right place at the right time," said Bryscoe with a smile. "For example, I wouldn't be at all surprised if Princess Jessalyn was conceived during one of her parents' periodic tours of Fyngree, while they were traveling from one city to another."

"You don't think that having Threaded parents has *anything* to do with it?"

Bryscoe shook his head thoughtfully. "I wouldn't say that. Having such parentage might well improve the odds of a child being gifted with the Thread. Perhaps after a certain number of generations, some bloodlines are as apt to pass down the Thread as they are to pass down blonde hair or brown eyes. But I still maintain that it all begins with place."

"But why wouldn't *all* children conceived in these places, these locations that you describe almost as natural lakes of magic. . . . Why wouldn't children immersed in such waters *all* grow up to become casters?" she asked. "And what of the Tusk twins? Why is Artemys threadbare and his sister not?"

Bryscoe gave her a rueful grin. "I haven't figured that out yet."

"Perhaps they aren't lakes," said Traejon.

Tabytha turned to the shadow. He'd been quiet for much of Bryscoe's oration, but now he was pacing back and forth himself, his face alight with some internal calculus. "Perhaps all of Tempyst is like a great river in winter," he continued. "Most of it is blanketed with ice and snow. But here and there the currents running beneath leave only a thin skein of ice. Places where the magic seeps up, bestowing minor casting abilities on those who tread on the ice above. And the current shifts over time, thickening the ice in some areas and thinning it in others. But suppose that there are a few bends in the river where the current courses so consistently that it creates permanent pockets of open water. Pockets like Kylden Hall and the House of Clouds and Stormheel Hall. And when the moonlight shines on these open waters at just the right angle, Threads of great and lasting power emerge, entwining themselves around the limbs of those conceived in that moment. If Aleyda Tusk was conceived even a second before her brother, perhaps that made all the difference."

Tabytha stared at Traejon. "And so all this time we've been mistaking good fortune for good bloodlines."

"That sounds about right."

"Traejon's words ring true," said Bryscoe. "I believe the Thread operates very much along those lines. It would--"

Bryscoe stopped at the sound of approaching footsteps, and a moment later Clattermoon entered the room, accompanied by a slight, dark girl of fourteen or fifteen years.

"Lylah!" declared Bryscoe with undisguised pleasure.

Tabytha snapped to attention at the mention of Lylah's name. The girl was dressed simply, her slim body floating inside light trousers, loose shirt, and a faded vest that looked several sizes too large for her. The girl's long black hair spilled around her shoulders, framing dark features that were pleasingly arranged. She was a pretty girl, if a little on the waifish side, and a shy smile stole across her face as she crossed the room with Clattermoon.

"Well, she's finally back," Clattermoon said, his voice heavy with irritation. "And now that she's here, I'm going to bed. She's all yours, Bryscoe." And with that the caster turned on his heel and stomped out of the chamber.

Lylah rolled her eyes and pulled a piece of chalk and dark slate out of a leather satchel that hung from her left shoulder. She scribbled for a moment, then held the slate out for them to see.

HELLO AND WELCOME!

Tabytha grinned broadly. "Hello, Lylah. Tis a pleasure. My name is Tabytha."

"And I'm Traejon." He stepped forward and extended his hand in greeting. Lylah brought up her right hand, but when their hands touched the girl's eyes widened and she pulled her hand loose, her smile fading as she studied the tall shadow. Tabytha looked sideways at Traejon, whose expression had turned from friendliness to puzzlement.

"Are you all right?" he asked.

Lylah stared at Traejon for another moment, then turned back to her slate. Tabytha watched her closely as she wrote. Had her hand trembled in that manner when she wrote her first message?

YES. JUST TIRED.

Tabytha exchanged glances with Bryscoe and Traejon, trying to make sense of the strange tension suddenly drifting through the room.

Bryscoe felt it too. "Where did you go tonight, Lylah?" he asked, the question clearly meant to smooth the girl's faintly furrowed brow.

HERE AND THERE. VISITED SHYMMER.

"Shymmer is Lylah's familiar," explained Bryscoe. Lylah nodded, a faint smile returning to her face. The girl seemed to be slowly recovering from whatever had upset her a moment before, but Tabytha noticed that she kept stealing glances at Traejon. It was if she couldn't help herself. This wasn't a case of a young girl swooning in response to the shadow's handsome features, though. Tabytha had no idea what had transpired, but it was much more than an instant infatuation. And Traejon knew it. She could see that underneath his casual demeanor, their encounter had unsettled him.

"Did Clay fill you in on the arrival of our guests?"

Lylah nodded again as she bent her head to write. A moment later she flipped the slate up, beaming.

EXCITED TO MEET PRINCESS!

Bryscoe chuckled. "She's excited to meet you as well. But that will have to wait until morning. She's sound asleep now, I hope." He gestured in the direction of Traejon and Tabytha with his right hand as he hoisted the lantern with his left. "As our other guests should be. Could you show them to the library, Lylah? I want to check on our watchmen before I turn in. Myles Sourtongue is not our most reliable sentry on any night, and he drank a little more wine than he should have this evening."

Lylah nodded and made a "come-with-me" gesture to Tabytha and Traejon, her gaze skittering on and off the shadow yet again. The girl's expression was now one of poorly disguised fascination, as if Traejon was some exotic beast or flower that she had never seen before.

They had just reached the room's arched entryway when the faint echo of pounding feet reached their ears. They paused and peered down the hall as the sound intensified, and a moment later Clattermoon came flying around the corner. He pulled to a stop before them, his face scrawled with dread.

"Emmalyn's lynx just came in and woke her up," he panted. "The child stroked his fur for a moment, then cried out in terror. She says the forest is thick with soldiers, all pouring forth in the direction of the Sanctuary. They're dressed for battle, and from what Emmalyn described, they'll be here by morning."

"Smoke and Ash," breathed Bryscoe. "We've been discovered. But how could Whytewender's forces have reached us? Even if they've broken across Tucker's Front, it would take weeks for such an army to penetrate the Matchstycks!"

"Perhaps it is a mercenary army paid for out of Whytewender's coffers," Tabytha managed through the tumult of her thoughts.

"What does it matter?" cried Clattermoon. "No matter where their swords were forged, they'll run us through just the same. We must flee now!"

"And go where, Clay?" demanded Bryscoe. "We can't outrun them. Half our number are children or elderly. And we'd have to leave my wagon behind. How will we feed everyone without those supplies?"

"They won't get all of us. Not if we scatter."

"Said the man without children or elderly parents to care for," Bryscoe returned.

"Are you calling me a coward?" rumbled Clattermoon.

"Doesn't matter whether you're a coward or the bravest man alive," said Traejon conversationally. "Neither one's going to outrun a condor."

Clattermoon wheeled on Traejon. "Shut up, foameater. You brought them here. We were safe until you arrived."

Traejon smiled, but Tabytha could see a dangerous glint enter his eyes. "Are you really so much of a fool that you believe that?" he said. "This trap has been hidden under the leaves for a long time. The only reason it is being sprung now is the quarry they want finally stuck its leg between its jaws. You're just the dangling meat meant to draw us in. Whoever's out there, they've known of your Sanctuary for weeks."

As Clattermoon blinked and sputtered, Tabytha moved between the two men. She placed a restraining hand on Traejon's arm, felt the corded muscle bunched under the cloth of his shirt. Clattermoon needed to withdraw before Traejon took him apart. He might be a caster, but in these close quarters the shadow could cut him down before he even began to conjure a spell. "Traejon, this bickering isn't getting us anywhere," she said in a low voice. "They'll be upon us in a matter of hours."

Traejon looked down into her upturned face, and after a moment the gathering storm in his eyes faded. "You're right, Tab," he said contritely. "I'm sorry. I'm angry with myself. I should have forced Jess to leave the forest when I saw the condor."

Tabytha pressed a hand against his chest and left it there. "Um, I'm not sure that would have been possible. Reaching here was an obsession for Jess. You know that. And none of that matters anyway. The question is, what do we do *now?*"

Traejon looked at her for a long moment, then turned to Bryscoe. "How many adult casters do we have? Four? Five? Perhaps if we use them for a rearguard defense—"

A loud cough erupted behind them, and all eyes pivoted toward Lylah as if spun on gears. The first thing Tabytha noticed was that the girl's expression was calm—serene, almost. The second was the slate that Lylah held extended toward her.

Tabytha reached out and took the slate from Lylah's hand as Traejon, Bryscoe, and Clattermoon watched silently.

Then she held it up to Bryscoe's lantern so they could all read it.

DONE RUNNING, it said.

And beneath that:

LET THEM COME.

35

The Curtain Rises

"**I**t's beautiful, isn't it?" Thylus Whytewender said.

Glynt turned to his monarch. The king's face was raised to the pre-dawn sky, his eyes locked on the full moon hovering low over the sea's rippling surface.

"Yes, Your Majesty," said Glynt as he exchanged a glance with Tumdown, who stood on the other side of the king. They were standing on a low ridge buttressing the north end of the sprawling encampment, midway up a thick fang of slanting rock that provided them with a fine vantage point over the proceedings below. "Truly, it portends the birth of a new world," he added, knowing that the sentiment would please Whytewender.

The king had chosen a striking outfit for the coming festivities. He wore gleaming black armor forged to closely follow the contours of his body, its inky surface filigreed with swirling lines of reddish gold. Draped around his neck was a long cape in the same colors, its length billowing and snapping behind him in the night wind. The braids in his dark beard, meanwhile, were adorned with an even greater number of beads and gems than usual. They twinkled in the moonlight like flashing fish in dark water, as did the various rings he wore on his long, slender fingers.

Glynt smiled to himself. On several occasions these past weeks, their war preparations had seemed reminiscent of a vast theatrical production, but never more so than tonight. Whytewender reminded him of some wealthy patron of the arts on opening night. The indulgent benefactor of some half-starved, long-anonymous playwright, come to the theatre to see whether the coin-filled purses he'd tossed the playwright's way had been money well spent. Would the action on stage reveal a soaring imagination? Tell a gripping story? Or would it be some trite, hackneyed test of audience endurance? Would the playwright weave a tale powerful enough to transport his sponsor to another world? Or would it chase him from the theatre and into his carriage before the third act even began?

Of course, the analogy was an imperfect one, for tonight Whytewender was both patron *and* playwright. True, Glynt and a few of the king's generals had helped build the stage scenery, and they had even convinced Whytewender to change a line of dialogue here and there. But Glynt was under no illusions about the authorship of this particular production. King Thylus had been painstakingly crafting this play for nearly two decades. Rewriting entire scenes until his fingers blackened with ink. Sewing costumes deep into the night. Checking the oil and wicks in the footlights.

So with the curtain finally about to rise on his masterwork, who could blame him if he dressed up for the occasion?

Glynt turned his attention to the crowded plain laid out before them. Only the faintest smear of light could be detected on the eastern horizon. But the moon and stars still shone overhead, and the illumination was sufficient for Glynt to make out the broad contours of both armies' encampments, as well as the black gash separating them in the middle distance.

In the foreground, on their side of Twenty Night Canyon, the Rojenholdean camp was a turbulent hive of activity, with horses, soldiers, and siege weapons all winding past one another under a shifting mosaic of shadow, firelight, and moonlight. The flickering shadows, combined with the faint babel of shouting, neighing horses, clanging metal, and groaning wheels, gave the impression of disarray, if not outright chaos.

But Glynt could see the patterns beneath.

He saw how the massive training tents were being emptied of their conscripts, and how those freshly minted soldiers were being funneled to the front lines. They poured into the rear entrance of the stone gatehouse standing sentinel at the foot of the Span, then spilled out through the open portcullis to the other side, coming to rest mere steps from the faintly glowing stonework of the Span.

He also saw how the stars and moon cast a deceptive gleam on the helmets and mail and weapons of those conscripts; in this dim light even other conscripts would have difficulty discerning the advanced age of their fellows' weapons and gear.

And he saw how cavalry on armored horses were positioning themselves around the legions of conscripts, pressing them up against the Span and the edge of the gorge and coastline like a garrote poised around a man's neck.

"They've noticed," said Tumdown, pointing to the south rim of the gorge with her right hand as she held a spyglass to her eye with her left.

Glynt and Whytewender both pulled out looking glasses of their own to study the Fyngrean army on the far side of the gorge. Usually the lights of their campfires and lanterns shone steadily in the pre-dawn hours. But now, with black forms rushing back and forth in front of them, they winked in and out of sight like fireflies. The faint sound of trumpets wafted across the canyon to Glynt's ears, and he immediately recognized the notes from his days in Kylden's military. It was the Fyngrean call to battle positions. Either their sentries or one of their winged familiars—or most likely, a combination of the two—had alerted General Splyntbell to the sudden escalation of activity along Rojenhold's lines.

The three of them watched intently for several minutes before King Thylus finally spoke. "Can you tell who Splyntbell is putting at his front?"

"No, Your Majesty," said Tumdown, bringing down her glass. "But he is a prideful man. He won't want to let your army set foot on the Fyngrean side of the bridge. Desecration of Fyngrean soil and all that. And the Span is a natural bottleneck. Choking off our advance there is the obvious strategy. So he'll almost certainly put battle-tested divisions there. Archers too. And he'll back them with his best cavalry."

"And meanwhile, it appears that Valyedon's late arrival on the field has convinced Splyntbell to keep them in reserve," said Glynt. "See there, at the far end of their encampment? Those fires still burn whiter than the others."

Whytewender nodded. "Yes, I see them," he said.

That had truly been a masterstroke, thought Glynt. In Whytewender's most recent Tiding Horn to Preston Excque, commander of Valyedon's forces, he had instructed him to treat all his army's firewood with a special resin that bleached the flames of the burning wood. It made for a subtle but clear marker confirming Excque's location in relation to the rest of Splyntbell's army.

Glynt could see that the eastern horizon was growing noticeably lighter now, erasing the stars from the sky one by one. But the Gryphon's Eye continued to shine brightly, as if ignoring the approaching dawn by sheer force of will.

They watched silently for the next several minutes as the armies moved into their respective positions. Rojenhold made no effort to disguise its intent; on their side of the Span, Whytewender's officers were arranging the front edge of their troops like a battering ram. Arrayed behind them sat two columns of massive siege weapons—trebuchets, ballistae, and catapults—and several wagons bearing ammunition for the fearsome engines.

Over on the Fyngrean side of the bridge, meanwhile, Glynt could see tiny figures lining the ramparts of the gatehouse fortress. And further in the distance, behind and to the sides of the gatehouse, thick lines of shield-bearing infantry, archers, and cavalry taking up supporting positions.

"Splyntbell has to be confident of victory," observed Tumdown.

"Why wouldn't he be?" said Glynt, his grin flashing in the gloom. "He appears to have every advantage. And the casters traveling with him should have nothing troubling to report from the familiars that have been patrolling over our heads these past weeks. He sees no flanking maneuvers to counter. No army of mercenaries pouring down out of the Speartips to tip the scales of war."

"No reason to fear us at all," Whytewender murmured.

"He's just been waiting for us to get hungry and frustrated enough to lash out," said Glynt. "At which point he thinks he'll teach us a lesson, like a parent would an obstinate child. After which we'll skulk home to Stormheel in humiliation and he'll return to Kylden to a hero's welcome. As far as

Splyntbell is concerned, the outcome of this battle is not in the slightest doubt. It's preordained. A matter of everyone fulfilling roles already written in the stars."

Glynt stopped at the sound of footsteps behind them. He, Tumdown, and King Thylus turned as one as Prince Teryk and a dozen archers came into view. Glynt saw with amusement that the archers were giving Teryk a fairly wide berth. No matter. They were up here to defend him from threats from the sky, not swordsmen. They didn't have to stand shoulder to shoulder with the prince to do that.

The boy was wearing his ever-present cowled cloak, the hood masking his features in a pool of black. And as usual, the cloak about his shoulder seemed to have a half-life of its own. Its length billowed and rippled independently of the winds raking across the exposed outcropping upon which they stood. As if the cloak was responding to winds from another world.

"Hello Father," said Teryk.

"Good morning," said King Thylus. "Are you ready?" he asked, and for the first time, Glynt heard an undercurrent of nervousness in the king's voice. "You will do as you've promised?"

Teryk did not answer him. Instead, he brushed past his father, walking to the edge of the precipice to take in the moon, the ocean, and the armies arrayed below them.

"Do you remember the first thing you ever killed, Father?"

Turned away from them as he was, Teryk's voice should have been carried off by the wind before it could reach their ears. But the words seemed to float about their heads, as if caught in some strange eddy in the air's currents. *"Was it a fly? A mouse?"* He paused, then added slyly, *"A person?"*

"I don't recall, Teryk. "

"No? How about the first time that you ordered something killed. Back when you were a mere stripling of a prince. A cat that scratched your tender flesh? A stubborn horse unwilling to submit to your crop? Or a childhood friend that displeased you in some way, perhaps?"

King Thylus sighed, but even in the dim gray light Glynt could see his face go pale. "Teryk. I think we should focus on the task at hand."

Teryk turned back to them, his hood slipping off his head seemingly of its own volition to reveal his faintly glowing eyes and scar-ravaged cheeks. Several of the archers took an involuntary half-step back at the sight.

"Quite so. Forgive me, father." The boy smiled faintly. "My mind wanders to the strangest places sometimes. Are the festivities still scheduled to begin at dawn?"

"Yes."

"Wonderful." Teryk turned to Glynt and gestured to the archers behind him. "These gentle souls are here for my protection, yes? In the event any winged familiars from Fyngree seek to do me harm?"

"That's right, Your Highness," said Glynt.

"My father must love me very much to take such precautions," said Teryk. "Wouldn't you agree, Captain? That your king loves his sons with all his heart?" And then he grinned broadly, as if he was enjoying witty banter with friends down at the local tavern.

Glynt glanced at Whytewender, unsure of how to respond. King Thylus sensed his unease and stepped forward. "Teryk, let Captain Glynt attend to his affairs while you attend to yours. I want your attention on the Span, please."

Teryk's smile vanished. "I'll be ready when the moment comes," he said sulkily, then turned his back to them and walked away, back to the very edge of the precipice.

Grateful for Teryk's withdrawal, Glynt spent the next few minutes positioning the archers at various points along the ridge. But once that chore was done, there was nothing for him to do but wait with Whytewender and Tumdown. He joined them where they stood at a short remove from Teryk, and for the next several minutes his gaze jumped restlessly from the prince to the Span to the ocean, where the horizon line was steadily brightening. The wait felt almost unendurable to Glynt, so great was his anticipation of the events to come. And he could feel the same tension pulsating off of Whytewender and Tumdown.

And then the first sliver of the sun's fiery body appeared on the watery horizon line.

And the trumpets of Rojenhold's army sounded in response, like an unholy congregation of crowing cockerels.

The echo of the trumpets still lingered in the rocks when the portcullis of the Rojenhold gatehouse was raised. Seconds later, the first legions of Rojenholdean troops emerged out onto the broad Span like a great colony of ants setting off on a high roof beam. Glynt gave a low grunt of satisfaction. The past weeks of drill had not been a waste of time. The farmers and housekeepers and chandlers hidden beneath all that armor looked for all the world like veteran troops as they began their march across the great bridge. Then, even as the conscripts continued to pour through the gate, siege weapons appeared behind them one by one, pulled forward by great teams of straining horses covered head to hoof in heavy armor.

Glynt turned his looking glass to the far side of the Span. He didn't have long to wait. Less than five minutes later, the leading edge of the army of Fyngree stampeded onto the bridge from the gate of its own fortress, yellow and blue pennants snapping in the wind. But unlike Rojenhold's ponderous advance, Splyntbell's forces were led by columns of armored Fyngrean cavalry. They galloped forward up the bridge's incline, a thousand riders or more, the hooves of their steeds booming like war drums on the ancient Elvish stone. They were nearly a quarter of the way across the Span before the first Fyngrean foot soldiers and siege weapons began to roll out of the gatehouse behind them.

Glynt took a quick glance at Whytewender, whose own glass remained fixed on the Span. Whytewender sensed his gaze, though, and he offered a thin smile. "They're taking the bait."

"Yes, Your Majesty. They are." And with that Glynt brought his glass back up to his one good eye to watch the show unfold.

As expected, Splyntbell had organized a decisive response to Whytewender's attack. He could not allow Rojenhold's siege engines to gain the crown of the Span; from that height they would not only be able to bash the Fyngrean gatehouse into rubble, but bombard the Fyngrean encampments beyond.

But as far as the Fyngrean general was concerned, Whytewender and his commanders had made a grievous error. Whytewender appeared to be counting solely on his infantry to secure the crown of the bridge for his siege weapons. He apparently intended to keep the entire Rojenholdean cavalry in reserve during this initial assault.

Glynt could see that Splyntbell intended to make Whytewender pay for that decision. The Fyngrean general aimed to claim the crown of the bridge first with his fast-moving cavalry. Then sweep down from the high ground with that same cavalry—any one of which was worth a dozen foot soldiers in combat—and tear Whytewender's infantry apart as he established his own ballistae and trebuchets along the Span's crown. As long as Splyntbell's forces rebuffed any belated mobilization of enemy cavalry, they could use their claim over the Span's high ground to pound away at the Rojenhold position with impunity. Splyntbell might even be harboring dreams of battering Whytewender into submission before the day was out.

And as Glynt watched the Fyngrean cavalry race across the Span, sprinting rabbits in comparison to Rojenhold's tortoise-like infantry, he felt a certain cold serenity flood into his bones, washing away the last of his anxiety.

The leading edge of the Fyngrean cavalry had just materialized over the crown of the arching bridge when both armies unleashed their first salvos of arrows. They rained down on each side, spilling the first blood of the day on the Span's lime-green expanse. Along each edge of the bridge, Glynt saw tiny figures stagger and tumble down into the abyss below.

And then the armies crashed into one another—if one can describe a dagger being punched into a soft belly as a "crash." The Fyngrean cavalry pounded down the incline and tore through Rojenhold's leading line of infantry with little resistance, horses and riders leaving trampled limbs and sword-slashed bodies in their wake. Fyngrean infantry followed a few minutes later, rolling downhill in the cavalry's wake in a gleaming surge of spears, swords, axes, and morningstars. They disposed of Rojenhold's siege weapons as they went, either steering them off the Span into the blackness below or setting them afire. As the catapults and ballistae caught fire, black clouds of smoke erupted and swirled around the bridge.

To be sure, it was not a total slaughter. The conscripts had no choice but to fight, as they knew they would be cut down by their own countrymen if they tried to retreat. And

Whytewender had had the good sense to sprinkle his conscript divisions with minor officers of fanatical zeal. Men and women perfectly willing to march to their deaths in service to a new age of Rojenholdean glory—especially after they consumed the contents of the decanters that Tumdown had distributed to them a few hours earlier.

So here and there along the Span, Glynt could see pockets of fiercer resistance. Areas where clots of conscripts were rallying together to ward off the death bearing down on them. Was it courage that led them to fight like that against such hopeless odds? Terror? It didn't really matter, thought Glynt, as he watched one such clot dissolve under the slashing blades of several Fyngrean cavalrymen.

In the end they were just meat.

And then the moment that Glynt had been waiting for arrived. It was almost imperceptible at first. A mere slowing in the pace of slaughter at a few isolated spots along the blood-slickened Span. But then he could see the realization pick up speed and sweep across the triumphant Fyngrean cavalry and infantry, cutting through their ranks like a sudden, sour gust of wind.

What was it that triggered it? Did the number of oddly old—or young—faces at the ends of their swordtips and spearpoints finally sink in? Did the Fyngrean troops finally realize that the screams of some of the conscripts pushed off the edges of the Span sounded more like the voices of children than veteran warriors? Or perhaps it finally dawned on a few blood-spattered Fyngrean commanders that the continued lack of a counterpunch on the part of Whytewender's army—a cavalry attack, a fusillade of fire from the trebuchets arrayed along their edge of the canyon, *something*—despite the disaster unfolding on the bridge might not mark an appalling paralysis of military leadership, but something else entire.

Like a trap.

Whatever the trigger, Glynt heard the thin, faint sound of Fyngrean horns over the wind once again. In a matter of seconds, the Fyngreans disengaged and began a slow retreat back up the bridge. The withdrawal was orderly and unhurried, which made it easier for them to pick their way through the mounds of unmoving soldiers and horses and burning artillery littering their path. Here and there Glynt saw Fyngreans stop to provide aid to wounded comrades. Meanwhile, the crews manning the siege weapons at the top of the Span began settling in to their new home. With that commanding vantage point under their control, the Fyngreans could still pulverize the Rojenholdean gatehouse below whenever they pleased.

Glynt heard another sound behind him. A titter of laughter, followed by a rush of strange words from a language he didn't recognize. He turned to where Teryk stood at the end of the outcropping.

And felt his knees turn to water.

Teryk Whytewender floated three feet above the ground, his long black hair whipping in the wind, his cloak wriggling and snapping like a sheet of spasming black flame. The prince held his arms spread wide and curled at the elbows, as if he held invisible buckets of water, and his long spidery fingers flashed from one contorted position to the next.

Teryk was looking out over the Uncrossable Sea, as if searching for something in that great steel-gray immensity. Glynt turned to follow his gaze and saw a strange ripple on the water's surface, far out to sea. At first it was hard to make sense of the sight. It was as if the horizon line had been artificially raised. But as the line continued to rise Glynt recognized it for what it was: a rogue wave that was increasing in size with each passing second as it barreled toward the mainland. It was hard to tell from this distance—the wave was probably still a half-mile offshore—but it already looked as if it was four or five stories tall. And it was heading straight for the rift in the coastline known as Twenty Night Canyon—and the gleaming bridge that spanned that gorge.

Thunder and Thorn, Glynt muttered to himself, drawing a ragged breath of relief that he was on high ground. To what manner of dark creature was the prince threaded?

A moment later the approaching wave penetrated the consciousness of the thousands of Fyngrean and Rojenholdean soldiers on the Span. One moment the last remnants of Whytewender's conscript army were dragging themselves back down the bridge's Rojenholdean side as the victorious Fyngreans gathered at the crown of the Span to consolidate their position. The next moment they were all madly scrambling to get off the bridge before the approaching wall of water hit.

Some of the Fyngrean cavalry nearly made it. Frantically digging their heels into the flanks of their chargers, they sailed past the soldiers running on foot as if the latter were standing still. A few of the riders might even have drawn near enough to hear the exhortations of their comrades atop the parapets of the gatehouse. But then the monster wave reached landfall.

It rose up over the Span, a moving mountain of foam-marbled water. As if suspended from invisible hooks, the wave loomed over the bridge for a long second, blotting out the low-hanging sun so that the entire length of the Span was plummeted into darkness.

And then the wave spawned by Teryk's malediction broke over the bridge, obliterating cavalry and soldiers and horses and siege weapons with a deafening thunder that seemed to come from the deepest trenches of the ocean. From there the tidal wave pushed deeper into the canyon, punching through the rocky corridor with such volume and force that a great gout of water exploded out of the gorge's western terminus. Glynt felt a light spray of water from the geyser settle on his head and shoulders.

The water then withdrew in a great burbling shudder, revealing a gleaming bridge that had been scoured clean of all the blood and gore that had been spilled on it that morning. As well as every soldier, horse, and siege weapon that had been standing on it a minute earlier. Not even a stray sword remained to blemish the surface of its great expanse. The Span looked pristine and new, as if its Elvish creators had just completed their work that very morning.

Glynt shook his head in wonderment. The wave had claimed a third—perhaps even half!—of Fyngree's entire cavalry, not to mention untold numbers of infantry and many of its best siege weapons. And what had Rojenhold sacrificed? A handful of older siege engines and a few thousand worthless peasants. A pittance, given the immensity of the blow they had just struck.

Truly, Act I had exceeded every expectation.

He turned back to Teryk, who had sagged down to his knees, his head bowed as if in prayer. His thin form swayed slightly, as if he were naught but a bag of bones rattling in the wind. Glynt studied the fallen prince, his face impassive but his thoughts a blur of possibilities. Had the spell exacted too high a price? Had it permanently damaged him in some way—or perhaps even sent him spiraling toward death? The notion was a pleasing one. With Splyntbell's army broken and the Jailer's Key now Whytewender's for the taking, Teryk was no longer essential to the king's plans. And if he were to expire now, or in the next few days, Glynt would no longer have to endure his company.

At that moment Teryk slowly raised his scarred, moon-pale face and turned Glynt's way. His lips peeled back from his gums in a leering grin that quickly reddened due to the blood trickling into his mouth from his left nostril. Glynt turned away, chilled by a dark intuition that the ruined prince knew exactly what he'd been thinking.

The rest of the morning took on a dreamlike quality for Glynt. Each moment seemed to bring something new to savor. And after a while the images intertwined in his mind like scenes from some dark and fabulous mural painted in garish hues of blood:

Such as when Preston Excque and his Valyedon forces tossed their Fyngrean banners in the dirt, raised the pennants of Rojenhold in their place, and slashed into the unprotected rear of Splyntbell's forces.

And when King Thylus cast a spell that rolled away several boulders on the Fyngrean edge of the Pauper's Way, revealing the entrance to the subterranean tunnel that Whytewender had spent the last sixteen years constructing.

And when armored Rojenholdean solders came boiling out of the tunnel like beetles from hell to wreak havoc on Fyngree's vulnerable left flank.

And when the Rojenholdean cavalry finally took to the empty Span, rolling forward with monstrous siege engines that began bombarding the Fyngrean gatehouse from positions at the crown of the bridge.

And when a lone eagle came spiraling out of the clouds toward a capering, singing Teryk, talons poised to rake out the prince's eyes, only to disappear in a burst of light after being struck by a barrage of arrows.

But the image that stayed with Glynt the most—the one that returned to him again and again over the course of the day—was not of any of these. Instead, it was of a long-ago morning when he and his brother Traejon had gone exploring in the woods behind their home. They had been aimlessly following the shoreline of a pond when Traejon had stopped in his tracks, his little head looking down at something at his feet. Glynt had stepped forward and looked down himself to see the corpse of a duck in the grass.

The duck had not been dead long. The green and gold plumage on its head and along its wings still retained some of its vivid brilliance. But Glynt had hardly noticed the vibrant color of the bird's feathers. His eyes were drawn instead to the legions of pasty white maggots, and how they squirmed as they feasted on the bird's cooling body.

3 6

Mad Jack

Ben returned to wakefulness in fits and starts, prodded to dawning consciousness by scattered sensory signals that emerged as if from a deep fog. First, the crackle and pop of burning logs. Followed closely by a dim realization of pleasant, steady warmth on his skin, like the feel of the sun on a bright spring morning. Then the unmistakable aroma of fresh-baked bread and . . . could that be some sort of spicy stew? He felt his mouth begin to water as he sleepily pondered the possibility.

Then a disordered tangle of memories suddenly surged up and out of the darkness of his mind. Memories of the crushing cold and endless horizons of the Puzzle. Of approaching lantern lights across the ice, and of a looming giant garbed in heavy furs. A dim shard of memory of being loaded onto a large sled. And of lying flat on his back, staring up at the stars as they floated by overhead. And then . . . darkness.

Ben opened his eyes.

The room in which he lay was large and rectangular in shape, its high ceiling supported by pillars and beams of thick pine. Beyond his feet he could see a large oaken table with chairs, several rough-hewn but sturdy looking cabinets, and an assortment of shelves and smaller tables laden with half-spilled bags of onions and potatoes and stacks of fire-blackened skillets and pots. Several lanterns suspended from the ceiling and atop a small corner table cast that end of the room in a warm honey glow.

Ben shifted his head to take in the far side of the room. It was dominated by a large hearth fire that cast light on more shelves—these crammed with books and papers—lining part of one wall. Another long section of wall was festooned with snowshoes, skis, fishing gear, and canoe paddles. An assortment of spears, swords, and daggers leaned against one of two comfortable-looking chairs spaced in front of the fire. Atop the back of each chair sprawled a cat—one a gray tabby, the other a calico. The calico was sound asleep. The tabby, though, was intently studying Wynk, who was sprawled out on a thick rug before the hearth, her flanks rising and falling in a steady cadence. And evenly spaced around the room entire, a set of moderately sized windows that revealed snow-covered pines. By the slanting quality of the light, Ben judged that the sun was either rising or preparing to depart for the day. He was so disoriented that he couldn't hazard a guess as to which was more likely.

"Sit up, boy," a deep voice rumbled off to his right. "Bout time you stirred."

Ben started, then slowly pushed himself to a sitting position on what he saw was a long bench that had been padded with blankets and furs. Ben looked down dumbly at his clothing. He was wearing a man's shirt, but it was so enormous that it hung on him like a nightshirt. And he was naked underneath. Before he could do much more than register this embarrassing fact, however, his eyes settled on his feet, and he felt a wave of bewildered but genuine relief sweep over him.

Before he had slipped into unconsciousness, his feet had been frozen blocks of ice. There was no doubt in his mind that all of his toes had been lost to frostbite. But now they looked and felt as if they had never experienced anything worse than a chill breeze. Ben wiggled his toes experimentally, an involuntary smile rising to his lips as they moved up and down painlessly.

Then a shadow fell across his lap and he looked up. The man standing before him was tall and heavy with muscle, dressed in a light shirt and trousers, with bear-sized hands upon which glistened several thin rings of a deep cerulean hue. He had a great mane of light brown hair, lightly threaded with silver, that swept back from his forehead all the way to his shoulders, and a short beard of equally prodigious density. His features were more striking than handsome, all sharp angles and sun-leathered skin. But as Ben's eyes skittered across the face of the stranger, he saw that the dark brown eyes looking down on him appeared to hold no threat.

The man thrust a large plate toward him. "Here you go, sleepyhead. Eat up. You look like you need it."

Ben accepted the plate, which bore the hallmarks of heavy use. Chipped and scratched, it looked like it might be older than him. But the plate held two warm slices of dark bread, hunks of butter melting in the center of each one. And in the center of the plate sat a fat mug of steaming stew that smelled absolutely marvelous.

"Thank you," Ben said after a moment. "Do you have a spoon I might use?"

"Spoon? No. Don't believe in 'em. One less thing to wash. You know how to lift a mug, don't you?"

He doesn't believe in spoons? "Uh, yes, sure." Ben raised the mug to his lips and took a big slurp. It was a creamy concoction full of vegetables and hunks of fish and sausage, and it tasted just as delicious as it smelled. Ben suddenly realized that he was ravenously hungry, and he took another couple mouthfuls from the steaming mug. Then he set it down and looked around. "Where am I?" he asked with dawning curiosity. And then his eyes widened as his groggy thoughts finally cleared enough for him to remember who he had been traveling with. "Where are my mother and brother?" he demanded, his heart suddenly hammering in his chest.

"Tut, tut," the man said mildly. "They're in the other room," he said, jerking a thumb over his back, "still sleeping off your little stroll through the Puzzle. They're fine. I cleaned up their frostbite as well. That was taxing. Had to take a little nap myself after treating the lot of you."

The man nodded toward the nearest window. "As far as your location is concerned, you're in the southern Speartips. Far below the worst of what these mountains have to offer. In Fyngree, according to the mapmakers. Valyedon lies a week to the west."

The man pulled out one of the table chairs and sat down heavily. "You're safe here, son. Folks don't come to this valley. It's cursed, they say. Herders seeking summer pastures, miners looking for an undiscovered lode, they all steer clear. Or at least they've steered clear since I came here." A hint of a smile came to the man's lips. "Funny what a few well-placed enchantments can do to darken a place's reputation. Even the gargoyles learned to give it a wide berth. Though that took a while. Stubborn lot, they are."

Ben slowly resumed eating. It was strange sitting here clad in nothing but a stranger's shirt, stuffing his face under that same stranger's gaze. But he was famished, and the stew was very good.

"So no one else lives here? In this valley, I mean?"

The man shook his head. "All to myself. Oh, once in a while visitors come through. People unaware of its notoriety." The man frowned. "Had a few soldiers pass through a couple weeks back, as a matter of fact. But a couple spells were sufficient to get them riding around in circles until they departed. They might have been more of a nuisance if they'd had a decent caster among them, but their ranks contained nothing but threadbares."

Ben nodded, then turned the mug up and polished off the last of its contents. "Where are my clothes?" he asked hesitantly.

The man snorted and made a floating away gesture with one hand. "Gone. Burned 'em. They were disgusting. Couldn't be salvaged. We'll get your bum covered soon enough, though. I'm almost done with your trousers."

Ben looked at him blankly.

"I make my own clothes, boy. Most of them anyway. Easy enough to make some for you and yours. Already finished some clothing for the woman who was accompanying you—I assume she's your mother." The man grinned. "No worries, boy, I have more. And it won't take much fabric to cover those skinny shanks of yours."

Ben's face reddened, but he didn't say anything. The man was probably speaking truthfully. By those last days in the Puzzle, their clothing and furs had become so stiffened and stained with sweat and grease and blood that they probably were unsalvageable. If the man really was making new clothes for them . . . well, that was good news, he guessed. Provided he knew his way around a needle and thread, as he claimed.

Ben picked up one of the pieces of bread, his eyes wandering around the room. "What are your cats' names?" he finally asked in an effort to break the lengthening silence between them.

"Lankhmar and Carsultyal."

"Those are unusual names."

"They're unusual cats."

The man leaned forward, placing his forearms on his knees. "All right, boy. You've got a full tummy now, and you've taken a full inventory of your fingers and toes, and I trust that they're all in good working order. So it's time for you to answer a few of *my* questions. What's your name? And how did the three of you—and that big cat of yours—end up all the way out there in the Puzzle?"

Ben tore off a big hunk of the last piece of bread with his teeth and chewed slowly as he considered the questions. There was no doubt that this stranger had saved their lives by whisking them out of that nightmare of snow and cold. But there was no telling where Ben and his mother and brother *really* were at the moment. Were they truly in Fyngree? The presence of snow on the boughs outside suggested that they were in the Speartips somewhere, but they could still be in Rojenhold for all he knew.

And to what crown did this man swear allegiance? It was impossible to tell. Most residents of the borderlands traced their heritage to the same distant ancestors, and there was little in the way of physical characteristics, accents, or mannerisms to distinguish citizens of the two kingdoms from one another. And whatever his nationality, might the man be angling to see if the family he had rescued had a price on its head?

Or worst of all, might all this be a ruse? Ben felt a cold chill run down his back. What if this man was a member of the Faithful Shield, orchestrating some elaborate charade to draw Ben back into the Shield's embrace—or to punish him for fleeing?

And if the stranger *was* one of Whytewender's agents, could Ben best him in battle if it came to that? The stranger's physical advantages were obvious, but that alone did not particularly faze Ben. As long as he could get a little distance between the two of them—ten yards, say—he would have time to complete any number of castings capable of crippling or even killing the hardiest of warriors, now that his hands were in good working order again.

But this wasn't just some muscle-headed mercenary sitting across from him. Clearly, the man was a formidable caster in his own right. Even if his claims that he had littered the valley with enchantments were false, healing spells were well beyond the capability of minor wizards or witches. And their host appeared to be in the prime of his casting life, with years of experience with the Thread to draw upon. Ben, on the other hand, was still learning daily about the nature and extent of his powers. An unpleasant sensation of mingled frustration and apprehension stole over him as he realized that, for the moment at least, they were at this stranger's mercy.

The man sighed and scratched at his beard. "Perhaps you should renew your Thread with your familiar, son. Then maybe we can talk."

Ben looked over to where the snow leopard lay in front of the crackling hearth. "Wynk?"

The big cat instantly rolled up to her feet, as if she had been just waiting to be called. She indulged herself with a long, slow stretch, then padded over to Ben's side, her big golden eyes locked on him all the while.

Ben placed his hand on the beast's shoulder, and a flood of images rushed through the corridors of his mind. He watched through Wynk's eyes as the wolf-drawn sled drew up to Ben, his brother, and his mother out on the ice and snow; as the stranger carefully strapped them onto the sled; as the man and his team of wolves, led by a black wolf larger and stronger than the others, carried them out to the edge of the Endless Empty, through a narrow notch in the mountains—the fabled Keyhole?—and deep into the Speartips; as they fetched up at a large single-story cabin nestled deep in a grove of pines; as one by one, the man quietly healed their cold-ravaged skin and laid them down to sleep; and as the stranger roamed around the big cabin, preparing food and sewing clothing.

Ben dropped his hand from Wynk's shoulder, fighting back tears of relief and gratitude. The stranger pretended not to notice. Instead he stood up and walked to the cabin's main door, where the leopard had sauntered after completing her interactions with Ben. The man opened the door and Wynk bounded out into the snowy woods. He looked out the doorway for a moment longer, then gently shut it and turned back into the room. "Your familiar never left your side the past two days," he rumbled. "She must have been going mad being cooped up in here like that."

Ben watched the man return to his seat by the table. "Thank you for saving us," he croaked, swallowing hard.

The man smiled, big white teeth flashing. "My pleasure, boy. But if you really want to show your appreciation, you'll tell me how you and your family came to be wandering in that wasteland. Because I don't think you got lost picking blueberries. So how about you start with your name?"

And so Ben spent the next hour recounting the series of events that had nearly resulted in their demise. Wynk's arrival and their subsequent departure from Hanken. Glynt's menacing visit and Tumdown's tutorials. Ben's dreams of the mysterious girl and their flight from their father and the torments of the Puzzle.

It was hard at first, given his innate shyness and the stranger's imposing appearance. But after a time he became more comfortable, especially when he saw how attentively the man was listening to his tale. The man asked him a few questions seeking clarification on one detail or another—and Ben could have sworn that his mention of the girl in his dreams triggered *something* in the man's eyes. But for the most part he just listened silently.

Ben had just finished his account when his mother walked into the room, Rowan held tightly in her arms. He leaped to his feet and ran over to them, and the three of them dissolved into a scrum of fierce hugs and happy tears and joyful exclamations. His eyes returned again and again to those of his mother, and his heart soared at the way they shone with love and pride and life. Ben felt as if he could hug them forever.

After several minutes, though, he reluctantly stepped away from his embrace of his mother and younger brother to study them more closely. Malkyn's hair was disheveled and her features were drawn, but there was no hint of frostbite on his mother's face or hands. And Rowan looked the same. His face was pale and his hair was a chaos of corkscrews and cowlicks, but his skin no longer bore the markings of the Puzzle's searing cold. And while his little brother also appeared to be draped in one of man's shirts, he saw with considerable relief that his mother was still garbed in the filthy, sweat-stained clothing that she had worn under her furs throughout their journey.

At that moment the stranger walked to the table carrying a large tray heaped with mugs of stew and thick slices of bread. He set the tray down and began dispersing the items around the table. "Dinner's ready," he said gruffly.

Malkyn tore her gaze away from her eldest son to take in their host. "And this must be our rescuer," she said, her eyes shining with fresh tears. "We are forever in your debt, sir. Please accept my deepest thanks. I don't know how I can ever repay you."

This time it was the wizard's turn to look uncomfortable. "Any man with a beating heart would have done the same," he grumbled. "And in truth, your son's familiar deserves much of the credit. If Ramblefoot—my own familiar—had not seen the leopard hunting at the edge of the Puzzle, where the ice meets the mountains, I never would have known of your presence."

Malkyn smiled. "You are being modest, Master . . . ? I'm afraid I am at a disadvantage, sir. I was in such a rush to thank you that I did not give Ben the opportunity to make proper introductions."

The man smiled and took a step back so that he could look at all three of them at once. "Thrynjack Brymborne, at your service," he said breezily.

Ben felt the blood drain from his face upon hearing the name, and he heard his mother gasp. Brymborne smirked at their shocked expressions. "Yes," he intoned in a mocking voice. "You've fallen into the clutches of old Mad Jack, the bone-eating hermit himself."

✝ ✝ ✝

Brymborne shook his head as he refilled their goblets with water from a big ceramic pitcher. "Tumdown's main purpose with those lessons was not to improve your spellcasting, Ben. She may have helped your focus a bit, and tempted you with dribs and drabs of instruction in alchemy." He gestured to the far end of the room, where lines of books and dark jars of cloudy liquid filled the shadowed shelves. "But any well-stocked conjurer's library can provide you with a grounding in spellbinding. The Thread remains a live thing that blossoms of its own accord. The alien words, the hand motions, they issue forth out of you like water from an underground spring, do they not?"

Ben nodded, his eyes widening in recognition. "Yes. Yes, it is kind of like that. Or like breathing. One doesn't think of working one's lungs to sustain himself. One just does it. My casting has started to feel a little like that. The words just come unbidden to my lips. I don't even know what they mean. They just rise and escape from my mouth when my mind curls around a given spell." He looked down and worked his fingers back and forth. "It is the same with my hands. I can *feel* how they want to make certain motions to complete a casting. I used to fight that feeling. It felt so strange at first, as if someone else was trying to control my hands. But I'm learning to let go. To let them do what they want to do. It's like . . . like swimming with the current instead of fighting against it."

Ben looked across the table to his mother and they smiled at one another. She had been listening to their discussions of castings and the Thread for an hour, and she looked no less fascinated now than when they had begun.

And unlike Ben and Rowan, who were still walking about in nothing but Brymborne's shirts, Malkyn was sporting new clothing from head to toe. Before sitting down to eat, Brymborne had first given her a shirt, tunic, and trousers, all made of soft, comfortable fabric. When the caster had presented her with the clothes Ben thought that it might prompt a fresh outpouring of tears. But his mother had simply gawped at the man for a moment, then thanked him and scampered back into the bedroom to change and use the wash basin that he had filled for her. A few minutes later she had returned to the main room dressed from head to toe in new clothing—all of which had been perfectly tailored to fit her form.

"Swimming with the current," said Brymborne meditatively. "I like that. Very good. And you've learned that without benefit of Tumdown's 'lessons.' No, her primary purpose in visiting you was indoctrination, Ben. To immerse you in the poisonous creed of her masters. Whytewender's creed, which holds that any road to power and glory must be sowed with the tears and blood of others. And that the road must be replenished with those elements again and again to keep the pathway clear. The bastard."

Ben nodded somberly, but Brymborne's harsh words had no effect on the cloud of euphoria on which he was floating. Not only were he and his mother and brother safely in Fyngree, far from the reach of Faxon Glynt or King Whytewender. But he was discussing magic and familiars and spellcasting with one of the most legendary wizards in all of Tempyst as if they had known each other for years. He felt a secret hope flare to life within him once again. A hope that his Thread might actually prove to be a gift rather than a curse.

A squeal of laughter exploded behind Ben, and he turned in his seat. Rowan was huddled under several blankets that had been propped up into a makeshift fort by a latticework of chairs and canoe paddles. Carsultyal and Lankhmar were prowling around the perimeter of the fort, pouncing whenever Rowan poked a hand or foot out from the blankets.

Then Ben heard a rough scratching at the door, and both of the cats scurried into the fort with Rowan. Brymborne strode over to the door and opened it. Ben caught a glimpse of darkening sky and black pines in the door frame, and he realized that evening was approaching. And then an enormous black wolf with silver markings on its face and chest padded into the room in a swirl of snowflakes and frigid air.

Ramblefoot stopped a few feet from the table, ice-blue eyes turning from Ben to his mother without expression. Brymborne walked over and laid one big hand on the wolf's shoulder. He closed his eyes as he slipped into the beast's consciousness, then spent the next several seconds standing silently, his hand still on the wolf. Then he opened his eyes and smiled at Ben's mother. "All quiet, Malkyn. No one in the valley tonight. And between Ramblefoot and your son's familiar, we'll know of any visitors who venture into any of the neighboring valleys as well."

Ben heard a squeak of fright from behind him, and he turned just in time to see Rowan's head withdraw behind the blankets of his fort. He walked over and kneeled down next to the entranceway. "Rowan?" he said. "There's nothing to be afraid of, little brother. The wolf is a friend to Master Brymborne. The same way that Wynk is my friend. She helped save us when we were lost in the snow." He looked back over his shoulder at Ramblefoot, whose eyes were watching him with an unblinking intensity that, whether he wanted to admit it or not, gave him a little thrill of unease.

"Would you like to come out and meet her?" Ben continued. "We can go over together and thank her for helping us."

The fort was silent for several seconds. Then Rowan shuffled out on his knees, using one arm to sweep back the blanket, the other to keep the calico cat pinned against his chest. The cat—was that Carsultyal or Lankhmar?—looked resigned to being transported about in this undignified fashion until she saw Ramblefoot. At which point the cat instantly wriggled out of Rowan's grasp and darted into the kitchen, ignoring the boy's protests.

Ben took Rowan's hand and coaxed him over to Ramblefoot. He murmured words of thanks to the wolf from a respectful distance and Rowan solemnly followed suit, his eyes wide and shining. The familiar paid them little heed for the most part. At one point, though, she swiveled her big head around and looked at them as if noticing them for the first time. Rowan took a deep shuddering breath and stepped forward, one little hand extended to touch her fur. But Ben gently pulled his brother back. "No, Rowan," he said quietly. "Ramblefoot is our friend. But the only person she wants touching her is Master Brymborne."

"Why?"

"That's just the way it is, Rowan. Wynk's the same way, remember? My touch is the only one she welcomes."

Rowan looked up anxiously into his older brother's face. "But Ramblefoot still likes me, right?"

Ben smiled and tousled his brother's hair. "Oh yes. There's no doubt about that."

Ben glanced over at Brymborne, who nodded slightly in what he hoped was acknowledgement of a situation deftly handled.

Brymborne went back to the door. "All right, out you go," he said briskly as he opened it wide. "Sentry duty awaits." The big wolf promptly turned, padded over to the doorway, and slipped back into the night. The caster watched her for a moment, then shut the door and turned back into the room with a grin. "Didn't have to ask her twice, did I? She hates spending more than an hour or two in here. She likes the fire, but the cats drive her barking mad. Figuratively, I mean."

3 7

Trapped

Traejon climbed the stairs of the manor's lone standing tower and walked to one of the empty window wells. Seating himself on its stone sill, he surveyed the rustling roof of the vast forest laid out before him, feeling not unlike a sailor atop the crow's nest of a ship riding the swells of a great sea.

Tendrils of fog hovered around the ruined manor and dissolved into the woods. Further in the distance, scrawls of smoke from trees that had burst into flame overnight drifted languidly to the east. Yet despite the fog and smoke, the Matchstycks still shimmered red and orange and yellow, cutting through the murk as if the stems and veins of every leaf were suffused with liquid light. Traejon decided that it was both a stirring and disquieting sight.

Songbirds darted to and fro along the edge of the woods, their distant chirps and trills just barely reaching his ears. Usually he liked the sound. But this morning their warblings sounded oddly discordant. Jarring even. Like foolish musicians playing a lighthearted reel when a storm warning was called for. Or a funeral dirge.

Such had been the hue of his thoughts throughout the nighttime hours. Unable to sleep, Traejon had wandered throughout the derelict manor house. His steps had not been aimless; he had used the time to examine the sightlines of every corner and vantage point, study the layouts of the various rooms for possible points of entrance and escape. And now, as the sky slowly brightened, Noxon and Max and a few of the more able-bodied refugees were tucked into the best of these spots, swords and bows and full quivers in hand.

The sound of approaching footsteps reached his ears, followed by Tabytha's warm voice. "Ah, there you are," she said. "Mind some company?"

Traejon turned and smiled, pushing his black thoughts away. "Good morning." Tab's features were shadowed by weariness, her hair drawn back in a short, careless ponytail that had failed to capture several stray locks. But her big dark eyes still shone, and Traejon's gaze lingered over the light sprinkle of freckles across her nose and cheeks and the pleasing curve of her lips.

Tabytha joined him at the window well, and the two of them spent the next moment or two in companionable silence, watching the valley slowly wake up.

"I feel like I'm looking at a dreamscape," Tabytha finally said, her breath puffing in the chill morning air. "Beautiful but kind of unreal. Like something conjured out of a fairytale."

"Yes. You know what I find most strange?"

"What's that?"

"Fallen leaves. There are no fallen leaves to crunch under your feet out there. Nothing floating down from the branches. Nothing for the wind to pile up into rustling drifts. I miss that."

"Hmm. That's true, isn't it? How did I not notice that?" Tab scanned the forest's edge for even one stray leaf. "They just cling there on their branches, their colors deepening with each passing hour, until they explode into flame. Perhaps that's part of the unreality of this place. A forest where a leaf never falls."

Traejon turned to look at her and felt his chest suddenly constrict at the knowledge that she—both of them— would in all likelihood be dead within a matter of hours. They had never lain with one another during these past weeks—had never even kissed—but the thought of seeing her cut down and borne away to the Far Shore filled Traejon with a sick fear that made his throat tighten. And following close on the heels of that dark thunderhead of foreboding, a desperate but diamond-hard resolve to bring them both through this somehow. If only to see Tab's bright smile again.

So this is what love feels like, he thought heavily. Like having your heart exposed to the raw open air.

"Tabytha," he said.

She turned to him then, a half-smile on her lips. But when Tab saw his expression her smile faded and she drew in her breath. Traejon stepped toward her, long-suppressed desire sweeping over him in a flood. She opened her arms hungrily and they fell into a long, deep kiss, their hands moving over each other's arms and shoulders and back as if seeking to memorize each curve and plane on the other's body. Until finally, gently, they broke apart and opened their eyes to one another.

"Thunder and Thorn," said Tab huskily. "I hope we get to do that again."

Traejon managed a small smile, his pulse hammering now in a way that it never had in combat. "Me too."

Tab took his left arm and raised it up, then curled herself under it until she was nestled tightly against his side. She looked out over the forest below them. "Let's stay here forever," she said quietly. "Right on this spot. Right in this moment."

Traejon nodded, not trusting himself to speak. He stroked her hair as they watched the birds wheel and dart at the edge of the wood. Two trees in the far distance erupted into flames within seconds of one another, and Tab took his other hand in hers.

They stood like that for a full three minutes. Until Emmalyn's lynx familiar came streaking out of the forest and into the castle. A moment later they heard faint shouts below indicating that the approaching soldiers were only thirty minutes out.

As forevers go, it left a lot to be desired.

They kissed again briefly, murmured promises and encouragements, then reluctantly parted ways—Tab to the half-collapsed ruins of the keep's other tower and Traejon down to the front gateway. He found Lylah standing at the entrance, Clay Clattermoon and Dayna Bossory on either side of her. Traejon nodded to them absentmindedly, still savoring the taste of Tab on his lips, but they didn't appear to notice him. Lylah's head was bowed over her slate tablet. The other two casters were peering over her shoulder, reading her jottings as they unspooled on the gray surface.

Traejon left the manor and went outside. He tramped through the tall, frost-silvered grass and spider webs of fog until he reached the lone cloaked figure standing beside the remnants of an old waist-high stone wall that must have once marked the perimeter of the manor's front courtyard.

"Good morning, Jessalyn."

Jess turned away from the forest below and mustered a tight smile of greeting. He saw that Clattermoon's sleeping spell had done its work. The princess looked well-rested—refreshed even. "Good morning, Traejon."

"Everyone's ready. Or as ready as they'll ever be. How about you?"

Jess's smile vanished. "I've been better," she admitted, raising one trembling hand into the space between them. Traejon felt a rustle of unease at the sight. He had never met the Tusk twins, but they were reputed to be an intimidating, imperious pair. If she was already shaking, how would she perform when the time came to stand before them?

Traejon cast about in his mind for a new topic of conversation. "I saw you with Lylah earlier this morning," he said, nodding back toward the manor.

"I helped her prepare some binding spells for the Sanctuary. Bryscoe's wagon didn't have all the materials I would have liked, but I improvised. I was able to scrounge up enough of what we needed to establish defensive wards in the first floor windows and the servants' entrance at the back. But there wasn't enough for the main entry or the breach in the wall at the north tower. We'll just have to fight them off there if it comes to that."

Traejon frowned. "Why does she need such materials at all? If her Thread is so strong, why can't she cast a spell to protect the entire Sanctuary?"

Jess gave him a surprised look. "Because wizards and witches can only cast one enchantment at a time. And that spell only endures as long as the casting continues. Did you really not know that?"

"Uh, no. Casters aren't known for sharing their secrets with threadbares, Jess. I think your station made you a bit of an exception."

"Sorry," Jess said sheepishly. "Well, if a caster launches a spell conjured by word and hand and then stops for any reason—to sleep, to eat, to cast another spell, to scratch her nose, whatever—then the original spell expires. Unravels. So while such enchantments are wonderful for retrieving an item from across the room without leaving your seat—or snaring wolves in quicksand, as Gydeon did back at the Widow's Torch—they aren't so effective at maintaining a spell for long periods of time. Even an hour is difficult. Let alone a week or a year or a century. Your hands and voice get pretty tired after a while."

"I suppose."

"That's why spells of greater duration require a whole different set of casting skills and knowledge. It's a separate branch of magic known as alchemy or spellbinding. *Those* enchantments, whether they are meant to keep intruders from entering your home or—in my father's case—to enter into a state of oblivion, require special materials to keep the spell in motion. As well as a potion or a physical object in which the spell can be housed." She glanced down at his left hand. "Like your rings."

Traejon nodded his understanding. "That explains why Lylah was laying links of chain on all the windowsills this morning."

"Exactly. Once I prepared the solution into which the chain links could be submerged, all Lylah had to do was use her Thread to spellbind them."

"So you collaborated on the spell."

Jess shook her head. "I just prepared the solution. It was nothing but a broth of inert ingredients until she infused it with purpose."

"But why did she need *you* to prepare the solution?"

A faint smile returned to Jess's lips. "Lylah might possess a powerful Thread, but her knowledge of alchemy is practically nonexistent. She didn't have the faintest idea how to prepare the spell. Wherever she came from, she didn't have a tutor or mentor to instruct her in the alchemical arts."

"Well it sounds like she has one now."

Jess grimaced, as if he had said something utterly ridiculous. After a moment, though, her expression became thoughtful. "Perhaps she does," she said slowly, as if the sentiment was some strange object that she had taken in hand so that she might examine it from all angles. Then she looked up at Traejon, her eyes clearing as they returned to the present.

"So tell me again how this is all going to go?"

Traejon gestured in the direction of the ruins. "Most of the casters and their families are already with Bryscoe at the back of the manor house, in the old kitchen. They've gathered their familiars back there too. All but Dayna and Clattermoon. They're with Lylah. And a few parents who insisted on joining Tab, Noxon, and Max in the north tower."

Jess nodded, but her expression was one of puzzlement. "Why are the casters keeping their familiars so close at hand? That doesn't make sense to me."

Traejon frowned. "I don't know. I agree that they'd be too exposed on the open ridges behind us. But when Bryscoe and I counseled them to send their familiars deep into the forest, Lylah objected. She insisted that all the animals stay out of the Matchstycks this morning."

"Why?"

"I don't know. If things don't go as hoped this morning, they will be that much easier to capture or kill if they're bottled up in the Sanctuary. But Lylah was adamant that *no one* was to enter the forest. And those folks listen to her."

Jess was silent for a moment, and Traejon could tell that she was pondering the mute girl who had drawn them all to this place. The princess didn't know quite what to make of her, either.

"Where is she anyway?" Jess finally said.

"Just inside the main entrance. Hidden away but close enough to hear us when the time comes."

Jess looked at him appraisingly. "You don't trust her very much, do you?"

"No, it's not that. I just don't *know* her. Or her full capabilities. So the idea that she's largely shaped our preparations for the soldiers approaching our doorstep feels like madness. Raven and Crow, she's only fifteen years old. And we only just met her last night. "

"She is a mystery," Jess said. "But I have no doubts about her loyalty."

"Nor do I," he admitted. "Not after watching the way she reacted to meeting you this morning. I thought she was going to faint when Bryscoe introduced her to you."

"Yes, that was something. Felt just like being back at Kylden Hall."

Traejon raised his eyebrows at the note of sarcasm in her voice.

"Where I'm celebrated for my bloodlines, not my deeds." Jess managed a small smile. "Don't misunderstand me Traejon. I'm proud to be my father's daughter. But the silks and trumpets that trail behind me at Kylden Hall are not due to anything *I've* done."

Traejon frowned. "Give yourself a little time, Jess. You . . . ." His voice trailed off as he caught a glimpse of movement out of the corner of his eye. Turning his head to the forest, he saw a form flying low over the treetops.

"The condor's back," he said. They watched as it approached, skimming low and then climbing high into the sky just before reaching bow range. Traejon and Jess watched the giant bird carve a broad circle over the manor house and the surrounding lands. It slowed briefly as it passed overhead, floating in an eddy of air. Then it turned back toward the forest, beating its wings languidly.

"One final scouting foray," guessed Traejon. "They're very close now."

As if on cue, the condor spiraled down from the heavens and disappeared into the forest no more than a hundred yards from the edge of the woods.

"The bird has returned to his compeer to report," Traejon murmured. He rolled his neck and shoulders in anticipation, felt the reassuring weight of the quiver and bow and sword on his back. "You're confident it's her out there? Tusk? Not some other caster?"

"Based on the descriptions provided by Emmalyn and Clattermoon it has to be her. I've met Aleyda and Artemys Tusk on two occasions. They don't exactly try to blend into the crowd."

"Well, I'm still skeptical of the wisdom of this, Lylah's confidence notwithstanding. I'd rather you were back there with the others." Traejon ran a hand through his hair and sighed. "But I suppose I'm getting used to taking orders from young ladies these days."

"This is still my father's kingdom," Jess said. "And the Tusks and their soldiers are still nominally subjects of my father. I need to at least give them a chance, Traejon. To reconsider. To turn back and leave us in peace. You understand that, don't you?"

Traejon sighed and looked away to the sky, where the condor had returned. It floated high above them again, a black smudge against the gray clouds.

Jess waited for him to respond, and when he didn't she returned her eyes to the forest. "They're probably going to kill us all anyway," she said. "Or haul us away in chains. But before they do so, I want them to at least have to admit their treachery. Acknowledge their treason to my face."

Then Jess lifted her right hand until the small crossbow she held peeked out of the folds of her cloak. The pointed steel head of an already loaded bolt gleamed in the cold morning light. "And maybe if I'm lucky, I'll finally hit something with this thing before I go. All those hours of practice with Tab. . . . It would be nice to put those to use. Besides," she continued after a moment, "if anyone should be back there in the Sanctuary it's you. Standing beside Tabytha. Not down here with me."

"And leave you to face the Tusks alone? Nah. I wouldn't miss this for the world."

The two of them exchanged melancholy smiles, then turned back to the forest. They watched the wood silently for a minute, then two.

Far in the distance, three more dragon oaks flared into flame in quick succession, casting clouds of spiraling, fiery leaves into the heavens.

A gust of wind sent the treetops swaying.

And then the first soldiers appeared, materializing like wraiths at the edge of the wood.

Traejon studied them as they filled the shadows at the forest's edge, their mounts chuffing great drifting clouds of white vapor. Here and there the glint of chainmail and helmets could be seen, but for the most part they were garbed in cloth and leather. The soldiers and their horses were outfitted for speed. That was something at least. If they had been garbed in full armor, Tab and the other archers behind them would have been rendered fairly toothless.

"How many?" asked Jess in a low voice, her eyes riveted on the soldiers gathering below her.

"A hundred? Maybe two. They're keeping to the forest to disguise their numbers. And neither Emmalynn nor Clattermoon could really provide us with an estimate other than 'a lot.'"

As they watched, two riders on sleek black horses cantered forward into the clearing a few steps and then stopped, as if presenting themselves for inspection. Which they might well be, Traejon speculated. Their entire arrival struck him as carefully choreographed to ratchet up the fear and tension among anyone watching from the Sanctuary's ramparts.

The rider on the left was a slim man who looked to be in his mid-thirties. His clothing was dark and finely tailored, and the hilts of two crossed swords jutted out above his back. The man's hair was long and braided, and so blonde that it was almost white, while his short beard—black in jarring contrast to his hair--followed the contours of his narrow face to a sharp point. His dark eyes surveyed Traejon, Jess, and the manor looming behind them with a cold, predatory air.

The other rider was a woman, similarly slender in form. Her hair was coiled in great alternating blonde and black ropes atop her head. She looked up the slope with eyes of the same near-black hue as those of the man next to her. Her mouth was a slash of red on her pale skin, and it was set in a wintery smile. Without taking her gaze from the scene before her, the woman began speaking quietly to her companion.

"The Tusks?" Traejon said, already knowing the answer.

"Yes."

Artemys Tusk casually touched his heels to his horse's flanks and began strolling toward them. His sister Aleyda remained motionless as half a dozen riders emerged from the forest, passed her, and fell in behind her brother.

"She's not coming," said Jess in puzzlement.

"She's staying out of bow range. She's probably armed herself with some manner of protection against arrows, but arrows can be given magical properties as well, can't they?"

"Yes. But imbuing an arrow with such capabilities requires materials we don't have here, even with Bryscoe's wagon of conjuring ingredients on hand." Jess looked up at him with a hint of a smile. "I checked."

Traejon shrugged. "That's all right. The fact that she's hanging back means they're not as confident as they're trying to appear. They know we don't have numbers. But they also know that some of the people here are casters. And the Tusks are not quite sure of their capabilities."

"Even so, be mindful of Artemys. His sister may be the one with the Thread, but he is reputed to have devoted himself to the warrior arts with fanatical zeal over the years. He's not some foppish peacock who has spent his life farting into silken pillows."

Traejon snorted. "Neither am I."

They smiled at one another, then fell silent as Artemys Tusk drew closer, his horse pushing through the tall grass. He halted about thirty feet away and his guards followed suit, their horses snorting and shaking their great heads. Artemys looked down at them from his perch for a moment, then swung lightly out of his saddle and to the ground. He walked forward until he was no more than five feet from them, an insolent grin spreading across his face.

"Well, well. Owyn Suntold's little girl," he said in mock surprise, his eyes shining. "You're a long way from Kylden Hall, princess. Are you lost?"

Artemys glanced over at Traejon, sizing him up and down with a theatrical sneer of distaste. "And this must be your private legion of guards. Reduced now to a lone soldier of mongrel heritage, by the looks of him. You've wandered far from the Tomorrows, foam-eater. You should have stuck to diving for pearls and mending fishing nets, like the rest of your kind."

Traejon regarded Artemys impassively, his heart beating no more swiftly than it had before Tusk's approach. As taunts go, he had heard much worse.

Tusk's eyes lingered on Traejon for another heartbeat, but once it became clear that his goading had not drawn blood, he turned back to Jess. "You really need to pay a little more attention to your appearance, my dear," he said, spreading his arms out toward her in a caricature of concern. "Truly, it's distressing to see you in such a fallen state. Tell me—have you forsaken the proud steeds of King Owyn's stables for half-blind donkeys as well?"

"You forget yourself, Master Tusk," Jess said. Traejon was relieved to hear her words ring out high and clear. And if there was a slight tremor to her voice, he sensed that it stemmed as much from anger as fear. "I'm not much for standing on ceremony these days, but you will address me as 'Your Highness.' Out of respect for my father. The king to whom both you and your sister have sworn your allegiance."

"Ah yes, that." Artemys brought a hand up to his neck and pulled a thin leather loop over his head. He held it out to Jess. At the end of it dangled a small sounding weight. "I don't think I have any need for this now. You can find someone else to wear your father's choke collar." He tossed the oathstone at her feet. "As of this morning, the banner of Rojenhold flies over Valyedon again. After all these years, we are reunited with our Rojenholdean sisters and brothers. We stand together again, as we did when we drove the elves from the north so many centuries past."

"So the House of Tusk has chosen the path of treason," Jess said heavily. The news was not unexpected. But Traejon could tell that actually hearing it spoken aloud had hit her like a physical blow. "You and your sister will pay dearly for this, Artemys," she continued. "When my father--"

"Your *father* is on his deathbed," Artemys hissed. He cocked his head at her. "You little fool. You really have no idea what's been going on while you've been skipping through the countryside these past weeks, do you?"

"Enlighten me," Jess said coolly.

"Oh, where to start. River and Sea, there's so much to tell. Well, King Owyn already lies in state at Kylden Hall." Jess's face hardened in displeasure at his gleeful tone, but Artemys misinterpreted her expression as one of stunned disbelief.

"Oh, his lungs haven't gotten the message yet," he said, his voice a burlesque of reassurance. "They're still wheezing in and out at the moment, so far as I know. Your father's fetid breath still pollutes the air. But that won't be the case much longer. Seems his familiar did a disappearing act. Flew the coop, so to speak."

Jess's face was deathly pale, but her eyes blazed with hatred.

"But that's not the best part," continued Artemys. "The best part is that at this very moment . . . The Throneholder's vaunted army is taking its last breath as well."

Traejon and Jess glanced at one another. "What do you mean?" said Jess, frowning.

Artemys smiled thinly. "The armies of Rojenhold even now pour into Fyngree, wiping their boots on the bodies of your father's soldiers under the pale light of the Gryphon's

Eye. I wouldn't be surprised if King Thylus has already fashioned the spine of General Splyntbell into a walking stick."

Traejon felt his gut twist at Artemys's words. Could it be true? Had Rojenhold's armies really crossed the Span and overrun Tucker's Front?

"You're a liar," accused Jess, but her voice was thick with horror at the possibility.

"Am I?" Artemys said mildly. "I suppose we'll see about that, won't we?"

His eyes lifted to take in the crumbling building behind them. "Now on to the matter at hand. I'll give you twenty minutes to bring everyone in yonder manor house out. All the familiars as well. No one will be harmed. Though everyone in your merry little band will need to submit to some precautionary measures."

Without taking his eyes off of Jess, Artemys spoke over his shoulder. "Show them, Krestoph." A tall, bearded rider to Tusk's left lifted up a pair of strange-looking devices. Small, flat discs of iron out of which five thin bars sprouted. An assortment of clasps and straps hung from the metal contraptions as well.

Traejon gleaned their purpose immediately, but he saw the confusion on Jess's face. Artemys noticed it as well. "To immobilize their fingers," he said in the tone of a schoolmaster dealing with a dim student. "As I said, a simple precaution to ensure against any mischievous casting."

"Those look like torture devices."

"Not at all," Artemys said lightly. "They're painless. Well, relatively painless. But if you object, I suppose we can just chop off all of their hands instead. I'd prefer to avoid such senseless bloodshed, though. Wouldn't you?"

"They're not going anywhere with you," said Jess. There was no tremble in her voice now. It rang out like a bell in the gray morning, strong and pure. "Go away now. Leave before the casters behind me lose patience with you. Because if they do . . . no one will ever find a trace of you and your sister."

Traejon saw a flicker of uncertainty skim across Artemys's face, like the shadow of a flying bird across the surface of a pond. But then it was gone, replaced by smoldering anger. "Not much of a bluff, Jessalyn. We know what manner of familiars your friends are threaded to. Porcupines. Geese. Foxes. Your casters are capable of little more than parlor tricks."

"Then why bother with them at all?" asked Jess. "If they are so weak, so very pathetic, why not just let them all be? Go on your way and leave them in peace."

"Because King Thylus wishes them brought to him. To see how they might be most usefully employed in his new empire, I would imagine. You, on the other hand? A threadbare princess whose world has crumbled under her feet? I think he just wants you as a trophy. A trinket to play with."

"You're just as threadbare as I am, Artemys," she spat. "Which makes you nothing more than an errand boy for Whytewender and your sister." Then Jess smiled and leaned forward as if sharing a carefully guarded confidence. "Are you *sure* you're not wearing a choke collar anymore?" she said softly.

Artemys's expression darkened, but he restrained himself with visible effort, and after a few seconds he even managed a wolfish half-smile. "We all serve one master or another, Jessalyn. Even you. Now are you and your friends coming with us voluntarily? Or do we have to drag everyone away? Personally, I've come to hope that you choose the latter. Because I promise you that if we have to pry them out of those ruins there will be casualties. Heavy casualties."

Jess stared at him for a moment. "Let me consult with my friends," she said in a tone of barely suppressed fury. Then she drew her cloak close around her, turned on her heel and began walking back to the manor, her legs swishing in the long grass. Traejon cursed silently as he fell in behind her, walking backwards so as to keep Artemys and his riders in his sights. Jess had ended the encounter too abruptly. Instead of conveying a posture of possible surrender that would allow the two of them to return to the manor unmolested, the princess had shown her true feelings. There would be no surrender on this day.

And Artemys knew it. Traejon saw the mouth of Artemys open in surprise at Jess's sudden angry withdrawal. . . saw the bloodlust fill his eyes . . . and knew what was coming before Artemys said a word.

Traejon filled both his hands with daggers as Artemys turned back to the forest, to where his sister and their warriors waited. "Warriors of Valyedon!" he bellowed. "Capture who you can, kill who you must! All except for the princess. Battered and bloody is fine. But if you kill her you'll answer to King Thylus!"

The soldiers in the forest roared in response, stabbing their swords and spears towards the heavens.

But then came the faint sound of chanting at Traejon's back, and a smell of sulphur so powerful that he found himself blinking away tears. Followed by a frantic eruption of songbirds out of the forest canopy.

38

Reborn

As Jess strode through the grass toward the manor, her heart hammering in her chest, she saw Lylah step into the archway at the entrance, her hands weaving patterns in the air.

Even from where she stood, Jess could see that the young girl's mouth was forming words. Strange words that floated to her ears in faint scraps. Jess was so stunned by the sight of Lylah speaking that she slowed for an instant. Had the girl been deceiving them all this time? Or was her Thread so powerful that it could even overcome her affliction? But these questions had no sooner formed in her mind than they were dispersed by the smell of sulphur, strong and sudden, as if she'd been plunged into an impenetrable fog of the stuff. And in an instant, she knew what that bitter smell portended.

Jess broke into a run. The manor suddenly seemed an impossible distance away, and she felt the first coppery taint of panic in her blood. Even as she fled up the hillside toward Lylah and the others, though, she could not resist the impulse to glance behind her.

A few yards downslope stood Traejon, his broad back to her as he covered her retreat. Beyond him stood Artemys and the six riders who had accompanied him out onto the grassy slope. The riders surged past Tusk, who was only now remounting his horse. They pounded up the slope toward the shadow with swords and axes aloft, their chargers tearing through the high grass. But these images reached Jess only dimly, because her gaze was pinned to the forest beyond.

To the clouds of songbirds frantically streaming out of the treetops and into the gray sky.

To the millions of rustling leaves dipped in dyes of red and gold and orange.

And then every dragon oak that had not already burned itself out for the season erupted into fire with a tremendous thundering sound that seemed to shake the earth itself.

Every single one.

As far as the eye could see.

Jess flinched and averted her face at the blinding flash of light and ear-splitting roar. A wave of heat rolled over her a second later, and cottony warmth invaded her lungs as she stumbled to the ground. She rolled up onto her knees in a burst of hacking coughs. But even amid her coughing and the titanic roar of the burning dragon oaks, the sound of screaming men and horses reached her ears.

Using one hand to shade her eyes, Jess looked to the woods again. It was as if a chunk of the sun had broken off and plummeted to earth. The entire forest was on fire, vomiting up great lunging spirals of flame from one end of the great valley to the other. Even the pines at the crest of the valley's rocky ramparts were not spared. The heat generated down in the valley by the fire was so great that burning leaves floated up higher than ever before. They nestled into the needled arms of the dark pines and set them alight too. And above the ocean of flames, great pulsating walls of black smoke piled high into the sky. The easterly wind carried much of the smoke away from the Sanctuary. But even so the scene before her was veiled in a kind of glowing twilight, as if the world had been suddenly entombed in amber.

Squinting and blinking away tears, Jess could see that most of the soldiers at the very edge of the Matchstycks had escaped the conflagration, although they were struggling to control their terrified horses and put out glowing embers in their hair, beards, and clothing. But many of the horsemen accompanying the Tusks had been hidden deeper in the forest when Lylah cast her spell. Several of these soldiers came staggering out of the inferno on foot, hacking as they rubbed furiously at their eyes and frantically beat at their singed hair, beards, and clothing. But of mounted soldiers Jess saw no sign.

Their steeds were more fortunate. Whereas the heads and shoulders of the riders had skimmed the lowermost branches of the trees, the heads of even the tallest of the horses had a few additional feet of clearance. Saved by these critical few feet of space, riderless horses flowed out of the forest in a steady stream. They stampeded across the tall grass as if possessed, manes smoking, eyes rolling in terror. Here and there, a panicked horse dragged a burning figure behind it in its stirrups. Small brushfires flared up and down the slope as well, the dry grass ignited by dragged bodies or burning leaves. Within the paddock, meanwhile, the horses belonging to the residents of the Sanctuary were racing around the stone wall in a panicked, stampeding gyre.

River and sea, she thought numbly. To what manner of creature could Lylah possibly be threaded? This was magic on a scale that seemed inconceivable. Even at the height of his powers, her father would not have been remotely capable of casting such a spell. Jess felt herself slipping into a kind of paralysis, as if the heat baking the air around her had petrified her bones. With power such as this, Lylah might some-day crack the world in half if she so desired . . .

Traejon was suddenly standing over her and shout-ing. His voice sounded very far away, muffled by the roaring of the flames.

"Run to the manor!" he bellowed, his voice shining a light into the abyss into which her mind had slipped. She nodded and rose shakily to her feet as Traejon spun back to-ward the forest. The six riders who had accompanied Tusk were pounding up the hillside, swordblades raised. Moving with blinding speed, Traejon slung one two three of his throwing daggers into the chests of the first three soldiers, knocking them off their horses like dominoes. The next two tried to trample him underfoot, but the shadow dispatched them quickly in a blur of daring feints and deadly sword strokes.

Traejon wheeled to face the last rider, the one that Artemys had called Krestoph. But this horseman had more sense than to test his blade against that of the shadow. In-stead he had used the distraction of the others to pull up about twenty feet from Traejon, a loaded crossbow up to his shoulder. As if in a dream, Jess watched his finger as it squeezed down on the trigger. Her hand twitched on her own crossbow, but she knew in her heart that she could not raise it in time.

Then an arrow appeared in the center of Krestoph's chest as if by magic. An arrow adorned with the snow white fletchings of Tydewater. And Jess understood reflexively that the arrow had come from Tabytha's bow.

Krestoph fired his crossbow a split-second later, but Tab's shot had done its work. Krestoph's quarrel thunked deep into the ground a few feet to the left of Traejon. The horseman looked down at the arrow protruding from his body, his expression one of deep bewilderment, before slumping out of his saddle and falling bonelessly to the ground.

Jess bolted the last few yards to the manor's open main doorway and ran into the foyer. Ducking to the left, she pressed her back against the cold stone wall, panting to catch her breath. A moment later Traejon came sprinting inside and joined her against the wall. "Find Lylah," he said. "If she can burn an entire forest down with a spell, she ought to be able to hold off the Tusks."

"Lylah is in no condition to provide further assistance," said a familiar voice—Clattermoon's—from an open doorway to their left. Jess exchanged a quick glance with the shadow, and they both ran over to the doorway and looked inside.

The chamber looked like it might once have been some sort of drawing room for entertaining, to judge from its size and the tattered tapestries that hung from the walls. Now, though, it held only three guests. Lylah lay sprawled unconscious on the floor, half in and half out of a square of bright, wavering light cascading in from one of the room's tall windows. Her features looked slack and haggard, and both of her nostrils were rimmed with blood. Kneeling on either side of her were Clattermoon and Dayna.

"What happened to her?" Jess asked Dayna, joining her on the floor.

The carpenter's widow looked frightened out of her wits, but when she spoke her voice was steady. "Lylah collapsed as soon as she completed her spell, the instant the woods went up in flame."

"She warned us beforehand," growled Clattermoon. "Said that we'd need to revive her or she'd be out for days. That's what she was doing this morning. Honing our healing castings so as to help speed her recovery. Fat lot of good it's doing."

Dayna scowled at Clattermoon's skeptical tone. "She said—wrote—that it might take a while," she said pointedly. "She told us to keep trying."

"Then keep trying," said Traejon from the doorway. "The Tusks are advancing. Lylah's casting made it pretty clear that there's more than just a few hedge witches in here. Even so, they're still not as frightened of us as they are of failing Whytewender. They'll take the Sanctuary or die trying."

"How many of them are left?" asked Jess, dreading the answer.

"Three or four score at most. Lylah's casting took a heavy toll, and our archers are further thinning their ranks. But we also have the Tusks to contend with." Traejon's piercing jade-colored eyes locked on hers. "Jess, they're ignoring the main gate and making for the ruins at the base of the north tower. That damned condor's reconnaissance must have convinced them that our defenses are weakest there. I need to go."

"I'm going too," said Jess, rising unsteadily to her feet. She hefted the crossbow to underscore her determination, even though she felt that it had come to weigh about a thousand pounds. Raven and Crow, her fear was so great that she thought that she might lose control of her bladder at any moment. But anger was coursing through her veins as well. Righteous anger, clear and bright and iron-hard. She seized the feeling to her breast, wielding it as a cudgel to keep the fear at bay. Come what may, she wasn't going to tuck herself away in some musty corner of the Sanctuary and wait for someone—friend or foe—to tap her on the shoulder after this was all over.

Traejon saw the look in her eyes and sighed. "I don't have time to argue. Come on."

Jess followed Traejon as he sprinted to the once-grand staircase at the center of the manor. He took the stairs three at a time, leaving Jess hopelessly behind. But the shadow paused at the second story landing, his eyes searching the dark corners of the cavernous space, until Jess had reached the top herself. Whereupon he promptly took off again. She fell in behind him, cursing Traejon's long legs. They pounded down several long dark corridors, their footfalls echoing on the stones even over the throbbing roar of the fire outside. Once Traejon pulled back into a mere trot so that he didn't lose her completely, and Jess felt a mix of gratitude and self-conscious irritation at the gesture.

And then they turned into a hallway unlike the others. Down at its far end, the corridor terminated in a ragged circle that framed an expanse of stone wall washed in fiery light. And echoing forth from the opening came ugly, desperate sounds of cursing and screams and steel on steel.

Traejon charged forward, sword in his right hand, another throwing dagger in his left. Jess fell in behind, her breath coming in ragged bursts as she tried to keep up. Then Traejon stopped in his tracks as the stone floor ended, giving way to empty air. She skidded to a halt by his side, her left foot nearly slipping off the edge entirely. Panting for air, she looked around to get her bearings . . . and reeled at the madness swirling below them.

She and Traejon stood at what had once been a second-floor entranceway to the manor's north tower. But the roof and second floor of the collapsed tower were gone, as was a good portion of its west-facing wall. Exposed to the elements here on this perch high over the rubble, Jess could feel the heat of the forest fire on her face and clothing, and the wind tugging at her hair and cloak with insistent hands. She pushed her hair out of her face so that she could see the Matchstycks, still roaring and burning in the distance with otherworldly intensity. Above the towering flames loomed clouds as black as night, fiery leaves glowing like dying stars as they floated through their depths. Tusk's condor was up there too, soaring and banking among the burning leaves and black smoke.

Far below the bird, next to the remnants of the old stable, the Tusk twins sat on horseback watching the siege of the manor house. From this distance Jess could not make out their expressions. But she knew they were not out there shedding tears for lost warriors. No, they were probably debating whether the casters who had set the Matchstycks on fire had spent themselves completely. Or whether they might yet have a spell or two in reserve. Jess was certain that they hadn't entertained the notion that the conflagration might possibly have been the work of a single caster. She could still hardly believe it herself.

Jess tore her gaze away from the witch and her loathsome brother. Down on the ground floor, soldiers of Valyedon were slowly slashing their way inside through the gaping wound in the side of the north tower. They leaped and writhed forward like spawning salmon, their faces haunted and determined by turns. But their progress was slowed by the great slabs of granite that had fallen inward from the tower's walls—as well as by the accumulating bodies of those already slain. From Jess's vantage point she could see that the stones and bodies had combined to transform the space around the breach into a deadly bottleneck. A compact, nightmarish maze through which the invaders had to pass. And thus, an ideal location for the Sanctuary's defenders to make their stand.

Frantically sweeping the chaotic scene with her eyes, she found Noxon, Max, and a bald, bearded man that she recognized as a father to one of the younger casters cutting and stabbing furiously at the soldiers squeezing through the passage. All of them were splashed with blood, but Jess had no idea how much of it was their own. Then she spotted Tabytha, kneeling directly below her on a slab of broken stone. Jess watched as Tabytha coolly fired an arrow just over Noxon's shoulder into the blood-rimmed entranceway. A Valyedon soldier fell away with a howl of pain, an arrow buried deep in his bicep.

Then Jess's gaze drifted right as if pulled along by some irresistible current, skittering across the floor until it settled on the still forms of two men and a woman. She recognized them immediately as parents to young refugee casters hiding back in the kitchen. Children who would never again feel their parents' embrace or hear their voices.

Jess felt a lump rise in her throat and she lifted her crossbow to push it back down. Feed the anger now, save the sorrow for later, she thought. She lifted the small weapon to her shoulder, searching through the chaos below for some opportunity to strike a blow. It was only then that she realized that Traejon had left her side. Leaping from ledge to ledge, he had found a path to the floor below. He moved now like flowing water through the maze of stone, hurling daggers into the enemy-clogged opening as he ran forward.

The shadow reached the spot where Max had stood only a moment before, and Jess saw why Traejon had rushed to the line. The bald, bearded man was frantically dragging Max away into the back of the room. The scout's shirt was dark with blood, his eyes clenched tight in pain.

Jess looked back to where Traejon and Noxon now stood side by side. She could see the weariness in Noxon's slumped shoulders, and in the sloppiness of his form as he battled to keep the dam from bursting inward with invaders. Traejon, though. . . . Traejon moved like quicksilver. Using the shattered remnants of wall and pillar as shields, the shadow waded past Noxon, his sword and daggers cutting down enemy soldiers with every other step. He advanced implacably toward the breach in the wall, littering the floor behind him with crumpled warriors and pushing the remaining invaders into grim retreat. Jess shook her head in disbelief when he reached the gash in the wall, his sword gleaming a brilliant ruby red as it emerged out of the shadows of the tower walls and into the firelight. To Jess he looked like the Ferryman incarnate, come to fill the hold of his ship for his next sojourn to the Far Shore.

And then something made Jess lift her eyes beyond the rubble of the tower to the stable in the distance. To where the Tusk twins sat their horses.

Was it a premonition? Some instinctive response deep in her being to a movement that hadn't even registered in conscious mind? Whatever it was, Jess's eyes settled on Aleyda Tusk's black-gloved hands. She watched as if hypnotized as the witch's hands sliced and curled in the smoky air.

A few yards to Tusk's left, a bushel of arrows shook themselves loose from the quiver of a fallen soldier as if pulled free by an invisible hand. They hovered in the air for a half-second, their points reflecting the forest's hellish light. Then they swooped forward in the direction of the tower, flying in concert like a flock of streaking starlings. . . .

And Traejon staggered out of the firelight and back into the gloom of the tower, his chest pincushioned with a half dozen arrows.

Jess felt the blood drain from her face as Traejon staggered, then crumpled to the floor. She slumped against the near wall and slid to the floor herself, limbs heavy and numb. The roar of the burning forest faded away to a droning murmur, like the sound of distant surf.

Even Tabytha's screams of horror sounded far away.

Jess watched hopelessly as Tabytha scrambled down from the scree-like ruins upon which she had been stationed, keening no no no as she went. She ran to Traejon and knelt over him, her hands frantically moving from arrow shaft to arrow shaft, as if they were pieces of some monstrous musical instrument that had exploded out of him. Traejon's eyes were wide and filled with pain, and bubbles of blood appeared on his lips. But Jess saw how he tried to smile at Tab—and how he murmured words that set her entire body convulsing with sobs.

Some unknowable length of time passed by. A few seconds? Minutes? Days? Jess found herself unable to even ponder the question. All she seemed able to do was watch Tabytha weep over her dying love as he looked up at her, brushing at her tears with one blood-striped hand.

Then several Valyedon warriors walked through the now undefended breach and into Jess's field of vision, swords at the ready. They faced no resistance as they fanned out across the chamber. Jess's eyes wandered over the room below until they reached Noxon, who was clutching his stomach and seemed barely able to stand. Next to him slumped the bald bearded man, who was in only marginally better condition. Neither man held a weapon. Jess understood. Without Traejon and Tab their cause was hopeless. The soldiers herded Noxon and the other man into the far corner of the circular room, where Max already lay groaning.

Only then did Aleyda and Artemys enter the ruined tower. They strolled in as if the blood-soaked chamber was a banquet hall filled with a cheering throng. Their pace was casual, unhurried. But Jess could see the fury in their eyes. The smile on Artemys's face looked as if it had been carved into his flesh with a paring knife, so ragged and unnatural was its appearance. Aleyda looked even more enraged. Her mouth was set in a thin bloodless line, her shark-like eyes fixed on Traejon and Tabytha.

The Tusks moved forward until their shadows loomed over Traejon and Tab. But her friends seemed oblivious to the presence of the twins. She heard the low rustle of Tab's voice, insistent and beseeching, followed by a murmur from Traejon, who was somehow still drawing breath.

Aleyda signaled to one of the soldiers. The warrior strode over, grabbed a fistful of Tab's hair, and began dragging her away to where Noxon and the others huddled. Tab struggled and spat, and one well-placed kick crumpled the soldier into a groaning ball. But two other soldiers set upon her before she could claw her way back to Traejon's side. One of them struck her a vicious blow that sent her reeling onto the floor next to Noxon. The soldier towered over her, brandishing his sword as if he wanted nothing more than to run her through. Tab gathered herself to rise, but then Noxon reached out with his one good arm and pinned her to his side. She struggled for a moment . . . then dissolved against him in a storm of tears.

Satisfied that Tab had finally been defanged, Aleyda turned back to her brother. "He fought well," she said, nodding down at Traejon. Jess could see that the shadow's chest was barely moving now, and that he had closed his eyes. As if now that Tab's face was not hovering over him, this world no longer interested him.

"He's talented at the arts of war. Perhaps even more talented than you, brother."

"Don't be ridiculous," Artemys snarled. "He fought like a savage. I would have spitted him like a pig if you had allowed me to face him. If you hadn't lost your nerve."

Aleyda's eyes flashed in displeasure. "Perhaps you haven't noticed the toll that this day has taken? How many able-bodied men do we have left, brother? A dozen, perhaps? Wouldn't you agree that it would be nice to have a few men to guard the prisoners during our return to Valyedon? Especially given their evident capabilities."

"I suppose," Artemys said grudgingly. "Although I still say we should just hack all their hands off. Eliminates the risk of casting while still preserving the familiars."

"Don't start in with that again. As I've reminded you more than once, Thylus wants to look at them first, see if any are salvageable. And I daresay he has a point. If they managed to combine castings in such a way that they could burn a forest down, who's to say they couldn't help bring down the walls of Kylden Hall? So let's get on with it and gather them up. While they're all still exhausted from their little playing-with-matches escapade."

"Very well, sister," said Artemys. He drew his sword out of his scabbard and placed the point of his blade on the shadow's throat. He pressed down until Traejon's eyes fluttered open at the pressure.

"Wakey, wakey," Artemys said. "Where's your little collection of misfits hiding? And the princess. Can't forget about her."

Traejon remained silent as he stared up at his tormentor, his eyes shining with defiance.

Artemys grinned and cocked his head as he looked down at the helpless man. "This doesn't have to be hard. Everyone here will be well provided for. The casters hiding in these walls are resources, not enemies. But I'll be vexed if you force us to search this cobwebbed dump room by room. So if you won't tell me where your friends are holed up . . . " He jerked his head in Tabytha's direction, then leered back down at him. ". . . I might have to find a way to amuse myself while our soldiers look around. What do you think? Is your nurse-maid game for that? She can listen to your death rattle as I have my way with her."

Jess rolled away from the lip, tears of frustration welling in her eyes. Smoke and Ash, what a nightmare. Trae-jon, Tab, Noxon, and Max were doomed. The Tusks would never spare them. The only items of value here were the cast-ers and herself. Hauling other threadbares along would only complicate the task of the guards.

But what could she do? She still had the crossbow. But Jess knew it wasn't nearly enough. Not against Artemys and a roomful of warriors. And certainly not against Aleyda, who had undoubtedly taken precautions to protect herself from such weapons.

Should she run? The thought came skulking in unan-nounced, only to instantly take root in Jess's mind, feeding off her fear and mounting feelings of hopelessness. What good was she doing here? Why not flee this horror? If she could reach the ridgeline above the castle undetected, per-haps she could find a hiding place somewhere in the rocks. The smoke from the fire was so thick that Tusk's familiar might not see her flight. And if she could elude the Tusks long enough, they might even depart so as to deliver their other prisoners to Whytewender. Tab and Traejon would under-stand, she told herself. They wouldn't think less of her. They would *want* her to save herself. She should run. Run. Run!

But try as she might, Jess found herself unable to step back into the dark corridor and disappear. Her eyes refused to cooperate. They just kept looking down on Traejon and

Tab and Max and Noxon, who had stood by her side unflinchingly these past weeks. Never cowering in fear, never turning away in search of an easier path. And as she stared down at her friends, she felt the rationalizations that she had been frantically telling herself loosen their hold on her heart. No. She would not abandon them. She would stay, even if only to bear witness to their bravery and grace in their last moments of life. They deserved that much from her.

Running a sleeve roughly over her eyes, Jess flopped back into her previous viewing position. As she did so, she caught sight once more of Aleyda Tusk's familiar, an inky black silhouette against the smoke-filled sky. The condor was circling over the manor as if it were a just-discovered piece of carrion. And other birds were slowly returning as well. Far out over the forest, Jess could see a smaller winged form drawing steadily closer. It flew in and out of pillars of smoke, appearing then disappearing again. It wouldn't be long until the skies were thick with vultures, she thought miserably.

"Tell us where they are, and I'll put you out of your misery and spare her," said Artemys. "Otherwise, I'll fill this tower with her screams—and yours." He clattered his blade through the thicket of arrow shafts poking out of Traejon's chest for emphasis, and the shadow writhed in pain.

It was that gesture—that casual act of cruelty—that galvanized Jess into action. Feeling something splinter and snap inside her, she rolled up onto her knees and brought the crossbow up to her shoulder, taking aim at Artemys Tusk. And as she did so, her chaotic thoughts crystallized into a single hard nugget of desire: to make certain that even if she spent the rest of her life in chains, she would know that she had spent her last moments of freedom defending her friends, father, and kingdom.

As Jess aimed her crossbow and squeezed down on the trigger, both of the twins looked up simultaneously. Identical looks of recognition flitted across their faces, but then their expressions diverged. Artemys's features twisted into disbelief as the crossbow bolt slammed deep into his left shoulder. His sister gaped in shock as the impact of the bolt spun Artemys against a stone pillar. His forehead smashed into the rock and he sank to the floor with a low moan.

Aleyda looked down at her brother's body for a long moment. Then she swung her gaze up toward Jess, mouth moving, hands carving runes in the air.

Jess felt the cloak around her neck instantly tighten into a deadly noose. She staggered back against the wall, dropping her crossbow so that she could use both hands to loosen the steadily intensifying constriction. But it was no use. Even as her fingers frantically pulled at the material, the cloak continued to tighten its grip around her throat. She felt the metal clasp pierce her skin, felt the warm trickle of blood that followed, felt the intensifying pounding of blood in her ears.

Clawing frantically at the strangling material, Jess raised her chin in a desperate bid to somehow cram a finger between her flesh and the cloak. Her eyes opened to the dark skies overhead, and as her consciousness began to flicker, her gaze snared once more on the fast-approaching bird that she had noticed a few moments earlier.

Watching it emerge out of the last of the clouds of smoke to join the condor, Jess dimly realized that it was not a vulture, as she had originally thought. The bird was too small, and its plumage was a chaos of orange and red and white.

And then the strangest thing happened. An event that Jess's blood-starved brain could not make sense of. All she could do was watch it unfold.

The second bird carved a wide high circle in the sky, as if seeking to keep out of the condor's field of vision. Then it aimed itself toward the condor and accelerated, its bright wings a flashing blur. It slammed into the condor's side and the birds plummeted out of the sky in a tumbling tailspin, the strange bird's talons clamped on the condor's right wing and shoulder.

They were less than a hundred yards over the tower when the strange bird burst into flame. The condor's screech of agony reached Jess's ears at the same instant that the noose loosened around her throat. She fell to her hands and knees, coughing and gasping for air. Even so, she never lost sight of the birds. The flames coming off the strange bird grew until the creature was a virtual ball of fire, its heat and light enveloping the condor as well. Then the fiery bird disappeared in a cloud of black ash, leaving only the condor. Virtually bereft of feathers, it slammed into the ground like a pumpkin being dropped from a silo.

Right next to the broken, motionless body of Aleyda Tusk, the former high sentinel of Valyedon. A moment later, the smoking body of the familiar vanished in a spray of shimmering lights.

The soldiers who had been guarding Noxon, Tabytha, and the others looked at each other with stupefied expressions. "Warriors!" Jess shouted down to them hoarsely, and as one their faces lifted to her. She coughed and rubbed her throat, then continued. "The Tusks have been vanquished. Lay down your arms now and your lives will be spared."

"You should listen to her highness," said a deep voice from the shadows of the breach in the wall. A moment later Clattermoon and Dayna entered, flexing their fingers meaningfully. And then they stepped aside, revealing the small but upright form of Lylah Rendsong.

Lylah looked even more sickly than her companions. Stray locks of hair were pasted to her forehead by sweat, and she walked into the room gingerly, as if suffering from some lingering pain. Nonetheless, the soldiers hastily dropped their swords and spears and backed away with hands upraised. For perched on Lylah's thin and trembling left arm was the bird that had brought Aleyda Tusk's familiar down. It was impossible. Jess had seen it disintegrate into ash with her own eyes. But there the creature stood, glaring around the room with a fierce intensity that made Jess's arms break out in goosebumps.

Clattermoon stalked over to Artemys Tusk and kicked at him roughly. "He's still alive," he announced, and pulled a dagger out of his belt. "But not for long."

"No!" barked Jess. "Put your blade away, Clay," she said. "Care for his wound and place him with the other prisoners."

"What?" Clay said, his features contorting in confusion and outrage. "Why would you spare this wretch?"

Why? Because he might possess valuable information. Because he really was no more than a pawn in the schemes of his sister and King Thylus. And because whenever Jess finally succeeded her father as Throneholder, she did not wish to preside over a kingdom that executed helpless soldiers as if they were hogs for butchering. No, she would not drink from the same goblet as Thylus Whytewender. But her throat hurt too much to say all of this. So instead she just fixed Clattermoon with a stern look of warning and croaked: "Because that's not who we are."

Clattermoon glowered at her for a long moment. Then he sighed, bowed stiffly, and reluctantly sheathed his knife. At which point the chamber dissolved into yet another flurry of frantic activity. The bald, bearded man who had fought beside Max and Noxon ran to retrieve Emmalyn to aid in the healing. Clattermoon marched the surrendering soldiers outside, accompanied by Lylah's familiar. Dayna scurried over to Noxon and Max to tend their wounds. And Tab ran back to Traejon's side as Lylah knelt down and began ministering to him.

At first Jess thought that Lylah was too late. There were so many arrows, and Traejon had lost *so* much blood. But as the young girl's casting took hold, Tab gently pulled the arrows out one by one, each wound closing tight as each arrowhead departed.

It took about fifteen minutes, and Jess sensed that at several points, Lylah's strength, diminished so much by her spell over the Matchstycks, nearly failed her. But finally, Traejon's eyes fluttered open, and as he looked up into Tabytha's laughing, crying face, a faint smile crossed his own features.

Traejon has been reborn, thought Jess. Just like Lylah's familiar. And then Jess smiled. For she felt more than a little reborn herself.

39

Home

A s the morning sun climbed the sky, its rays bronzing the eastern flanks of the Marching Mountains, the Gryphon's Eye dissolved into the rising blue.

Here there were no forests afire. No tidal waves carrying broken bodies back to the deep. Just warm light and a cool breeze that ruffled the liquid skin of the range's rivers, lakes, and streams and the fur of the bears, foxes, and elk wandering its valleys.

The western flanks of the mountains remained pooled in darkness. Still, if one looked closely enough, one could see pocks of darker black along the mountain walls and ridges. Openings into the caves—some small and isolated, others offering entry into vast subterranean networks—that riddled these mountains.

It was out of one such opening—a small one, located midway down a ridge peppered with similar openings—that Nomad emerged.

She studied the land laid out before her to the west. The last time she had seen the woodlands and shining river that beckoned to her now, they had been cloaked in twilight. But now, with the shadows of the mountains receding by the minute, they seemed to be calling to the sun.

Nomad felt that they were calling her as well.

It had been weeks since the Daughter and the One Who Follows had sent her to be reunited with the man to whom she was bound. Weeks since the gargoyle had descended upon her and nearly captured her. Nomad had felt the gargoyle's presence just in time, and she had managed to evade its grasping claws. But even a glancing blow from the gargoyle had been enough to send her into a tailspin that culminated with her smashing her right wing into a slanting rock face. If not for the cave opening next to her, she never would have escaped. As it was, she barely managed to hop and flutter into its black interior before the gargoyle could pluck her off the mountainside.

For a while, the gargoyle had tried to dig her way in. Using her fists as hammers and her claws as chisels, she made steady progress. But the cave in which Nomad had taken refuge was not a single shallow notch in the mountain. It opened up into a wider network of caverns that offered numerous hiding places for the falcon. And when the gargoyle penetrated deeply enough to see that, she had withdrawn. Nomad had detected no sign of her since.

Nomad, though, had no choice but to remain in hiding. Her wing didn't work right. And so day after day she had remained in the dark, even as she felt her once-vibrant Thread to her compeer slowly dwindle down to a few fraying strands.

Until today.

Nomad shook her wings tentatively, felt the cool mountain air course through her feathers. Her wing was still weak, and she felt a throbbing pain when she tried to flap it too vigorously. But her entire being shivered with the knowledge that her compeer did not have much time left. So she would do her best.

And with that she launched herself into the air, her gaze fixed on the distant horizon as she crossed out of the dark mountains and into the light.

For more information on Kevin Weston and the Casting Shadows Trilogy, go to kevinwestonbooks.com.

71180839R00266

Made in the USA
Lexington, KY
18 November 2017